Pirate

ABOUT THE AUTHOR

Ted Bell is the former Vice Chairman and Creative Director of one of the world's largest advertising agencies. His three Alex Hawke thrillers, *Hawke*, *Assassin* and *Pirate* are all *New York Times* bestsellers. Visit www.tedbellbooks.com

Pirate

TED BELL

**POCKET
BOOKS**

LONDON • SYDNEY • NEW YORK • TORONTO

First published in the United States of America by Atria Books, 2005
First published in Great Britain by Pocket Books, 2006
An imprint of Simon & Schuster UK
A CBS COMPANY

3 5 7 9 10 8 6 4 2

Simon & Schuster UK Ltd
Africa House
64–78 Kingsway
London WC2B 6AH

www.simonsays.co.uk

Simon & Schuster Australia
Sydney

A CIP catalogue record for this book is
available from the British Library

ISBN-10: 1-4165-2244-1
ISBN-13: 978-1-4165-2244-7

Printed and bound in Great Britain by
Cox & Wyman Ltd, Reading, Berks

For Page Lee Hufty

Acknowledgments

Many people helped make this book possible, and I am happy to acknowledge their contributions. I will never forget how lucky I was to get a start, and for that I have to thank Emily Bestler. She went a considerable distance out on a very green limb and dropped a great big ladder. Also, my thanks to Judith Curr and Louise Burke, who have always been so supportive and helpful. Also at Simon & Schuster, Carolyn Reidy and Jack Romanos—thank you.

A note of thanks to English teachers everywhere. You bear a far larger burden now than you endured with my generation and I appreciate your dedication and fervent belief in words and stories. We are all lost without you.

A few folks helped on this book in particular. My friend Stefan Halper, former White House and State Department official, and now senior fellow at Magdalene College Cambridge. His wise counsel and deep understanding of the challenges presented by China in this century were invaluable. M. Boicos, many thanks for helping me retrace Napoleon's footsteps in Paris and at Malmaison. Chief of Police Mike Reiter and the Palm Beach Marine Unit were very helpful in matters of harbor security. My good friend and agent, Peter Lampack, contributed, as always, enormously to this manuscript.

To my wife, Page Lee Hufty, who has been steadfast and unwavering in her love and support of me and this book, I express my deepest gratitude.

"It doesn't matter if it is a black cat or a white cat.
If it can catch mice, it's a good cat."

—DENG XIAOPING, CENTRAL COMMITTEE LEADER,
COMMUNIST PARTY OF CHINA, DECEMBER 1978

"From our view, the dominance of the West since the Renaissance
was a five-hundred-year mistake that will soon be corrected."

—HIGH-RANKING CHINESE COMMUNIST PARTY OFFICIAL TO
U.S. AMBASSADOR, 2005

Pirate

Prologue

Marrakech

HARRY BROCK SPENT HIS LAST HOUR OF FREEDOM IN PARA-dise, sipping orange-scented tea in the loamy shade of a grove of date palms. He was reclining against the base of a palm on a tufted cushion of grass, soaking his sore feet in a sunken pool of cool water. White and yellow petals floated on the surface. Moroccans were great believers in flower petals.

They scattered them everywhere, especially in fountains and in the various hidden pools that dotted the property. The pretty maids even sprinkled them on the pillows of his bed whenever he left his room to go down to the bar, or go for a walk in the hotel gardens like he was doing now.

After a hard sleep, he'd awoken that morning to the sound of distant motorcycles cranking up somewhere beyond the orange groves. *Vroom-vroom.* At least, that's what it sounded like when the muezzins began calling the faithful to prayer. He could hear wailing from atop slender minarets. Needles, pointing at the sky, and white domes were visible beyond the walls of his current residence.

He'd cracked one eye at the clock. He'd been sleeping for sixteen straight hours. It took a moment to remember that he was still alive and recall exactly where he was; to realize that he was conscious again.

It was a pretty ritzy place, his current residence, way too expensive for his current pay grade, but, hey, if he got out of this joint alive, he was going to put in for it anyway. Beluga for breakfast? Why not? Kir royales and mimosas? Hell, he was entitled after what he'd been through.

By God, was he ever entitled.

Brock had donned the fluffy white robe and gone straight down to the pool, swum fifty laps, then strolled among citrus groves heavy with fruit. He was careful to keep within the high ochre-colored walls of the hotel, La Mamounia. And he tried not to look over his shoulder every five seconds, though reflexive behavior was pretty standard in his line of work.

Harry Brock was a spy. And, not to be overly dramatic about it, but he was marked for death. Big time. Nothing new and exciting about that, he imagined, not around here. Spies went for a dime a dozen in this neck of the woods. Hell, maybe even cheaper.

The 1920s-era Art Deco hotel, smack dab in the heart of beautiful downtown Marrakech, was, itself, no stranger to spycraft or wartime military secrets. The lavish brochure up in his room proudly proclaimed the fact that Winston Churchill and Franklin Roosevelt held secret meetings here during World War II. You could just picture the two of them, huddled in a corner, speaking in hushed tones, working on a pitcher of ice-cold martinis at l'Orangerie bar. Beat the hell out of Washington or London in December.

The hotel's bar must have been spy heaven in those days. Yeah, back in those good old Bogart days when everything was still black and white. When the fundamental things still applied. And a kiss was just a kiss.

There was nothing remotely heavenly about the fix Harry Brock was in. Right about now, Harry was up to his ass in secrets. Hell, he had more secrets than ten men could safely handle. He needed to unburden himself in a hurry. The guy he now worked for in Washington, guy name of General Charlie Moore, no doubt thought Harry was dead. He needed face time with Moore, fast, before someone really did take him out. Harry was sitting on something very big and it wasn't his butt. He had learned that America's old pals, the European Axis of Weasels, had themselves a new silent partner.

Namely, China. And to stop Harry from delivering this juicy tidbit to his superiors, the boys in Beijing were pulling out all the stops. Find Harry; silence Harry, before he blows his little whistle.

Harry found the simple fact that he was still breathing to be mind-blowing. He was living proof that human beings were much harder to kill than people gave them credit for. Maybe he wasn't long on brains, but old Harry knew how to deal, hold, and fold. Yeah,

Harry Brock, creeping up on forty, could still take a licking and keep on ticking. So far, anyway.

There was a train leaving Marrakech station for Casablanca in two hours. Somehow, if his luck held and nobody killed him, he'd be on that train. His normally puppy-dog-brown eyes were red, filigreed with strain radiating out from the irises. Harry was beat to shit, literally and figuratively speaking, and he couldn't find a thing that didn't hurt like hell right now except his little friend, Mr. Johnson.

To complete his laundry list of physical complaints, he had such a cocktail of drugs pumping through his system, he was humming like a goddamn high-tension line. Some kind of meth they'd injected him with, a mix of truth serum and speed, and he couldn't get it out of his system.

Time to hit the pool.

Brock had spent the preceding few nights in far humbler circumstances. He had lain on bare ground under the stars, freezing his balls off and listening to his camel fart. Having skirted the two walled towns of Tisnet and Goulemain, he'd reached a desert plateau cradled in the foothills of the snow-capped Atlas Mountains.

Exhausted, he tied his foul-smelling beast to a handy scrub bush and collapsed on the rocky ground. Below his mountain, he could see the hazy lights and minarets of Marrakech in the near distance and the coast of Morocco in the far. He slept hard, woke up with the sun, and started down.

At eight the previous morning, having given his noxious camel away to the first reasonable facsimile of a decent-looking kid he saw, he'd presented himself and his remaining cash at the reception desk. The dark-eyed beauty behind the computer flashed a winning smile. He'd cleaned up a little first, in the Gents' off the lobby, washing a couple of continents' worth of dirt out of his long brown hair. Couldn't do much about the beard or the clothes, but he'd flirted his way into a room with a big marble bathtub and a balcony overlooking the gardens. A bowl of rose petals by the tub: paradise, just like he said.

He was so close, now, so close and yet so goddamn far.

He heard a noise above him and looked skyward. A jumbo was on final, Air France, bringing in another boatload of tourists for *le weekend.* Down from Paris to hit ye olde Kasbah. Drop a few thousand Euros at the rug and hookah shops in the Medina. Two hours on the ground and the big Frogliner would load 'em up again and fly away home.

Au re-fuckin'-voir, mes amis. French bastards. When General Moore's JCS munchkins and the seventh-floor suits at Langley heard Harry's epic tale of harrowing adventure, they would not effing believe what their erstwhile "allies" were up to now.

Brock had a plane to catch, too, but his was an unscheduled departure at an airport short on amenities. Like runways. And, in order to catch that little crop duster, first he had to get on that train to Casablanca.

Brock International, as he'd dubbed it, lay about thirty-five miles out in the open desert, due north of Casablanca. It was a dried-up oasis called Dasght-al Dar. This garden spot was where an underground spring used to form a wadi, nothing more than a forgotten pinprick on a few old maps; even parched-brain camel-drivers hadn't bothered to visit the site for a century or more.

At eighteen hundred hours today, just at dusk, a two-seater biplane with no markings would touch down and taxi across the hard sand, stop, and turn.

The pilot would wait exactly ten minutes. If no one instantly recognizable to the pilot ran out of the clump of palms by the oasis in that time, the pilot would take off solo. Harry had one shot. One shot only. Going once.

They had a name for CIA guys like Brock. He was a NOC. That seldom-heard acronym stood for Not on Consular. It meant if you got caught, like he had been five days ago, you were dead and gone. Forgotten. Your name did not appear on any consular lists. In fact, your name did not appear anywhere. If you ever called your actual boss, in his case, Sweet-Talking Charlie Moore, the head of the Joint Chiefs, and said, hey, somebody has a gun stuck in my ear, Charlie would say, "Harry who?" and hang up. A NOC, operating behind enemy lines, was the deepest of the deep, and the deadest of the dead should he or she be captured.

No NOC funerals in Arlington, no-sir-ee bobtail.

Brock had been captured all right, three fucking times. Once in Tianjin on the Gulf of Chihli, that was the second time, trying to get the hell out of the Chinese prison system. He figured he could survive the beatings and other shit maybe one more day, so he'd gone over the wall. They caught him, tried to kill him again, and he escaped again. Made it to the waterfront. An old guy, a longshoreman with a scow, was supposed to ferry him to a French freighter anchored out in the crowded harbor.

The longshoreman geezer turned out to be a PLA, People's Liberation Army, informant, like every other rat in that godforsaken cesspool port town, and Brock had to kill him, too, just like he'd wasted all the other rodents. He slit the bastard's throat with his well-honed assault knife and held him under the stinking water until the thirty bloody pieces of silver lining his pockets made him sink out of sight.

Harry then made his way through the heavy fog to the freighter, poling the scow by himself. It was not a skill they taught at Quantico or the Farm, two places where he'd attended classes on his way to becoming a case officer. Put scow-poling in heavy fog in the training manual. Yep. He'd have to drop that one in the seventh-floor suggestion box if he ever made it home.

But he found the right boat at least, without the Chinaman's navigational help. He held on to the anchor rode, kicked the scow away, and did a hand-over-hand up a slimy ratline. It was two in the morning. He knew by that time the captain, a rummy from Marseilles named Laurent with whom he had a passing acquaintance, would be passed out dead drunk in his bunk. Brock hauled himself over the rail and dropped silently onto the deck at the stern. He made his way unchallenged to the bridge deck and slipped into the Frenchman's darkened cabin. Laurent had covered the single porthole with his blanket, probably hoping to sleep it off in the morning.

Sorry, *mon ami. Je m'fucking 'scuse*, pal.

It was pitch black in there.

It stank to high heaven, too. But Brock didn't differentiate the bad smells in the captain's boudoir, which was his first mistake. No, he simply dumped a half-full pitcher of water from the nightstand in Laurent's face and simultaneously put the point of his blade up under his stubbly chin. The man positively reeked of fish and sweat and gin and needed a bath anyway.

"Who got to you?" Brock asked the captain, one hand clamped

down on his shoulder, the other twisting the blade tip in the soft folds of grey skin hanging loosely around his grimy neck. "You gave me up, you sonafabitch! Why? Tell me!"

"Piss off, mate! I'm already dead," Laurent hissed through clenched yellowed teeth.

"Correct," Brock said, and made all of the captain's well-founded assumptions come true. He had barely finished wiping the blood off his blade and sticking it in its nylon ankle holster when he realized just how badly he'd just this minute fucked up.

"Mr. Brock?" a voice said in the darkness, and Brock figured it might be over for him, too. Game, set, and match. The head. He hadn't checked the goddamn toilet. The door to the fricking head had been closed. It was open now. He could see a lighter shade of grey in there, and the guy standing by the toilet. Christ. Two guys.

Harry instinctively turned sideways to present a smaller target. He had his small Browning Buck Mark already out. His handgun skills were modest, but, luckily, the Browning shot a whole lot better than he did. He raised his arm to fire. He got one round off in the general direction of the silhouetted guy's mouth when the flat of a hand came down on his wrist and broke it. Shit. The gun clattered to the steel deck and whoever had hit him danced back into his corner. He still had his knife, of course, but he'd stowed it inconveniently in his ankle holster.

"Pick the gun up, Mr. Brock, and put the barrel in your mouth. Then put your hands above your head."

Gun in his mouth? These guys were endlessly inventive.

"If I put my gun in my mouth, I'll use it." He would, too, put his brains on the bulkhead. Had no intention of going back to the "Potsticker," the guy who liked to duck Harry's head in a pot of boiling water, or worse. He always carried an "L" pill on him, a Lethal for little emergencies just like this one, but he hated to swallow the damn thing until he saw exactly how this was all going to turn out.

"Let me get a look at you, Trigon."

Trigon was his cryptonym in all the agency dossiers. Everybody in the agency had three names: the one on their birth certificates, the one on their files, and a dumb codename like Trigon. Damn. He'd been in China for six months, two of which he'd spent in prison. He was finally on his way out. And he'd been stupid enough to think he was clean. And trust a Frenchman.

Will we never learn?

He heard the soft click of a switch and an overhead light came on. Buzzing fluorescent. There were two of them in the cabin with him. A tall, elegant Chinese gentleman in a neatly pressed white mandarin jacket was seated in the hard wooden desk chair. His long khaki legs were encased in old-fashioned leather boots laced up to his knees, polished to a mirrorlike finish.

He was tall for a Chinese, something over six feet. His hair was dead straight and blue-black. A thick comma of it lay on his forehead, the skin of which was the familiar shade of flat light yellow. His eyes, a shade of pewter grey, were hooded and thickly lashed. A northern type, Brock thought. Tibetan, perhaps, or Manchurian. He'd seen this face somewhere. Yeah. He'd seen the guy's picture in a dossier at Langley. Hell, the guy was practically famous in certain international terrorist circles.

Say hello to General Moon. A charter member, at least as far as Harry was concerned, of the World Hall of Fame of Flaming Assholes.

This would be the dashing General Sun-yat Moon, all right. He was a man Harry had managed to learn something about in the last six months. Like any good case officer, especially one assigned to the chairman of the Joint Chiefs, Brock had done his homework. Before his insertion into China, he'd committed every line on the man's face and every filling in his mouth to memory. Even knew his favorite movie: *Bridge on the River Kwai*.

It was starting to come back to him now.

General Moon, fifty-six years old, was born in Jilin, Manchuria. He was a widower with two grown daughters, twins, both of whom had been trained in the shadow arts since childhood. Rumor had it, they were both high-ranking Te-Wu officers. That's secret police in Chinese. Their current whereabouts were unknown, but both were believed to be on assignment in the field.

Moon was a seasoned battlefield commander. He'd come up through the ranks. But more important, Sun-yat Moon was deputy chief of the much-feared Special Activities Committee, People's

Liberation Army. A vicious, hard-line Communist, known even in Beijing for his extremist ideological stands, Moon was now in operational command of more than a million Red Chinese, for want of a better description, storm troops.

And, he was second in command of the Te-Wu. Tough outfit, to put it mildly. Harry couldn't even imagine what a badass the number-one guy must be.

The gentleman now getting ready to kill him was also the officer who had commanded the Thirty-eighth Home Brigade, responsible for the slaughter of thousands of demonstrating students in Tiananmen Square in 1986.

Busy boy.

Moon's mission was to suppress dissidents on mainland China. Which Brock figured was about as tough as being on the California Raisin Board like his step-dad had been before he retired to a sun-kissed casita in Santa Rosa. There just aren't that many bad raisins, Pop. And there just weren't that many fucking dissidents period, end of report, in Red China, either. They'd all learned to keep their mouths shut at Tiananmen. It didn't hurt to cover your eyes and plug your ears, either.

Moon's sidekick, a nasty little horror-show featuring a bald head ringed with greasy black locks, leaned casually against the sweaty bulkhead, whistling a pretty ditty. This bullyboy was semifamous, too, an assassin from the sewers of Hong Kong named Hu Xu. Couldn't forget that name. When Brock had repeated the name on hearing it in a Foggy Bottom briefing room, he had tried a number of different inflections but it had always come out sounding like a question Abbott might ask Costello. *Who's who?*

The four-stars and the Pentagon suits just looked at him and said, "It's not funny, Agent Brock."

It isn't?

Hu Xu was, according to his resume, the assistant consultant of interrogations, and looked like an Oriental Peter Lorre starring in a bad sideshow gig with the Ringling Brothers. This was the little chipmunk who'd just broken Harry's wrist. Both of these Commie agitators had ugly snub-nosed Sansei .45 automatics aimed at his gut. Brock knew at that precise moment that he was dicked, double-dicked, and redicked. Made him slightly sick to his stomach.

"We've been waiting patiently for your arrival, Mr. Brock," General Moon said in clipped Oxbridge English. He lit a cigarette and stuck it between his thin lips. He kept talking, just letting it burn down without taking a puff. It was kind of cool, actually. "This is my associate, Hu Xu. He will help me find out what I need to know from you. He is a doctor of sorts. A semiretired mortician, actually, who works on both the living and the dead. You seem uninterested, Mr. Brock. Bored. Distracted. Are you?"

"I'm pretty busy figuring out how to kill you two shitheads and get off this fucking boat. That tune your little pal is whistling. Catchy. What is it?"

"Beethoven."

"I like it."

Moon laughed. "I'm curious about you, Mr. Brock. You've been difficult to arrest and you have caused my Te-Wu officers some embarrassment in Beijing. Let's talk for a moment before Hu Xu dissects you, shall we? Have you learned very many of our secrets? You'll tell me everything under Hu Xu's injections and expert scalpel anyway. What exactly do you know, Mr. Brock?"

"Enough."

"Tempelhof?"

"What about Tempelhof?"

"The Happy Dragon?"

"Never heard of him."

"Leviathan?"

"Leviathan? What Leviathan?" Brock said. Moon just looked at him, reading his eyes for a minute. You could tell he'd spent most of his career doing this stuff and was really, really good at it.

"Given China's explosive growth, you can hardly blame us for our current political actions, Agent Brock. China is the second-largest consumer of petroleum on earth. You know that. The CIA tracks our consumption numbers on a daily basis."

"You're hooked on oil, pal. Welcome to the club."

"China has only an eighteen-day strategic petroleum reserve. Whereas you Americans have 180 days. We find this inequity unacceptable. You have the Saudis. You have Iraq. And, soon, you'll occupy Iran, or Sudan, and our new oil contracts with those countries will be null and void."

"Life sucks when you're a junkie, doesn't it, Comrade?"

"China intends, as you have no doubt learned during your recent travels, to redress this gross injustice in the Gulf."

"May I sit on the bed with the deceased?"

"Please. It's your deathbed, too, Harry Brock."

"Thanks. Hey, here's one for you. What is the significance of the numerical sequence one-seven-eight-nine? I keep seeing that in the middle of a code break. That one has got me stumped."

Moon ignored him. Time for a new tactic. Brock sat on the edge of the bunk and let his hands fall between his legs, a man who knew he'd been bested. After a few long seconds, he looked up at Moon with tired, bloodshot eyes.

"America will never allow you into the Gulf, General," he said. "Never. Trust me on that one."

"Really? Are you quite sure of that, Mr. Brock?"

In reality, Harry knew, China was already headed to the Gulf to get her fix. Yeah, China had the oil monkey on her back now, big time. Harry had recently glommed on to the fact that the Reds had moved more than half a million troops into the Sudan. More were arriving every day. This "secret army," disguised as "guest" workers, millions of them, was slipping into Africa serving as cheap labor. Here was the thing about the Sudan: It was just three hundred miles across the water from the Saudi oilfields.

But Brock didn't want to go there. He had to concentrate on more important stuff, like survival. Somehow, he had to live long enough to bring home the bacon. The Chinese weren't stupid. They knew an American spy satellite couldn't distinguish between a soldier and a Sudanese migrant worker. The bastards had it all figured out. Only Harry could spoil this Chinese tea party. But first he had to disembark with his head intact.

Right now, the only thing standing between the world's shaky status quo and a total collapse of the global economy was the Saudi royal family. If the Chinese rolled from Sudan and into Saudi Arabia—or into any Gulf state—well, you don't want to even think about that. Where Brock came from, counting on the Saudis was what was called leaning on a slender reed.

Harry thought about all the things he could say at this point, and then he decided on, "Forget the Gulf, General. How about

Mother Russia? Or Sister Canada? They've got a lot of sweet crude."

Moon had chuckled at "Sister Canada." He had a sense of humor, you had to give him that. A lot of these Commie four-stars did not.

Moon said, "We know that America will never allow China into the Gulf. But they will allow our ally to do it, Mr. Brock."

"Really? What ally is that? You don't mean France?"

Okay, this was the part that really pissed him off. The French. Their behavior toward America in the last decade or so had been despicable. First, their UN votes were bought and paid for by Saddam's billions. Then, during the early going of the Iraq war, French diplomats were selling details of meetings with U.S. diplomats to the Iraqis! American boys were dying because of French duplicity. It made his blood boil. And he wasn't the only one in Washington who was hot and bothered.

General Moon laughed again. "That cowboy in the White House is capable of many things, Mr. Brock. But nuking Paris is not one of them."

He had a point. Wolf Blitzer broadcasting CNN images of the Eiffel Tower leaning at a severe angle would not be well received back home.

Brock said, "Don't be so sure about that, General. The prez is kind of pissed off at your little French pals right now. That whole 'oil for food' scandal, you know. Bugs some people in Washington. How many billions did it cost Saddam to buy French votes at the UN?"

"Enough, Brock."

"I'll say enough. The 'City of Light' could take on a whole new meaning, *Mon General.*"

"What do you mean by that?"

"I mean, General Moon, that if you and your little French pals don't watch your step, that town could light up like the Fourth of July."

Harry saw the thermonuclear light bulb go off in Moon's mind. "You're not serious."

"I'm not? Just try us, General. Keep pushing."

Moon never saw the knife. Never saw a human being move as fast as the American spy. All the general felt was the searing pain in his thigh as the blade sliced down to the bone. Then Brock had his gun and he fired at Hu Xu, who was a blur moving sideways away from Moon and toward the door, trying to get a shot at the American without endangering the life of the second-most-powerful man in China. The little cretin fell back against the bulkhead, gouts of blood erupting from the side of his neck.

Brock smashed him to the floor going out the door. A second later Moon heard a splash. He ran out to the rail and looked down at the surface of the water. He fired Hu Xu's pistol into Brock's rippling point of entry until it was empty.

Moon smiled, pressing his knotted handkerchief against the wound in his thigh. He went back to Hu Xu and tightly wound the blood-soaked cloth around his neck wound. He would live. This American was good fun. Te-Wu reported that he was working alone. He was on the run. He would be caught again before he could escape China, and he would be killed before he could tell anyone what he knew. Even now there was an impenetrable ring around the city of Tianjin. He whipped out his cell phone and speed-dialed the port security commanding officer. The noose started to tighten even while Harry Brock was swimming through two miles of floating garbage.

But Harry was a resourceful guy. He had slipped through the general's noose. And he had slipped through another one at the Mongolian border crossing into Kazakhstan when a guard ran out of the guardhouse with a faxed picture of his handsome mug. The AK-47s opened up and Harry dove into the back of a covered truck they'd just opened the gate for. The guy behind the wheel apparently decided the Red Guards were shooting at him, zigzagged, and floored it. So that worked out pretty good. They'd entered Kazakhstan on two wheels.

After a little adventure on the stormy Caspian Sea, and a few other high and low points, Harry had finally made it to Morocco. And there he was, daydreaming of home under a date palm tree, when a waiter in a wine-red fez bent over to pour him a cup of tea and instead slammed a hypo into his neck. Boom, like that, Harry Brock had found himself back on a slow boat to China.

Chapter One

Le Côte d'Azur

AN ILL WIND LAY SIEGE TO THE PORT. HARD OFF THE SEA IT blew, steady and relentless. For days the strange weather had spooked the ancient harbor town of Cannes, driving everyone indoors. You could hear the icy wind whistling up the narrow cobbled streets and round the old houses and shops that clung to the hills overlooking the bay; you could feel it stealing down chimneypots, seeping under window sashes, rattling doors and the inhabitants sealed behind them.

All along this southern coast, dust devils and dried leaves, desiccated by the unseasonably cold wind, swirled around the *grande dames* standing shoulder to shoulder as they faced the sea. Le Majestic, Le Martinez, and the legendary Hotel Carlton. The nor'westerly worried, rattled, and shook acres of expensive hotel glass, the seaward windows of perhaps the most glamorous stretch of real estate in the world, the Côte d'Azur.

Le mistral, the locals called this foul sea wind, wrinkling their noses in a Gallic gesture of disgust. There was no stench, not really, but still it seemed a frigid plague upon the land, and the man in the street, if you could find one about, kept his collar up and his head down. This wind carried the kind of relentless chill that worked its way deep into the marrow.

Some seventy kilometers to the west of this meteorological malaise, however, the warm Mediterranean sun was smiling down upon a singularly happy Englishman.

The cheerful fellow behind the wheel of the old green roadster was Alexander Hawke. Lord Hawke, to be completely accurate, though you'd best not be caught using that title. Only Pelham, an ancient family retainer, was allowed use of "m'lord" in Hawke's presence. And that was only because once, long ago, he'd threatened to resign over the matter.

Hawke was a good-looking enough sort, something over six feet, trim and extraordinarily fit. He was still fairly young, in his early thirties, with a square, slightly cleft jaw, unruly black hair, and rather startling arctic-blue eyes. His overall appearance was one of determination and resolution. It was his smile that belied the tough exterior. It could be cruel when he was crossed or took offense, but it could also betray a casual amusement at what life threw his way, both the good and the bad.

Women seemed attracted to, rather than put off by, Alex Hawke's rather bemused and detached views on romance, the war between the sexes, and life in general. Because he was quite wealthy, his liaisons with the fair sex were varied and well documented in the British tabloids. He had ventured down the matrimonial aisle just once. That had ended in horror and sorrow when his wife was murdered at the very outset of the marriage.

A goodly number of men seemed to find him reasonably companionable as well. He was athletic enough to compete seriously when he cared to, and he enjoyed strong drink and a good story. However, most of the truly interesting Hawke stories were known only to a few. He never spoke of his childhood. Unspeakable tragedy had struck the boy at age seven. It didn't kill, or even cripple him. It made him strong.

All in all, the sorrows of his past notwithstanding, Alexander Hawke remained an improbably cheery fellow.

If you were to ask Hawke to describe what he did for a living, he'd be hard-pressed for an honest answer. He was the titular head of a large family business—a sizable conglomeration of banking and industrial entities—but that job required only a light hand on the tiller. He had carefully chosen able commanders to helm his various enterprises and he wisely let them command.

As for himself, Hawke did the occasional deeply private favor for HM Government. When his particular skill set was required, he also did odd jobs for the United States government. Among his fellow Royal Navy aviators, it was said of him that he was good at war.

There was never anything on paper. No buccaneer's letter of marque. He was simply called in whenever they needed someone

PIRATE · 15

who didn't mind getting his hands dirty. And someone who could keep his mouth shut afterward. He was, in fact, rather like one of those seafaring eighteenth-century scoundrels from whom he was directly descended, adventurers who plundered ship and shore in the name of the king. Hawke was, in short, nothing more nor less than a twenty-first-century privateer.

Gunning his Jaguar eastward along the French coast toward the old city of Cannes, Hawke felt like a schoolboy sprung for Christmas. It was, after all, just another unexceptionally beautiful spring day on the Côte d'Azur. The wide-open road that hugged the shoreline, curving high above the blue Mediterranean, beckoned, and Hawke hungrily ate it up, one hundred miles of it every hour or so. Gibraltar had long since receded in his rearview mirror. And good riddance, too, he thought, to that monkey-infested rock.

And, while he was at it, good riddance to the stuffed-shirt navy as well.

Hawke was the kind of man to prefer bread, water, and solitary confinement to just about any kind of organized meeting. He had just suffered through two solid days of DNI briefings at British Naval Headquarters on the Rock. CIA Director Patrick Brickhouse Kelly, the guest of honor, had given a sobering presentation on the final day. He had identified another serious crisis brewing in the Gulf. The nub of it was, Red Chinese warships were headed into the Indian Ocean for a rendezvous with the French navy.

China and France? An unlikely alliance on the surface. But one with grave implications for stability in the Gulf region. And thus, the world.

No one in Washington was exactly sure when, or even if, this much-ballyhooed naval exercise would occur. But all of the blue-suit Royal Navy boys at Gibraltar were quite exercised about it. The very concept stirred their blood. Not a few of them were fantasizing a re-play of Nelson's great victory at Trafalgar, Hawke thought. And Blinker Godfrey had provided more than enough charts, facts, fig-ures, sat photos, and mind-numbing reports to whet their brass whis-tles. Endless stuff.

Why? Hawke had wondered, squirming in his chair. It was not a difficult concept to comprehend: France and Red China, sailing jointly into the Indian Ocean. You can actually express that notion in one sentence. Maybe ten words. Most situations Commander Hawke dealt with were like that. Straightforward and not irreducible. In Royal Navy parlance, however, that one sentence had translated into forty-eight hours of squirming around in a smoke-filled room trying to find comfort on a hard wooden chair.

British Naval Intelligence, Gibraltar Station, had an especially nasty habit of providing far too much unnecessary detail. This tendency was personified in one Admiral Sir Alan "Blinker" Godfrey, a pompous chap who never should have been let anywhere near a PowerPoint computer presentation. Even back in the day, when the old walrus had his antiquated overhead slides to present, he simply didn't know how to sit down and shut up. More than once he'd caught Hawke at the back of the briefing room fingering his BlackBerry and made unpleasant remarks about it.

So, overbriefed and underslept, Hawke finally escaped. He cleared the Spanish border checkpoint at the Rock and headed out along the sad and condo-ruined coast of Spain. As he wound up the C Type's rev counter, he found himself turning over the salient points of the prior evening's brief in his mind.

The bloody French were at the heart of the matter. Their Foreign Trade minister, a corrupt and virulent anti-American somehow related to Bonaparte, was a constant worry. No surprises there; the man had been making relations with France increasingly difficult for some time. No, the truly worrisome mystery at this point was French involvement with the Red Chinese. Eyebrows were raised when Brick Kelly called them that; but "Red" was an adjective CIA Director Kelly had never stopped using, since, as he said in the briefing, "If that group of Mandarins in Beijing ain't red, then I don't know who the hell is."

Kelly then put up a chart: in the preceding year, Red China had quadrupled her military budget to eighty billion U.S. dollars. She was buying carriers and subs from the Russians and building her own nuclear missile submarines as fast as she could. In the preceding months, Kelly said, hard American and British intelligence had shown France and China engaging in secret joint naval exercises in the Taiwan Strait on seven different occasions.

Christ, what a stew.

The Taiwan Strait, between the People's Republic of China on the mainland and that offshore thorn in her side, Taiwan, was as dangerous a stretch of water as there was; it, rather than the Gulf, got Hawke's vote as the place most likely to spark a world war in years to come. Not that anyone in the Admiralty was asking his opinion. He wasn't paid for his geopolitical savvy. He was in Gibraltar for the briefing solely at Kelly's request. There was, the director said, a new assignment. A matter of some urgency, he said.

As his dear friend, Ambrose Congreve of Scotland Yard, had observed on numerous occasions, it was simply cloak-and-dagger time again. This notion, the prospect of his immediate assignment, a hostage rescue, soon had a salutary effect on his mood. Hawke had always found the classic covert snatch to be one of life's more rewarding endeavors. The former hostage's appreciative smiles upon rescue were priceless reminders of why one played the game.

This particular hostage was exceptionally lucky. According to Kelly, only the actions of an alert station chief in Marrakech had alerted the Americans that one of their own was in trouble. He'd been stepping out of his car at La Mamounia just as a drunk was being loaded into the rear of a black sedan. The drunk looked American, the two men "helping" him were Chinese. Sensing something was amiss, the station chief jumped back into his car and followed the sedan for hours, all the way to the harbor at Casablanca.

Armed guards at the foot of the gangway made intervention impossible, and he'd watched helplessly as the unconscious man was hauled up the gangplank of the *Star of Shanghai*. He'd called Langley immediately. His suspicions were confirmed. The drunk was likely one of their own all right, due out of China a week ago and presumed dead.

Feeling much rejuvenated (driving at speed also worked wonders), Alex Hawke found himself grinning foolishly after only an hour or so behind the wheel. The sun was shining, his recently restored C Type was screaming along the Grand Corniche straightaway at 130 mph, and, for the moment, all was right with his world. His two hands firmly positioned at quarter to three, Hawke relished the notion that he was officially back in the game.

A sign marker flashed by: Ste. Tropez. Only a few hours from his destination, the old resort at Cannes. Executing a racing change down into second gear, going quite quickly into a built-up S-bend, Hawke inhaled deeply.

Provence was delightful in June. Glorious. Somewhere, bees were buzzing. He'd always felt a certain kinship with bees. After all, were they not similarly employed? Zipping around all day, doing the queen's work, ha?

Indeed.

Spring itself was in the air. Not to mention the scented vapors of hot Castrol motor oil wafting back from one's long, louvered bonnet. Good stuff. The feeling of raw power as one smashed one's shoe to the floorboard and, whilst exiting a descending-radius curve, hearing the throaty roar of the naturally aspirated 4.4-liter XK Straight-Six responding beautifully. He'd been listening to the newly rebuilt motor carefully all day and had yet to hear any expensive noises.

Nor did he, until he arrived in Cannes and checked into the fabled Carlton and heard the chap at Reception say how much his bloody seaside suite would cost him per night.

Chapter Two

Hampstead Heath

AMBROSE CONGREVE LAVISHED A DOLLOP OF TIPTREE'S LIT-
tle scarlet strawberry preserve onto his warm toast and held it up for
closer inspection. Satisfied, he contemplated the two three-minute
eggs in their Minton blue china cups with unbridled relish and a
shudder of warm satisfaction. Songbirds trilled outside his sunny
windows and the teapot was whistling merrily on the Aga. To say that
Ambrose was enjoying his early breakfast in the sunny conservatory
of his new house would be gross understatement.

It was pure, unadulterated bliss.

Moments precisely like this one, the legendary New Scotland
Yard criminalist reflected, had been the stuff of keen anticipation for
lo these many months.

Just as there had been times, shivering with damp cold in his
drear little Bayswater flat of many years, that he'd never dared dream
these happy domestic circumstances might ever come to pass.

His present situation, newly acquired, was a lovely brick-and-
stone cottage in Hampstead Heath. The house proper, and some of
the outbuildings, had been bombed almost into extinction by the
Nazis during the Blitz. It had been the property of his late aunt, Augusta. The dear woman had spent the last half of the century in a lov-
ing restoration of house and gardens completed just a few short
months before her sudden death at age ninety-seven. Augusta had
died peacefully in her sleep. Ambrose, standing at the graveside, had
hoped this exit method ran in the family.

Attending the reading of the late Mrs. Bulling's last testament at
her solicitor's drab offices in Kensington High Street, Ambrose's re-
morse had been tempered by the vain hope that he might inherit.
There was, after all, a complete set of Minton china she'd promised

him decades earlier, and he sat there feigning composure, hoping she'd not forgotten him.

She had not.

Rather, from the cold grave, Aunt Augusta had stunned all present by bequeathing Heart's Ease cottage and the entirety of its contents to her dear nephew, Ambrose Congreve, instead of to her sole issue, her son, Henry Bulling. A stupefied silence descended upon the lawyer's office. Henry Bulling, the assumed heir and a minor diplomat by trade, sat for some few moments in goggle-eyed shock, taking quick, shallow breaths. He shot Congreve a look that spoke volumes, all of which would have made for unpleasant reading, and then rose somewhat unsteadily on shaky pins and made for the door.

The solicitor, a Mr. Reading, coughed into his fist once or twice and shuffled documents atop his large desk. There was a lavatory down the corridor and the door could be heard to slam loudly several seconds later. There was a muffled gargling noise, a retching actually, and the lawyer quickly resumed his reading. All ears were turned in his direction. There was a calico cat, Reading continued, apparently not well, which would be solely entrusted to Mrs. Bulling's son, Henry. The cat, Felicity, and the princely sum of one thousand pounds.

This current incident was just the latest in a long chain of disappointments for Henry. Ambrose had known him since birth. He was a boy who'd seemed positively doomed from the very beginning.

Augusta's only son was plainly one of life's born unfortunates. A lackluster hank of orange hair lay atop his pate. He had not been blessed with the strong jawline and prominent chin that most Bulling men were known for leading with. He'd struggled in various public schools and been sent packing down from Cambridge for debauchery. Which is what they called in those days being discovered in a coat closet with a don's wife in a compromising (and difficult to achieve) position.

Born to Augusta in Bruges, by one of her husbands, a no-account count, a Belgian noble of some kind, Henry was a notorious layabout as a young man. It had gotten so bad that, at one point, Ambrose simply gave up on finding the boy a job he could hold for more than a month. Ambrose took to referring to his wastrel cousin as the "Belgian Loafer" after a shoe of that name. Actually, Ambrose thought the nickname did the eponymous shoe a disservice. The comfortable handmade shoes (a favorite of Congreve's) were very stylish and wore quite well. Henry fit neither description.

Migrating to Paris, Henry had spent a few years dabbling at the Sorbonne, and he had dabbled in the arts, too. Setting up his easel on the quay beside the storied and moody Seine, he had produced a series of dramatically large canvases that were, to Ambrose's practiced artist's eye, scenes of mindless violence.

In the eighties, Henry Bulling lost a good portion of his mother's money in the Lloyd's debacle. Penniless, tail twixt the hindmost, he returned to his mother's cottage in Hampstead Heath and moved into the small flat above the gardener's shed. Later, he moved to an apparently rather unsavory place in town. He remained nonetheless an effete snob, in his cousin Ambrose's opinion. His character was not enhanced by the faux French accent. Nor by the hundred-dollar pink Charvet shirts from Paris he could ill afford on the clerk's salary he earned at the French embassy in Knightsbridge.

His role there was not an exalted one—he worked in transportation and trade relations—but he was in a small way useful to queen and country.

Henry Bulling was a spy. He earned the odd extra shilling or two keeping an eye on things at the French delegation, reporting on a regular basis to the Yard. Since Ambrose was Henry's first cousin, it fell to him to listen to the weekly gossip and examine the purloined copies of generally useless documents Bulling had secreted in his briefcase before leaving for lunch. It was Ambrose's habit to meet his cousin on various random but prearranged benches throughout St. James' Park. It wasn't sly and sophisticated tradecraft, but it worked well enough.

Congreve's new housekeeper, May Purvis, a sturdy, sweet-faced Scotswoman from the Highlands, was bustling about in the adjacent kitchen. After breakfast, she would begin her daily rounds, plumping pillows, dusting and adjusting, keeping Heart's Ease cottage pristine for her beneficent employer. Curiously enough, Mrs. Purvis was, at the moment, wallpapering his drawers. That is to say, carefully scissoring bits of floral and scenic Chinese toile wallpaper and placing them into the bottoms of all the cupboards and drawers in his new kitchen.

May had a habit of whistling as she worked, and Ambrose found it quite cheery. She would pick up in the middle of a tune, stick with it for an hour or so, and then move on to some fresh melody in her seemingly inexhaustible repertoire. He watched her bustling about every morning and tried to imagine if this current scene was an accurate representation of married life. Cozy, tranquil, comforting. An idyll, in fact. Even Mrs. Purvis's bashful smile as she hummed and hoovered was—well, he sometimes wondered if there might not be . . . someone, out there. His other half.

He supposed not, or he would surely have found her by this stage of the game. He was, after all, on the wrong side of fifty.

The happy detective bit into his slice of toast, heaved a sigh of contentment, and dove back into today's *Times*. The economic news in Europe was grim. The cornerstones, Germany and France, were both reporting stagnant economies. France, amazingly enough, was pulling out of the EU! And it was rife with turmoil after another political assassination. There were sniffs of panic at EU headquarters in Brussels. Et cetera, et cetera, page after page. He sometimes wondered why he bothered with the damn newspapers. They were uniformly gloomy on a daily basis.

But, to be sure, all was right with his world. His sunny little corner of it, at any rate. His musty old flat in Bayswater was already receding into the mists. In its place, this sturdy brick pile in the Georgian manner. A gabled slate roof with imposing chimneys standing sentry at either end, and a lovely fanlight over the front door. It was by no means a large house. No, it was small, but handsome. He had a few acres or so of sun-dappled grass and beds of peonies, lilies, and space, when he got around to it, to cultivate his beloved dahlias. Yes, an abundance of them. Polar Beauties, Golden Leaders, and his favorite, the Requiems.

Everything in his life, it seemed, was brand new. His recently acquired dog, Ranger, a handsome Dutch Decoy Spaniel, lay puddled round his slippered feet, sleeping in the warm yellow sunlight. He had reached down to idly stroke the dog's head when Ranger looked up suddenly and growled loudly.

"Good lord, what on earth is that, Mrs. Purvis?" Ambrose sputtered.

"What is what, Mr. Congreve?"

There had come down the hall such a pounding and banging at the front door as ever you heard and yet the woman was blissfully unaware, snipping away at the blue Chinese toile paper.

"That infernal pounding. At the front door, I believe. Is the bell out of commish?"

"Let me find out, sir. Did the bell ring?"

"Mrs. Purvis, please."

"I'm just going as fast as I can then, aren't I, sir?"

Ranger raced down the worn olive-green Axminster carpet of the hallway ahead of her, barking furiously. Congreve, nose buried in the *Times*, tried to ignore the muffled conversation coming from the front hall and concentrate on an article he was reading. Apparently, the bloody French were holding naval exercises with the Chinese. And it wasn't the first time. This was the seventh. Something was clearly afoot with England's irksome neighbors across the Channel. After years of trying to forge a united Europe, they seemed to be striking out on their own. It was a hoary tale, but a true one. Perhaps he'd lean on young Bulling a bit more heavily in future.

"It's two gentlemen to see you, sir," Mrs. Purvis said, returning.

"About what?"

"Didn't say, Mr. Congreve. Only that it was a matter of some urgency."

"Good lord, is there no escape?" Congreve said, getting to his feet and zipping up the wool jumper he'd slipped into against the early morning chill. "Tell them I'll be right there, Mrs. Purvis. Invite them inside, offer tea, but keep an eye on them. And see if you can call off the dog, please. It wouldn't do to have him bite a policeman."

"Policemen? How'd you come by that?"

"I may have mentioned that I am a detective, Mrs. Purvis. It's my nature to take a mystery and bend it to my will."

"But—"

"Men in pairs, Mrs. Purvis, are always coppers."

"Or they may be a nice gay couple, mayn't they be, Mr. Congreve?" she said, with a twinkle of her blue eyes.

Chapter Three

Cannes

TONIGHT, THE TRAFFIC ALONG LE CROISETTE, THAT BROAD, palm-lined boulevard that hugs the shoreline of this normally glittering village, was minimal. It was fiendishly cold. A few desultory black Mercedes taxis cruised the big hotels and, now and then, a startlingly red Ferrari or chrome-yellow Lamborghini with inscrutable Arabic license tags would roar up under the porte-cochere of the Majestic or the Hotel Carlton and disgorge a leggy blonde just down from Paris to visit her "sick uncle."

Thing about all these bloody sick uncles, Hawke had noticed on prior occasions, was that they seldom if ever emerged from their shuttered lairs to take the air. So, what on earth did they do in there with those leggy nieces all day?

At just after ten that evening, a Friday night in early May, in a gilded grey-and-white bedroom at the Hotel Carlton, Alexander Hawke, recently arrived, and a woman, recently encountered, were making noisy love, thrashing about on an ornate and very rumpled bed. Kissing the woman hard on the lips, he stole a glance at the faintly glowing blue dial on his wrist. The dive watch confirmed the atomic clock in his head, an internal biological device that was usually accurate to within one minute.

Yes. Time to get a move on.

"*Du vent,*" the woman murmured, pausing in her own fluid rhythms to gaze at the louvered shutters banging violently against the French doors of the terrace. The howling cold wind had to be gusting upward of thirty knots.

"Yes," he said, gently stroking her cheek. "What about it?"

"*C'est terrible,* eh?"

"Hmm," Hawke said, a bit preoccupied at the moment.

Hawke's back arched involuntarily. A cry escaped his lips. She was still breathing hard, sitting astride him, and he admired her strong ivory profile in silhouette. She was naked save for the black sable stole draped over her shoulders, loosely fastened at the neck with a diamond brooch, probably an old Van Cleef by the look of the setting. Beads of sweat formed a rivulet between the hills of her dark-tipped breasts and there was a light sheen of moisture on her high forehead.

She was strikingly beautiful. Astonishingly so. Her name, Commander Hawke had only recently discovered, was Jet. She was, apparently, a celebrity sufficiently famous to have but a single name. A film star of some magnitude in China. Hawke, who favored the luminous black-and-white motion pictures made on Hollywood back lots or at Shepperton Studios before and during the war, had never seen one of her films. Nor did he care to. His idea of a one-name star was Bogart.

In fact, beyond her dark eyes, her red lips, the soft contours of her body, and the confines of this vast bed, there was very little he did know about the woman.

They had met that very afternoon at a posh luncheon at the Hotel du Cap over at Antibes. A German tycoon named Augustus von Draxis had hosted the affair (held on the green lawns beneath the pines of his pale blue Villa Felix), and he had graciously ferried a few guests over from the Carlton pier aboard his sleek Riva launch. As it happened, Hawke and the woman were seated together in the stern for the short and stormy voyage across the bay at Cannes to Cap d'Antibes. It was spectacularly rough going, and he had admired both her cheek and her cheerful nonchalance.

"Well, you've certainly got good sea legs for a woman," Alex Hawke said to her. Her expression hinted that she did not take this as a compliment.

"Il fait froid," she said, shivering. She was eyeing his somewhat shabby Irish fisherman's sweater. Besides his navy kit and dinner jacket, he didn't have much in the way of wardrobe. The woman was wearing a very short black dress, raw silk, with bare shoulders and a necklace of large Tahitian black pearls in graduated strands. Quite expensive baroques, Hawke thought, noticing their irregular shapes. Jet had not dressed for heavy weather. She had dressed for men.

"Sorry," he said, pulling the thing over his head and handing it to her. "How thoughtless." He still had on his old blue flannel shirt, which offered a modicum of protection from the wind.

"Right," she said, somehow donning his thick woolen sweater with only minimal further disturbance to either her severely styled black hair or her dramatic makeup. He found himself watching her every move. Her gestures were economical, almost balletic, and Hawke found himself mesmerized. He knew quite a few men who were besotted with Oriental women. He had never quite understood the fascination until this very moment.

Looking perhaps at his own thick black hair and sharp blue eyes, she interrupted his reverie. "You are Irish, no?"

"No. I'm a half-breed. English father, American mother."

She seemed to consider that briefly, but gave no reply. She did, however, adjust her black pleated skirt, giving him a glimpse of lush pale thigh and filigreed stocking tops held up by black suspenders. It was a fashion statement he'd always found profoundly appealing.

"Staying at the Carlton, are you?" Hawke asked. He wasn't all that accustomed to flirting (if that's what this was), and he felt awkward. If his poor attempts at conversation with this beautiful woman sounded like so much cheap tin to his own ear, he could only imagine what they must sound to hers.

Anyway, she managed a half smile.

"No. I went ashore to shop. I am a guest aboard that yacht out there. We came for the film festival and stayed. The owner likes it here."

"*Valkyrie*, I believe, isn't she?" Hawke said, gazing across the water at the astounding white sloop. He knew exactly which boat she was, but it seemed far more sporting to feign ignorance. The German yacht was famous. Just shy of three hundred feet length overall, with a forty-foot beam, she was the largest sloop-rigged private sailing yacht on earth. Built in strict secrecy in Hamburg by von Draxis's German yard, she had three fully automated carbon fiber masts and carried twenty-six thousand square feet of sail. Hawke had heard rumors she could do well over twenty knots per hour under sail.

"Yes, that's *Valkyrie*. She belongs to our host, Baron von Draxis. How do you know him?"

"I don't. Someone slipped his invitation under my door."

"Ah. Schatzi is an old and dear friend. You seem to like his yacht. Perhaps I can arrange a tour."

"Tour? I'd rather sail her. I'd give my eyeteeth to sail that boat, to be honest," Hawke said, his pale sun-bleached eyes devouring the boat from stem to stern.

"You are a sailor, *Monsieur*?"

"An old navy man," Hawke said, hating the sound of that, and he looked quickly away. An "old navy man"? He wasn't that old. And he wasn't strictly a naval officer any longer. He was more of a contract advisor. How ridiculous and fatuous he sounded. Good God. He was instantly ashamed of his transparent and hollow efforts to charm this woman. The jolt of guilt deep in his gut had shocked him, as if he'd swallowed a live battery.

For two years, Hawke had been trying to suppress a brutal memory of overwhelming loss: the murder of his beloved bride, Victoria, on the church steps within minutes of their wedding. The event itself, the graven images of blood and lace, had been bulwarked against. But the vicious specter of pain remained, lurking on the outer edge of his consciousness, lingering, grinning hungrily, breathing hotly. He had tried to run away and failed.

He had come to call this specter his "black dog."

Six months after his wife's murder, there was a brief and illconsidered rekindling of an old relationship. It was unforgivable, but it happened. The woman involved, an old and dear friend named Consuelo de los Reyes, no longer spoke to him. Would not return his calls nor acknowledge his flowers. He didn't blame her. After a period, he gave up and retreated within his own walls.

Fate, and its accomplice tragedy, had finally won the lifelong battle. At barely seven years of age, Alex Hawke had witnessed the horrific murder of his beloved parents on a yacht in the Caribbean. Pirates had come aboard in the middle of the night. His mother had been raped before her throat was slashed. His father was crucified upon the very door the boy was hiding behind. He had seen it all. Behind his door, he kept silent to stay alive.

He kept silent about it now, for much the same reason.

For nearly two years, Hawke had simply disappeared from his own life. He locked up his house in Gloucestershire and fled. He ran to escape his feelings, to repair his heart. As far as he could run. Tibet.

Malaya. Burma. A tea-and-vegan lifestyle, no liquor at all. The daily yin-yang discipline of tai chi. Mountain climbing. Meditation. Fasting. A Zen retreat on the beautiful Thai island of Koh Samui. It didn't work, none of it.

Alone in his one-room hut by the Gulf of Martaban, when the night was dead still, he could hear the black dog. Could see him crouching there, just inside the green edge of the leafy jungle, panting, all pink gums and bared fangs. Ready to pounce. He ran home. Opened the house in Belgrave Square. Once back in London, he'd tried liquor. Mr. Gosling's rum. Barrels of the high-proof stuff. That hadn't worked, either, and he'd felt like hell every morning in the bargain.

His closest friend, Chief Inspector Ambrose Congreve, had told him perhaps this period of mourning was growing unhealthily long. Perhaps it was time to begin to see other women.

Looking at Jet in his bed now, he thought that, yes, perhaps the world-famous detective had solved yet another of life's mysteries.

It was time. Hawke was the kind of man who needed a woman. Perhaps this one was the one he needed.

Chapter Four

Cap d'Antibes

AT ONE OF THE PINK LUNCHEON TABLES SCATTERED RAN-
domly beneath a copse of whistling pine trees, Hawke gave chase. Jet
was a girl, he now thought, who wanted to be caught. His grandfather, a font of enduring wisdom, had said to Alex at a tender age,
"Never chase a girl who doesn't want to be caught." The nine-year-
old boy hadn't really understood the lesson then. He did now.

The sun had returned to the sky, as pale as a waning moon. He
was glad he'd come. He tried to be witty and charming throughout
the bouillabaisse and poisson du jour and sorbet au citron.

It wasn't easy. He felt like a two-bit stage actor who kept flubbing
his lines. Out of practice, he thought.

After the luncheon, the two of them had strolled up a freshly
washed gravel path bordered on either side by manicured gardens of
alyssum, salvia, and lobelia. The wide path rose up a gentle slope and
led to an exquisitely beautiful hotel sitting atop the breast of a leafy
hill. The Hotel du Cap definitely lived up to its billing.

It had been a pleasant enough afternoon. The girl was stunning.
Hawke had eaten a dozen *portugaises* and washed the delicious oysters down with cold white wine. The black dog was nowhere to be
seen.

Popping an oyster into his mouth, he had said to Jet, "You know
who's the bravest man who ever lived?"

"Let me guess. You."

"No. The first man ever to eat an oyster."

And, somehow, there had been more oysters and then more
champagne on the return voyage to the Carlton pier and then at dinner and in Le Petite Bar downstairs and somehow the beautiful Jet
had ended up here in his bed.

"Le vent," she said again now in the darkness of the Carlton bedroom.

"What about it?" Hawke said, stroking back a lock of her hair, black as a crow's wing and cut on the diagonal across the sharp planes of her cheeks.

"C'est mal, this wind."

"Winds have a habit of blowing themselves out sooner or later," Hawke said. "Like men, I suppose."

"Where do you live?" she asked him.

"Oh, London and thereabouts. How about you?"

"I have a flat in Paris. The Avenue Foch."

"Very posh."

"This is not your suite, Mr. Hawke," Jet said, athletically disengaging her body from his, rolling over, and firing a cigarette, sucking hungrily, her dark eyes flaring in the glow of the red coal.

"Really? Why on earth do you say that?" he asked, his own keen blue eyes laughing.

"No toothbrush. No razor," she said, exhaling a plume of harsh purple smoke toward the ceiling. He looked at her carefully. She had the blackest eyes. He liked to believe he could read people through their eyes. He assumed most people felt that way. He'd been trying to read Jet's eyes all day long with no success. Inscrutable was the word.

"Ah. Well, there's that," he said.

"And the name on the card. Out in the hall by your door. You wrote it yourself. It's not the engraved placard the hotel concierge provides for guests upon arrival."

"Guilty as charged."

"You are a—what do you call it—a cat burglar?"

"No, my dear Jet, I am not. I hate cats," he said, swinging his long legs off the edge of the bed. "Besides, they'd never allow pets in this pretty palace."

"Where are you going?"

"Out to the terrace to check something. I have an old acquaintance sailing for Shanghai on the evening tide. I have to make sure he misses the boat."

"Don't let me keep you, Mr. Hawke."

He didn't bother with his shirt and trousers, just shouldered into his dinner jacket and slipped out through the French doors, grabbing a pair of rubber-coated Zeiss Ikon military binoculars he'd left hanging by a strap from the doorknob. Raising the glasses to his eyes, he saw the sea whipped into a frenzy. Strange weather was, Commander Alexander Hawke knew, not at all unusual in this corner of the world.

The entire Mediterranean Sea passes through the eye of a needle. Only fifteen miles of water separated Ceuta in North Africa from the Rock, that headless limestone sphinx crouching on the tiny peninsula of Gibraltar. The ancients called the rockpiles standing on either side of the straits the Pillars of Hercules. Beyond them lay chaos, the dark and spooky ocean they called *Mare Tenebrosum*.

Spooky enough out there tonight, Alex Hawke thought. The roiling sky was a bruised color, yellowish and grey on the horizon.

He allowed himself a thin smile. There was something in him that loved bad weather. Sunny days were a dime a dozen in the South of France and this night he was glad of a little mood and drama. Besides, foul weather might keep a few prying eyes and ears battened down and out of his way. His mission tonight was certainly straightforward enough. A simple hostage snatch demanding basic techniques that were, once learned the hard way in the Special Boat Squadron, never forgotten.

But, as usual in the life of Alexander Hawke, the implications of failure were enormous.

He swung the Ikons west to the harbor proper and found what he was looking for in the crowd of grand yachts, fishing boats, and a thicket of sailboat masts. An ancient rust bucket called the *Star of Shanghai*. She'd arrived from Casablanca and was en route from Cannes to Aden and then on to Rangoon. Aboard her, he'd learned two days ago, was an involuntary American passenger. A CIA chap, whose very life was hanging by—

"Alex?" Her voice floated out from the darkened bedroom. She spoke both English and French with a lilting Chinese accent. The words came to him like a tinkling wind chime.

"Sorry," he said above the wind, scanning the horizon with the Ikons. "Just give me a moment, dear. Have some more champagne. The bucket is by the bed."

In his mind's eye, he saw his old friend Ambrose Congreve smirking at that one. Caviar, champagne, fancy rooms at the Carlton. And in his bed—

He would never have taken the wildly expensive suite (ever since his first stint in the navy, he'd loved small bedrooms with single beds and crisp white linen) had not the corner rooms offered one very specific advantage. The eighth-floor terrace of Suite 801 happened to present a panoramic view of the entire harbor. From this luxurious perch, Hawke could monitor the comings and goings of every vessel in the harbor, unseen. And so he had done for the last two days.

His own boat, *Blackhawke*, lay anchored in deep water a half mile from the harbor entrance. To all appearances, she was simply another rich man's play toy in this glittering Côte d'Azur yacht harbor, a seagoing Mecca for the extravagantly wealthy. In reality, she was more of a small warship cleverly disguised as a megayacht by the Huisman Yard in Holland.

The yacht's unusual name had not been chosen lightly. She was named in honor of Hawke's notorious ancestor, the English pirate, Blackhawke. John "Black Jack" Hawke, born in Plymouth, had gone to sea as a cabin boy serving under the infamous "Calico Jack" Rackham. This worthy buccaneer was known as much for his colorful calico cotton clothes as for his beautiful pirate wife, Anne Bonny. Years later, Calico Jack was hanged for piracy in Port Royal. Young Hawke, already prized for his heroism and amazing luck, was the crew's unanimous choice to succeed Rackham as captain.

"To whom does the sea belong?" he would ask.

"Blackhawke!" was the unanimous reply.

Over the years, as his reputation grew, Black Jack Hawke would come to be known by a shorter, more memorable name: Blackhawke. He operated in the Caribbean, commissioned by colonial authorities in Jamaica, preying on Spanish possessions. His hearty band became known as "the brethren of the coast." Tens of millions in gold and booty buried by the brethren remain hidden to this day along the rocky coast of what was then the island of Hispaniola.

"Fortune favors the fast," was the young pirate captain's motto, and he made good on it. Blackhawke had light sloops called balandras

specially built in his home port of Plymouth and rarely had trouble overtaking even the fastest quarry. Once he'd spied you, and his ship *Revenge* was bearing down, you'd do well to start making peace with your maker.

Ferocious and merciless in battle, Blackhawke was one of the very first to fly the Jolly Roger, a hand-sewn black flag emblazoned with symbols taken from old gravestones in his native land: skulls, crossed bones, and an hourglass to warn prey how rapidly their time was running out.

Blackhawke's enormous success was later attributed by scholars to atypical pirate behavior. He was highly intelligent, drank only tea, never swore in front of women, and regularly observed the Sabbath. For all that, he was condemned to the gallows in the Old Bailey for striking a mutinous crewman on the head with a bucket and killing him. His corpse was hung on the banks of the Thames as a warning to all who would take up the pirate's life.

It was a warning his bloodline had found difficult to heed.

Blackhawke had been steaming all day en route from Corsica. Hawke's yacht had arrived on station according to schedule, just after nightfall. Hawke had spoken to his chief of security, Tom Quick, and ordered all unnecessary lights aboard doused. From Hawke's luxurious perch at the hotel, her darkened silhouette resembled some hulking, uninhabited island lying just offshore.

The *Star of Shanghai* had arrived in Cannes harbor the afternoon before. Hawke had observed minor comings and goings aboard her, nothing too intriguing. She was now moored along the long narrow breakwater that curved out to sea from the eastern edge of the harbor. Hawke focused on the *Star*, swept the glasses back and forth, stem to stern.

From this cursory appraisal, he was surprised she was still afloat. What the hell were they loading? It looked like huge barrel-shaped sections of polished steel. According to his dossier, some kind of Renault factory assemblies. She was riding low in the water, down by the head. On the dock, more massive steel O-rings secured with bright orange tarps. Looked innocent enough but you never knew.

She wasn't scheduled to sail for another hour. But schedules in French ports didn't always behave properly. Time to go, at any rate.

Hawke lowered the glasses, noting the sudden lack of breeze on his cheeks. The wind had vanished just as capriciously as it had sprung up forty-eight hours earlier. And now, as the temperature rose perceptibly, a thick, viscous fog bank the color of charcoal was rolling in from the sea. Hawke turned and ducked back into his bedroom through the French doors, his brain ticking over rapidly now.

"What are you doing now?" Jet said with some annoyance, sitting up in bed and vainly attempting to cover her quite beautiful breasts with a corner of bedsheet.

"Sorry, dear girl. I've got a meeting," Hawke said, stepping into his skivvies and then his black trousers. He pulled open a dresser drawer and removed the new nylon swivel holster that held his pistol. He'd spent long days down at Fort Monkton, the Royal Navy's Field School near Portsmouth, assassinating video projections in the simulator. He could now comfortably draw and fire in no more than one-quarter of a second. It was his fondest wish to shave one-fifth off that. He had no urge to spend his last moments on earth counting the bullet holes in his tummy.

He wore the gun just behind the right hipbone, the position he'd found most suitable for the fastest draw. The gun was a lightweight Walther TPH only recently acquired and he hoped it was as effective as advertised. Tom Quick, a U.S. Army sharpshooter and weapons expert before joining Hawke's security staff, had assured him it was good for close work. Assuming one used Quick's own hand-loaded ammunition, which Hawke most assuredly did.

"So. You are some kind of spy, or counterspy. Is that it?"

"Over-the-counter spy would be more like it."

"Meaning?"

"For sale without prescription," he said, checking the heft of the fully loaded mag and sliding it with a satisfying click into the butt of the gun.

"What?"

"Readily available, you know, generic espionage. Mundane stuff, I'm afraid. Tedious corporate snooping and the like. A dull business, I assure you. Might as well have studied the law."

"And the gun?"

"Strictly precautionary. Might encounter some archfiend of the industrial espionage world out there."

"Bullshit."

He cut his eyes toward her. The word didn't fit the face. Women had every right to use the same language as men. He wasn't being priggish. He just didn't find it attractive.

"Really? How on earth do you know that, my dear?" he said, reaching behind his back and slipping the weapon into its high-tech scabbard. Then he reached for his knife.

It was an item acquired a few years earlier in Qatar. A long-bladed dagger called the Assassin's Fist. He wore it strapped to the inside of his right forearm with a quick-release device his friend Stokely Jones had perfected in the Mekong Delta. The knife had seen a lot of use. He'd recently replaced the original blade with six inches of the finest Sheffield steel.

"So. You have a meeting?" the actress pouted. "At this hour? Ridiculous."

"Yes. Quite sorry, darling," Hawke said, pulling a thick black turtleneck jumper down over his head. "Offshore work, you see. That's the problem with freelance. Dreadful hours."

He gave her a peck on the cheek and withdrew his face before she could slap him.

"You'll find my office number in London scribbled inside," he said, handing her a gaudy matchbook from the Casino Barriere de Cannes. "I do hope we'll see each other again. A quiet dinner at Harry's Bar, perhaps."

"You are the most—"

Hawke put his finger to his lips and then said, "I know, I know. Unbearable. A cad. A fiend. I can only hope you'll forgive me. You see, my dear girl, nobody quite knows this yet, but there's a war on."

"War?"

"Hmm," he said, and started to turn away. She grabbed his sleeve and put a small white card into his hand.

"What's this?"

"An invitation. The baron is hosting a small private dinner party aboard *Valkyrie* tomorrow evening, Mr. Hawke. To celebrate the launch of his newest ship. An ocean liner. Perhaps you would like to come, yes? As my guest, of course."

"On one condition. You must promise never to say that word again, darling," he said. " 'Bullshit.' It's most unattractive coming from that pretty mouth."

He crossed the darkened room swiftly and pulled the heavy mahogany door softly closed behind him. Then he plucked his handwritten card from the brass fixture by his door, stuck it inside his pocket, and made a quick dash for the marble stairway.

The *Star of Shanghai* was scheduled to sail on the tide at midnight. His old friend Brick Kelly, the CIA director, had informed him that somewhere deep in the bowels of that old rust bucket was a captured American operative formerly working deep cover. A dead man walking who just might be able to save the world.

His name, Hawke had learned in Gibraltar, was Harry Brock.

Chapter Five

Paris, 1970

WHAT A FRIEND ARCHITECTS HAVE IN SNOW, THE CORSICAN chuckled to himself, climbing out of his taxi. Almost a foot of the white stuff had fallen. Even the Gare d'Austerlitz, an ugly duckling by Parisian standards, looked beautiful with its frosting. The barrel-shaped man slogged across the Place Valhubert to the station's entrance. No boots, just tired leather shoes, his icy wet socks sagging around his ankles in the slush. He'd left the taxi running. His fellow drivers at the stand would look after it, no problem.

Yes, there are many grand railway stations in Paris, Monsieur Emile Bonaparte considered on this freezing December night, brushing wet snow from his eyes with the back of his hand, but this one, this ugly duckling hiding under its mantle of winter white, this one is all mine.

A vaporous yellow light hovered inside the main hall's soaring web of iron. A cloud of iridescent steam rose above the damp and overheated woolens of the teeming crowds. Surprisingly busy for a Sunday evening, he observed. There was a hubbub of noisy passengers as throngs departing for the South of France, Spain, and Portugal surged against travelers arriving from those selfsame destinations.

Like the battlefield ebb and flow of charging armies, the old soldier imagined, firing a soggy unfiltered Gauloise. Emile felt a certain stirring of his blood, pleased with this ironic, militaristic turn of thought. In the café earlier, he'd spied a lengthy piece in *Paris Soir* and relished every word of the account, chewing it carefully with pride, seeing the action.

On this very day in history, he saw, the second of December, 1805, his glorious ancestor Napoleon and his Grande Armée had defeated the Austro-Russian armies above the small Moravian town of Austerlitz. A sublime trap it had been. A feint here! There! Suddenly, the genius Napoleon had lured the Allies to the Pratzen Heights, had rushed in his III Corps to crush them! Ah, yes. Long ago and far away, but still shining through the mists of memory and history.

An army on a hill. The glory of it. *La Gloire!*

He looked up at the sudden shriek of a whistle. A massive white-sugared engine, heavily laden with snow, rumbled in amidst a cloud of frosty vapors. A rush of porters and people meeting the Nice–Paris train brushed by him. He jammed the cigarette into the corner of his mouth, shot the cuffs of his rough brown leather jacket, and joined the tide. Ahead, he saw the doors of the second-class carriages open, and his heart beat a little faster. He slipped on his heavy tortoiseshell glasses with brown, tobacco-stained fingers and scanned the emerging passengers. Was that—could it really be?

Luca.

Emile Bonaparte watched his son step down from the train and hardly recognized him. Well, he's grown, hasn't he? Emile thought. My God, he's almost as tall as I am!

"Papa! Papa!" the boy cried. Emile grinned as his son shouldered between two jostling women struggling against the tide. One of the two, the beefy one who'd dropped her string bag full of baguettes, shouted angrily, wagging her stumpy finger at his son. But the fifteen-year-old, seeing an opening, laughed merrily at her and darted and dodged ahead, making his way toward his father.

Two very large men in loud sport jackets remained between father and son. Emile shoved past them and stepped forward and, with his arms spread wide, embraced his child. He was startled at the hard knots of muscle at his back and shoulders.

"Luca!" Emile said, clasping him happily to his breast. "Did you bring it? You didn't forget, did you?"

"Don't be stupid, Father! You only need look in my sack."

Emile released his son from the embrace (Luca was plainly embarrassed by such a show), and his son handed him the parcel. Inside, four brown bottles of Pietra, the beer of his native Corsica, difficult to find in the small shops in the St. Germain des Prés.

"Eh bien, you must be hungry, eh?" he said, tousling the boy's thick black hair. *"Alors.* Give me your knapsack. Let's go eat some

supper." He picked up the boy's battered valise and they headed for the exit. "Get ready. Cold as a witch's tit, out there."

Outside, slogging through heavy snowfall back to the taxi rank, Emile was glad of his leather jacket and worried about Luca's worn woolen one. With a nod toward his friend Marcel, who'd been guarding his old Renault taxicab, he motioned to his son. *"Allons! Vite!* Quickly! You'll freeze!"

"Good boy, Pozzo," Luca said, opening the door and seeing the dog up front.

The dog, a scruffy old mutt with one eye, but a good watchdog, growled his assent and the boy slid into the front seat beside him. It was filthy in his father's taxi and smelled of sweat and black French tobacco, yes, but it was warm, and even Luca, who considered himself a true Stoic, was glad of it after trudging through the deep snow. With a single sweep of his short powerful arm, Emile cleared the fresh accumulation of glistening powder from the windshield, and climbed behind the wheel. The ancient engine turned over reluctantly and they were off.

"Maurice is holding a table for me at Le Pin Sec," Emile said, taking a left out of the car park and maneuvering the old Renault into the rutted snow of the Quai d'Austerlitz. "I know you like it."

"Papa, no, no. Lilas. I insist."

"Are you crazy?"

"It's expensive. Yes. But I will treat you. I have made some money. Doing some jobs."

"Jobs, eh? What kind of jobs?" Emile looked at his kid with a sidelong glance. The bookworm had finally started working?

"I write articles for the papers," the boy said, his face turned to the frosted window. "Political articles. They don't pay much but I've saved it."

"Political, eh? More love poems to Lenin and Trotsky? You and your Brigade Rouge. I hoped you would have outgrown this romantic infatuation with Communism by now."

"There is a deep schism in the Corse, Papa," Luca said. "The old, which is you. And the new, which is me. The Brigade Rouge."

"A *schism*? Is that what you said? Schism?"

Luca just smiled and stared out at the passing images of his favorite city.

"No comment, eh?" his father said. He coughed something up, rolled down his window, and spat it out. He said, *"Eh bien.* No politics. I'm right and you're left. I love you anyway. We'll go to the Lilas. Give you and your fucking Red Menace the night off, eh, boy? Ha-ha!"

Somehow, the old man managed to open a bottle of the Pietra with one hand, and he swigged it while he drove.

"Merci bien," he said, toasting his son with the bottle as they slid around a corner. "You want some?"

"Merci bien à tu, Mon Cher Papa," the boy said, taking the bottle and tossing back a swig, his dark almond eyes shining in the glow of the dashlight. Emile laughed. His youngest son had the glossy dark hair, long thick eyelashes, and sallow complexion of a true Corsican. Yes, here was a boy weaned on olive oil; you could almost catch the fragrant scent of the pine forests of the *maquis* in his hair. As his father drove and drank from his bottle, Luca squirmed uncomfortably.

"What—there is something here—" There was a hard object on the seat, poking Luca's hip. He raised himself up and grabbed it. A small black automatic pistol, he saw, holding it up to the light. It was flat and deadly looking. And, loaded, too, Luca could tell by the weight.

"Give me that," Emile said. He flipped the empty bottle over his shoulder into the back and stretched out his hand.

The boy did as he was told and said, "A job, Papa?"

"Phut, it's nothing," he said, slipping the weapon inside the side pocket of his leather jacket. "Some foreign crazies making too much noise is all. One of the New York families, I think. You know the types. Wiseguys. Foreign bullies. Busybodies. Think they can waltz onto our turf and intimidate me."

"Right," the boy said, looking at Emile carefully. His father did dangerous things for dangerous people. He was an enforcer in the oldest and most feared crime family in all of France, the Union Corse. His father had been shot and stabbed many times in his long career. When they swam in the sea, you could see that his body had been—

"Well. How was the ferry over to Nice?" Emile asked. "A nice boat?"

"Ça va," Luca replied matter-of-factly. And then, in English, he said, "I prefer horses to boats."

So, Emile thought, casting a sideways glance at his son. The boy's mother had been working on his English, eh? The child had a gift for languages. Hell, he had a gift for everything. Philosophy. Literature. A genius, some people even claimed. He'd always been the most curious boy. Always with his nose in a book. History. Art. Science. When Luca was seven, and just falling in love with his maps, a teacher had asked which he preferred, history or geography.

"They are the same," the boy replied matter-of-factly, "geography dictates history."

Hah! That was a good one. But, when he told it later that night, standing with his mates at the bar, they'd just stared at him blankly. Idiots. All his comrades were idiots. *Campesinos.*

And now, politics. The boy had drifted dangerously to the left for his father's tastes. Writing fucking Communist manifestos. No way to make a living, pamphlets, that much was for certain. If Luca envisioned a career in politics, which he had confided to his mother that he did, he'd better start steering a middle course. That way, like any good politician, he could go whichever way the wind blew.

"So, you've been riding?" Emile said, not wishing to spoil the reunion mood. He slowed down and turned right into the rue George Balanchine. "That's good. A man who cannot sit a horse well is not to be trusted. How is your dear mother, eh?"

"She hates you."

"Ah," Emile said, and made a sound like a wet finger touching a hot iron. "Love is like that."

M. Bonaparte managed to find parking in the snowy street. A few minutes later, father and son were sitting at a small window table at the bistro Lilas. It had a narrow red facade on the street and the rear door opened onto the catacombs, a convenient exit when you needed it. Emile ordered for both of them, sliced Lyonnais sausages and roast Bresse chicken with cornichons.

The stained vanilla-colored walls and the big zinc bar gave the place a prewar feel that older Parisian cabbies like Emile enjoyed when they were feeling flush. He saw familiar faces, but tonight he kept to himself, delighted just to bask in the rays from his brilliant and newly prosperous son.

After they'd eaten, Emile ordered another demi of the delicious Châteauneuf-du-Pape to celebrate his son's arrival. He refilled their glasses, hung a Gauloise from his lips, and said, "It's good, eh, Lilas? The food? The wine? Like you remember it? *Molto buono?*" Emile, like many Corsicans, often switched seamlessly between Italian and French.

Emile was enjoying the expensive food and drink and seeing his handsome son all grown up, employed, picking up the tab. He'd even taken tonight off, called in sick. In addition to his taxi, Emile worked five nights as a security guard at the Hôtel des Invalides, the massive old soldiers' home that stood along the Seine. With the two incomes, he could afford to have a pretty good life here in Paris and still send enough to Corsica each month to help Flavia care for Luca.

"*Alors.* You're all grown up now, eh? Fifteen."

"Sixteen. Papa—who is that man?" Luca said. "Do you know him?"

"What man?" Emile replied, looking around inside the crowded, smoky bistro. There were few women in the place, many men. Which one—

"No. Outside. At the window. Staring at me."

Emile looked around and saw a man standing just outside, his nose an inch from the glass. The stranger smiled at Luca, then blew a plume of cigarette smoke against the glass, hiding his face. Emile rapped the window sharply with his knuckles and the face reappeared. The man, he looked like a skeleton with black holes for eye sockets, turned his ugly smile on Emile and crooked his finger, beckoning.

"Some crazy," Emile said to his son. He pushed back his chair and got to his feet. "Don't move. I'll go see what the devil he wants."

"Be careful," Luca said.

He watched his father take his brown leather jacket from the hook by the door and push through out into the snow. The face at the window disappeared once more into the snow. For a time, Luca sat blowing his warm breath against the glass and scribbling problematic mathematical equations with his fingertip. After some minutes, the *garçon* appeared. Where had his father gone? He wanted to know. Was he going to pay? Was something the matter?

The skeleton suddenly appeared behind the waiter, staring at

Luca. He had a long red scarf wrapped around his neck and he had snow on his shoulders. His face was bright red from the snow and cold and his curly, wet yellow hair was plastered to the sharp angles of his skull.

"On your feet," the soggy sack of bones said in American English to the boy.

"Who the hell are you?" Luca asked, loudly enough to be heard by the boisterous group at the next table. A few heads swiveled in his direction.

"Gimme the fuckin' check," the skeleton hissed at the waiter, eyeing the young Corsican for a few moments. The waiter went off and returned with the bill. The yellow-haired man pulled a wad of francs from his pocket and handed some to the waiter, who mumbled something and disappeared. Luca cast his eyes about the diners. No longer was anyone paying attention to him or the stranger.

"Where is my father?"

The man bent forward and whispered into Luca's ear.

Luca made a face and nodded his head, then followed the stranger outside into the snowy street. No one inside had said a word.

There was a long black car parked at the curb. It wasn't a French car, Luca saw, but an English one. A Rolls-Royce, a very ancient one with brass headlamps up front and a single violet carriage lamp mounted on the roof above the windshield. Like a hearse, he thought. Luca could see the black shape of his father seated in the rear between two large men.

The bony man opened the driver's side door. There was another man on the passenger side, big, the collar of his black raincoat turned up. Luca could make out a shaved head, a bashed-in boxer's face, and a close-cropped beard. The yellow-haired skeleton slid behind the big wheel, started the car, and turned on the headlights.

Outside, all was blurred white.

"I'm sorry, Father," Luca said, turning to his father in the rear.

"Shut your piehole, kid," one of the two men sitting in the rear on either side of Emile said. It was New York English, the kind you often heard in movies but seldom in Paris. They were wearing very colorful sport coats and Luca remembered seeing them on the platform at the station. His father nodded his head, staring at Luca, telling him to obey. Yes, he would be quiet all right. That would be best. In fact, no one spoke as the big car slid through the snowy streets and crossed the river at the Pont Neuf, some of the turns very tight in the great long car.

"Hey, Joe Bones," the big man next to the window said in the thick accent of a movie gangster. "What's wrong with this right here?" He spoke without looking over at the driver, pointing out the side window.

"I ain't Joe Bones yet, boss. Just Mama Bonanno's boy Joey."

"You will be after tonight, kid, I'm telling ya. Make your frigging bones at last."

"So, whaddya want me to do?" the skeleton behind the wheel said out of the side of his mouth.

"Pull over, for chrissakes. I want you should park it here. Nice and close. It's fuckin' freezin' out there. Christ, snow in Paris? Who knew? Right here. Awright, Joey?"

"Whatever blows your hair back," Joey said, and pulled the big wheel over to the right. The black Rolls skidded to a stop next to a massive nineteenth-century cannon in the southwest corner of the cobblestone courtyard.

"Well, kid, this is us," the big man said, sucking in his gut and looking at Luca through a haze of cigarette smoke. He said, "Napoleon's Tomb. I'm lookin' forward to seein' it. I hear it's even bigger than my friggin' mausoleum at Mount Olivet in Queens. Hey, how you doing, kid?"

"Who are you?" Luca said.

"Who, me?" The man stuck out his big meaty hand. There was a massive gold nugget on the small finger.

"Greetings from Gangland, U.S.A., kid," the big bald man said, grabbing Luca's hand and pumping it. Luca whipped his hand away, rubbing it on his trousers, and stared into the man's eyes until the American gangster averted them.

"What did you say?" Luca said coldly.

"Name is Benny," the man said, and shrank back from Luca's gaze. "Benny Sangster."

Chapter Six

Cannes

HAWKE SLID HIS GREEN AMERICAN EXPRESS CARD UNDER the hotel cashier's grate and waited for the clerk to raise the dreaded issue of whether one had raided the bloody honor bar. It was a universal travel wrinkle he loathed. He found it unbearable, in the process of checking out of a hotel, that one must stand there trying to recall if one had eaten any peanuts or opened a bloody Perrier before turning in.

Having paid, he strode across the lobby and informed the concierge that he was leaving, discreetly slipping the mustachioed man a sealed hotel envelope containing one hundred Euros, informing him that the lady, his—guest—might be staying in his rooms until next morning.

"Mais oui, monsieur. Pas de problème."

Hawke emerged under the hotel's porte-cochere entrance, pausing for a moment. On assignment abroad, one expects to be watched. He saw no quickly averted head, or raised newspaper, however, so he turned right, descending the gently curving drive that led to the avenue. There was little traffic and he sprinted across the four lanes and grassy median to the beach promenade. Following the curve of the harbor west along le Croisette, he kept the *Star* in view on his left. From this distance, it looked like normal departure preparations were well underway.

Beyond the twinkling lights of the Vieux Port, the glittering coastline lay like a necklace beneath the dark sky. He was, he thought, ready. It promised to be a simple business, to be sure, but it was not in Hawke's nature to pursue any objective with less than the maximum of his ability.

He walked as quickly as possible without attracting undue attention. A pair of rope-soled espadrilles had replaced his evening shoes. Here in the South of France, the thin canvas shoes were conveniently stylish and stealthy. Approaching the palm-lined fringes of the marina, he spoke softly into the lipmike of his wireless Motorola.

"Hawke," he said.

"Quick," the distinctly American voice of his security head replied in his earpiece. "Good evening, sir."

"Hi, Tommy," Hawke said. "How do we look for this thing?"

"All the telephoto surveil monitors look good, sir. Normal last-minute activity aboard the subject vessel. Ship's radio officer has been monitoring the *Star*'s transmissions and reports business as usual. Idle chit-chat. A pair of cargo cranes loading the midships hold now, as you can probably see from where you are. Looks like heavy equipment. She got her final departure clearance from the port authority an hour ago, confirmed a midnight sailing."

"Good."

"Skipper, again, I have to urge you to reconsider some backup. I don't want—"

"It's a civilian vessel, Tommy. Not military. The hostage is being smuggled out to China by a single guard. I'm good."

"With all due respect, sir, I really gotta say—"

Hawke cut him off. "I'm allowing myself just twenty minutes. Time. Mark."

"Yes, sir. Time: coming up on 23:29.57 GMT . . . and . . . mark."

"Mark. Twenty-three-thirty GMT. Twenty minutes. Mark."

"Sir, I confirm a fast Zodiac standing off the vessel's portside stern at precisely twenty-three fifty."

"Zodiac mission code?"

"She's mission-coded Chopstick One. Twin Yamaha HPDI 300s. She'll get you out of there in a hurry. I say again, sir, I believe there should be at least minimal backup. If you'd only—"

Hawke cut him off again.

"Tommy, if I can't handle a simple snatch aboard an old rust bucket like this I really ought to pack it in. Chopstick One stand by and confirm pickup at eleven-five-oh. Okay? Chop-chop!"

"Aye-aye, sir. There is one thing—"

"Make it snappy. I'm about to do this."

"If you look back up at your hotel, sir, you'll see someone standing out on your terrace with binoculars trained on you. One of my guys has a long telephoto on her now. She's . . . uh . . . not wearing much, sir."

"That will be all, Sergeant," Hawke said.

He snapped his mobile shut and quickened his pace. He had deliberately left the Ikons hanging on the balustrade, left behind like all the few recently acquired and untraceable possessions in his suite. But why the hell would she— He paused and looked back at the Carlton. With the naked eye, he could just make out Jet's tiny black silhoutte standing at the balcony of his suite. There was a glowing orange dot, her cigarette. He smiled and waved. The glow was immediately extinguished. Interesting behavior. Was she sad that he'd left or curious about where he was going? Make a mental note, old boy.

Hawke made his way past the long row of charter boats, all moored stern to in the Mediterranean style, and then out along the curvature of an outer breakwater that culminated in a deepwater pier. There was a trickle of passersby, mostly lovers linked arm in arm, out for a stroll now that the weather had changed. Otherwise, the harbor was quiet. The only activity was dead ahead where the *Star of Shanghai* was moored. Lights atop a pair of very tall cranes created an oasis around the ancient steamer. At her stern, the faded red flag of the People's Republic of China hung limply in the light breeze.

All the intel he had from Admiral "Blinker" Godfrey at DNI Gibraltar and his old friend Brick Kelly, the director at Langley, suggested this nocturnal visit of his would be a complete surprise to the Chinese operative on board the *Star*. He was a man operating under the name of Tsing Ping. He was a Te-Wu secret police officer whose dossier Hawke had read twice just to make sure he wasn't seeing things. The man, whose base was an ancient enclave on the Huangpu River, was apparently a human killing machine.

CIA had assured Hawke that both the Te-Wu man and the Chinese skipper aboard the old tramp steamer had no idea the Americans were on to them. They knew that the Americans would think Brock had simply missed a pickup in Morocco, that's all. Happened all the time. Besides, this guy Brock, whoever he was, was a NOC. Normally such agents, captured in the line of duty, were simply dead men, no questions asked, no answers given.

Unless Hawke got him out tonight, his slow death at the hands of the world's most sophisticated torturers was a given.

More important, Brock's superiors in Washington would never learn what secrets were imprinted upon his brain. Kelly wanted him alive. Badly.

Hawke stepped over a mooring line running from a hawser on the *Star*'s stern to a bollard on the deepwater pier and brought the scene before him into focus.

A couple of seamen were lounging at the stern rail, smoking cigarettes, watching the fog roll into the harbor. Most of the crew was engaged with the loading going on amidships. There was a single lookout standing at the bow. They'd posted a pair of standard-issue guards at the foot of the gangway. Both were wearing greasy orange slickers with rain hoods. One of them was looking at him now, carefully observing his approach. Unlike most such practitioners in his chosen field, this one looked almost alert. Hawke plastered a drunken smile on his face, dropped his right shoulder, and walked loosely toward the man, concealing the narrow blade along the inside of his right forearm.

"Beggin' yer pardon, Cap'n," Hawke said slurrily to the big fellow, laying his left hand easily on his shoulder. "This wouldn't be the HMS *Victory*, now would it? Nelson's barky? Seems I've lost me bloody ship."

The guard sneered, showing his unfortunate teeth, and reached inside his slicker for a weapon.

Hawke instantly inserted the long thin blade precisely five millimeters below the man's sternum and upward into the thoracic cavity on his left side, found the heart, and ruined it. One small gasp and his eyes went vacant.

Before the first man knew he was dead Hawke had turned and performed an identical procedure on the second, smaller guard. He caught the newly deceased by the collar of his orange waterproof and let him fall silently to the concrete, the dead man's arms sliding out of the sour-smelling garment as he did so.

In a trice, Hawke shouldered himself into the slicker and raised the hood so that his face was in shadow. As he did, he stifled the wave of self-disgust that usually accompanied such vicious and unexpected violence. He actually hated killing, though it was duty. He took pride in doing it well. It was scant consolation.

Tendrils of fog snaked into the harbor from the sea and wrapped around the old steamer's stacks as Alex Hawke ascended the slippery gangplank. The *Star*, save the loading activity amidships, was quiet. Having gained the deck, he paused and looked up at the dimly lit bridge. Shadowy figures moved behind the grimy yellow glass of the pilothouse. Two men at least, maybe three. He would start his search for Harry Brock there. He looked at his watch. He was two minutes in, right on schedule.

To his left, a steep corrugated stairwell leading up, more of a ladder than a staircase. He raced up it, and another like it, and arrived on the starboard-side bridge wing. He paused and listened, feeling the faint shudder and thump of the engines beneath his feet. Inside the pilothouse, he could hear muffled voices and laughter. The door was slightly ajar. He shot out his left leg and slammed it inward, stepping inside the hot and stinking bridge with the Walther extended at the end of his right arm. The look on the faces of the two Chinamen told him his information from Brick was indeed hard fact. They were hiding something. And surprised.

"Evening, gents," Hawke said, kicking the steel door closed behind him. "Lovely night for it, what?"

"Huh?" said a squat man in grimy coveralls who now moved in front of the fellow in a sheepskin coat who was levering noodles from a box to his hungry mouth. The boxlike man advanced toward Hawke, protecting his captain.

"Bad idea," Hawke said. Somehow, the gun was now in his left hand and a long blood-stained dagger had appeared in his right. The man kept coming and retreated only when Hawke flicked the blade before his eyes. He had little interest in killing these men, at least until he learned the location and condition of their prisoner. Then he would dispatch them without mercy.

"I'm looking for a reluctant passenger of yours, Captain," he said to a leather-jacketed man wearing an ancient captain's cap cocked rakishly over his bushy black brows. "Chap who was shanghaied in Morocco yesterday. Where might I find him?"

The Chinese captain stopped eating his noodles, and, placing the container and chopsticks carefully on a stool, stared at him. Hawke saw something in his eyes and instinctively dove for the floor as rounds from the captain's silenced automatic pistol stitched a pattern in the bulkhead inches above his head. Hawke rolled left and fired the Walther, putting one slug in the captain's thigh and sending him crashing back against the wheel.

There was little time to celebrate. Five fingers that felt like steel bolts sank into the ganglia at the back of his neck. He relaxed, then sucked down a lungful of air at a new sensation: the cold press of steel at his temple. The pressure increased and he dropped his own gun.

"I Tsing Ping," an oddly musical voice whispered in his ear, "you dead."

"This is all a bit more complicated than I was led to believe," Hawke said, twisting his body carefully and smiling up at the man. His eyes were like a pair of small coals. Tsing Ping racked the slide on his gun.

"Easy, old fellow," Hawke said calmly, getting one foot under him. "Easy does it, right? I'm going to get to my feet now and—" He never finished the sentence.

There was a sudden screech of metal and then a terrific jolt as the ship's entire superstructure shuddered under the violent impact of something slamming against it, just below the pilothouse. Hawke, trying to scramble to his feet, was slammed hard against the bulkhead. The impact was sufficient to send Tsing Ping and everyone on the bridge flying across the wheelhouse and tumbling to the floor. He heard shouts from the pier below and then shots rang out, bursts of automatic fire.

Hawke crabbed his way across the chaos of the wheelhouse, managing to recover his Walther from under a sheath of loose documents and navigation charts and broken glass. Then he was up and out onto the bridge wing. Standing at the rail he saw that one of the two dockside cranes, the one directly abeam, was now coming under intense fire from crewmen standing on the starboard rail. Then he saw why. Some madman was at the controls of the crane. The cab had revolved away and now was spinning toward the *Star*'s hull again, the cable taut, and the crazed operator was about to smash the heavily laden pallet against the ship for the second time.

Hawke could see by its trajectory that, this time, the violent impact was targeted at the pilothouse itself. With maybe three seconds to spare, Hawke turned and simply dropped through the stairway opening, hitting the deck hard, and raced aft.

He didn't look back at the violent sound of metal on metal and shattering glass as the crane whipped around and smashed its payload directly into the four angled windows of the *Star*'s bridge. Agonized screams were heard as bodies were smashed in the twisted metal.

He reached the stern rail. On shore, he could hear the keening high-low sirens and see flashing blue lights approaching the harbor from every direction. *Les flics* to the rescue. Everyone aboard the old tub appeared to have run forward to see what was going on. He looked at his watch. The Zodiac rendezvous was in six minutes. In the pitted bulkhead behind him, a rusted door hung open, steps leading down. Brock had to be down there somewhere. Guarded? Absolutely. It seemed he was expected after all.

How the hell had he imagined this was going to be simple?

He had one thought as he raced down the steep metal steps.

He'd gone soft. Lazy. Cocky.

Chapter Seven

Paris, 1970

ALL WAS BLACK INSIDE DES INVALIDES. THE GREAT COMPLEX of buildings housed a veterans' hospital and the army museum. And, in the center, a great church, the Church of the Dome, where the emperor was buried. The skeleton named Joe Bones had forced Luca's father to use one of his keys to open a security door at the rear of the Musée de L'Armée.

They entered the museum at the end of a long dark *allée* where no lights shone. But now the snow had stopped and a bright white moon had emerged from the clouds. Pale light flowed through the tall windows and Luca could hear the powdery silence outside.

"Move yer ass, Joey," Benny said to his gunman. "History awaits us."

"Yeah, yeah," Joe Bones said, and shoved the gun in Luca's father's back, nudging him forward. The two mute goons brought up the rear.

Everywhere Luca looked, in shadowy display cases, were relics of the vanished Grande Armée. Uniforms, muskets, cannon, and swords. Cavalry mounted on horses. The stuff of Luca's dreams. The stuff of *La Gloire*. In other words, his bright and shining future, if he survived this night. His heart quickened.

Their footsteps were a hollow echo on the vast marble floors as they made their way past the endless rooms of the museum, moving relentlessly toward the great Dome. Luca willed himself to show no emotion whatsoever. It would do no good in any case to let these monkeys see anything.

His father was walking ahead of them all, his head down, like a condemned man approaching the gallows. The dog Pozzo trotted happily alongside his owner. Joe Bones held his gun extended at the end of his arm, trained on the back of his father's head. Luca had never seen the old man look so forlorn and defeated. Except now, amazingly enough, his father had begun to sing. Softly at first, then with a full throat. The French National Hymn, "La Marseillaise."

> *Arise children of the motherland*
> *The day of glory has arrived . . .*
>
> *To arms, citizens! Form your battalions!*
> *We march, we march!*
> *Let their impure blood water our fields.*

It was almost unbearable, the pity Luca felt for his father at that moment. Almost. Finally, they came to a wide corridor at the end of a long hallway. Inside the church proper, now, Luca thought. The huge round room of the Dome was full of moonlight as they entered. There was a waist-high white marble balcony circling the room beneath the towering dome. Pale blue moonlight streamed down from above, falling on a single sculpted monument rising up from the floor below.

"Holy Jesus," Joe Bones whispered, awe in his voice. "Lookit that!"

He took Luca by one shoulder and pulled him toward the balcony. Luca closed his eyes and placed his hands on the cool marble railing. Breathing deeply, he emptied his mind. When he was ready, he opened his hungry eyes and feasted on the vision of his noble ancestor's final resting place.

The tomb of his beloved emperor.

Luca took a deep breath. Napoleon Bonaparte's real bones were inside this beautiful monument. His heart was pounding against his ribs as he took it all in, almost forgetting about his father for the moment.

Arising from the lower depths of the church, the emperor's great stone sarcophagus, the captured wave, rested atop a high marble plinth. Above the tomb, the circular cupola rose some two hundred feet. Although the space was chill and airless, Luca could sense a thrilling presence here. Almost a living presence. Menacing. It was as if Napoleon was not resting here, but *lurking.*

Luca saw that a thick rope descended out of the gloom of the top of the dome. It hung directly above the crypt and now one of the goons had a long shepherd's crook and was reaching out over the balcony, slowly pulling the rope toward his father. He sucked down a lungful of cool damp air. They were going to hang him? His heart rate zoomed even higher and his mouth went dry, but still he showed nothing.

"Luca!" he heard his father cry now. "Run! Run!"

"Don't worry, Father, I'm coming," Luca said. As he slowly circled the curved balustrade, a passing cloud covered the moon, filling the dome with purple darkness.

Luca, his eyes shining, strode round the balcony to where Benny and his men stood in a small circle around his father. The son walked up to the father, stared deeply into his haunted eyes, and turned to the man in the black raincoat.

"Monsieur Benny," Luca said in a voice so low it was barely audible, "if you would be so kind as to ask Monsieur Bones to give me his gun."

His father stared at him, his face a mask of confusion.

Luca leaned forward and kissed his father on the left cheek.

"What? What is—" His father's eyes went wide and he strained violently against the two men who held him in their grip. He struggled for breath. His lips formed words that would not come.

"Luca?" Emile cried out as the skeleton handed Luca the pistol. "Luca! What are you—what is happening—I am a loyal soldier of the Corse! I—"

"You are loyal to the Corse, Papa," he said, his voice barely over a whisper, "but you killed a brother of the Brigade Rouge."

He raised the automatic until it was aimed between his father's eyes.

"Luca, no. Listen to me. You don't know what you're doing."

Luca increased the pressure on the trigger.

"Put the gun down, son. Listen to your father. Whatever your crazy Brigade Rouge people are saying, it isn't true. I made some mistakes, yes. But, not—this. Don't do this, Luca. I love you."

The boy couldn't do it. He lowered the muzzle slowly, never taking his eyes off his father's own pleading eyes.

"My son! What—"

"The Brigade Rouge has no forgiveness for traitors," Luca said, his voice flat.

"The party! Wait! You don't—let me—"

The gun came up.

"Luca! For God's sake! You can't—"

Luca pulled the trigger.

The muzzle flash was brilliant and the crack of the explosion reverberated throughout the great domed chapel. His father was blown back against the balustrade, a bubble of blood forming on his lips as he sank to his knees. Luca looked down, letting the gun slip from his hand and clatter to the marble floor. His father lay gasping on the cold stone. In the dim light, the spreading stain on his chest was thick and black. He was vomiting blood. Luca stepped back and the two goons bent to their work. They looped the thick rope over Emile's head, forming a heavy noose around his neck.

"You got balls, kid," Joe Bones said, looking down at the dying man. "I gotta give you that."

Emile Bonaparte's right leg was still jerking spasmodically and he was taking shallow ragged breaths. Luca knelt beside him, taking his father's still-warm hand and holding it to his cheek. Luca made every effort to force his eyes to fill with tears. It was the one test he would fail on this historic night. He could not cry on demand.

"Arrivederci, Comrade Papa."

A fresh gout of blood erupted from his father's mouth, and Luca's hands were covered in the thick warm fluid. It had to be this way, he said to himself. In just this place, in just this way. He pinned a red floret to his father's lapel and got to his feet.

"Do it," Luca finally barked at the skeleton. "Finish the damn thing. Hang him."

Then the two large men—Luca recognized them now as the two men who looked like brothers from the station platform—bent and picked up his father's body. One had the feet, the other held his wrists. They began to swing the body to and fro, in ever greater arcs, the blood looping out of his father's mortal wound.

Luca watched in stony silence as his father's body sailed high out over the curvature of the balcony. He moved to the railing and looked down as the rope snapped taut, taking the full weight of the old man's body.

Emile Bonaparte jerked to a stop at the end of the rope, his body swaying gently just a few meters above Napoleon's sarcophagus. A cloud shifted high above, and blue moonlight once again lit the scene. Two dead Bonapartes, one grave. A red floret pinned on the traitor's lapel. It was all intended to send a message to those in government who had something to fear from the Brigade Rouge. It was also a call to arms to Luca's fellow conspirators, to unite in their struggle to overthrow the old leadership of the Corse.

"Wait till the cops get a load of this little picture," Joe Bones said, staring at the scene. "I mean, this shit is friggin' dramatic!"

Luca felt Benny Sangster's big rough hand on his shoulder.

"You got the money, kid? I know you popped him. But we got expenses to cover."

Luca handed him the envelope containing the ten thousand dollars, U.S. The price the Brigade Rouge had put on his father's head.

"I never would have believed it, kid," he said, pocketing the cash. "I told them Red Brigade Corsicans you was too wet behind the ears. You know. That you didn't have the moxie. I mean, c'mon. What kind of kid could—"

"I am capable of absolutely anything," Luca said, in a voice as cold as stone. "I am a son of Napoleon."

And, in that pit where his soul would have been if he'd had one, he truly believed it.

"Well, you certainly made your bones the hard way, kid," Benny said. "Never seen anything like it."

A death rattle came from the twisted throat of the man hanging by his neck in the moonlight.

"Whoa," Joe Bones said, digging his knuckles into his sunken eye sockets, "this shit is intense."

"This is just the beginning," Luca Bonaparte said as he walked away into the shadows.

Chapter Eight

Hampstead Heath

SOME FEW MINUTES AFTER MRS. PURVIS HAD ADMITTED THE two policemen, Ambrose was seated comfortably in his worn leather armchair; it was situated behind the walnut desk in his book-lined study. Beneath a sunny south window stood his painting table where all of his watercolor materials were laid out just so. The low stone fireplace, swept clean this time of year, would be crackling merrily with nice pine logs come the first fall chill.

The room was his favorite. It housed, among its treasures, not only his collections of Buchan, Ambler, Dorothy L. Sayers, Zane Grey, and Rex Stout, but the complete first edition of Conan Doyle, and his Holmes memorabilia collection as well. A rare Moroccan bound edition of *Hound of the Baskervilles* lay on his desktop, and he drummed his fingers upon it impatiently.

Blast. He was not in the mood for company. He was in the mood for eggs.

The two young coppers (they were MI5, surprisingly, not the local constabulary as he'd deduced) had moved the side chairs up to the desk and were getting into their topic rapidly. Ambrose had retired only recently from New Scotland Yard as the Number One, so his bona fides had been quickly dispensed with at the door.

He was pleased to find that, despite a few years of assisting his dear friend Alexander Hawke in some messy undercover work abroad, he still enjoyed something of a reputation at Thames House, the MI5 headquarters building, and in the British law enforcement community. Or so it would appear by the sunny look of adulation on the face of the young chap opposite.

This eager junior man, Agent H. H. Davies was his name, was

ogling Ambrose as if he might be some aging exhibit in the Yard's Legends of Crime museum.

"The Georgi Markov affair, Chief Inspector," Davies said, shaking his head in wonder. "When the KGB took out the Bulgarian dissident waiting for his bus. Ricin pellets in the umbrella tip. No one had ever even heard of the stuff and yet you, you—"

"Well," Ambrose smiled, "I can hardly claim credit for—"

There was a loud cough from the other chair.

"So you know this Henry Bulling, Chief Inspector," the senior agent, George Winfrey, interrupted, glowering at Davies. "Your nephew, I believe."

"Ah. Facts, Winfrey, facts. He's not my nephew. He's my cousin, in point of fact."

"And you were running him? For the Yard? Looking into the Chinese connection? I know that's Topic A with you fellows these days."

"Chinese connection? You mean, with the French? Really. I've no idea what you're talking about. I am a detective, not a spymaster."

"But you were running him, were you not?"

"In a very minor way . . . gossip, mainly. It is France, after all; in my view, merely a demented version of Italy. We do keep an eye on them, however. Especially, of late, this Bonaparte chap who's causing so much trouble. A man to be watched very carefully. Now, tell me, gentlemen, what's the gen, here? Is young Henry in trouble?"

"The gen?" Davies asked, leaning forward as if he expected some priceless gem of spy-speak to come spilling forth onto the master's desk.

"Hmm. An Americanism I picked up from the author Hemingway via Lord Hawke, who devours his books. Gen. As in, intelligence. I mean to say, what's up with Bulling?"

"He's bolted, sir. Vanished. The French at the embassy are up in arms. Certain documents have gone missing from his department."

"He's on his own, then," Ambrose said, tapping some Peterson's Irish into the bowl of his favorite pipe. Firing it, he puffed out, "The Yard has no involvement in this, I assure you."

"He hasn't contacted you?"

"Certainly not."

"He wasn't directed to remove documents pertaining to China?"

"Asked and answered."

"Did your cousin have reason to wish you ill, Chief Inspector?"

"Ill?" Ambrose said, suddenly looking up from a careful study of his signet ring. "Why do you ask that?"

"We tumbled his flat. Milk Street. Southeast London. We found a recently purchased weapon. A cheap target rifle with a 10X scope. Wrapped in oilcloth and stowed under a loose floorboard."

"Under a loose floorboard. How original of him. And?"

"And these photographs, sir."

Davies slid over a manila folder and Ambrose extracted six glossy eight-by-ten photographs. They were grainy telephoto black and whites. All six were taken on separate occasions by someone who had secreted himself deep within Hampstead Heath forest. And all of these long-lens photos depicted Congreve walking his new dog, Ranger, in the lovely hour just before sunset.

"Anything else?" Congreve asked, sliding the folder back to Davies without comment.

"A good deal else, Inspector," Agent Winfrey said, pulling a wad of brochures from his leather satchel. He held one aloft. "Your cousin left his flat in quite a hurry. He was quite possibly abducted. There were signs of a struggle. We found this tract and others like it in his coat closet. All political. Pro-Chinese, Pro-French. Anti-American. Written, we've gone to a great deal of trouble to learn, by the French Foreign Trade minister in Paris, the same chap you mentioned a moment ago. Bonaparte. Translation Section is just getting round to translating this bit this morning."

"Hand it over," Ambrose said. "French is one of my languages, unfortunately." Congreve had in his youth been a language scholar at Christ College, Cambridge, but tossed it all for a street beat with the Metropolitan Police. A decision he'd seldom regretted on his way to legendary status at the Yard. Never one to view a mystery from afar, rather he held the thing pinched between two fingers beneath his nose, sniffed the bouquet, then swallowed it whole.

He perused the overwrought anti-American polemic for some moments, then slipped it inside his opened red leather day diary. Something called OMOCO had published the self-serving diatribe on behalf of some radical French group calling themselves the Brigade Rouge. OMOCO. Somewhere, that name rang a bell. Oman—something or other. Oh, well, it would come to him.

"Anything else?" he asked, smiling. Mrs. Purvis had slipped silently into the room and was carefully gathering the empty cups and saucers. He was grateful for her quiet, efficient demeanor and, catching her eye, murmured a silent thank-you. The woman was good cheer and grace personified.

"With all due respect, Chief Inspector," Winfrey said, "that pamphlet you've just taken is evidence in a missing persons case."

"I'm well aware of that, Agent Winfrey. For professional reasons, I'd like my friend Alex Hawke to have a look at it. I'm happy to sign for it if you insist. One final question for you chaps before you go, if I may."

"Shoot," Davies said, earning a look from Winfrey. *Shoot?*

"What the blazes is the 'Brigade Rouge'?" Congreve asked. "That's a new one on me."

"A spinoff of the old Union Corse crime family from Corsica. Quite fanatical. Ultraleftist paramilitary chaps, all former Union Corse foot soldiers and Foreign Legionnaire types, a few ex–Deuxième Bureau. Been around for years but raising holy hell of late. Rumored to be responsible for this latest spate of political assassinations in France. We can't prove it yet, but we're working on it. Henry Bulling never mentioned that lot, eh?"

"Never."

"Well. You'll let us know straightaway should Henry Bulling contact you, won't you, sir?" Winfrey said, getting to his feet.

"Unless he contacts me with a bullet to the heart, I shall indeed endeavor to do so."

"If I may, sir. Until we find your cousin, I'm sure I need not say this. But do keep your eyes open, sir. I'd be happy to assign one or two of my men to sit outside for a few days. Unobtrusively, of course."

"Won't be necessary, but thank you for your concern. I've got young Ranger here. First line of defense in my personal homeland security system." The dog emitted a rough bark as if on cue.

"A great honor meeting you, sir," Davies said, rising from his chair and sticking out his hand. "The man, the legend."

Ambrose waved this ridiculous piffle away and picked up his beloved Conan Doyle first edition. He was just about to thumb open the thing when there came a sound next to his ear of an angry hornet and a neat round hole suddenly appeared smack dab in the middle of his precious Holmes.

At that precise moment, he saw Mrs. Purvis collapse to the carpet. The tea tray and its contents flew from her hands. A bright red stain appeared just below her starched white collar and spread rapidly. She moaned once and went silent.

"Mrs. Purvis!" Congreve shouted, knocking his armchair over backward as he leaped to his feet.

Chapter Nine

Cannes

HAWKE RACED DOWN THE DESERTED COMPANIONWAY, A grim corridor lit only by a few naked bulbs suspended from loose wires dangling from the overhead. Doors hung open on either side, small flyspecked cabins with double- or triple-tiered bunks, empty. At the far end, a large door in the bulkhead opened into the galley. He stepped inside. The stink of cabbage and rancid grease was overpowering. He was about to turn and retrace his steps when his eye caught a thin edge of yellow light between two tall cabinets loaded with rusty canned goods, stocks that appeared to be long past their best-by date.

He ripped at the shelving and dodged heavy falling cans of undoubtedly exquisite Chinese delicacies. The cabinet swung open easily, revealing a tiny broom closet of a room, no bigger than six by four. There was a metal rack upon which lay a man, pale and gaunt, who looked as if he'd neither eaten nor slept during his days in enemy hands. A tin plate with what appeared to be dried vomit rested on his chest, just below his chin. A foul slops bucket stood under his bed. At the sight of Hawke, he made to sit up, and the thin scrap of blanket fell away, revealing his legs. They were severely bruised and made fast to the frame with strips of heavy canvas.

The man smiled weakly up at Hawke as he entered.

"What part of China you from, mister?" he said, slurring his words.

"I look Chinese to you?" Alex said, and he had the knife in his hand, cutting the canvas from the frame, starting with the left leg.

"Can't see too well. Where are you from then?"

"Place called Greybeard Island. Little rock out in the English Channel."

"English, yeah. Thought so. A limey. I'm Harry Brock. From L.A."

"La-la land. Never been there. Have they been torturing you, Harry Brock?" Hawke asked, inspecting his horribly swollen feet and ankles.

"Nothing Dr. Scholl can't fix," he said, laughing weakly. "I don't know. Been on the run. Can't remember much of the last few days."

"Drugs, Mr. Brock. Chlorides. Pentothal. Anything broken? Can you walk?"

"I think so. Any chance at all of us getting out of here?" the man said. The fear that this might not be so was writ large in his dilated blue eyes.

"That's the general idea," Hawke replied, cutting the last of the bonds. "On your feet, Mr. Brock. Let's get off this tub before it sinks."

"Sounds good," the American said, and, with Hawke's help, he swung his legs painfully off the frame and got his feet under him. He swayed and Hawke put one arm around him.

"I won't be much good to you in a fight. I think the bastards have broken my wrists. One of 'em, anyway."

"We're going to make straightaway for the stern. As fast as you're able. Over the rail. I've got a man waiting below in a Zodiac. He's expecting us. Now. Can you make it?"

As he said this last, Hawke heard a now familiar high-pitched voice behind him. He whirled, and his right hand came up in a blinding motion, the Assassin's Fist already on its deadly way. Tsing Ping appeared to move his head less than an inch to the left and Hawke's blade twanged into the wooden shelving, the knife handle vibrating just by Tsing Ping's ear.

"You are knife fighter?" the man said in his disturbingly childlike voice. "Good. I, too."

An ugly serpentine dagger appeared from the folds of Ping's black pajamas, and he flicked it playfully before his face. Hawke, who still had his left arm supporting the American, was going for the Walther on his right hip when he heard certain death whizzing his way. The point of the Chinaman's blade was perhaps an inch from piercing Alex's heart when it struck something solid. There was a metal thud and Hawke glanced down to see the dented tin plate that had saved his life still in Harry Brock's hand and the assassin's dagger falling harmlessly to the deck.

"Thanks," Hawke said to Brock.

"Don't mention it," Brock replied, and then both men looked up to see the most extraordinary sight.

Tsing Ping, now writhing in anger, had been lifted a good three feet off the deck. Both hands were above his head, pinioned in the one-handed grip of a giant black man. This man, who was now standing in the doorway looking at him from head to toe with intense curiosity, seemed immovable; as solid and still as a black marble statue.

"Hey! Listen up!" the black man said to Tsing Ping. "What you got against soap and water, boy?"

"Stokely!" Hawke said, barely able to contain his joy at the sight of the man. He hadn't seen his old friend in more than a year. "What in God's name are you doing here?"

"Saving your ass again, looks like to me. Speaking of which, we got to go. I got a couple of mines going off in about a New York minute."

"What mines?" Hawke asked.

"Limpet mines, you know, that somehow got attached to the hull. This old tub's going down, boss. What shall I do with this little guy? Hey, you! Stop that!"

Tsing Ping was making horrible guttural sounds and scissoring his legs viciously at Stokely's groin. Stoke put an end to that with a short, jabbing motion of his arm. He slammed the Chinaman bodily against the bulkhead twice and then dropped him like a sack of broken sticks to the deck. He didn't move after that.

"Ugly little critter, ain't he?" Stoke said, looking down at Ping. "What is he?"

"Dead, I hope," the American said, looking pleadingly at Hawke. "He ought to be if he's not. Sweet Jesus. Somebody shoot him."

Hawke holstered his pistol. He may have had pirate blood in him, but cold-blooded murder had never held any appeal.

"Be dead soon anyway," Stoke said, looking at Alex with understanding in his brown eyes. Stoke didn't want to murder the man either.

"What do you mean?" Brock said.

"I mean when this old piece of scrap iron goes to the bottom in, say, oh . . . let's call it three minutes now," Stoke said, looking at his dive watch. "When he wakes up, he'll be dead enough."

"Let's go," Hawke said, and he and Stokely helped the American move quickly aft down the companionway.

"Nice of you to show up," said Hawke.

"Not much else to do on shipboard," Stokely said. "Not since I gave up duplicate bridge."

"How'd you come to be aboard *Blackhawke* anyway?"

"Got picked up in Corsica. Taking care of some business there and saw her in the harbor. Tom Quick said he was making a run over here to pick you up. I didn't see a good reason to turn down the invitation."

"And tonight?"

"He said you needed backup."

"Damn it, why does no one listen to me?"

" 'Cause you the boss, boss."

The stern was deserted. A thick fog had rolled in, making the decks slippery and the rail wet to the touch. Hawke leaned over the rail and saw the large black Zodiac, the outboards idling, hovering in position. It was a twenty-foot drop to the oily black water.

"I'll go first," Hawke said to the American, climbing up on the rail. "Then you, then him. Watch where I land and do the same. Stoke, you get him up on the rail. I'll help him into the boat. Oh, and Brock?"

"Yeah?"

"Try to land on your butt. It'll hurt your ankles a lot less."

Hawke dove and surfaced three feet from the Zodiac. Tom Quick left the helm of the center console and helped him aboard. Having been nervous about this whole operation, Quick had decided not to entrust this pickup to anyone else. And he'd invited Stokely to come with him. He knew the skipper would later say this was overkill and decided to keep his mouth shut for the time being.

"Now!" Hawke shouted up to the two men waiting at the stern rail. "Go!"

Stokely helped the American over the rail. He jumped, awkwardly but effectively, splashing bottom first and coming up easily within Hawke's grasp. At that moment, lead started thumping the water very nearby in a neat circular pattern fired from above. Looking up, Hawke saw a single man with an AK standing on the upper deck directly above Stokely's head.

It was Tsing Ping.

Hawke instantly saw the thing unfolding: Stoke in the act of looking up to see who the hell was still shooting at them and the muzzle of Tsing's automatic weapon coming down to greet him with a lethal burst of fire. In a half second, Stoke's head would explode into a fine red mist. Zero chance of survival at this range. In a nanosecond less than the allotted time, Hawke whipped the Walther from his hip holster and put three quick rounds through the Chinaman's heart.

Tsing managed a harmless spurt before he pitched forward over the rail. He plunged, dead weight, into the black water.

Stoke, never one for lengthy mourning, shouted a hearty "Yo!" and saluted snappily. He then turned his back to the rail and executed a perfect Navy SEAL backflip, entering the water with an astoundingly minimal splash considering his size.

Hawke, mentally calculating the time it had taken to draw his weapon and fire, smiled inwardly. Slipping, perhaps, yet gaining a bit of traction.

A minute later, they were all three safely in the stern of the Zodiac, and Tom Quick shoved the throttles forward. The twin 300-HP Yamahas roared. The big inflatable went instantly on plane and two seconds later they disappeared into the fog. There was sporadic fire from the bow of the *Star;* Hawke could see the faint wink of harmless muzzle flashes from her direction disappearing into the fog. In ten minutes, he'd have the hostage safely back aboard *Blackhawke.*

"Tommy, get on the radio," Hawke said. "Tell them the hostage is out and alive. Dehydrated, malnourished, with possible fractures of the wrists. No other casualties. Have sickbay standing by to receive him. And someone get on the horn to Langley. Tell them we have Harry Brock alive."

Hawke pulled a nylon blanket from the stern locker and got the American wrapped in it, then held Brock's head while he sipped from an emergency water ration Hawke had found in the locker. Two seconds after that, he heard the muffled underwater explosions of the limpet mines Stokely had affixed to the *Star's* hull.

"Any particular reason you decided to sink that boat, Stoke?" Hawke asked, as secondary explosions rocked the old steamer and licks of fire and thick black smoke from the midships hold climbed into the murky sky.

"Cargo she was carrying. I didn't like the looks of it. Some kind of super-sized gun barrel. And nuclear reactor shit headed from France for North Korea. Damn French. Why the hell they selling this stuff to those people for, got at least four nukes already? The world ain't dangerous enough for they ass?"

"That was you? Operating the crane?" Hawke asked, deciding to hold his questions about the cargo for later. DNI's intel about the Renault auto assemblies was clearly inaccurate.

"Hell, yeah, it was me. I ain't too good operating heavy machinery, as maybe you noticed. I saw you up there all alone in that wheelhouse. Situation looked a little iffy up there, all those shadows moving around and gunfire and shit, so I started throwing my weight around, tried to distract everybody."

Hawke laughed out loud.

"Skipper?"

The tone of Quick's voice brought Hawke scrambling to the console. "What is it, Tommy?"

"That," Quick said, putting the tip of his right index finger on a tiny greenish blip moving across the radar screen.

The large color Navstar display showed their position relative to the mother ship. The GPS indicated they were a quarter of a mile outside the harbor mouth waypoints, a half mile from where *Blackhawke* lay at anchor. And there was another vessel bearing down on them at high speed. Suddenly, phosphorescent tracers were sizzling overhead, glowing in the fog.

A second later, a round caught Quick in the right shoulder, spun him around and slammed him backward into the console. He collapsed to the deck. Hawke grabbed the helm with one hand, knelt on the deck, and placed the other hand on Tom Quick's bleeding wound. Using two fingers, he probed deeply for an exit wound, and found it, all the while keeping his eyes glued to the bright screen.

"Make a fist and press it here," Hawke told Quick, guiding his hand to the blood-soaked depression. "There. Harder. That should hold you till we get you to sickbay."

"I'm all right, sir. Just a sting. You got the helm okay?"

"Yeah, hold on. I'm going to lose these bastards in that fog bank." Hawke firewalled the twin throttles and swung the boat hard starboard, catching the backside of a cresting wave and getting the big

RIB momentarily airborne. "Stoke, you have that man battened down?"

"I got him, boss," Stoke shouted above the roaring engines. "You go on ahead and open her up!"

"Good God," Hawke said a moment later, his eye tracking the narrowing gap between the two moving vessels on the vivid color display. "What the hell is this, Tommy? A launch from the *Star*?"

"I don't think so, Skipper," Quick said, struggling to his feet. "Way too big. She's got to be some kind of—holy shit!"

"What?"

"Whoever they are, she's painted us! We're all lit up!"

"Who the hell—"

Hawke put the helm hard over and the inflatable curved a tight radius cut to port. Immediately, he veered hard starboard, initiating a violent zigzag course in a desperate effort to elude more incoming enemy fire. A steady warning tone now came from the Zodiac's onboard systems and a half dozen panel lights began flashing rapidly.

Hawke thumbed the radio mike.

"Blackhawke, Blackhawke, Chopstick's under attack . . . repeat . . . under . . . *attack* . . . we are taking evasive measures . . . copy?"

"Skipper!" *Blackhawke's* fire-control officer replied, "we're not believing this, sir. I think they—yeah, they are launching! Get out of there!"

"She just *launched*," Hawke said, disbelief palpable in his voice. They were off the coast of France, for God's sake. He yanked the wheel once more hard to starboard. "A surface missile! Are they all bloody insane around here?"

"Can you lose it, sir?" Quick asked, eyeing the screen in utter disbelief. He clenched his shoulder and staggered every time they went off a wave and exploded through a wall of water. The big props dug in once more and they shot forward.

"I don't know—depends—if it's heat- or radar-guided and—you know what, to hell with this . . . *Blackhawke*! Talk to me!"

"Roger that, Skipper," came the cool voice of the crewman manning the ship's fire-control and commo operations center. "Missile has no active radar . . . it is heat-seeking . . . we, uh, we have lock-on with the attacking vessel . . . they, uh, the attacking vessel not responding to repeated verbal warnings, sir."

"Who the hell are they?" Hawke demanded, curving an impossibly tight right turn.

"Refuses to identify herself, over. Visual ident impossible in this thick stuff, sir."

"Are these outboards hot enough to pull that missile in?"

"Maybe not . . . it's going to be close—hard left now!"

Hawke looked back at Stokely and the rescued American holding on for dear life in the stern of the Zodiac. He needed to get Harry Brock to safety. He'd do what he had to do. He put the damn thing halfway up on its side the turn was so tight.

The missile passed harmlessly not ten feet aft of his stern.

"*Blackhawke*, sink the attacking vessel. Fire when ready."

"Aye, aye, Skipper. We confirm that. *Blackhawke* is launching—"

"I cannot believe this shit!" Stokely shouted. "Man, we—nobody shoots a damn missile at a little rubber boat!"

The Zodiac was lifted upward on a roiling mound of water by the massive explosion aboard the attacking boat. The soupy grey fog surrounding them instantly became an incandescent orange and the shockwave nearly ripped the four men from the small inflatable.

Whoever had had the nerve to shoot at him no longer existed.

The sea-skimming Boeing Harpoon AGM 84-E missile fired at Hawke's command by *Blackhawke* was carrying nearly five hundred pounds of Destex high explosive in its warhead. The Harpoon unerringly found its target. Seven of the attacking vessel's crewmen were killed in the initial explosion, two drowned, and one died from severe burns some hours later in a Cannes hospital. The ship burned for twenty minutes before she rolled and went to the bottom.

If you even glanced at the papers next morning, although it hardly seemed possible given the events of the first few years of the twenty-first century, the world seemed to have slipped its moorings yet again.

Somehow, a French vessel had been sunk off Cannes. Hawke would later learn she was *L'Audacieuse*, No. 491, a type P40 attack cutter on patrol for the French navy. *L'Audacieuse*, it was claimed in an appearance by the French Foreign Trade minister, Luca Bonaparte, was on routine patrol off the port of Cannes, when, without provocation, she was deliberately and viciously fired upon and sunk with all hands by a British vessel believed to be in private hands.

If you paid much attention to the screaming headlines in French newspapers or the endless state-run France Inter Radio or France 2 television reports, you would believe that France and England were on the brink of war over the incident.

At the center of this new international storm, a certain captain of British industry named Alexander Hawke.

Chapter Ten

London

AMBROSE STOOD IN THE COLD RAIN ON THE GLISTENING pavement. Traffic on Lambeth Palace Road, just outside the south entrance to St. Thomas's Hospital, was heavy. He was waiting for Inspector Ross Sutherland to appear. The man was a good ten minutes late and Congreve, who had spent the last four hours sitting by the comatose Mrs. Purvis's bedside in a dreary wing of St. Thomas's Hospital, was not in the sunniest of moods. He was about to step from the curb and hail a taxicab when the dark-green Mini Cooper appeared, careening around the corner at a high rate of speed and skidding to a stop one foot from the curb.

Sutherland club-raced the thing weekends out at Goodwood and Aintree and the car still had a large number 8 stuck to the side of the door. Ambrose had never in his life imagined owning a car, but he thought of buying one at that very moment. A dark blue Bentley Saloon, prewar, with walnut picnic trays that folded down in the rear. Yes. It would look lovely parked in the gravel drive at Heart's Ease. He could motor out to Sunningdale for his Saturday foursome or to Henley on Sundays, pack a basket, a chilled bottle of good—

The numbered passenger door flew open and Congreve bent himself down and over, contorting his comfortably large corpus so that it miraculously folded inside the rolling deathtrap. His umbrella was another matter. It refused to collapse without a Herculean effort and snapped shut only after a pinched thumb and a few well-chosen words from its owner. Only then did Ambrose pull the door shut, find what comfort he could by adjusting the rake of the barebones racing seat, and acknowledge Ross Sutherland's presence behind the wheel.

"He stoops to conquer," Ambrose said with a wry smile, strapping himself in. He'd learned long ago that complaining to Sutherland about his beloved Mini was air he could save for more fruitful use elsewhere. Ross murmured something vaguely apologetic, noisily engaged first gear, and accelerated at an astounding rate of speed until he was able to insert the damnable machine into an invisible hole in the stream of traffic humming along Lambeth Road. Congreve ran his fingers through his damp thatch of chestnut hair, heaved a sigh of relief at getting out of the rain, and pulled his briar pipe from an inside pocket of his sodden tweeds.

"Sorry I'm late, sir," Sutherland said, eyeing his superior out of the corner of his eye. "A holy fuss at the Yard and I couldn't duck out until quarter past."

"Late? Really? I hadn't noticed." Congreve was packing his bowl with Peterson's Irish. His voice was flat. "I assumed I was early."

"Well," Sutherland said, shifting gears, his bright tone suggesting a change of mood and subject as well, "how is dear Mrs. Purvis getting along, sir?"

"Expected to recover fully, thank God."

"What are the doctors saying, sir?"

"The bullet nicked her heart."

"Good lord."

"Left ventricle. She was extremely lucky. A centimeter northeast and she'd be bound for glory."

"I'm so—sorry, Chief. I know how fond of her you are. Whoever did this—"

"Bastards."

"Plural?"

"I may be wrong."

Sutherland knew better than to even chance a reply to that one. Congreve was seldom wrong, but never in doubt. After ten minutes in heavy South East London traffic, they were making quite good time motoring south along the Albert Embankment. The clouds had lifted, forming a clearly defined purplish grey line beneath which lay a band of orange sky. The sun had dipped below the visible horizon and the Thames was bathed in a red glow, a long black barge chugging slowly downstream toward Greenwich. Eventually Congreve said, "Next turning. That's it, right here. Moreton Street. It's a shortcut."

A few minutes later they pulled to a stop in front of Henry Bulling's former home at Number 12, Milk Street. Large puddles of standing water dotted the street and the downpour had eased, replaced by a vaporous rain, cold and invasive. The house itself was a halfheartedly mock Tudor wedged between an ugly rash of modern bungalows and two-story boxes of variegated flesh-toned brick. Ambrose had been subconsciously hoping the Bulling residence would surprise him with a cheery, pleasant facade. It did not.

He still felt a twinge of guilt at his good fortune in the matter of Aunt Augusta's will.

"Do you have the key?" Ambrose asked as they mounted the wooden steps. A few soggy copies of the *Times* and the *Daily Mirror* lay against the entrance. Congreve noted that the most recent edition was five days prior. Who had canceled service?

"Aye, here you are, sir," Sutherland said, putting his murder bag down on the peeling floorboards and fishing the marked evidence envelope containing the key out of his pocket. Sutherland, sans the pleasant Highland burr, was a dead spit for an American. A former Royal Navy aviator, Hawke's wingman during the first Gulf War in fact, Ross had the fresh crew-cut looks and brisk bonhomie one generally associates with England's cousins across the sea. He'd turned into a fine copper, however, and the two men had notched a few successes together. Most recently, they had succeeded in identifying the murderer of Alex Hawke's bride, the late Victoria Sweet. That foul murder, a grotesque act of vengeance, had occurred on the steps of the chapel as the beautiful bride had emerged into the sunlight. It still rankled, it still hurt.

Ambrose and Ross had cracked the case, true enough, but it was Ross Sutherland, along with Stokely Jones, who had brought the man to summary justice on a remote island in the Florida Keys.

Congreve and his colleague had retained Yard offices in Victoria Street, but both were on semipermanent loan from Scotland Yard, enlisted in the service of Alex Hawke on an as-needed basis. It seemed to Congreve that Hawke needed him constantly, as the boy was always getting into the middle of one scrape or another.

Ambrose, along with the Hawke family retainer, Pelham Grenville, had practically raised the child since the murder of his parents by drug pirates in the Caribbean. The boy had been just seven years old when he witnessed the murder. Congreve would never admit to it, even to himself, but his feelings toward young Hawke since their first meeting could reasonably be described as paternal.

Ross inserted the key into the lock and swung the seamed and weathered oak door inward. He paused and looked over his shoulder before crossing the threshold. Long shadows of purple dusk fell over the quiet street. The only sound was a chattering of starlings. Stunted beeches stood on the bare soaked ground in front of a few houses. If there were neighbors here on Milk Street, they were all hidden away inside, electric fires burning in the grate, huddled round the supper table or the telly.

"You didn't sign that key out, did you?" Congreve asked Ross, switching on his powerful torch, and swinging it into the gloom of the front hall as he stepped inside.

"No worries, Chief. I just borrowed the key from Evidence."

"Good lad," Ambrose murmured his approval, glad as always to keep the Yard at arm's length in these situations.

Congreve stepped inside and flared his nostrils, processing the myriad odors of the place. Tobacco, primarily (Henry smoked like a fiend) and pungent old carpet, seldom if ever hoovered. Dusty furniture and draperies, boiled beef and cabbage and Brussels sprouts from the back of the house where the kitchen would be. There'd been a cat at one point, perhaps several, and possibly a canary if the moldy scent of soggy Hartz Mountain seed was any indication.

Nothing surprising, really. No coppery scent of blood at any rate. No odd gases or poisonous chemicals.

There was one thing. A scent most startling to his finely attuned olfactory organ, a very faint trace of some expensive perfume. Odd. A female visitor? Yes. Sophisticated, and of sufficient means to afford *les parfums Chanel*. It was the new one, he thought, not the one he loved, No. 5. No. Allure. That was it. So she was younger rather than older, fashionable, and well-heeled, to boot. Henry? She must have had the wrong house.

Sutherland turned on his flashlight and beamed it up the narrow stairwell. Ambrose watched the beam's ascent to the dark at the top of the stairs. The flowered stair carpet was worn and stained and gave off an unpleasant scent of age and dirt.

There was heavy oak paneling and hideous Victorian sconces mounted on all four walls of the small foyer. He flicked the three brass toggles on the switchplate. Nothing. The electricity had been turned off. And probably the gas as well, Ambrose imagined. Most likely when the leaseholder had been informed by an MI5 agent investigating Bulling's disappearance that his tenant was probably not returning to the premises in the foreseeable future.

"There's the lovely parlor," Congreve said, swinging his flashlight's beam to the right. By the cheery tone of his voice Sutherland could tell the clouds had at last lifted. The old bloodhound already had the scent, it seemed. "Why don't you start in there, Ross? A good lesson in Gothic decor for you. I'll work the kitchen down there at the rear and then we'll go up and toss the boudoir as an *ensemble*. Good hunting. *Bonne chance!*" he said, and bounded off.

Inspector Sutherland smiled at Congreve's ironic French usage. Rumors were flying. Something was up with the damnable froggies and it wasn't good. He began his inspection of the dreary sitting room knowing full well that MI5 had been there many times before him, had vacuumed and bagged and logged every microscopic particle, used black light and Luminol on the walls and furniture looking for blood spatter and done as thorough a job as was humanly possible. That, he thought with a grin, was usually where Ambrose Congreve came in. He was an inhumanly gifted forensic investigator.

It was only a matter of time before Ross heard the familiar telltale exclamation from the kitchen at the rear.

"A-ha!" came Congreve's jubilant shout.

Sutherland continued with his own search, turning over cushions and probing them with his fingers, tweezering the odd particle or fiber into a glassine envelope, giving Congreve time to relish and contemplate his own discovery, whatever it might be. They had their routines; they had worked side by side long enough to form them.

Ten minutes later he heard the expected summons issued from the kitchen. "Ah, young Sutherland, would you mind joining me back here?"

He found the Chief sitting at the kitchen table. On it were two mugs of tea and a small thin envelope made of silver mylar with a plastic zipper seal. Ambrose was drumming the fingers of his right hand upon the envelope and staring at a mustard-colored prewar ice box standing against the wall beneath the high rain-streaked windows. His mien was one of benign contemplation.

Sutherland sat in the chair opposite and lifted the mug to his lips. It was tepid, as expected, brewed by Congreve with whatever hot water remained in the pipes. But it was welcome and he drank it down. Putting his mug on the table, he looked at Congreve and saw that the man's gaze remained fixed on the half-century-old appliance.

"What have you got here, sir?" he asked. Congreve turned and looked at him with his bright blue baby's eyes.

"An enigma," Congreve said, rolling the end of his waxed mustache between two fingers.

"Ah. One of those."

"Not *an* enigma, really. The Enigma. I am considering the Nazi cipher machine your Royal Navy chaps found aboard that sinking U-boat seconds before she went down. The one that saved England's bacon. You do know how they cracked that one? Figured out the Nazi encryptions embedded in that infernal machine?"

"Crossword puzzle geniuses, wasn't it, sir? Psychics? Mind readers? Something like that. All gathered down at Bletchley Park, as I recall, trying to crack the code. And we did, too."

"It wasn't a code, Sutherland. Codes substitute whole words. The Enigma substituted individual letters. It was a cipher machine."

"Sorry, sir."

"And it wasn't British codebreakers who cracked it, the opinions of assorted dime novelists to the contrary. Polish mathematicians cracked the Enigma, Sutherland. They'd begun intercepting the German Enigma transmissions in Poland in the early twenties. Poles found mathematical techniques could attack the problem of finding the machine's message key. By exploiting the Nazis' cryptographic error in repeating the message key at the start of each transmission, they—"

"Fascinating stuff indeed, sir, but—"

"I was just thinking that perhaps one of the reasons I've been able to offer some assistance to Alex Hawke all these many years is our complementary skills. On my end, my absolute hatred of mathematics. I like logic well enough, but numbers, no thank you. Alex is quite good with numbers. You have to be, I suppose, to fly an airplane as well as he does. Celestial navigation or what have you."

"Chief—"

"Warm, hot-blooded mysteries are what ring my bell, Sutherland. Human mysteries. Like that one over there on the floor at the base of the freezer. That puddle of water. The machine started defrosting some time during the early morning hours. So, the electricity was on until then. Just shut off this morning. Which is why your MI5 chaps missed this little silver envelope. Someone pulled the plug about, oh, six and one-half hours ago. Who? Why?"

"You found that envelope in the freezer?"

"I did. Inside a defrosted crown rack of lamb, to be precise. In the center of the thing, under a mess of jellied madrilene. Fairly clever of Henry, if you must give the devil his due."

"Good work, sir! Let's have a look."

"In due time. A man like Henry Bulling has three lives, Sutherland. Many men do, I suppose."

"Three?"

"Yes. There is his public life, you know, the facade, the persona he dons every morning in his shaving mirror before sloughing off to his sad cubby at the embassy. A chimera. And then there is his private life. Much of that can be adduced by simply observing the artifacts in this house. These chairs, for instance. There is a dark, Gothic cast to that mind, isn't there, Inspector Sutherland?"

"Indeed, sir."

"And then there is his third life."

"Yes?"

"His secret life."

"You mean the envelope?"

"Yes. Please open it."

Sutherland picked the thing up with thumb and forefinger and slid the plastic zipper open.

"It's a DVD disc, sir. Two of them. Unmarked."

"Yes. That's what it felt like to the touch. You have one of those laptop computers in your murder bag, I believe."

"Back in a flash, sir."

Ambrose sipped his tea, contemplating the enigma that was Henry Bulling, keen with anticipation as to what might be encoded on the discs. He had a feeling it wouldn't be prize-winning dahlias.

"Here you are, sir. Let's see what we've got."

Ross inserted the first disc into the small Sony laptop, and Congreve heard the faint whir as the thing spooled up. Both men leaned forward as the screen came to life.

"It appears to be a very large oil refinery, sir," Sutherland said, disappointed that the image was not salacious or at the very least intriguing.

"Go to the next one," Ambrose said.

"Same refinery, different angle."

"An infamous French refinery, Inspector. Can you zoom in on this area here? The small sign above this lorry?"

Sutherland used the cursor to create a small shaded box on the area Congreve had indicated. Then he used the zoom to enlarge it.

"A-ha," Ambrose said, "the center of the storm. Our Henry may have gotten in a little over his head here. This is juicy stuff indeed. Keep clicking."

"I'm not with you, sir."

"Oil is a very hot topic these days, Sutherland. This is the famous Leuna oil refinery, built by the French and Germans in Eastern Germany. Operated by Elf Aquitaine, the largest corporation in France. Publicly owned. In reality, an extension of the French government. Leuna was at the center of a huge scandal involving the French Foreign Trade minister a few years ago. The infamous Monsieur Bonaparte."

"Right. Budget irregularities. Kickbacks to African countries, as I recall," Sutherland said, excitement starting to color his voice. He continued to scroll through the disc, which contained countless scenes of pipelines, tankers, and the like.

"That's it. A tawdry romance involving Bonaparte and his German counterpart."

"That German shipbuilder. Giving African politicians cash for every barrel extracted."

"Ah, yes, our old friends, the French and the Germans."

"The new Europe," Sutherland said, looking up at his superior.

"Don't forget the Iraqis," Ambrose said. "Billions traded hands illegally. The oil-for-weapons transactions. France got oil. And cash, of course. Iraq got French Mirage fighter jets and restricted French nuclear technology and power plants. It was the biggest French scandal since the war. Now, what do you suppose our Henry is doing with pictures of French refineries in his freezer?"

Sutherland clicked through to another photo. "Good lord."

"What?"

"Look at this thing, sir. A bloody big supertanker. Never seen one half this size. Certainly has a head of steam, though."

"Yes, I was just noticing the size of that bow wave. Just leaving the Strait of Hormuz, it would appear. What's her name there on the side? Can you make it out? Zoom in."

"The *Happy Dragon*, sir. Sounds more Chinese than French. She's not putting out any smoke, sir. No visible stack at all."

"Nuclear? That's an interesting notion. Let's have a look at that second disc, shall we?" Ross said, ejecting the first and inserting the other. An image appeared, and this time he wasn't disappointed. It was both salacious and intriguing.

"Good heavens," Ambrose said, looking carefully at the image. "Henry, you naughty fellow, what *have* you been up to?"

Sutherland stared at the picture. It was a starkly lit amateur color photograph of some kind of fancy dress ball. Very grand, judging by the opulent interior design and a few famous faces from the tabloids. In the foreground, a very thin chap, all but naked, with shockingly bright orange hair. Plainly the infamous Cousin Henry. He was wearing some kind of choke collar. Not a few of the costumes seemed to involve leather and studded chokers.

The other end of the leash was in the hand of an extraordinarily beautiful Oriental woman, a peroxide blonde wearing nothing but a smile, high-heeled shoes, and a black leather bustier. He clicked to another image, then another. The woman smiled back from each photo.

"She is rather exquisite," Sutherland said.

"Bianca Moon is her name," Ambrose said, leaning forward to examine her more closely. "Not to be confused with her twin sister, Jet. A very senior Whitehall chap came a cropper in Bianca's company. One of Her Majesty's closest aides. He fell in love with her. The daughter of a high-ranking official in the Chinese PLA. A spy, in fact.

Worked for something called the Te-Wu. Chinese secret police. The tabloids all called her the 'China Doll.' I've always wondered what became of her."

"What on earth is the China Doll doing with your cousin Henry Bulling?"

"That's rather obvious, isn't it?" Ambrose said, his keen blue eyes sparkling with satisfaction at his little joke. It wasn't a joke at all. He knew very well what Henry and the beautiful Chinese woman were up to and it was certainly no good.

"Good one, sir," Sutherland said.

"Hmm, yes, isn't it? It would appear the chinless wonder has given us the Chinese connection at last. Do you see that bottom portion of a large painted picture portrait in the upper right of the photo? Mostly gilt frame, but you can make out the hem of a blue silk gown and one silk-slippered foot."

Sutherland leaned forward, peering at the image. "Yes. You mean this section here."

"Hmm. A rather famous portrait, Sutherland. John Singer Sargent's study of the great beauty of her age, Lady Cecily Mars. It still hangs in the Great Hall at Brixden House. Lady Mars's great-granddaughter, Diana, lives in the house now, I believe."

"Yes, I've heard of it. A 'stately,' I believe. Just west of Heathrow, isn't it? One of Britain's more celebrated country houses, if I'm not mistaken."

"Quite right. Bit more notorious than stately, from what I've heard, however. Brixden's been the scene of many wild nights, orgies and the like, according to what one hears. Somehow, the current Lady Mars has managed to keep the whole unsightly mess out of the papers. She's quite something, from all you hear."

"Have a look at this one, Chief Inspector," Sutherland said, looking at one of the seamier photos from Henry Bulling's private collection.

"What is it?"

"What are they doing with that demitasse spoon?"

"Good heavens!"

Chapter Eleven

Cannes

"GET THIS MAN TO SICKBAY," HAWKE SAID TO A YOUNG crewman, stepping from the bobbing Zodiac onto the floating dock extending from *Blackhawke*'s stern hangar bay. "His pulse is irregular. Malnourished. And he's dehydrated. Check for fractures, left wrist specifically."

Stokely stood on the gently rolling deck with what was left of Harry Brock cradled lightly in his arms. The broken man was out cold, his head lolling against Stoke's broad chest. Stoke was broad all over. Hawke liked to say Stoke was as big as your average-sized French armoire. Maybe. Stoke had seen a couple of French armoires in his day and hadn't been all that impressed.

"I think he's sound asleep," Stoke whispered, lowering Brock carefully to the waiting stretcher. "Probably had him down in the sleep-deprivation spa for a few days. Had the boy on that alfalfa diet. Shoots and leaves. You can't help but lose weight, you on that program."

Hawke looked at Stokely and shook his head at the big man. Ex–Navy SEAL, ex-NYPD, Hawke couldn't remember how many scrapes the man had bailed him out of, but each one of them had been a special moment. Beginning with that very suspicious warehouse fire in Brooklyn, when New York Detective Sergeant Stokely Jones, Jr., had carried an unconscious Alex Hawke down six flights of burning stairs. Hawke had been the victim of a kidnap gone bad. After refusing to pay his own ransom, he'd been bound by his Colombian abductors and left to die on the top floor of the deserted warehouse.

"No worries, Skipper, we'll take good care of him," said one of a pair of young Aussie sickbay orderlies, stepping forward. "Ship's surgeon is standing by, as ordered. How about yourself, sir? Nasty cut below that left eye."

Hawke swiped at his face with the back of his hand and was surprised to see it come away bright red. No memory of the wound.

"Tell commo to put me through to Langley, please," Hawke said to the nearest crewman. "The director. Secure line. Straightaway. Five minutes. I'm going to my quarters."

"Aye, sir," the man said and took off at a run.

"Tommy," Hawke said, looking at his security chief who was now hoisting the Zodiac aboard. "Well done. If someone told me you could outrun a Harpoon missile in a rubber boat, I'd have suggested they seek psychiatric treatment."

"Thanks, Skipper. Six hundred horsepower works wonders sometimes. Sorry about our surprise guest here. Mr. Jones, uh, seemed like a good idea at the time."

"Thanks, Tom. Stoke is always a good idea. So, who the hell do you think took a shot at us?"

"Military, sir. Had to be, a weapon like that."

"Right. Let's hope the terrorists don't have sea-launched guided weapons systems quite yet. But *whose* military, Sergeant?"

"That is an extremely interesting question, Skipper."

Ten minutes later, Hawke was in his quarters. He'd stripped off his clothes, taken a steaming hot shower, and stretched himself out on his bed. He picked up the secure line to the CIA director, his old Desert Storm buddy and former ambassador to the Court of St. James, the Honorable Patrick Brickhouse Kelly. Brick was a tall, soft-spoken Virginian who cloaked his fierce intellect behind a veil of old-fashioned southern style and manners.

"Hi, Brick," Hawke said. "Lovely night for international incidents."

"So I hear. Casualties?"

"No good guys. You can delete the *Shanghai Star* from your current edition of Lloyd's International Ship Registry, however."

"Out of commission?"

"Out of commission at the bottom of Cannes harbor."

"You had to sink her?"

"It happened."

"Brock?"

"We got him off first, luckily enough," Hawke chuckled. "He's down in our sickbay. A bit worse for wear, I'm afraid."

"How bad is he?"

"Nothing life-threatening. The Chinese are good at torture. I'm sure they were saving all the really good stuff for some hellhole prison in Shanghai. He'd clearly been drugged, however."

"Sweet Jesus. Okay. I'm going to call Jenna and his kids right now, tell them he's okay. Is he mobile, can he get around all right? I'm ordering a chopper airborne to medevac him."

"What the bloody hell is going on, Brick? After Stokely and I got Brock off that Chinese junker, somebody gave chase and fired a surface missile at us. At our bloody Zodiac. Right outside the bloody harbor."

There was a silence as Brick Kelly absorbed the import of what Hawke had just told him. He said, "You were fired upon. Okay. But a surface-to-surface missile? Are you absolutely positive about that?"

"Yes."

"Then what?"

"We evaded. Lucky for us, it was heat-seeking and our outboards don't put out that much. *Blackhawke* counterlaunched. Sank the attacking vessel before she could launch another one."

"You sank two boats inside Cannes harbor."

"One inside, one outside. Affirmative."

"Christ."

"Exactly. That's why I brought up that international incident idea."

"You know the identity or nationality of the attacking vessel?"

"I do not."

"Educated guess. I'd say it was the French navy."

"The French? What the hell is going on, Brick?"

"The Napoleonic Wars with a new Bonaparte at the helm. I'll tell you all about it when you get to London."

"Me? I thought you wanted Brock."

"Both of you."

"London isn't in my travel plans. I've got a date tomorrow evening."

"Rain check. You're acquainted, aren't you, with *Big John*?"

"The USS *Kennedy*? Yeah, I landed my seaplane on her once. Bit of difficulty. I don't think they like me much aboard that carrier. Certainly the air boss would not number me among his favorite sons."

"That's what happens when the Royal Navy tries to land a single-engine seaplane on a U.S. Navy carrier deck, Hawkeye. You are a legend on that boat. At any rate, she's the closest thing we've got to you in the Med. I'm going to put a helo down on *Blackhawke*'s aft pad. *Big John* is sending a Sea King to retrieve you two. She should be in the air in an hour. Once you're aboard the *Kennedy*, I'm putting you on the first thing smoking to London."

"Lucky me. I hate the Riviera in June."

"I'll have a medevac navy Gulfstream warming up her engines on *Big John*'s flight deck. Once you leave the *Kennedy*, you'll be in London in four hours. Get some sleep now. We'll debrief Brock here in D.C. at Walter Reed. Before and after his brain scan. Is he talking much? What kind of stuff is he saying?"

"Not much. He's in and out most of the time."

"Someone should scribble down everything he says, everything he's said since you first found him. That would be very helpful, Alex. We're going to be looking for inconsistencies."

"Why?"

"The Red Chinese are big into autosuggestion and cranial implants these days. Our HRT guys bring back schizos all the time. You don't know who's talking, your guy or the microchip embedded in his cerebrum. Hard to keep track of who's still on your side once they've met the Chinaman."

"Yeah. Manchurian Candidate stuff. No such thing as science fiction anymore. All right, Brick. See you in London. Come out to Hawkesmoor for a day or two. We'll do some shooting."

"I'll do that. Listen, Hawkeye, your new pal Brock is a very big deal to us. You'll know just how big when I see you."

Before going to bed, Hawke met Stoke topside for a late drink at the small aft bar. They stood on the upper deck under a dense net of stars. It was the first good night in over a week. The mistral had departed, the ill wind disappearing as quickly as it had arrived.

"Thanks again, Stoke," Hawke said, raising his brandy.

"De nada," Stoke said.

"One does not expect to get one's arse shot at by the French navy."

"No. One's arse definitely does not. Not after Normandy and all that other conveniently forgotten history we got going back. You know, Omaha Beach, Ste.-Mère-Église, distant, foggy memories like that. Makes me nuts, boss. You really think that's who it was fired at us? A French navy boat?"

"That's what Brick thinks. He's pretty good at this stuff."

"France ain't exactly my idea of a perfect ally, but shooting at us is taking the game to a whole new level."

Hawke nodded in agreement, sipping his brandy, watching a shooting star blaze and die overhead. He said, "Sky look strange to you, Stoke?"

"Nope. Same old, same old."

"Really? Look at the constellation Orion. See how it's tilted? See that? Like our planet's shifted a few degrees on its axis. Christ. I'm beginning to think it has."

"You okay?"

"No, I don't think I am, quite."

"You want me to stick around with you, buddy? When you go meet with the director in London? I got nothing on my dance card but a trip to Miami to see the next Mrs. Stokely Jones, Jr."

"The lovely Fancha from Cape Verde."

"Girl got a legitimate shot at the title, boss."

Hawke nodded. "I think we all ought to stay in close touch. You, me, Sutherland, Ambrose. Something tells me we are embarking on a long and dangerous journey, Stoke. Here. Your first assignment."

"Every dangerous journey begins with a single step," Stoke said, looking at the small envelope.

"An invitation to a dinner party tomorrow night. Aboard a very fancy yacht moored off the Hotel du Cap. I'd like you to go. See what you can find out about a Chinese movie star named Jet. She lives aboard. Ever hear of her?"

"Nope. Don't see many Chinese movies."

"She's very cozy with some character named von Draxis. German chap who owns *Valkyrie*. Some kind of industrialist. Shipbuilder. Owns a lot of newspapers and television stations in Eastern Europe as well. I read an SIS document about him some years ago. A Saddam stooge in those days, getting oil vouchers for political favors. I think he's dirty. She may be, too."

"Why do you say that?"

"I was with her just before I boarded the *Star*. She may have tipped them—I don't know. They seemed to be expecting me. Anyway, I'd like you to check it out. Have a good look round. See what you can get by being your sociable self."

"You mean you want me to go over to that fancy yacht and just sort of 'blend in.' "

"Right, Stoke, just blend in," Hawke said. "Disappear into the crowd. Lose yourself . . ."

After a beat, the two of them eyed each other and burst out laughing. The only place on earth Stokely Jones might be able to blend in would be the Olympic wrestlers' locker room.

Stoke was well over six-foot-six and weighed nearly two-sixty, not an ounce of it fat. He'd started life in the projects and on the streets selling product and muscle. A wise old judge gave him the navy as an alternative to Riker's Island. He did his SEAL training at Coronado and ended up as a river rat in the Mekong Delta in '68. Coming home, the New York Jets signed him as a walk-on running back. He got hurt in his first game and spent an unhappy year on the injured reserve bench. Then he joined the New York City Police Department.

"Yeah. I like this part," Stoke said. "Spy stuff. Hey, boss, I never got to tell you about Ambrose."

"What about him?"

"Somebody trying to kill him."

"Any idea who?"

"Nope. But he's taking it personally."

Hawke laughed. "I would, too."

"I mean he's on the case himself."

"He's got the right man for the job."

Chapter Twelve

Hong Kong

THE VERY BEST PART OF HIS DAY WAS NIGHT. THE SMELLS OF the harbor coming through the small window to his left included salt brine, dead plankton, marine fuel, the flotsam and jetsam of centuries, rotting sea organisms, human waste, and much, much more. He closed his black eyes and inhaled, sucking these particulate fumes into the very cellars of his lungs. After a seeming eternity, the small black eyes embedded in the twin hollows above his razor-thin nose reopened.

He took a deep breath, creating a wet sucking noise through the narrow vertical slits that constituted his nose. He opened the wide horizontal gash of his mouth. And, through that hole like an open grave, he exhaled. What did they say? In with the good air, out with the bad.

His name was Hu Xu. He was nearly sixty years old and a death artist by trade. He called himself the "diener," pronounced DEE-ner, the old German name for autopsy attendant. It can also mean "responsible manservant" or even "slave," but he was neither of those. It was a private joke. As a young man, living with his parents in America, he had for some years been an autopsy assistant in Tempe, Arizona.

Traditonally, any man (or, rarely, woman) who works in this capacity is called by the German word. To be the diener means pushing the gurneys around and hosing down the table. It means unzipping the body bags. It means sawing open bodies and learning their secrets, the tales of the dead. Hu Xu loved those secrets. It was in his blood.

In Tempe, when the sheriff and his men had discovered his secrets and were chasing him, they called him simply "the Chinaman." A

Chinaman on the run in Arizona has a hard time hiding. Here, in his homeland, he was invisible once more.

Standing now before a pedestal containing a tin basin full of hot soapy water, Hu Xu stared deeply into the steam-misted mirror and regarded the perfect beauty reflected there. Just the sight of his own wondrous face brought shudders of pleasure rippling up his short and slightly deformed spine.

Yesssss, he hissed through his small, evenly spaced, and very sharp teeth.

I am the beautiful diener.

Indeed, in his natural state, as now, he was a wonder to behold. His body, from the neck down, was decorated in a brilliant tableau of interwoven and intricate tattoos. On his chest, descending beneath the black Tao cross, a two-headed Chinese dragon etched in shades of yellow, crimson, and emerald green. The dragon on his belly spouted twin licks of orange fire that divided to encircle Hu Xu's small and malformed penis. Despite, or perhaps because of, the warped shape of the organ, his sexual appetites were varied and enormous. His sense of touch was inhumanly acute. As were all the others, taste, hearing, vision.

He grinned, baring his teeth, and murmured his approval at the rewarding sight. Perfect white dentures hid his own stubby points. As to hair, there was a wispy black goatee at the chin and a fringe of stringy black locks at the base of his skull. Normally, he plaited the sparse tresses adorning his tonsure with seven sterling silver skulls that clinked softly whenever he moved his head.

Now, he shaved off the goatee and stretched a latex skullcap over his hair and the tresses disappeared.

Tonight, the perfectly sculpted skulls were in a small silk pouch secreted upon his person. The tinny sound of tinkling skulls: the last sound countless victims heard before they stepped off. Hu Xu smiled, flipping at will through vivid memories of past glories engraved in his diener's memory bank; no, stop, back up, there, *that one.*

He passed his hand over his bony skull, slick with perspiration, licking his thin dry lips. He must hurry. It wouldn't do to be late for his appointment with General Moon, and he'd much to do before he could leave his barge.

A red leather bag sat on a small wooden table by his dresser. It contained the protean secrets of Hu's unusual life. He reached inside.

Delicately extracting another rubber prosthesis and any number of jars and tubes of foundation cream, greasepaint, and powder, Hu Xu began to make himself disappear. He liked to sing while he worked, something he had learned as a child in Arizona from the Seven Dwarfs in the movie *Snow White.* A song popped into his head and he gave voice to it, beautifully, as it happened. One of his many skills was an uncanny gift for pitch-perfect vocal impersonations. And so the soulful voice of Eric Clapton began to waft through the floating house.

> *She puts on her makeup*
> *And brushes her long black hair . . .*

Twenty minutes later, the wizened assassin had ceased to exist. In his place was a diminutive woman from the upper echelons of Shanghai society. Her name was Madame Li, and she had all the papers to prove it. Elderly and stooped, wearing a black raw silk dress with pearl buttons, Hu Xu leaned forward and studied himself carefully in the mirror. His cheeks were lightly rouged, his eyelashes long and thick with beautifully applied mascara. An artful application of lipstick fleshed out his lips, and his wig of hennaed black hair swept back into a tight chignon held in place by a tortoiseshell pin.

Off to Paris, dearies!

An old Louis Vuitton bag hung from his shoulder. Inside, a forged passport and fifty thousand Euros in cash. The old ship's chronometer in the next room tolled. Eight bells. It was time to go. General Moon was expecting him at half past the hour. But first, he must bid fond adieu to the desolate creature waiting so patiently in the dark and fetid spaces beneath his feet.

He pulled open the concealed hatch in the barge's galley and paused to savor the lovely stink that erupted into his nostrils. Below, a sewer of fear awaited him. His studio. He stepped carefully (he was wearing modest heels) onto the wooden ladder and began his descent. Halfway down, he heard a muffled cry of hope from poor Marge. Grandmother's coming, Margie! He had expected this confusion on her part and it delighted him no end. Did Marge really believe this elegant septuagenarian was coming to the rescue? The answer was yes!

The bilges of Hu Xu's floating residence, an aging two-story barge indistinguishable from thousands like it in Hong Kong's crowded Victoria Harbor, were the death artist's sanctuary and workplace. In the bowels of his barge he would complete his masterpieces in solitude, working through the night, his subjects lit only by guttering candles as he molded and reshaped their forms and limbs with his scalpels, bread knives, pruning clippers, and, noisy old thing, a vibrating bone saw.

It was dark down here, he saw. All but two of the large candles had expired. Still, it was lovely by candlelight. The walls were lined with large and small jars of formalin holding organs, bits of tissue, and carefully excised body parts. There was a central drain in the floor leading to a holding tank below. The tank emptied into a macerator, the same kind used on larger fishing boats to grind fish guts into thin gruel before the bloody soup was finally pumped overboard into the harbor.

In the center of his busy autopsy suite sat a brand new table. It was the very latest thing in morgue decor. It had two tiers. The top slab, where Margie was now, was simply a perforated metal sheet. The perforations allowed flowing water and bodily fluids to seep through to the lower tier. This level was also metal and served as a catch basin. A pump ensured a continuous flow of water over the lower tier, keeping it clean.

This one's name was Marge Goodwin. Stupid-sounding name, he felt, even for an unattractive and overweight American. She was the wife of a corrupt corporate executive near the top echelons at the Bank of China. General Moon had demanded one million dollars for the dear wife's safe return. The deadline had expired. No word from the disobedient banker. It was assumed he had gone to the police. Pointless, since the new chief, like many others in the new Hong Kong, was in Moon's pocket.

Alas, Moon had decreed death for Marge Goodwin.

The general, through his aide, Major Tang, had forwarded this late-breaking information to his most prized assassin earlier in the evening. It arrived via an encoded message. It was usually a simple transposition code, based on the fact that it was the third day of the week and that the date was the fifteenth of the sixth month. It was also, as always, hand-delivered by an anonymous fisherman on an anonymous sampan.

There were thousands of such nondescript men and women living on sampans in the harbor, large numbers of them on the general's secret payroll in one capacity or another. In a recent move to solidify his position in Hong Kong, Moon had decided to equip this army of coolies with automatic weapons and grenade launchers. Concealed, but, still, they were a formidable secret militia.

Decoding Moon's unusually lengthy message in his small study, Hu had further learned that he was to have a new and most exciting assignment. In Paris, yet. *Très chic, n'est-ce pas?* He was so thrilled, he noted the news in one of his black leather notebooks. He wrote much of this diary in haiku form, the poetry being one of the extremely few things Japonais that Hu had cause to admire.

Hu was expected at the Golden Dragon tonight at precisely nine o'clock. A quiet dinner with the general's aide-de-camp, Major Tony Tang. Tang, whose westernized first name and chic appearance made him a glamorous society figure in Hong Kong, would provide his itinerary. Efficient preparations had already been made on his behalf by the general's secretarial staff.

According to the general's message, he was prebooked, first class, on the British Airways flight to Paris next morning. There was a deluxe suite waiting for him at the George V hotel. The loveliest flowers in that hotel, he thought. Brilliantly arranged. He'd have to find out who did them. Buy the boy a drink and then, who knew?

But he had to tidy up his nest before he left, of course. Hu Xu had been only too happy to learn he was to put the distasteful victim out of her misery. As was his habit, he just took his own sweet time doing it.

He'd been her host for just forty-eight deliriously happy hours. She was almost complete. A few finishing touches here and there tonight and, voilà, pop her in the oven! My, but wasn't she the noisy one? He had grown tired of all the fretful blather. He had ceased to be interested in the sound of her. Pausing on the bottom rung, and looking coyly over his shoulder at Marge, he finished his work tune with a dramatic tremolo flourish.

I say, my darling, you look wonderful to-ni-i-ght . . .

She screamed. Who wouldn't? A seventy-year-old grandmother who sounded exactly like Eric Clapton? It was enough to drive anyone in their right mind stark raving mad.

First things first, he thought, stepping off the bottom rung and turning toward her. Yes, he was running a little late. But if there was one thing he'd learned at the University of Tempe medical center, it was that it pays to be methodical and organized. A place for everything, and everything in its place.

He plucked the oversize green hospital scrub suit and disposable plastic apron from the hook on the wall beside the table and put them both on. On his hands he snapped thin latex gloves. Over his lovely shoes, little paper booties. He stood for a moment and regarded the woman, shaking his head from side to side as she fussed. Oh, my, what a fuss it was. She'd seen the old woman's eyes and known at once that it was not her savior who stood gazing longingly at her now. No. In her pale blue eyes, realization bloomed in the widened irises.

"Upsy-daisy, my dear," he said, sliding a hand under Marge to lift her torso. With the other hand, he inserted a black rubber block under the middle of her upper back. This raised the throat and tilted the head back.

He whipped the delicate knife back and forth, scraping the edge against the whetstone.

Oh, yes, my dear. That tongue will have to come out, I'm afraid.

Shhhh, he said, and raised the scalpel.

Chapter Thirteen

Gloucestershire

SUTHERLAND SPED ALONG THE TAPLOW COMMON ROAD, slowed imperceptibly at the turning, and whipped through the main gates. After a moment's study of the National Trust signs, they were motoring at a snail's pace along the broad curving drive leading to Brixden House.

The drive wound its way through hundreds of acres of formal gardens and parklands, dotted here and there with classical statuary, some of it quite voluptuous, and the occasional temple or folly beyond the odd pond. Dappled June sunlight on the lawns, lakes, and beds made the thing picturesque in the extreme.

It was all a bit much for Congreve's tastes, but then, he was prepared not to like it. The Brixden Set, as they were called, had quite a reputation. Séances. Masked balls. Orgies. He inclined his head and looked at Sutherland, who seemed quite keen on this visit. Orgies, indeed.

"We might need to stop once or twice for petrol before we reach the house," he observed, tamping down his fresh bowl of tobacco.

"Impressive," Sutherland agreed.

"Built originally by the second duke of Buckingham," Congreve said, suppressing a disapproving sigh. "A scoundrel and rake if ever there was one. Dodged a bullet in a duel with one of his mistress's husbands, then died shortly thereafter after having caught cold pursuing his second great love after women, foxhunting. He seems to have set the tone."

But the peach orchards they now drove through and the gardens spoke to Congreve of another age, dotted as they were by extensive greenhouses with walls of nectarines, mind-bending displays of orchids and bromeliads, rare fuchsias and almost extinct varieties of cyclamen, rare Lorraine-series begonias, and benches draped with thick strappy-leaved clivia and yellow Vico. When finally he spied a bed of his beloved dahlias, he found himself softening a bit toward Brixden House, if not its owner.

Anyone who shared his love of dahlias couldn't be all bad.

The house itself was imposing when they finally caught sight of it. It was in the classic Italian style, and even Ambrose had to concede it was lovely. Built originally in the mid–seventeenth century as a hunting lodge, and rebuilt many times, the present Edwardian country house stood on great chalk cliffs with views of the rolling green Berkshire countryside. The main house overlooked an idyllic bend in the Thames while a large guesthouse in the Tudor manner, Spring Cottage it was called, sat right on the riverbank.

Sutherland drove briskly round a grand fountain at the head of the main drive, down a wide path of crushed stone, and into the car park. He tucked his Mini in the shadows between a spanking new Bentley Continental in racing green and an enormous 1980 Aston Martin Lagonda. Ambrose, despite all efforts to control himself, bent over and had a peek inside the Bentley. This notion of owning an automobile had quite taken him over, and he found himself admiring the rich interior and picturing himself behind the wheel. He now knew how addicts must feel, catching a whiff of burning opium or a sniff of glue.

"Come along, Sutherland, we've no time to dawdle," he said, righting himself and buttoning his tweed jacket. He was wearing a stylish young check for his meeting with Lady Mars. A black-and-white dog's-tooth pattern, three pieces, and, on his feet, his favorite double-buckle Derbys. The fine brown calf leather shoes were bespoke, John Lobb, and were slender with a beveled waist and a delicate hourglass contour. Precisely the kind of footwear, he reflected, a man with a vintage Bentley might wear on a country sojourn.

They were expected and shown immediately into the Great Hall to wait for her ladyship. Sutherland gravitated to the famous Singer Sargent portrait of Lady Diana Mars's great-grandmother hung to the left of the fireplace while Ambrose inspected a fine suit of Spanish armor, one of a pair standing guard at the foot of a great sweeping staircase. You didn't see armor much these days. It had become such a cliché in the mid–twentieth century that it had largely disappeared.

Congreve, noticing the delicate filigree work on the breastplate, thought perhaps the stuff was due for a comeback.

"You must be Chief Inspector Congreve," he heard a voice at his back say. "I'm delighted to have you here at Brixden House."

"Lady Mars," Ambrose said, turning to face her. "I am—" The words froze on his lips. He felt as if he had slammed into a wall of beauty.

"You are quite a celebrity, is what you are," Lady Mars said, quickly covering for his obvious embarrassment. "I googled you just this morning, Chief Inspector. The 'Demon of Deception,' one newspaper called you. 'The International Master of Mystery.' My, my. I shall certainly have to watch my every word around you, shall I not?"

The chief inspector was beginning to perspire. "Well, I shouldn't go that far, Lady Mars, I—I think anyone in my circumstances would have done as much. Why, these criminal cases I'm handed are all simple logic usually and—and—"

"Yes?" she said.

Sutherland, seeing his colleague's inability to supply further dialogue, came to his immediate rescue. "Good afternoon, Lady Mars," he said loudly, crossing the room in a single bound. "Detective Inspector Ross Sutherland, Scotland Yard."

"How do you do, Detective Sutherland? Another good-looking policeman. I'm so very pleased to meet you. Diana Mars. Would you two like tea? A cold drink? You've come a long way and it's brutally hot out, isn't it? I believe service is waiting in the library."

Sutherland looked at Congreve, who now seemed wholly incapable of responding to even the simplest question, and said, "That would be lovely, thanks very much."

"Follow me, then, won't you?" Lady Mars said, and then she was gliding over the highly polished parquetry floors and disappearing through a set of gleaming double doors.

Sutherland looked at Congreve and found him rooted to the spot. "Do I need to run get the defibrillator out of the boot, then, sir?" he asked.

"What? What's that?"

"Are you quite all right, sir?"

"Indeed. Yes. What seems to be the problem, Sutherland?"

"Lady Mars is serving us tea. In the library. It's over there."

"What is your point, Sutherland?"

"She's waiting in there for us, sir."

"Ah. Well, let's get moving then, shall we?"

"There you are!" Lady Mars exclaimed as they came through the doorway. "I thought I'd scared you two off. Come sit and have some tea, won't you? Oakshott here has provided us with a wealth of lovely cakes as well. Haven't you, Oakshott?"

"Indeed, Madame," Oakshott said. He was quite tall and thin, with blond, curly hair, and when he bowed slightly from the waist his boiled shirt rose up uncomfortably under his chin.

After the two detectives had been seated in a deep brocaded velvet sofa, Lady Mars poured for Ambrose and then Sutherland. Congreve lifted the cup to his lips, desperately trying to steady his hand. There was a noticeable rattle of cup and saucer.

"You like dahlias, I take it, Lady Astor?" said Congreve, managing a sip, but just barely.

"*Lady Astor?*" she said, smiling politely enough for a woman who'd just been wrongly addressed as someone who'd been dead for nearly four decades.

"Sorry. I mean, *Lady Mars.* How silly of me. You see, I'm feeling a trifle warm. Terribly sorry, but—"

"Good heavens," she said. "It is stifling in here. How rude of me. Oakshott, would you mind nudging the air-conditioning down a notch? The chief inspector here is burning up."

"Not at all, Your Ladyship," the butler said and, with a slight bow, he pushed his thick black glasses up on the bridge of his nose and slid silently from the book-lined room.

"You were speaking of dahlias, I believe, Chief Inspector," Diana Mars said, looking at him over the rim of her cup with her impossibly large china-blue eyes.

"Was I?" Congreve said, swallowing a mouthful of hot tea. He seemed incapable of supplying further dialogue.

"Yes," Sutherland said, somewhat frostily, "you were."

"Would you care for an eclair, Chief Inspector?" Lady Mars asked.

"What?"

"I said, would you care for an eclair, Chief Inspector."

"Oh. Right. Sorry. I was listening to your voice and not what you said."

Sutherland coughed discreetly into his fist.

"Lady Mars," the younger man said while reaching inside his navy jacket to withdraw a manila envelope. "We don't want to take up too much of your time. We've come here to Brixden, as I mentioned to you on the telephone this morning, to discuss a possible suspect in an attempted murder that occurred recently."

"Yes, Detective Sutherland. How may I assist you?"

"I'd like you to take a look at this photograph," Sutherland said, handing her a glossy eight-by-ten he'd had printed up.

"Yes?" she said, scanning the snapshot.

"Do you recognize anyone?"

"Of course. This photograph was taken right here at Brixden House. Last New Year's Eve, as a matter of fact. Right out there in the Great Hall. See? There's my great-grandmother's portrait on the wall."

"Why, she's quite right, Sutherland! The Sargent on the wall. Her great-grandmother."

"So," Sutherland said to her, with a glance at Congreve, who was still plainly trying to compose himself, "these persons are all, shall we say, friends of yours?"

"God, no. I just fling open the doors every year and see what fetches up. I've held this party annually since my dear husband died. He passed away on New Year's Eve, you see. One minute into the new millennium. Chunk of ham lodged in his throat. Choked to death. Dear Nigel."

"My condolences, Lady Mars," Sutherland said.

"So," Congreve said, rallying to the cause at last, "you are a widow, I take it."

"Excellent deduction, Chief Inspector," Diana Mars said with a warm smile in his direction. "Yes, I am."

"There are rumors afoot that you plan to sell Brixden House," Congreve said, mopping his brow with his soggy linen handkerchief. "Turn it into some sort of hotel."

"My dear man, it's always *been* a hotel."

"Getting back to the photo, Lady Mars," Sutherland said. "I'd like to ask you about this gentleman here. With the orange hair."

"Yes?"

"He's naked."

"So it would appear. You see, I retire precisely at the stroke of midnight. To be alone with my memories, as they say. The party, naturally, continues full bore into the wee hours. I usually import a band from the States. Last year it was Jimmy Buffett. He was simply marvelous. Breakfast is served at five next morning. What goes on in the house after witching hour doesn't interest me. Only that everyone wakes up next morning with a terrible head remembering what a splendid time they had in dear Nigel's honor."

"Marvelous," Ambrose stated for the record.

"Yes," she said. "As for me, I don't tipple. One reason I don't drink, you see, is that I do want to know when I'm having a good time." She looked from one man to the other, her eyes alight.

"If you drink, don't drive," Congreve said. "Don't even putt!"

"Now, that's a good one, Chief Inspector. Wonderful! You play golf, I take it? So do I."

"About the photograph," Sutherland said, with a hard glance at his superior.

"Yes, yes. Is there anyone that you do recognize, Lady Mars?" Ambrose asked, leaning forward with his hands on his knees. Sutherland breathed a sigh of relief. The man was back, or at least making a brief appearance.

"This woman here," she said.

"Which one?" Congreve said.

"This one. Bianca Moon is her name. Quite notorious. She's been here a few times, I think. She and her twin sister, Jet. At this party or that. Never for luncheon or supper, naturally."

"And may I ask why not?" Sutherland said.

"No one is comfortable talking about things in her presence, that's why. We all think she's a spy."

"Of course she's a spy," Congreve said, all his prior consternation seemingly vanished. "The question is, why is this particular spy so—interested—in an English employee of the French embassy?"

"Why, the Chinese and the French have gotten very cozy lately, it seems," Diana Mars said. "A big oil deal. Of course, you knew that. Everyone does."

"Of course," Congreve said, his innocent baby's eyes doing their utmost to convey genuine sincerity. "We knew that."

And, before he could stop himself, Sutherland blurted out, "We did?"

Chapter Fourteen

Hong Kong

MADAME LI ARRIVED AT THE GOLDEN DRAGON PROMPTLY AT nine o'clock that evening. He had traveled to the floating palace by water taxi, very fastidious in his white gloves and very careful not to smudge his beautiful pink suit or the pink pillbox hat he'd whimsically perched atop his coiffure. Perfect, he'd thought, spinning in front of his full-length mirror, for strolling the gay boulevards of the City of Light.

Dear departed Marge had taken a bit longer to dispense with than anticipated (that oven just wasn't working properly!), but still he'd managed to arrive at the appointed hour. After all, he didn't want to keep his "date" waiting.

I love Paris in the springtime . . .

The bustling harbor and the sky above it were absolutely filled with color and radiant light. So much so, that, en route, he was able to read his copy of the *South China Morning Post* (a good prop for his evening flight to Paris) as the water taxi made its way across the harbor through the maze of sampans and crisscrossing ferries.

I love Paris in the fall . . .

The Golden Dragon wasn't the largest floating restaurant in Hong Kong Harbor. Oh, no. That honor fell to the Jumbo Kingdom, a vastly popular tourist haunt. But, because it was not at all what it seemed, the Dragon was by far the most interesting. Four stories high above the waterline, and two below, the Dragon was over three hundred feet in length. It was lovingly decorated in the style of an exquisite Chinese imperial palace and festooned with every manner of gilded dragon and deity. One might dine there for years never suspecting the Golden Dragon was the official headquarters of the Te-Wu, the world's oldest and most brutal secret police society.

"Good evening," said one of the many handsome young maître d's fluttering around the ebony black reception podium, "I am Wu. Welcome to the Golden Dragon."

Hu Xu was delighted at the deferential treatment his new persona seemed to encourage among the staff. All the young men wore perfectly tailored evening clothes with soft black silk shirts. This one bowed with natural elegance, smiled at him, and said, in lilting English, "How may we serve you this evening, madame?"

The general, Hu Xu well knew, was obsessed with beauty in everything that surrounded him, and that obsession obviously extended to the human form. Everyone under his command, from his general staff to the busboys here at the Dragon, was a study in human perfection. There were exceptions for those with exceptional skills. A tattooed genius with a sketchy haircut, someone like himself, was tolerated. And even rewarded.

"Good evening," Madame Li said. "I'm meeting someone. I'm sure he's expecting me. Major Tang?"

"Ah," the beautiful boy said, and the flicker in his eyes was imperceptible to anyone but him. But there was a new sincerity and deference there. He picked up one of the pearlescent vintage telephones arrayed before him and spoke softly into it, waiting for and getting an answer.

"Certainly, madame," Wu said, his voice now barely above a whisper. "The major is expecting you. You will be dining this evening up in the Typhoon Shelter Bar. Will you be so kind as to sign our guest register and follow me, please?"

He signed and then followed the boy down a short roped-off corridor of gleaming and fragrant teakwood. At the far end was a small private elevator, the doors solid bronze and beautifully carved. Scenes, no doubt, of the farming village in the mountains where General Moon had been born and spent his idyllic childhood. Every carving, every painting, every work of art aboard depicted some aspect of General Moon's glorious life story.

Wu pressed the button and then clasped his white-gloved hands behind his back. This boy was just too pretty for his own good, Hu Xu decided, he needed some slight physical flaw in order to have some character. *I can arrange that,* he thought to himself as the doors slid open.

"Please, madame," Wu said, bowing and sweeping him into the elevator. "This will take you directly to the Typhoon Bar. I hope you have a lovely evening here with us."

"Oh, I shall," he trilled.

"And I hope to serve you again."

"Oh, you will, my child, you will indeed."

Alone in the elevator he threw his head back and roared with laughter.

He was such a romantic old soul.

The Typhoon Shelter Bar was on one of the uppermost decks, just below General Moon's suite of private offices. The views of the harbor at night were spectacular. And so was the food. And so were the martinis. And, knowing Major Tony Tang as he did, so would be the company. He was the most charming man on General Moon's staff. And one of Hu's closest allies.

He had dined with the major at the Dragon any number of times in other guises. On the main deck was a five-hundred-seat restaurant, the Dragon Court, decorated in classic Ming Dynasty style. The cuisine, if one could manage a reservation, was Cantonese and it was superb. Signature dishes included the White Shark's Fin and Seafood Soup with Bamboo Fungus. But the most celebrated entree on the menu, and Madame Li's personal favorite, was Chef Gong Li's Lobster, served whole, the bright red fellow served seated bolt upright, steaming in his own gilded wicker chair.

The Dragon proudly boasted onboard holding tanks containing live sharks and more than sixty kinds of sea creatures. There was even a UV light seawater sterilization system to ensure freshness and maintain hygiene. No expense had been spared. No detail had been overlooked. General Moon had seen to that. There was no reason a police station couldn't return a handsome profit.

The Golden Dragon was, in the tourist guides, or the eyes of thousands who passed through her portals each year, a glittering palace.

But, there were many sections not open to the public. These included a number of private dining rooms and banquet halls on the uppermost levels, but they always seemed to be fully booked. In fact, these rooms were bustling Te-Wu communications centers, bristling with high-tech gear and busy twenty-four hours a day. One deck was reserved for the general's private quarters.

The Dragon had been Sun-yat Moon's brainchild.

Under General Moon's direction, the PLA, the People's Liberation Army of China, had begun the multimillion-dollar construction in a Tianjin shipyard three full years before Britain ceded Hong Kong back to China. Engineers had assured Moon that at least five years would be needed to complete such an undertaking. He gave them three. Mainland Chinese workers at the construction yard at Tianjin on the Gulf of Chihli were sworn to secrecy about the massive undertaking on pain of death.

A great wall of secrecy immediately went up surrounding the project. All anyone in HM Government Hong Kong knew was that a very wealthy Chinese businessman was creating the most magnificent floating restaurant imaginable. The HK leadership was informed that at some point the great barge was to be towed from an unspecified location on the coast of mainland China and moored in Hong Kong Harbor. And that its arrival would coincide with the turnover.

Finally, on the historic day of the turnover to China, the Dragon miraculously appeared in the middle of Kowloon Harbor. Shrouded in canvas and secrecy, she had been towed into place by three tugs the night before. The harbor police looked the other way and patrol boats were mysteriously absent that night. The insidious power of the Te-Wu was already spreading its tendrils throughout the great city.

So, bright and early the next morning, the Golden Dragon, gleaming in the sun, was surrounded by sampans and private yachts, all hooting to celebrate her surprise arrival. Amidst a flurry of waterborne celebration, she was surrounded by fireboats that aimed great jets of water over her roofs and pagodas, sirens wailing. After sundown that night, a great fireworks display erupted from barges nearby.

The magic kingdom of General Sun-yat Moon was officially open to the public. And, unofficially, the new secret seat of power in Hong Kong was now open to the eager masters from Beijing.

The dreaded Te-Wu now had its long-coveted nest in the former Western stronghold.

"Welcome to the Typhoon Shelter Bar," another pretty boy said as the elevator doors parted to reveal the dazzling sight of Hong Kong at night.

"I believe Major Tang is expecting me?"

"Indeed he is. Right this way, madame."

Chapter Fifteen

The Cotswolds

HAWKESMOOR HAD PASSED DOWN TO ALEX WHEN HIS grandfather died at age ninety-one. The old Cotswolds pile, with countless chimneys and sweeping Corinthian south loggia by Robert Adam, stood against a backdrop of rolling green parklands in the heart of Gloucestershire. It was an idyllic setting for the somewhat terrifying tale now being told to Hawke by the director of the CIA. A black Bell Jet Ranger helicopter with no markings had swooped in and deposited Brick Kelly on a wide lawn, surrounded by lakes, streams, and *temples de l'amour.*

Two days had passed since Hawke's rescue of Harry Brock in the South of France. Hawke was shaving in his upstairs dressing room when he heard the big helo blades batting the air. He looked out his window and smiled. Summer days were always full of promise when a big black helicopter arrived on the lawn. He had dressed hurriedly and run downstairs to greet his old friend Brick.

At six o'clock that evening, Alex and Brick Kelly were seated in a library smelling richly of old leather and tobacco and countless decades of furniture wax. The ancient plane trees standing sentry outside the tall windows were black against a pale yellow sky. Pelham had laid a fire against the damp chill of the twilight hour. Hawke was sipping his customary Goslings rum, neat, while Kelly nursed a short whisky and soda.

The two men had just returned from a long afternoon's walk. The gorse and bramble on the hillside had been still damp from the morning rain. They'd carried a brace of twenty-bore Purdeys to the field but the birds weren't flying. Too wet. In their rambles they had covered, both literally and figuratively, a lot of ground.

"What else can I tell you, Alex?" Kelly said, settling deeper into the pale rose damask of the fireside sofa.

"A lot. Tell me more about this new French Foreign Trade minister Bonaparte," Hawke replied. "With every passing year he acquires a more Hitleresque persona."

Hawke, like everyone else, had long been reading newspaper and magazine accounts of Luca Bonaparte's miraculous ascent to power in France. His fiery speeches, his vision of a "New France," his visits with Castro and Chavez in Venezuela. His rumored secret ties to Beijing. But now Hawke wanted to hear the director's personal impressions.

The lanky red-haired Virginia gentleman laced his hands behind his head and stretched his long legs out nearer the fire.

"Luca Bonaparte," Brick said with a sigh, "is a goddamn time bomb. Your Hitler allusion is not that wide of the mark. The Foreign Trade minister's climb to power in the last few years has been nothing short of supernatural. He's got a magic name. He's good-looking, charismatic. But he's also had a lot of outside help. Our long-held suspicions on that have been confirmed. According to Harry Brock, he's getting it from the Chinese."

"Assassinations, rumor has it."

"They're not rumors. Brock is saying Chinese agents killed at least two of the ministers who stood between Bonaparte and his race to the top. We can't prove it, yet, but we will. That's today's real news flash. The French and the Chinese are not only in bed together, they're screwing each other's brains out."

"I'm not sure I can handle that image," Hawke said.

"No choice. You landed smack in the middle of this unholy romance when you grabbed Brock without asking permission. The Chinese are going to be gunning for you soon enough. Bonaparte already is."

"What's in it for the Chinese?"

"Oil. We think France, now that she's going it alone, is going to make some kind of move in the Gulf. China will back her. If the alliance proves successful there, Bonaparte will run France at China's pleasure. That's President McAtee's view, and most folks in Washington share it."

"The Chinese get a toehold in the Gulf and the French people get a direct descendant of their glorious emperor. It makes perverse sense."

"You bet. The name Bonaparte translates to priceless political cachet with the populace of France. France is sick to death of being marginalized politically. The last half of the twentieth century wasn't kind to them. The French people, and Bonaparte, despise being lumped in with 'Old Europe,' as the press now calls them. That's why they voted against the EU constitution."

"So the new France is really the old France."

"Exactly. Believe me when I tell you that Bonaparte uses this current nostalgia for past glory to full advantage. The man generates enormous excitement wherever he speaks. Verging on hysteria at times. Even the *ancien noblesse* seem to go all giddy about him. Aristocrats, farmers, academia. The whole country seems to see him as the second coming."

"Don't tell me he's got brains, too."

Brick nodded. "Brilliant politician. Great student of global military and naval history. Solves solitary chess problems every second he gets alone. That type. I wouldn't hesitate to use the word 'genius,' Alex. And you know I never use that word. I also believe he's batty as a bedbug."

Hawke said nothing, and continued to look at the photograph Brick had handed him, studying the man's face carefully. He had the same handsome cast of expression, the same hooded and dark almond eyes, as Napoleon. The eyes, that was the thing. They looked as if they could ignite the paper they were printed on. A dangerous opponent by any standard.

"Is he short, too?" Hawke asked, dropping the paper to the carpet as if it had singed his fingertips.

"No, but he acts like it."

"Napoleonic complex," Hawke said, grinning. "I didn't know Napoleon had any children, Brick."

"Not with Josephine. That's where most people get it wrong. The two of them couldn't bear children together. Her problem, not his, apparently. He strayed from the marital bed. When his mistress, Princess Maria Louisa of Austria, became pregnant with his son and heir, Boney dumped Josephine and married the princess."

"And she delivered?"

"Indeed, she did. Just what Boney wanted. A son. The kid was dubbed Napoleon François-Joseph Charles, heir to the French Empire and the king of Rome."

"You've done your homework. I remember now that there was a child with the second wife. But I thought the boy died young."

"Did indeed. Napoleon's son died of consumption at age twenty-one." Brick took another sip of his whisky. He was gradually warming the cold out of his bones.

"Twenty-one," Hawke said. "So, this Napoleon the Second would certainly have been old enough to have children of his own."

"Exactly. Never married, however. He liked to romp with the sporting ladies who frequented the arcades near the Ecole Militaire. His only known consorts were courtesans and hookers. One of them could easily have given birth to a boy and been paid to keep quiet about it."

"What do you think, Brick? Personally. Is this guy going all the way to the top?"

"He could. He's a star, Alex. You've seen his press. The country idolizes him, schoolchildren make up songs about him, and the current regime in Paris is terrified of him. And, rightly so. President Bocquet and his prime minister, Honfleur, were just reelected by a very slim margin. They've already got the long knives out for him."

"How so?"

"The Elysée Palace insiders aligned with Bocquet and Honfleur and their cronies in the mainstream French media now claim the golden boy, Luca Bonaparte, is a fraud. Worse yet, a Corsican. *Sacrebleu!* Dangerous. Unstable. Naturally they would say that. He's a clear and present danger to their tenuous grip on power. They've already taken to calling him 'Phony-Boney' in the right-wing press."

"The right wing doesn't like him because he's a Mao-style Communist. And the left doesn't like him because he doesn't play by the rules. I need to know which side I'm on in this goddamn fight," Hawke said, and Kelly smiled.

"You're on my side. Anyway, Boney actually is a bona-fide Corsican and everybody at Langley who has looked into it says, short of a DNA confirmation, he's probably a legitimate descendant of Napoleon Bonaparte."

"You must be digging up some real dirt on this guy, Brick. Knowing you the way I do."

"Yeah. And if we could prove it, we'd shovel it right to Honfleur and Bocquet. Let them do all the work. One of the stories we're checking is based on a rumor Brock paid a lot of money for while running down General Moon in China. The gist of it is that when Bonaparte was a kid in Corsica he was an assassin for the left wing of the Union Corse. Something called the Brigade Rouge. At fifteen, the kid supposedly murdered his own father. Shot him in front of Napoleon's Tomb, if you can believe that. Then hung him from the dome of the cathedral for good measure and left him there. Swinging in the breeze right above Napoleon's sarcophagus."

"Good God. Why?"

"Who knows? The way Brock heard it, his father got sideways with someone. One theory is his father was too right wing for his son's leftist sensibilities, so the kid popped him. The other is the old man had murdered an American capo from Brooklyn. In those days, the Mob and the Corse were eating at the same table. Sharp elbows. Luca's father crossed some line, and Luca took him out. He's definitely got a purge mentality."

"Sounds like he can't decide if he's Napoleon or Joe Stalin."

"Close enough. As you say, Luca Bonaparte, though he would never admit this publicly, is not the moderate left-wing French politician we've all grown to know and love. He's an old-style Stalinist Commie, Alex, with a dash of Chairman Mao thrown in for flavor. If he gets in power, watch out. We think this psychotic French fruitcake is hellbent on world domination and will gladly kill anyone who gets in his way."

Hawke looked at Kelly and said, "I know the world has passed me by when I hear 'French' and 'world domination' in the same sentence."

"It's not funny and it's not that far-fetched, Alex. Think about it. We now know for certain that Bonaparte is backed by the boys from Beijing. Beijing happens to possess one of the world's largest nuclear arsenals. We have absolutely no reason to believe they won't use it if we go to the brink."

"Why on earth would they ever go to the brink?"

"Oil. That's the imperative. They have to have it and they'll do absolutely whatever is necessary to get it."

"Risk nuclear annihilation?"

"China could lose a number roughly the size of the entire U.S. population in an all-out exchange and still have a billion or so souls to soldier on under the red banner. They are ascendant, the most powerful Communist dictatorship on earth, and the greatest threat we face in this century. Now they've got an ally in the heart of old Europe that wants to go along for the ride."

"Christ. Teetering on the edge again, aren't we, old Brick? If the Manchurian Candidate ever wakes up, we'll have to ask him for advice on how we go about stopping all this."

"While he's wired to a polygraph, obviously."

"Can we talk about this over food, Brick? I'm starved, and I think Pelham has our supper ready."

"Just one more thing. We think our guy is homicidal, maybe psychopathic. A lot of this kid's bodies are buried on Corsica. Even more family members, so rumor has it. And no doubt in remote corners of France, too, where his political rise has been a wee bit too meteoric."

"Can you actually pin anything on him?"

"Not yet. Boney's record has been scrubbed squeaky clean. Nobody's ever even tried to pin his father's murder on him, by the way. To this day, it's booked on the gendarmes' records as an unsolved homicide. They've still got it penciled in as a probable U.S. Mob hit."

"Patricide. At fifteen years old. That's fairly staggering."

"Yeah. If he actually pulled the trigger. Some of the New York families had deep roots within the Union Corse in those days. I've got an FBI file on my desk an inch thick. Maybe Luca somehow coordinated the hit on his old man with the Mob and then laid it off on them to keep his record shiny and new. He's had his eye on the throne for a long, long time."

"You could take him down that way, Brick. Legally."

"Yeah. We've been talking about that. At this point, it's all rumor and conjecture. It's too vague for Langley to pursue at this point. But Brock's source said there may have been a couple of eyewitnesses who are still around somewhere. I'd like you to bring Chief Inspector Congreve into this thing, Alex. Here's the file. It's a very cold case, but if anybody could prove Bonaparte murdered his own father, it's Ambrose Congreve. Do that, and Bonaparte might go down under his own weight."

Hawke took the heavy folder and placed it on the table beside his chair. He looked up at Kelly.

"Get the proof of this homicide into the hands of his political opposition in France. Let them take him down. And the U.S. keeps its hands clean."

"That's the general idea."

"Ambrose will be thrilled. I'll call him tonight. He's spent so much time planting dahlias lately he's bouncing off the garden walls."

Hawke got to his feet and placed one hand on the mantel. It had been a long day and his stomach was growling. Another rum was out of the question.

He said, "Brick, it stands to reason that Bonaparte's rise is behind all this heightened unpleasantness with France. They were bad enough before, God knows, with their support of that murderous Saddam. Not to mention actually supporting Hezbollah's right to raise money in Europe. But this is beyond the pale. Now it's personal. I mean, imagine shooting at helpless Englishmen on the open seas and all that sort of thing? Is it Honfleur and President Bocquet? Or is it the rise of Boney?"

"The military's loyalties are shifting rapidly to Boney. They see him as the long-awaited savior of France. Bocquet still sits in the big chair. And Honfleur is his big French poodle. But Boney's Chinese death squad is the one they're going to sic on you. You sank a French navy vessel, old buddy. And they don't admit to firing on you first. I had that scoundrel president Guy Bocquet himself on the phone this morning. They want blood."

"They keep this up, they'll get it."

"It's been suggested that you act contrite."

"Really? By whom? Not by my government, I assure you."

"No, mine. Your old pal the secretary of state for one," Kelly said, "Madame Consuelo de los Reyes."

"Conch? Rubbish. I don't believe a word of it."

"She's mad as hell at you. What happened between the two of you, anyway? For a while there, I thought you were going to get married."

"I don't want to talk about it."

"Conch said in a Cabinet meeting yesterday that she's got enough trouble on her hands with the Iranian-Syrian alliance, long-range missiles, and Kim Il Jong right now without you adding France to her shitlist."

"Me? Brick, damn it, I was doing a snatch for you. And somebody shot at me. I shot back. I don't give a damn about your bloody list."

"Easy, buddy. It ain't my shitlist and it certainly ain't my point of view. I told her exactly the same thing. You were on an approved mission for the United States of America and you acted in justifiable self-defense. What happened in Cannes is just the calm before the shitstorm."

"Meaning?"

"Two things. Right now, Conch has got her hands full trying to convince France and Germany to stop selling weapons and dual-use technologies to Iran and Syria. So France is already high on Conch's list. She just doesn't quite know how high yet. France's tacit approval of terrorism is an abomination and President McAtee, despite his proclamations of improving relations, is not going to stand for it. Put that together with the rise of Bonaparte and—"

Pelham had somehow floated into the flickering shadows of the room unseen and unheard.

"Dinner is served, m'lord."

Chapter Sixteen

Hong Kong

"MADAME LI, I PRESUME," MAJOR TONY TANG SAID, GETTING to his feet. Tall, imperious, and elegant, Major Tang was the pretty public face General Moon put on all of his ugly little secrets in Hong Kong. A PR flack, they'd call him back in Arizona. But he was far more interesting than that. He sat at the right hand of the king and he was the second-most-powerful man in Hong Kong. He was also frequently sent abroad to handle delicate situations. Major Tang had finesse.

"Yes, I am Madame Li, you wicked boy," Madame Li said, taking his proffered hand and shaking it delicately. "But tell me, Major, how did you know my new name?"

"Wu called me from Reception. Even now the Documents Section upstairs is preparing your travel papers, tickets, and a new passport. They are using the digital picture Wu took of you moments ago at the desk. And your signature from the guest registry."

"Flattering picture, I hope."

"See for yourself," Tang said, revolving his small Sony laptop so Hu Xu could see his portrait on the screen. Tang hit a button and the scene shifted back to a live feed from the communications center. He closed the laptop and pushed it aside.

"Charming photograph," Madame Li said, eyeing the man warmly. Despite (or perhaps because of) his powerful position and a noteworthy penchant for cruelty, Tony Tang was a very attractive human being. The type of man who could raise the temperature of any room he walked into. Oh, dear. He had to restrain himself from giggling at how easily he slipped into character.

"How silly of me. I should have known. Your staff is so very well trained."

Both enjoyed this little game of flirtation. Frequently, it was the major who vetted Hu's character choices and disguises before departure for a new assignment. When last they'd met, Hu Xu had been a portly and bespectacled petroleum geologist headed out to Oman on a fact-finding mission. The time before that, a middle-aged HKSB hedge fund manager on his way to Wall Street to assess the strength of the U.S. markets.

Tonight the major was, surprisingly, not in uniform. Rather, he wore a beautifully cut navy blue suit, crisp white shirt, and a navy silk bowtie. He was taller than the typical PLA officer, and exceedingly handsome. He had a strong chin and good high cheekbones that could hardly be improved upon. They made a handsome couple, Madame Li thought, smiling to himself. Possibly mother and son on some future assignment for General Moon? Thailand, perhaps, or Kauai.

"Please. Be seated here, madame, where you can enjoy the best view," the major said in flawless English, his smooth and gracious manners polished to perfection. The two often spoke in English, each trying to one-up the other with the latest Americanism. China's fate was to rule; it made sense to be fluent in the enemy tongue.

Tang pulled out a chair and he sat down, waiting to be pushed up to the table. Madame Li smiled up at him. This character Madame Li, for all the trouble and fuss she took to create, had its compensations. Perhaps, Hu Xu thought, folding his little white-gloved hands delicately on the white tablecloth, she should appear more often.

"So," Hu Xu said, smiling coquettishly at Major Tang, "Paris."

"Yes, Paris. I am envious."

All night, his expectations of Paris had caused a tingle down the spine. After all, there would be a suite at the George V and plenty of blood money to fritter away in the shops along the rue du Faubourg Saint-Honoré when he wasn't working. And there were darker treasures, too, antique medical instruments in dusty bins tucked away on side streets in St. Germain des Prés. He hoped he'd have enough free time to go exploring.

Collecting wildly expensive surgical antiquities from the far ends of the earth was certainly an extravagance, but, aside from occasional bouts of cannibalism, it was Hu Xu's only vice.

The view of the harbor from this table was exquisite, he noticed as a waiter approached with menus. The Typhoon Shelter Bar was built entirely of unsupported glass walls, and there were panoramic views of nighttime Hong Kong in every direction.

"I'll have a vodka martini," Madame Li told the waiter. "The French vodka, not the Russian. Grey Goose. And the lobster, please. How about you, Major?"

Major Tony Tang said, "I'll have exactly the same."

The waiter bowed deeply and departed and the two regarded each other with some amusement across the table. Tang, who had seen Hu in many of his manifestations, had never met Madame Li until this moment. He was obviously delighted with every aspect of this new apparition. Hu relaxed visibly, knowing his report to the general would be positive. Only a few diners had been allowed up to the Shelter Bar tonight, and they had all been seated a discreet distance from the major's corner table.

"Well," Major Tang said as their drinks arrived, "I must tell you that the general sends his apologies. He won't be dining with us this evening after all."

"I'm so sorry to hear that," he said. "Don't tell me he's ill."

"Busy. He has—how shall we say this—domestic problems."

"Double trouble? I thought he had those two girls under control."

The major smiled ruefully, nodding affirmation. "Yes. The terrible twins are at it again."

"Their Satanic Majesties. If they're not at each other's throats, they are at someone else's. Which one is causing him anguish this time? Jet? Or Bianca?"

"Both, I'm afraid. What a miserable trial he endures at the hands of those two."

"Bianca battles her own addictions, but she is a brilliant and loyal Te-Wu officer. Jet is the real trial, Major," Madame Li said, clucking like an old hen. "And yet it is the party who endures her. She is irredeemable, in my view. That wild debacle in Amsterdam should be proof enough of that. Jet is a Western culture junkie, no longer loyal to the party. She should be removed from her duties as a Te-Wu officer."

With that off his chest, he sat back and sipped his icy vodka.

There were few among the general's inner circle who could say such a thing about Moon's daughters without fear of losing his head. Hu Xu was plainly one of them.

The major's response was only a muted "Well, well. We shall see what we shall see."

"Someone was going to attempt to straighten Jet out. A cultural intervention, I believe it's called. I take it the attempt failed?"

Major Tang's shoulders seemed to sag with weight from the general's offices above. The general's troubles were his troubles by definition. And China's fortunes in the next month or so were problematic enough without two daughters who despised each other vying for the general's attention—and affection.

"You mean von Draxis. Yes, our German friend claimed to have gotten Jet under control. But, now . . . horrible news. Just hours ago."

"What happened?"

"A shipment from the South of France was unfortunately disrupted. Someone on our side completely bungled the security while the cargo was in port. We don't have all the facts yet, but we do know Jet let us down terribly."

"How?"

"She was supposed to eliminate a British agent in Cannes. For whatever reason, she did not."

"At some point, Major, the general is going to have to face reality where his beautiful daughters are concerned. Bianca is beset by her own demons. But her skill and her loyalty to her father and to the party are beyond question. Jet, it seems, has failed us again."

"The general will not acknowledge this, but it's true. The West has won Jet's heart. Jet, I think, has permanently slipped her moorings."

"Then Jet is very, very dangerous to us, Major."

"Yes."

"Let me know when action is required."

Major Tang nodded. "As we speak, the general is up in his office explaining what went wrong in Cannes to the CCP powers in Beijing. He never likes explaining the failures of subordinates. Especially when those involved are—"

"His own flesh and blood, yes. This disrupted shipment—that would be the American goods that Tsing Ping was handling? A transfer from Morocco?"

"Unfortunately, correct. A most vital shipment, as you well know. But these things happen. With your assistance, it shall ultimately be rectified."

"The goods were offloaded prematurely in transit, I take it?"

"Yes. The man responsible for the loss has already been identified. This bloody Englishman whom Jet let slip through her fingers. He will be dealt with once your mission in Paris has reached a satisfactory conclusion. You'll find digital photographs of him and his dossier in this packet." He slid a blue envelope across the table. The word PIRATE was stenciled in red on the outside.

"Pirate?" Madame Li asked, looking at the photographs inside.

"His name is Lord Alexander Hawke. General Moon himself gave Hawke the piratical sobriquet. He's been a bother to us on several prior occasions."

"Yes. I recall the name. That Cuban misadventure several years ago, was it not? The botched coup d'état?"

"Exactly. This Hawke is a direct descendant of the notorious English pirate Blackhawke. The scourge of the Spanish Main in the eighteenth century, according to our research gnomes and Mr. Google. Three centuries have not succeeded in washing the pirate blood out of Blackhawke's bloodlines. Especially that coursing through the veins of this man Hawke."

"Good-looking in a coarse way," Madame Li said, turning the photograph in his hands. "I suppose I shall have to kill him."

"In good time, yes, someone certainly will."

"And tell me about Bianca. She's still having problems in London?"

"Yes. Despite Bianca's well-known addictions to bizarre sex parties and opiates, she has in the past been an excellent field agent. Unlike her sister, she is, as you know, both efficient and lethal. Sadly, now, the opium seems to be winning the battle. Our French connection in London has been badly compromised."

"What happened?"

"We were, as you well know, running a highly successful operation there. But we recently discovered that a mole she planted inside the embassy last winter was doubling up on her. Bianca's agent-in-place, Bulling, was also toiling away for Scotland Yard. He had a weekly brush pass in Regent's Park with a man named Congreve. Retired from the Yard, now freelancing for MI6 and the man Hawke we discussed earlier. You'll find Congreve's picture's in there, too."

"What are you going to do?"

"For the moment, we are giving Bianca time to fix this mess. But the general's patience with her wears thin."

"Why doesn't Bianca simply eliminate both Bulling and Congreve and be done with it?"

A pained expression was visible behind the major's permanent smile. "She is involved with Bulling. Not romantically. Sexually. She confided the bizzare truth to me over dinner when she was last here in Hong Kong. The man is a hermaphrodite. Both sexual organs are extremely prominent but the male predominates—I, uh, well . . . there you have it."

"More, more!"

"I forget. You relish these oddities. At any rate, it's a perverse physical addiction to the man fueled by drugs. He beats her, yet she comes back for more. She has begged her father for time. She even ordered Bulling to eliminate Congreve in the hope he'll redeem himself. He has failed once. If he succeeds . . ."

The waiter had brought more drinks. Madame Li sipped his new martini and found it cold and delicious. "I take it her time is running out, Major."

"Yes. The general's frustration with both daughters has reached the boiling point. But, enough. Let us turn our attention to more pleasant subjects. Let's talk about Paris. Here is the brief prepared for you by the general's staff. Once you arrive, you will receive more detailed instructions from Minister Bonaparte himself."

"*Le Roi!* At last I get to meet this living legend."

Major Tang laughed.

"He will only succeed to the throne if you succeed first, Madame Li. First, you must successfully accomplish your mission in Paris."

"Tell me. Please don't make me wait to read it."

"The assassination of Prime Minister Honfleur and President Bocquet of France has been approved at the highest level."

"I am flattered."

"Who else would we trust to give the world a new Bonaparte?"

"I love my work."

"General Moon will be delighted to hear that," the major said, putting down his chopsticks. His handsome face and easy manner instantly lost all traces of levity. He stared at his principal assassin with flashing black eyes.

"Because without France," he said, "indeed, without Bonaparte himself, the general's great scheme for the future security of our country does not work. If the general's plan fails, Beijing will have his head. And, need I even say it, yours and mine as well."

"*Leviathan* will work, Major. It cannot fail."

"See that it doesn't, Colonel. After this dinner, I am to bring you to General Moon. There, he will impress upon you the absolute necessity of your success."

Chapter Seventeen

Cannes

STOKELY JONES HAD NEVER SEEN SO MANY RICH, BEAUTI-
fully decked out white folk jammed into one small location in his
whole damn life. Not only that, they were all floating. Of course, the
boat they were floating on had to have cost at least fifty mil, but hey,
this was the South of France! *La dolce vita* and shit.

He hadn't met Hawke's reason for his being here yet, some German baron or duke who owned this barge, but he'd sampled some of
the hors d'oeuvres (prissy-ass version of pigs in a blanket and assorted sushi that looked like little flower arrangements), and he'd finally managed to get himself something to drink from one of the
cute girls wandering around in short pleated sailor suits who didn't
speak word one of English.

A very tan couple was standing next to him sipping pink champagne. Lots of noisy gold jewelry. Major bling going on. Stoke had
seen a lot of topless action around, but this woman was actually
wearing one. Still, this being France, you could see right through it
and there was a lot to see. He decided it was impolite not to speak so
he said to the guy, "Hey, how you doing? Big boat, huh? What do you
think one of these goes for?"

"Mais oui," the guy said, *"c'est formidable, le* Valkryie. You are
Americain, n'est-ce pas?"

"Yeah, Ameri-*can.* I like that. Put the accent on the last syllable.
Who can? Ameri-can! We ought to try that. You guys are French, unless I'm very much mistaken?"

"Mais certainement, monsieur," the French guy said, as if this were
so damn obvious he couldn't believe anybody was even dumb
enough to ask the question. "My name is Marcel."

"Stokely Jones, nice to meet you. In that case, Marcel, let me ask you a question. Why the hell does everybody over here in Europe call this stuff I'm drinking here 'Coke Light' instead of Diet Coke the way we call it in the U.S. of A.? You got any thoughts on that? Maybe it's a marketing thing. Just curious. I had a hell of a time figuring it out. Almost died of thirst."

"*Pardon, monsieur?* I don't understand."

"No? Well, I mean, it's confusing. Let's take Bud Light, for example, what we Americans call the low-calorie Bud. You guys call that Diet Bud? I mean, just for instance."

The woman huffed out something that sounded like *Oof!* and turned away to look at the sunset. It did wonders for her transparent white blouse but Stoke didn't stare because the French guy was looking at him funny. Wanted to say something but not sure what. Like he couldn't get his mouth hooked up to his brain. Husband, Stoke decided. Definitely husband. Oh, well.

Having just about exhausted his small talk repertoire, Marcel lobbed a lame one from the foul line, saying, "You are staying at the Hotel du Cap, Monsieur Jones?"

"Me? Way out of my price range. No, I myself like to keep it low key. I'm up at the Plage Publique."

"The Public Beach?" The two of them looked at each other.

"You've heard of it, huh? Great views of the ocean. Cheap, too."

"I would imagine so, monsieur," the guy said. "Oof." *Oof* was a big word in France, Stoke figured.

"Well, I guess I'll let you guys circulate," Stoke said to him and began to move away. He stopped and looked at the guy over his shoulder.

"Hey, Marcel, you know what French word I really like?" Stoke said. "Sangfroid. Sang-*fwa.* Love to say that word. Ice in your veins. I can relate to that. Nice talking to you. Keep it real, you two."

Stoke made his way over to the starboard side and stood for a moment admiring the cockpit. The electronics and navionics and shit. Big flat-screen TV monitor in front of each wheel, which was something to see. Color GPS, weather sat, and radar displays. Underwater camera showing the bottom just below the boat in real time. Stoke looked at that for a second, thinking about why they might have that. Security? Maybe they did underwater exploration. Treasure hunters, maybe. Something.

He noticed the couple he'd been chatting with talking to a toady little man in a white jacket with brass buttons and epaulets and stuff. Looked like a baby admiral. He had two goons with him, big blond Teutonic types, muscle boys, wearing tight black T-shirts and shorts. The duke and duchess were holding their hands up in front to shield their mouths while they talked to the guy, but they kept looking over at Stoke so he could pretty well imagine who they were talking about.

The little egg-shaped admiral bobbed his head up and down. He had an expression of grave concern on his pink face as he headed through the crowd in Stoke's direction. The two storm troopers were right behind him.

"May I help you, monsieur?" he asked in a not-too-friendly way, moving close to Stoke so nobody could overhear him. That meant he had to crane his head way the hell back to look all the way up at Stoke's face.

"Help me? With what?"

That seemed to throw him.

"Are you finding everything you need?" he said. Translation, even though he was speaking plain, heavily accented English, I think you're at the wrong party, dude.

"Am I finding everything I need," Stoke said, smiling at the guy and putting one of his huge hands on the guy's shoulder as a display of international friendship. "Well, that's a damn good question and the answer is no, I'm not. Let me ask you something."

"Certainly, sir."

"Where all the black folks at?"

"I'm sorry?"

"Black folks. Brothers. Negroes. Where can I find them?"

The little guy was starting to puff up like an overheated pastry.

"I'm sorry, sir, I do not understand."

"That's all right," Stoke said, patting the guy on the back. He tried to be gentle but he thought he heard ribs cracking. "My name is Stokely Jones, Jr. You may have heard of my family. The West 138th Street Joneses of New York City? Ring a bell? No? We the ones everybody always trying to keep up with."

"Monsieur, I beg your pardon, but I—"

"Am I on the right yacht? Maybe I read this thing wrong," Stoke said, pulling the invitation Alex had given him out of his breast pocket. "It's in French so I may be mixed up. Here, you read it, see what you think."

The guy got all wide-eyed.

"You are Lord Alexander Hawke, monsieur?" the guy said, moving his lips while he read. Eyes, too, moving from the name handwritten on the card up to Stoke's face and then back at the invitation.

"Hell, no, I ain't!" Stoke laughed, pounding the guy so hard on the shoulder he almost drove him straight down through the teak deck. "But that's a good one! Am I Alex Hawke? I gotta remember to tell him that one!"

"Well, then—"

"I work for the man. He couldn't make it tonight so he gave me his invitation. That's his boat over there. See it? The big black one all lit up and shit. Kinda blocking out the horizon. Called *Blackhawke*. Hell, we're practically neighbors."

"You are Lord Hawke's guest." His mood brightened considerably at this idea.

"Technically," Stoke said. "But, since it's your boat, not. In reality, I'm your guest. See what I'm saying?"

"Well—"

"Listen. No harm done, Admiral. I'm not insulted. Hell, don't even think about it. Skin thicker than a New York City phone book. Yellow Pages. Hey, question, all right? Where's the host at? You ain't him, are you?"

"Certainly not, monsieur, I am the second chief steward aboard *Valkyrie*. My name is Bruno. The owner, Baron von Draxis, he is up on the bow. Giving a warm and welcoming toast to our guests at this moment. And unveiling an oil portrait of his newest project. An ocean liner. The world's largest. She will be launched at Le Havre in a few short weeks."

"Really? I'd like to catch that welcome toast. I love German warmth. But, listen, Bruno, do me a favor. I'm kind of a boat guy myself. Navy SEALs, shit like that. Do you think I could get a stem-to-stern tour of this thing? Just you and me?"

Stoke discreetly slipped a single Euro note into the guy's breast pocket, sticking out right behind his little puffed-out polka-dot hanky. Bruno looked down at it, saw it was five hundred smackers. He looked around, then shoved the note down in his pocket.

"I should be delighted, monsieur. Shall we start here at the stern?"

"Certainly. Who are your two friends here?" Stoke said, smiling at the huge evil twins and sticking his hand out to the one on the left.

"Guten abend," the guy said. He sounded like a German Barry White.

"Where are my manners? Damn! I didn't even say hello. How you doing? Stokely Jones, Jr., is my name. What's yours?"

"Arnold," the guy said, trying vainly to pulverize Stoke's hand. Stoke managed to extract it without permanent nerve damage and offer it to the other guy.

"Stokely Jones, nice to meet you."

"Arnold," the second guy said.

"You're Arnold, too? That must get confusing."

Bruno said, "They are in charge of the baron's security. Arnold and—"

"Listen, Admiral. Tell the two Arnolds you'll catch up with them later. Got it? We'll start at this end of the boat and work our way to the beginning. Lead on, Bruno," Stoke said, "I'll follow you."

"Very good, Mr. Jones."

"Auf wiedersehen," Stoke said, waving good-bye to the two Arnolds. And he really did get the feeling he'd be seeing them again.

Bruno led the way, grinning with pleasure, and gave Stokely a running description of everything they saw. The big stern section that swung open hydraulically, where they kept a whole lot of silver-painted wave-riders and two Riva launches. The walnut-paneled smoking room, the card room, the screening room, the antique-filled interiors designed, naturally, by the famous Luigi di Luigi of Milano and shit like that. The Bagni Volpi sheets, the Descamps towels, all those good-life things you saw in magazines.

Stoke wasn't too impressed by much of what he saw below. All boats, no matter how much money you throw at them, are pretty much the same below decks. Long passageways with closed cabin doors on either side. The galley, full of smiling Italian cooks and waiters, always happy to have visitors. A monstrous sparkling engine room where the chief engineer and his mates gave detailed information regarding the two massive diesels. It was, in Stoke's view, the most beautiful room on the boat. But Stoke had no time for that now.

"Where's this baron bunk his ass?" Stoke asked the admiral, gently squeezing his shoulder in a conspiratorial way.

"Ah, he has a full beam owner's stateroom just up at the end of this passageway. Afraid it's off limits just at this moment."

"Really? Why's that?" Stoke kept moving, leading them down the corridor leading forward until they reached the wide double doors.

"Surely you can understand that—"

"Man got to have his privacy, yeah, I can understand that. Question. What's below our feet? You got enough space down there for four or five New York City buses."

"It's just the bilges, very boring. Storage, fuel tanks. We motor a lot, so we have to carry many tons of fuel. Nothing very interesting, I assure you."

"I'm already interested. So, how you get down there? I've been looking for a stairway or elevator."

"I assure you it wouldn't be of interest."

"Maybe some other time, then. Hey, listen, this has been great. Fabulous. I've got to run along now, but I'd love you to do me a favor." Stoke fished inside his wallet. The guy rose like a trout.

"Of course, sir, how may I be of further assistance?"

"I really am dying to see the man's bedroom, see," Stoke said, putting a thousand-Euro note in the leaping hand. "I'm redoing one of my client's staterooms. Looking for decorating ideas, you understand. You don't need to stick around, just open it up for me and get back to your guests, okay?"

"Well—"

"Our little secret, Bruno old pal. Don't worry. Somebody sees me, I just got lost looking for the head."

"You're an interior decorator?"

"More of an interior designer. You may have heard of my firm. Jones and Jones of New York? I like these chairs, covered in white leather. Good look."

"It's not exactly leather," Bruno said. "It's the skin of whale scrotums."

"Whale scrotums?" Stoke said. "See, that's exactly the kind of decorating input I'm looking for!"

"The owner's thinking of doing these companionway walls in aqua. What do you think?"

"Bad idea."

"Really? How do you possibly know that without seeing it?"

"Tricks of the trade, Bruno. I don't have to throw up on the shag to know it's going to look bad."

"Monsieur Jones, I can see you are a man of exquisite taste. Just don't be too long in there. Five minutes, maximum."

"Max," Stoke said. "I'm not good, but I'm fast."

The little guy inserted a card into the reader and the thick, varnished mahogany door hissed open an inch. Soundproof, Stoke thought.

"*Merci beaucoup*, partner," Stoke whispered over his shoulder, pushing the door open and then closing it behind him.

The light was very dim but he was aware of beautiful paneling and what seemed like leather tiles beneath his feet. Leather floors! Now, that was serious decorating. The port lights were all shut and what light there was came from very low ambient fixtures hidden in the ceiling and bookcases. There was the dark shape of a large square bed against the far wall. Some kind of sheer curtains glimmering around it. A figure in black lay across the rumpled sheets. She was crying, sobbing softly into the pillow.

"Hey, what's wrong?" Stoke said, approaching the bed.

"Who are you?" she whispered in a fierce hiss. "Get out! I'll call someone!"

"Take it easy," Stoke said, holding up his hand and backing away. He had no interest in explaining his presence here. "I'm just a guy who got lost during the grand tour and—what the—"

He'd reached out to pull the sheer curtains back when his fingers brushed cold metal. The bed was surrounded on all three sides by pencil-thin metal rods that disappeared up into the ceiling. Stainless steel by the look of them, about an inch apart.

The bed was a cage.

And the woman caged inside was badly hurt. What Stoke had taken for dark clothing was in fact a blood-soaked sheet she'd wound around her torso.

"I'm going to get you out of here, is what I'm going to do," Stoke said, squeezing his fingers between two of the bars to confirm what he'd seen. Solid steel rods, all right. "You're hurt. You're in some kind of cage. You need a doctor."

"Who the hell are you?" she said, her voice ragged, druggy, and, come to think of it, not very damn appreciative.

"My name is Stokely Jones. Friend of Alex Hawke."

"Alexander Hawke?"

"Yeah, that's right. Who are you?"

"Jet."

"Jet? Tell me something, Jet. That cage supposed to keep you in or other folks out?"

"Both."

"Okay, Jet, it's a little weird, but I'll go with it. Tell me, what's the magic word that gets you out of the joint? You look like a girl longing to be free."

"Come here. Closer. Into the light. Let me see you."

"Awright," Stoke said, and did.

"My God, you are huge."

"Big."

"You're the biggest man I've ever seen."

"Glandular condition. How do I get you out of there?"

"There is a remote over there by the television. Next to that silver ice bucket."

"A *remote?*" Stoke said, shaking his head as he moved across the Italian leather tiles. He picked up the silver remote and pushed a couple of buttons. On the third try, the steel cage structure retracted silently into the ceiling and he dropped the remote into his jacket pocket.

Man, these rich people were into some weird shit.

Whale scrotums.

Chapter Eighteen

Paris

MADAME LI ENCOUNTERED ONLY MODERATE HEADWINDS EN route from Hong Kong to Charles de Gaulle and his BA 747 arrived at the gate twenty minutes early. British Air had been lovely. They'd done something marvelous to the first-class seating arrangements since he'd last flown the carrier. He'd had his preferred *placement*, Seat 4-D, the bulkhead window.

And now, when he'd finished his meal and was ready for sleep, an elegantly molded wooden partition rose up between him and the aisle seat at the push of a button. His seat had reclined to full horizontal and he'd curled up under a soft duvet cover and slept like a little angel.

Well, he thought, giggling silently, perhaps not *exactly* like an angel.

I love Paris . . .

The assassin breezed through Customs. After all, he held a diplomatic passport and the only thing he'd carried aboard was a valise containing his makeup, peignoir, and a few unmentionables. First thing in the morning, he was going to his favorite Chanel emporium near the Place Vendôme and pick up the requisite wardrobe for his stays in Paris and London.

He had his eye on a nice tweed suit he'd seen in the new *Vogue* on the airplane. He always bought ready-to-wear. And it was his practice to call ahead and give his sizes, changing rooms in Paris salons being so problematic. He'd had to kill more than one saleswoman who'd barged in at an inopportune moment. Messy.

Yes, a tweed suit, perhaps in black. With his white coif and pearls, he'd be ready for anything. And anybody.

It was Saturday morning, clear and cool, when he stepped outside

Terminal One. He was glad he'd brought the mink stole and he pulled it snug round his shoulders. He stood on the curbside for a few moments, eyes moving from side to side, a wealthy woman looking for her driver.

Not two minutes later, a German Maybach limousine slid to a stop in front of him, as long and black as a hearse. Diplomatic flags, one of them French, were mounted on the fenders just above the headlights. The other flag was one of the small Middle Eastern countries, though he couldn't remember which.

A thick armored door swung out and from within a deep voice said, "Get in."

Get in? So much for diplomatic courtesy and *politesse*. Madame Li was, after all, on a trade mission from Beijing. Her presence here was at the behest of the Chinese Politburo. The historic "meetings" she would hold with France's leadership in the next two days were matters of grave international importance, were they not? Her mission here in Paris could change the face of Europe forever. She was not unaware of her place in history.

And somebody, frankly he didn't care *who* it was, was telling him to "Get in"? In French-accented Chinese?

"That is certainly no way to address a lady, Comrade," Madame Li said as he climbed up and into the dark cavern at the rear of the automobile. There were two men inside, and he sat in one of the rearward-facing seats. It was obvious which one was Bonaparte; he looked like a tall, thin version of his famous ancestor. Olive skin, brooding expression. The other fellow was heavily muscled and looked immensely strong. The hard plates of his skull at first appeared to be devoid of hair, but now he saw that it was covered in fine red-gold down.

This would be the German, von Draxis, the man General Moon had charged with taming the wild daughter Jet. He looked fully capable of taming anything short of a herd of charging rhinos.

"Drive," the Frenchman said to the driver, ignoring Madame Li. The big car gathered speed smoothly and was almost instantly cruising at well over one hundred kilometers per hour, gracefully moving through the light morning traffic headed toward Paris.

The Frenchman pushed a button in the center console and a grey felt privacy panel slid up behind the driver's head. Then he fingered another panel of buttons, one that reclined his seat back to a more comfortable angle and another to dim the interior lights to a soft warm glow. A muted flat-screen monitor mounted on his armrest was tuned to local news. Some kind of procession was leaving Charles de Gaulle for Paris via the A-1 motorway. In the center of the procession, amidst a sea of flashing blue lights, a black Maybach limousine identical to the one Madame Li was riding in.

"I am Luca Bonaparte, madame," the Frenchman said, extending a stiff hand to be shaken. "This beautiful Maybach belongs to my dear friend here, Baron von Draxis. He was kind enough to volunteer his splendid vehicle for today's operations. He insisted on picking you up as he has heard so many interesting things about you."

"I'm a very interesting person. I am also not subject to anyone's approval. I am here to do a job and I intend to do it."

"Yes, yes, of course. Don't misunderstand. The baron here is a great friend to our mutual cause. So. You have a lot of work to do here in Paris. Are you fully prepared?"

Madame Li sat back and regarded the two men without a reply.

Bonaparte was as described by Major Tang. Good-looking enough to be a French film star, with a powerful intelligence burning within his dark eyes. His Chinese was beyond fluent. The German was beefy and bullet-headed but wearing a beautiful grey cashmere roll-neck sweater under a soft black calfskin jacket. Rich. Very, he decided. Rumor had it he'd made a fortune building supertankers for the French.

Madame Li crossed his legs and smiled. "Yes, I had a lovely flight, thank you for asking. The service was cheerful, the food delicious, although I detested the movie, something politically correct about Rwanda."

"Your sarcasm is ill-advised. Suppose you behave yourself."

"Suppose you let me explain something to you, Comrade Bonaparte," he said in flawless French. "I am attached to the personal staff of General Sun-yat Moon of the People's Republic of China. I hold the rank of colonel in the PLA. I am here at his behest, not yours. I am only in your country because of his personal involvement in your current situation. As it happens, his desires, and those of China herself, intersect with your own at this moment in history. That may not always be true. It is an alliance of convenience. You would do well to remember that."

"Are you quite finished with your geopolitical lecture, Madame Colonel?"

"No. I don't like surprises. You were supposed to meet me, not him. I know why he's here. You two are appraising me, deciding whether I'm up to the task. Well, I don't take orders from you, or him, or anyone else. I expect to be treated with the respect and courtesy befitting my rank and the current state of affairs between our two countries."

There was a brief silence as the French minister considered this. Bonaparte had asked the Chinese in Beijing for a supremely qualified assassin. Their best, in fact. He'd clearly gotten even more than he'd asked for. He looked at von Draxis and smiled, raising his hands in a gesture of helplessness. Male shorthand for "What can one do?" When he next spoke, his voice was gentle and well-oiled.

"Sorry, Comrade Colonel. My profound apologies."

"That's much better. Continue to use that tone and we shall get along splendidly. Now, precisely when does this operation commence?"

"It has already begun. If you push that button by your right hand, a small monitor will come up out of the armrest. Good. There is the newscast showing the motorcade a few miles up ahead. You see the vehicle similar to our own, yes? Inside that car is the sultan of Oman, who has just arrived for a state visit. I am personally awarding him the Légion d'Honneur at a ceremony tomorrow morning."

"Why are you telling me this?"

"As you know, we always field a decoy vehicle or two on such occasions. To thwart potential terrorist attacks."

"Naturally," Madame Li said. "Standard procedure."

"This morning, after a press conference at the Elysée Palace, a sécurité spokesman leaked a last-minute schedule change to a paid informant. He was told that I myself, and not Prime Minister Honfleur, would be greeting the sultan at the airport."

"*Ist gut, ja?* The media follows that car and not this one. That one on the television," von Draxis said in his thickly guttural German accent, "that is the sultan's."

"I made the connection, Baron," Madame Li said, unable to hide his irritation with this kind of condescension. "But why?"

"We want the media choppers following the other car," Bonaparte said calmly. "You'll find out why in a minute."

"Das ist sehr gut," the German said, amused at the little woman's impatience with them. He opened an aluminum case that was resting on his lap. Inside, nestled in black foam, a lightweight assault weapon and two rocket grenades. Von Draxis quickly assembled the weapon and affixed a grenade to the muzzle. A broad smile spread across the Teutonic features.

"Schatzi and his toys," Bonaparte observed with some amusement.

"You should see mine," Madame Li said with a coy smile. He found himself relaxing, having fun.

"Fasten your seat belt," Bonaparte said, "I see we are getting close." He lifted a receiver from its cradle and said a few words to the driver. The big car slowed perceptibly approaching an overpass over the A-1 motorway to Paris.

"Ach! Here zey come," von Draxis said.

A second later, another vehicle swerved into view beside them traveling at high speed. It braked hard, slowing to match the pace of the Maybach. A hooded gunman was visible by the rear window of the nondescript Citroën sedan. As the distance between the two cars narrowed to six feet or less, a bearded man lowered the tinted window and pointed the muzzle of a heavy automatic weapon directly at the Maybach.

Madame Li's instinct was to dive for the floor, but the seat belt and the meaty hand of the German on his shoulder kept him pinned to his seat. There was a muffled rattle from the sedan and heavy thuds as high-caliber rounds slammed into the door. The armor inside the door shuddered and stopped the bullets, but it was disconcerting, to say the least. He plainly saw the gunman, who wore a black balaclava, raise his sights, now aiming at the window inches away from his face.

"Get us the fuck out of here!" Madame Li screamed, and Luca

looked over at her, amazed. The genteel and aristocratic female voice was gone, replaced by that of an older man, crazed with fear for his life.

"Schatzi, if you don't mind?" Bonaparte said, pushing a button that retracted the large sunroof above their heads. Sunlight flooded the car and also the sound of a second automatic weapon at very close range. Another gunman was firing at the front-seat window, attempting to take out the Maybach's driver.

Von Draxis, frighteningly quick for his size, got to his feet with the stubby grenade launcher in his hands. At that moment, the first gunman opened up again. The passenger window by Madame Li's face instantly frosted over in overlapping starburst patterns as the heavy rounds slammed into the thick glass. Madame Li closed his eyes and waited for the next burst. There was a pause in the fire as if the terrorist shooter could not believe what he was seeing. He was firing from less than six feet away!

"Now, Schatzi," Luca Bonaparte said.

The German was standing now, his feet wide apart to maintain balance. He was tall enough so that his body from the chest up was outside the big Maybach. He raised his weapon and fired. As he did, the Frenchman lowered the shattered window so they could see.

A loud whoosh above Li's head and then a thunderclap explosion and a flash of fire lit the interior of the Citroën. The blast blew the roof off the sedan and thick black smoke poured from the blown-out windows as the car careened away, out of control. As the Maybach accelerated, Madame Li saw the burned-out sedan hit a bridge abutment head-on, and then the fuel tank blew. Flame and smoke climbed into the morning air. Out of nowhere, a motorcycle escort appeared around them and the big car surged forward and sped away from the carnage, quickly reaching a speed of 170 kph on the A-1 to Paris Centre Ville.

Madame Li sat back and closed his eyes. The powerful air-conditioning systems were quickly sucking the sharp smell of cordite out of the Maybach's interior. He was content to wait for the explanation he knew would come. In the meantime, he formulated the message he would encode and transmit to the Golden Dragon as soon as he was comfortably checked into his suite at the hotel.

For the next forty-eight hours, he would be working with a man who was absolutely fearless and unstoppable. General Moon's assessment had been correct. Luca Bonaparte was precisely the man Beijing had been looking for, for a long, long time.

"Well, that's done," Bonaparte said, and, with an appreciative nod to the German, reclined his seat once more. There was apparently a humidor in the console, because he extracted a cigar and fired it with a beautiful gold lighter. It was engraved with an ornate B encircled by an olive wreath.

Delusions of grandeur? This modern Bonaparte was many things, but Madame Li didn't think delusional was one of them. A twisted visionary, perhaps, nothing new about that. Expelling a cloud of pungent smoke, he said, "Sorry, how rude of me, Madame Li. Would you care for a cigar? Schatzi doesn't touch tobacco."

"I think not."

"A Vegas Robaina. A gift from my amigo, Fidel, during my last visit to his island paradise. A manly smoke."

"You are most amusing, Monsieur Bonaparte," Madame Li said with a wry smile. He'd dropped his guard during the heat of the moment and he'd caught it. *Madame* was a *monsieur*.

"Sorry if we alarmed you," Bonaparte said, "but there wasn't really time to explain."

"I think we have a few minutes just now," Madame Li said.

"Yes. By all means, let me explain. There was a young man in that Citroën named Philippe Honfleur. He was the youngest son of our current prime minister. He was the unwilling guest of a small cadre of rightist paramilitary types hired by me to attack this vehicle. Needless to say, they did not know that I would fight back. This outrageous attack on me by the prime minister's son and his would-be fellow assassins will be viewed as a blatant attempt to derail my negotiations with the sultan of Oman. The evening news will be full of the attempts on both our lives."

"Clever boy," Madame Li said, chuckling. In truth, he admired the ruse.

"Sometime in the next few hours, the badly charred body of the prime minister's son will be identified by the police medical examiners," von Draxis said, smiling broadly. "The press will go insane." He was busily putting his weapon to bed in the aluminum case.

"Very impressive," Madame Li said, and he meant it. The scheme was inspired. And the German clearly a man of great courage and cunning. "Will I see you again, my dear Baron?"

"My work here for the moment is ended, Frau Li," von Draxis said. "My plane is even now warming its engines at Le Bourget. I must get back to my beloved *Valkyrie*, my yacht, you see, so, I will be leaving you. I am only sorry that I won't be joining you for the fete at Château Belmaison this evening."

"A fete?"

"Mais oui, madame. I have invited the sultan of Oman to Paris. Tomorrow morning at the Palais he is to receive the Légion d'Honneur. Tonight, I am hosting a soiree to celebrate this great honor to be bestowed upon His Excellency, the Sultan," Luca said. *"Une bal masqué* at my country estate. You are invited to this masked ball, Madame Li."

"I accept with pleasure. We will miss you, Baron von Draxis," he said and offered the German his hand. The baron took it and smiled, his blue eyes crinkling in a most warm expression of goodwill.

Von Draxis added, *"Zo, Frau Li,* we have now this day begun the inevitable spiral toward a new world. This is what shall later be called history, madame. Enjoy it."

"Indeed. Who knows what reprisals against the current government we might expect? Or what the lunatic extremists who support me might extract in retaliation for this craven attempt on my life?" Bonaparte said, and expelled a cloud of smoke with great satisfaction. "We might even see another most unfortunate assassination."

"Or two." The baron chuckled. The car slid to a stop in front of a hangar at Le Bourget and the German climbed out. The driver shut the door, climbed behind the wheel, and the Maybach accelerated away. Luca reclined his seat and expelled a great cloud of Cuban cigar smoke.

"Bienvenue à Paris, Madame Li," Bonaparte said.

Chapter Nineteen

Hampstead Heath

CONGREVE, HIS VIVID IMAGINATION HOUNDED BY BASKER-villes, was racing across the haunted Grimpen Moor in the north of England, when the telephone jangled. He was so deeply lost in his beloved and well-thumbed Sherlock Holmes volume, he'd first thought the ring was part of the cracking good story. He looked up at the brass ship's chronometer mounted on the wall above his reading chair. There was a click and whir. Eight bells tolled midnight in the cozy sanctuary of his library.

He reached for the phone.

"Hullo," he said into the mouthpiece, and waited for whatever bad news was even now inexorably zipping along the wires in his direction.

"Is that Ambrose Congreve?"

"Yes, I suppose it is. Who's calling, please?"

"Oh, Ambrose, it's Diana Mars. I'm so sorry to ring at such a wretched hour. But I felt that I had to call immediately."

"Are you in some kind of danger, Lady Mars?"

"Call me Diana, please. No, I'm not. But I fear you may be."

"Ah, well, in that case, you needn't be alarmed. I'm quite accustomed to danger, you see. Goes with the territory, as they say in the, uh—territories."

"Ambrose, please, hear me out. I think your life may be in grave danger. If you don't mind, I'd—I'd rather not speak of this over the telephone."

"Well, I could drive over to Brixden House. At this time of night, it would take me only about—"

"No, no. Not in this house. I'll explain when I see you. I'd drive myself over to you but there's something wrong with the Bentley. It's the only car I have keys for . . . and, well, I don't want to rouse my chauffeur."

"A pub somewhere in between us? No, that won't work. Too late."

"All closed. I know what we'll do. We'll meet down at Spring Cottage. It's all shut up but I have a key, naturally. Do you know it? My summer house?"

"The Tudor structure on the river below the main house."

"Exactly. Can you meet me there in half an hour?"

"Half past. Jolly good. See you then."

He hung up the phone. For some reason, when he stood up, he tried to touch his toes. Hadn't done it in years, but he felt just spry enough at the moment to attempt it. Blast. No luck. Couldn't do it now, because his damn belly got in the way. Still, it felt pretty damn good to limber up a bit. Get the old blood flowing before one sprang into action. He stopped on his way out the door and shook his head, laughing at this picture of himself, the still-vigorous knight-errant taking up his battle-weary lance and entering the lists once more.

In his dressing room, shedding his navy silk pajamas, he paused by the small bow window seat and sat on the cushion. What does one wear to a secret midnight rendezvous in a deserted house? Considering a selection of tweed jackets, he chanced to notice through the window that lights were still on in Mrs. Purvis's bedroom. Upon returning from hospital, she had been installed in the rooms over the gardener's cottage some few hundred yards distant. It was decided that she would be far more comfortable there than in her prior digs, the small bed-sitting room under an eave on the third floor of Heart's Ease Cottage.

Mrs. Purvis not sleeping well? The doctor had said she'd be uncomfortable for at least another month. The bullet had torn a muscle in the chest wall that would be slow to heal. Poor dear. Ambrose had had no idea just how much her cheery presence meant until she was gone.

He chose a much-loved tattersall shirt, and a cavalry twill jacket over an old pair of flannels. Then, with a shudder of pleasure, he slipped on the brand-new pair of driving shoes he'd bought at Mr. J. P. Todd's establishment. They were red, a rather vivid shade, which Ambrose thought gave them quite a racy flair. Dorothy's slippers,

Sutherland had called them upon their debut, and Congreve, unlike Ross himself, had not been even slightly amused.

He switched off the lights in his dressing room and the single lamp beside his bed and headed for the back staircase. At the end of a short corridor was a door to a room he'd seldom entered until very recently. An enchanted room, full of magic and wonder he'd only just discovered. He took three long strides and was there, hand on knob.

He could hardly believe his zooming pulse rate as he entered his garage and reached for the light switch.

Click.

Oh.

Just the light reflected in the mirror finish of the long sculpted bonnet took his breath away. The car, his car, was a Morgan. The 1962 Plus Four Drophead. Forty-three years old, but she'd undergone a frame-off, rubber up restoration, whatever that meant. Wooden chassis, ash, stainless-steel wire wheels with spinners. A newish color one seldom saw on a Morgan, bright canary yellow for the body with a sort of Harrod's green for the fenders. Forced to choose a word to describe the paint scheme to someone, he might use the word "snappy." Yes, he thought, opening the driver's side door and climbing behind the wooden steering wheel, definitely snappy.

And he'd bought the two-seater machine off the Internet (actually, his pal Chappy Morris at the Crown and Anchor had done it all on the pub's office computer) for a good deal less than twenty thousand quid! Why, he'd simply stolen the jewels when you thought about it.

He sat there for a moment, just breathing in the smells of the thing. The leather seats, the grease on the wheels, the carnauba wax on the fenders, the fresh sawdust he'd sprinkled on the floor. Why, the entire garage was full of wondrous sensory inputs. The smell of old machine parts and oil and dirt in the dark space was intoxicating. How had he missed all this? This was the stuff of dreams.

This mechanical wizard (all right, it was dated) was nothing short of a personal rocket to the moon! He was free, in the bargain, free to roam, no longer held captive to the demonic Ross Sutherland and his midget racer. And, now, he was off to a midnight rendezvous with a beautiful woman—wait! He'd better let Mrs. Purvis know he was going out, lest she wonder if the new car was being stolen.

He'd had a wall phone mounted in the garage against the day when he'd spend more time out here, puttering around with wrenches and the like, cleaning the carburetors and whatnot. He climbed out of the Morgan and reached for the phone. He'd found this daunting egress far easier to accomplish with the top down, so he'd taken to leaving it down at all times. He'd already decided not to drive his dreamboat more than a mile from home if it even smelled like rain.

Someone was saying "Hello?" on the other end of the line.

"Oh, Mrs. Purvis, yes. I am so sorry to bother you at this hellish hour, but it's Mr. Congreve, as I'm sure you know. Saw your light on. I just rang to inform you that I'm about to go out in the new car. You know, the Morgan. Take it for a spin about the countryside. I didn't want you to worry needlessly on my account."

"Not at all, Mr. Congreve. I saw the light go on in the garage and I supposed that's what you were doing. I'm just tending to my needle-point. I must warn you that you've quite a surprise coming your way next Christmas. I am an absolute demon when it comes to needle-point."

"Ah. Well, splendid. I'm off then, Mrs. Purvis, with a roar and a chitty-chitty, bang-bang. Goodnight!"

He climbed back aboard the contraption and hit the ignition button. The Morgan roared to life (well, perhaps "roar" was too strong a word), and he engaged reverse and backed the thing carefully out of the garage. Reverse, he'd recently learned, was a damned tricky business. When one went backward, everything was the reverse of going forward. Eminently logical, but still. Took some getting used to, naturally, but he'd crack it. That crumpled left rear fender and brake-light assembly would be fairly easy to mend, he guessed.

Half an hour later, he'd found his way to the A404 to Marlow. From there, he simply followed his memory and swung through the stately Brixden House gates five minutes later. Moonlight turned the Roman sarcophagi in the gardens blue. After a seemingly endless succession of orchards and sloping meadows, he came to a narrow lane that ran east along the silvery Thames. He saw one of the tall brick chimneys through the treetops first. Smoke was curling out over the gabled slate roof. Lady Mars had apparently arrived at Spring Cottage first and got a fire going.

He turned right into a small car park beside the Tudor cottage. It was situated in a thickly wooded plot on a bend in the river. The many windows on the two sides he could see were dark, but there was an orange glow visible within the fanlight above the front entrance. He tried the door; it was open. He pushed inside and saw orange light licking the walls of a further room. The fire was the only light burning in the house. The smell of smoke cut through the musty odors of a place long closed and shuttered.

"Hello? Is that you, Diana?" he said, pausing in the doorway of the library. The fact that it might not be, he had to admit, had occurred to him. Someone, he still hadn't learned who, was trying to kill him. He sometimes found himself thinking like a mystery writer at times like these, and this deserted house by the river would be a perfect trap for the unwary victim. No one on earth knew he was here. Once he was done away with, it was simply a matter of weighting him down with stones and heaving him into the chilly dark waters flowing beyond the windows.

"Oh, Ambrose, I'm so glad you're safe. Come take a seat by the fire," Lady Mars said. Her voice was trembling.

There were two leather wing chairs facing the hearth. She was seated in the one to his left. In the firelight, her auburn hair had a reddish-gold glow. She was leaning forward, poking at the sparking embers with a fire-iron. On a low ottoman stood a many-faceted crystal decanter full of amber liquor and two glasses. He sat down and tried to speak. He realized that, having seen her face again, he could not.

"Er, well, here we are," he managed.

"I'll fill you in, dear, and then we'll have an adult beverage," she said, getting right down to it. "Does that suit?"

"Yes," he said, and shut his mouth. *Dear?*

"My head gardener came to see me earlier this evening. His name is Jeremy Pordage. He was my father's chief groundsman. He's eighty-three years old. I've known him since I was a child. I would trust him with my life."

"I see."

"Jeremy and his wife attended services at St. John's on Sunday as it was All Saints' Day. St. John's is a small chapel in the village of Upper Slaughter. Do you know it? It's the church where that horrific murder occurred last summer. Do you remember?"

"I stood up for the groom at that wedding. I was Alex Hawke's best man. Still am, I suppose."

"Oh! How perfectly awful for you, Ambrose. And that poor man Hawke. I'm so sorry. Did they ever catch the fiend who killed his perfectly lovely bride?"

"Yes. We did manage that."

"Ah. That's some small consolation, I suppose. They should hang him high, if they haven't already done so. At any rate, after church last Sunday, Jeremy and Alma decided to walk to Castle Combe for lunch. They took the country walk, not the roads. But, dear Alma twisted her ankle passing through a muddy stile. There was a small pub at the bottom of the hill. A place you'd certainly never go unless you knew of it."

"What was the name of this pub?"

"The Feathers."

"I know it. Please continue."

"The proprietor showed them to a booth and brought tea. Alma wasn't seriously injured, you see, she just needed to take the weight off the foot for a while. Shortly after they'd been seated, they heard the proprietor greeting another party. He seated them in the booth adjacent to the one Jeremy and Alma occupied. The seat backs were high, wooden, you couldn't see from one booth to the other."

"I understand perfectly. An overheard conversation."

"Yes. It was a man and a woman. Jeremy recognized the male voice immediately and almost spoke up. It belonged to my butler, Oakshott."

"Ah. The butler did it."

"Ambrose, be serious a moment. The conversation Jeremy overheard was about you. Oakshott began by telling the woman about your visit to Brixden House. She became very agitated. Wanted to know everything he'd overheard during your visit. He'd heard a lot, Ambrose. He's some kind of specter, I think, hears through walls. Oakshott told her all about that picture you showed me. The New Year's Eve party. The man with the orange hair."

"Stop. You were absolutely right to call me, Diana. Please continue."

"The woman sounded very frustrated with the lack of action since the failed attempt on your life ten days ago. Why didn't you tell me someone was trying to kill you? My dear boy, you're in danger!"

"Diana, this is not the first time someone has thought the world would be a sunnier spot absent Ambrose Congreve. Were any other names mentioned?"

"The name Henry Bulling came up. I vaguely recall meeting him at Brixden House. He's the fellow in the photo you showed me, isn't he?"

Ambrose nodded.

"Somebody wants you dead, my dear Ambrose. Bulling does. Or she does. I don't know. But they aim to kill you and they are apparently deadly serious about it."

"Over my dead body," Ambrose said, smiling.

The concern in Diana's eyes was most touching. He reached over and patted her hand, which was fluttering like a white butterfly above the folds of her skirt. "Which one really wants me pushing up daisies, Diana? Surely not young Oakshott the butler. I've never harmed a blond hair on his brutishly handsome head."

"Listen. Here's what Jeremy was able to gather. Henry Bulling was some kind of spy inside the French embassy. He was in fact working for the Chinese government. Passing along information. Something to do with oil. New French refineries being built. Capacity of oil tankers, et cetera. Does this make any sense?"

"Indeed, it fits perfectly. One wonders why the Chinese are so interested in French oil, since the French have virtually none of their own. They import all of it from the Gulf States, most notably, until the war, Iraq."

"I've no idea. But the Chinese secret police, who were running Henry, discovered that he was having secret meetings with British Intelligence. In St. James' Park. That Henry Bulling was a double agent. They abducted him from his flat and somehow got the truth out of him. Henry gave them your name."

"Ah, it all starts to make sense. The Te-Wu may well have issued a death warrant with my name on it," Ambrose said. "Sending a signal to MI6 to mind its own business. That wouldn't be unusual."

"Ambrose, how can you be so damned cool about this information? She, the woman, was apparently the one who orchestrated the kidnapping and did the interrogating. She gave Bulling a choice. She could kill him. Or he could kill you."

"He missed, didn't he?" Ambrose said, feeling a sudden pang for Mrs. Purvis. After all, the bullet that had nearly nicked her heart had been meant for his.

"Yes, and thank God he did miss, Ambrose. But I fear the next attempt will not be quite so catch-as-catch-can."

"You were very kind to call, Diana," Ambrose said. "And, wise. Now, let me pour you a brandy. I think we could both use one."

"I need to be clear in my mind. That man, the one with orange hair, Ambrose," she began, "is your cousin."

"Yes. Caught spying on the French by the Chinese. Who clearly have something to hide."

"Yes. And if he's dead, the woman is planning to kill you herself. Jeremy managed to sneak a peek at her when they left. She was Chinese, Ambrose. She was the woman in the photograph. That dreadful Chinese spy."

"Yes, I guessed as much. Hawke and I had a small run-in with the Chinese some years ago. Nasty affair. A lot of people ended up dead. We, Hawke and I, ended up on some kind of list in Beijing, according to MI6. Since I've been rattling their cage recently, I suppose it's possible the Mandarins have worked their way round to me again."

"Again?"

"Their previous attempts were unsuccessful. I thought they'd forgotten about me. It is not beyond the realm of possibility that my dear cousin Henry would sic this woman on me out of pure spite and malice. Or that he is himself very much alive and the true villain of the piece. He does have motive, after all. He is of the opinion that I stole his inheritance."

"Your lovely cottage."

"Yes. Heart's Ease. We shall see whether or not that shoe fits. Diana, you used the phrase 'running him' a few moments ago. Spy lingo. Do you enjoy such light entertainments? Spy thrillers and the like?"

"Well, I—"

There was a sound beyond the window. A dull thud, as if something heavy had fallen in the rose bed. Lady Mars leaped to her feet, her hand at her throat.

"Ambrose! Someone has been listening at that window!"

"Get down, Lady Mars!" Ambrose said, moving to the window and pulling his gun. "Get on the floor, now!"

The glass in the window exploded inward and a bullet tore into the plasterwork inches away from Congreve's head. He saw a dark blur of shadow moving quickly away from the window. He raised his pistol and fired once, twice, three times.

Chapter Twenty

Hawkesmoor

"GOOD MORNING, YOUNG PELHAM!" AMBROSE CRIED, STORM-
ing into the kitchen, the bright yellow scarf wound round his neck
fluttering behind him like a cricket pennant on opening day. "Come
out, come out, wherever you are!"

"He's in the butler's pantry, Chief Inspector," said a pretty young
woman in a toque blanche who was sitting at a counter sorting Brussels sprouts. A beam of pure sunlight was streaming down on her
white bowl of green vegetables and it looked like the kind of scene
that would have sent Vermeer or his like rushing madly for his
brushes.

"You'll find me back here, sir," Pelham's distinctive and fluty voice
floated from the pantry.

"A-ha!" Ambrose said, and headed in that direction, nodding and
smiling at all and sundry. "Good morning, all! Lovely day, isn't it?"

Congreve had awoken in a splendid humor. He wasn't sure what
was behind it. Still alive, for one thing. His marvelous new car, perhaps, or, chasing murderers in the moonlight across the grounds at
Brixden House. Or the kiss Diana had planted on his cheek when
he'd said goodnight. Whatever it was, life seemed full of sunshine and
bursting with promise.

"Good morning, sir!" the kitchen staff replied as one, their voices
hale and full of good cheer. This unbridled enthusiasm for the day at
hand was one of the reasons Ambrose so enjoyed these early morning
surprise visits to Hawkesmoor. The house was always a bustle of
happy activity on a clear, sunny summer morning like this one. In the
kitchens, in the gardens, in the stables, and throughout the house itself. Everywhere one went, someone was polishing something, dusting books, plumping pillows, making acres of glass sparkle in the sun.

It had become, Ambrose reflected as he passed through the bustling kitchen, a happy house once more. Vicky's untimely death had cast a pall over Hawkesmoor. Alex Hawke's doomed bride had been a great favorite in this house. Everyone was keenly anticipating the arrival of Lady Hawke, the new mistress of Hawkesmoor and the first woman to lay claim to that title since the death of Alex's mother, tortured and killed at the hands of pirates in the Caribbean in the seventies.

When you thought about it, as Ambrose did at that moment, Alex Hawke's entire life was just one long pirate story.

Victoria Sweet's horrific murder on the steps of St. John's Church had shocked and saddened everyone under this roof. And, indeed, many people throughout England still spoke of her loss with great sorrow. They had been a beautiful, popular couple. An aura of permanence and glamor seemed to surround them. It all vanished in an instant. After Hawke returned from Vicky's funeral in Louisiana, this house, once so full of youth and promise, had gone dark once more.

Alex left Hawkesmoor for good after weeks of grieving, vowing never to return to the scene of so much sorrow. But now, on this fine June morning, it seemed as if the very sun itself had once more come from behind the clouds. And, perhaps it had.

"Ah, there you are, young Pelham!" Ambrose said, and sailed his straw boater into the pantry, causing the aged retainer to duck his head.

"Morning, Mr. Congreve," the octogenarian said, giving the chief inspector a decidedly narrow look. In Pelham's personal view, the man sometimes bordered on the overly boisterous.

Pelham said, "I'm just on my way up to his lordship with the morning tray. Follow along, if you'd like."

"Having breakfast in bed, is he?" Congreve frowned.

"Hardly. His lordship was down for his breakfast at six, sir. Had it out there on the lawn with his papers, joined by a gentleman from the CIA, a houseguest who has since departed via helicopter. A helo, I believe he called it."

"Ah, what's this, then?" Ambrose asked, looking at the silver tray Pelham was preparing.

"A lemon, sir," the butler sniffed. He was long accustomed to Congreve snooping about the kitchen, lifting pot lids and sampling soups.

The two men had joined forces to raise the child Hawke after the loss of his parents and, finally, his grandfather when the boy was not yet twelve. Theirs was a long-simmering rivalry over the care and feeding of Alex Hawke.

"I can see that, Pelham, but what's it for?"

"He's going to eat it, sir. It's become his daily midmorning pick-me-up, as it were."

"Eat a whole lemon? Good lord. Why?"

"Some kind of new diet, sir. He is attempting to purge his body. I believe the word for his new regimen is 'holistic.' You'll have to ask his lordship, I'm afraid. I don't go there, as they say these days."

"Well, let's have it, then. Save your knees, my dear Pelham. I'll carry this noble feast up to him."

"You'll find him in the armory, Chief Inspector. He's been up there all morning long since his American friend Mr. Kelly departed."

"Really? What on earth is he doing up there?"

"Cleaning his guns, sir. He says we're going to war."

"War? With whom?"

"I believe he mentioned France, sir."

"France?"

"Yes, sir."

"Ye gods."

Ambrose mounted the smooth worn stone of the curving back staircase leading to the upper floors. Gaining the third floor, he paused at a door of carved oak to catch his breath. The design incorporated two animals locked in combat—the Scottish unicorn and the English lion. The door was slightly ajar and he pushed inside, using the tray. He saw Hawke at the far end of the room with his back to the door, standing beside a sunny window, burnishing an ancient pistol barrel to gleaming perfection. His beloved parrot, Sniper, was on his shoulder.

The walls of the great room were decorated floor to ceiling with spiral arrangements of antique arms. Just below the crown moldings were long ranks of stag antlers. And below that, a profusion of every kind of armament: swords, pikes, pistols, and long rifles. Perhaps a thousand weapons, from the fifteenth to the nineteenth centuries, lined the walls.

Other than the library, Congreve knew this was Alex's favorite room in the entire house. The heavy velvet draperies had all been tied back away from the tall leaded windows and sunlight flooded the room. On the far wall hung a collection of eighteenth-century pirate flags, including the grim Jolly Roger flown by Hawke's ancestor, Blackhawke himself.

"Morning, Alex," Congreve said upon entering the room with the tray. "I saw your personal black standard fluttering from the ramparts and assumed you were in residence. *'Fortune favors the fast.'* Blackhawke's noble sentiment."

Alex turned toward him and smiled. "And, so *true*, Ambrose! A fast ship and a star to sail her by, that's the winning ticket. How else do you think I came to sit atop this pile of ill-gotten lucre? Piracy, of course! Give no quarter, lads!"

"Am I interrupting some sort of . . . private ritual?"

"No, no, by all means, come in, do come in!"

"Where've you been hiding yourself, Alex?"

"I just returned from *la belle France* yesterday morning. I haven't rung you up because I've had Brick Kelly here, you see, and—what's that?"

"Your lemon."

"Right. Put it over there, if you don't mind. I seem to have lost my bottle for it this morning."

"One wonders why lemon, of all fruits," Ambrose said, putting the tray down amidst an array of partially disassembled sixteenth-century rifles and flintlock pistols.

Hawke ignored the question and picked up a rifle.

"You see this gun, Ambrose? Bloody marvelous, isn't it?"

"Stunning. What is it?"

"Wheellock rifle with breech-loader system, manufactured in Augsburg or Nuremberg in 1540. Belonged to some Prussian colonel named Andreas Teuffel von Gundersdorf. Glorious piece, I must say."

"Alex, speak to me of war. And the dreaded French. But first, speak to me of lemons."

"Ah. The latest thing," Hawke said, plucking it from the tray and dipping it in a bowl of white powder. "Plenty of bioflavonoids in lemons, not to mention Vitamin C. Especially good for you if you dip them in this stuff. Natural sweetener the Japanese have been using for centuries. Called *Stevia rebaudiana*. Produces a blood-sugar-lowering effect on normal nondiabetics. Give it a whirl."

"I'm trying to quit lemons, thanks very much, but don't let me stop you." Bioflavonoids? Japanese sweeteners? What on earth had the world come to?

Alex took a bite out of the thing and made an awful face. "I may give this up. Step closer to the window, Constable," he said. "I must show you something before we conspire to save the world from the Red Menace."

"What is it?"

"Look down there, in the courtyard," Hawke said, feeding the lemon to Sniper, a bird who would eat red-hot plutonium if offered the stuff. "I've just noticed something odd. See it, old thing?" He was pointing directly at the Yellow Peril, as Ambrose had privately named his new iron steed.

"Why, yes, I do."

"It's a Morgan, you know," Hawke explained. "A fairly old one, I think. The Plus Four. Wooden chassis. An absolute stunner, I must say. Brilliant paint scheme. I wonder what lucky fellow it belongs to. Pelham hasn't announced anyone."

"It's mine, actually," Congreve said, desperately trying to avoid looking smug.

"Yours? Don't be silly, Ambrose! You don't even know how to drive. You loathe any form of powered conveyance. You've not the least interest in—"

Congreve withdrew the keys from his trousers. They caught the light as he dangled them in front of Hawke's eyes. "Let's take her for a spin, shall we?"

"That machine actually belongs to you?"

"It does. I drove it here just minutes ago."

"Good lord, he's serious."

"Any interest in a high-speed run over to the Cock & Cork for a bevvy to celebrate? A midmorning eye-opener?"

"We will indeed, but for now we have to talk of more serious matters, Constable. Let's sit over there by the fire."

When they were comfortable, Hawke said, "Brick Kelly was singing your praises last night at supper. He gave me something for you; it's on my desk down in the library. A cold case file. A bizarre murder that occurred in Paris thirty-five years ago. Should you crack it, we could save the whole bloody world a lot of trouble."

"I should be happy to put this affair on my docket, Alex. However, there's another murder I'm bashing away at at the moment. My own."

"Don't tell me there's been a second attempt? This is serious."

"Very serious. This happened last night, in fact. I shot the bastard through a window. Down at Lady Mars's Spring Cottage. Only winged him, unfortunately. Scene-of-Crime officers are all over the place now. There was a bit of blood on the roses below the window. They've promised a report before day's end. The culprit escaped through the woods to a waiting car. I heard it start, ran to my own vehicle, and gave pursuit. Tried to catch it, you see, and very nearly succeeded. The Morgan is race-tuned. Something to do with the camshaft."

"Someone is making a concerted effort to kill you, Ambrose. We must put a stop to this. Any idea who it is?"

"I thought it was my cousin, Bulling. And it might well be. But there's also a Chinese agent involved, Alex, a woman. This might be an old wound reopened, I'm afraid. In which case, they're after you, as well."

"Ah. Last year's tour up the Yangtze River to the Three Gorges Dam. Lucky to get out of there alive, weren't we?"

"Possibly that unfortunate incident has come back to haunt us. On it's simply that this woman, Bianca, has it in for me."

"What's her beef with you?"

"Her beef? You sound like some kind of film noir gumshoe, Alex. Well. You no doubt remember my dear cousin, Henry Bulling? Formerly employed in a secretarial position at the French embassy in London."

"Chap whose chin was always trying to reach up to his mouth and finally gave up?"

"Exactly."

"Peeved about your aunt's will, was he not?"

"Hmm. My inheritance of Heart's Ease. At the beginning of this affair, I thought Henry was perhaps sufficiently peeved about the house to commit murder. Upon further investigation, Sutherland

and I have learned that it's a bit more complicated. A woman named Bianca Moon is intimately involved. 'Intimately' is not a word chosen lightly. Bianca, a Chinese agent, is sexually involved, God help us, with my cousin. She discovered that Henry and I were meeting for quiet lunches in the park. The Yard, as you well know, was running Henry. So, we now learn, were the Chinese."

"So Henry's a double. The Chinese are trying to warn us off."

"Henry *was* a double. Henry may be dead. Our Miss Moon was not at all pleased when Henry sent my new housekeeper, Mrs. Purvis, to hospital instead of me."

"Mrs. Purvis was shot? I'd no idea. Was she seriously wounded?"

"She's recovering nicely, thank heaven."

"Good news. I was thinking it was our Henry hiding in the rose-bushes at Spring Cottage. It sounds like his style."

"I thought about that, too. The only one on earth who knew I was leaving my house in the middle of the night was Mrs. Purvis. Henry could have been parked on the street and followed me, I suppose, but it's unlikely. I drove at high speed and watched the mirror the whole time. Nothing."

"There was one other person who knew you'd be at the cottage last night. The person who invited you to come there."

"Lady Mars."

"You said it, not me. It's no secret that Brixden House has been a hotbed of spies at various times in its history."

"Don't be ridiculous. Diana has nothing at all to do with this. She's quite lovely, in fact."

"So was Tokyo Rose, apparently."

"Please. Don't be absurd."

"Listen, Constable, you and Cousin Henry may have stumbled into something far more ominous than either of you anticipated. Something worth killing you both over. I'm talking about that disc you found in Henry's freezer. The French oil refineries and tankers."

"Yes. It's all about oil somehow, Alex. The whole bloody thing."

"I think the next world war will be about oil. And someone clearly wants you and me as early casualties of that conflict. Tell me what you've learned."

"The few computer discs in Henry's flat contained photographs of French refineries and pipelines. Supertankers in the Strait of Hormuz. Henry was passing Bianca Moon hard intelligence about current oil production at Leuna and French transport tanker statistics. It's a subject she has keen knowledge of, having been an employee of the French behemoth Elf Aquitaine."

"There was a scandal," Hawke said. "I knew I remembered that name. Bianca. She was the mistress, wasn't she, of the former French Foreign Trade minister who was disgraced in the matter?"

"Exactly. She was Honfleur's geisha. She absconded with millions and disappeared. Now, she appears to be back in spades."

"Likewise, Monsieur Honfleur. He seems to have rehabilitated himself. He's the new prime minister. That's a remarkable recovery, even in France."

"I was listening to the radio on the way here," Ambrose said. "The BBC is saying that Honfleur's son Philippe was killed yesterday in a terrorist attack on the latest French Foreign Trade minister, a chap with the old familiar name of Bonaparte."

"The French are killing each other, Constable," Hawke said, and turned to face the window. "Another Revolution. Another Bonaparte."

"It's worse. It's the dragon and the frog," Congreve said, thinking out loud.

"China and France," said Hawke, shaking his head sadly. " 'Let me not to the marriage of true minds admit impediments.' "

"A lovely sonnet indeed. But, something tells me you are going to be an impediment in this unholy marriage, Alex. You're going to spoil their bloody honeymoon, at any rate."

Chapter Twenty-one

Cannes

"PUT THE GIRL DOWN," STOKE HEARD A VOICE BEHIND HIM say. Major German accent. Sounded like Colonel Klink on that old TV show *Hogan's Heroes*. Stoke had Jet in his arms, having just lifted her from the bed. He'd wrapped her in the sheet, since she was buck naked except for a little pair of black lace panties. Girl had some nasty cuts and bruises in various places, but the blood had clotted up okay. In the mirrored wall behind the bed cage, he could see there was just one guy. The door was closed behind him. Big guy, weird blond fuzz on his head, and he had on a white dinner jacket and a rich man's thin smile on his face.

Thin smiles, thin watches.

"Hey, Baron," Stoke said to the reflection. "How's it going?"

"Drop her."

The German also had an ugly little black automatic in his hand. Austrian Walther. He had it pointed smack dab in the middle of Stoke's broad back. Hard to miss at this range. Like trying to hit a barn. Stoke was armed, but he couldn't think how the hell he could get to his weapon without putting Jet in the line of fire.

"She's hurt," Stoke said, keeping his back to the guy and watching him in the mirror. "She needs a doctor. You got a sickbay on this floating gin palace, boss?"

"Schweinehund!" Even in the dim light, Stoke could see him turning purple in the face. High blood pressure aggravated by people not listening to his ass say "jump." "I repeat, put her down. This is a private matter."

"How'd your speech go? Nobody gives more rousing speeches than you crazy Nazis when you're fired up. Man oh man, I'm telling you."

"I said, put her down!"

"I asked you a question. Is there a doctor aboard or not? I'm taking this girl to a doctor. Some of these cuts are deep."

"She is a guest aboard this yacht. She is here of her own free will. Now, put her fucking down."

"The tycoon himself. Sorry I missed that welcome speech. Bet you had 'em screaming for blood."

"Who are you? What are you doing on my boat?"

"Me? I'm a decorator. From Orlando. Just poking around, looking for fabric ideas. Chintz and shit. Toile. Found this lady who was hurt. You do this to her?"

"Drop her on the bed and turn around. Now."

"I want to know if you did this to her."

"It's none of your affair. A private matter, as I said. She disappointed me. She was punished. Simple."

"Punished? That what you call this? Punished?"

"She resisted and she got a little banged up. Nothing serious. Ask her."

"You were planning to leave her down here in a damn cage to bleed to death?"

"You have five seconds. If you don't do as I say, I will put one bullet in the back of each of your knees. Shatter the patella, sever the tendons. You won't walk again. One . . ."

"Do what he says," Jet said. "He will shoot."

"Hey—"

"Two . . ."

"Shit, man, you making this harder than it has to be."

"Three . . ."

"Damn, you Germans are stubborn," Stoke said, and then he dove across the bed with Jet tucked safely within the solid cradle of his arms. There was a rapid *pop-pop*, two slugs thunked into the thick mattress, and then Stoke and Jet were on the floor on the far side of the bed. He pushed her down with his left hand and drew his gun with his right. The Sig Sauer P220 was Velcroed into a nylon holster just above his left ankle. Aluminum alloy frame made it light, Black Talon ammo made it right.

Stoke figured he had two-three seconds before the guy came over the bed or around it. "Stay down on the floor, girl," he said to Jet, "no matter what." And then he just exploded up and sideways, planting one foot in the bed and using it as a springboard to the right. He fired the Sig while still midair, putting one in the German's shoulder, spinning him clockwise. Stoke caught the wall pretty high up and shoved off that by planting one foot, did a little half spin and flew into the German hard, using his right shoulder, hitting the guy just below the knees. There was a loud pop as the braced knee went and then the baron screamed a whole lot of unprintable stuff in German as he hit the deck.

Von Draxis was rolling around on his back, grunting with the pain of that bad knee and the shoulder. He still had the gun and he was pointing it in dangerous directions, so Stoke wrapped his hand around the man's pistol. He twisted the weapon, snapping the finger still inside the trigger guard. Oldest trick in the book, but the German hadn't seen it coming. The big fella howled in pain and Stoke sat back on his heels and tried to offer some comfort by patting him on the top of his big downy head.

"See? That's your problem, Baron, thinking you some kind of badass. You just a stereotype, son. Get over it. I'm serious. Relax."

Stoke removed the man's gun from his grip as gently as he could, trying to wriggle it free from the broken index finger. Still, you could tell it hurt a little bit when it came off. He pocketed the gun, got to his feet, and walked around to where Jet lay beside the bed.

"You can open your eyes now," Stoke said, bending to cradle her in his arms. "Fireworks are over."

"They'll never let you off this boat," Jet said.

"Really? We'll see."

"Where are you taking me?"

"I got a launch picking me up in about, oh, four minutes. We've got a great doc on board *Blackhawke*. Danish woman Alex hired because of her resume. Former Miss Denmark. She'll stitch you up. Then we'll see where you want to take it from there. Sound good? What do you think?"

"I think you are out of your mind."

"Yeah, most probably. Picking up strange women and taking them home when we hardly know each other."

"Let's go."

"Good idea. Hey, Baron. *Auf wiedersehen*, okay? I'll check up on you tomorrow. Thanks a lot for the party. I really enjoyed myself."

Stroke stepped over the German guy writhing on the floor on his way to the door. He could see the guy thinking about grabbing his foot or some crazy shit like that and then see him figuring out just how bad an idea that was, seeing Stoke's foot an inch from his head.

He got an idea. He took the German by one hand and dragged him across the leather floor to the bed.

"Alley-oop, *Mein Herr*," he said as he lifted the baron up and plopped him down right in the middle of the bed. Then he pulled the remote out of his pocket and lowered the cage back into place. As an afterthought, he dropped the remote on the floor and stepped on it, crushing it. That drove the baron crazy, beating on the cage and all with his good hand, but Stoke just let it go.

"Shut up, Schatzi," Jet said to the guy and, amazingly enough, he did.

"I like the name Jet," Stoke said to her as he carried her out into the passageway and closed the door on the stateroom behind him. "What's your last name?"

"Moon," she said. "But I don't use it."

"Jet Moon. That's cool. New wave. What do you do?"

"I'm an actress."

"Yeah? Like a model-actress or an actress-actress?"

"You tell me. Am I acting now?"

"That's a very good question, Jet. I guess we'll find out soon enough."

"You work for Alex Hawke, is that right?"

"You could say that."

"What do you do for him?"

"Blow things up. Kill people."

"My God, I can't believe this."

"What?"

"I'm just swapping one homicidal maniac for another."

Chapter Twenty-two

Château Belmaison

LUCA'S HISTORIC *BAL MASQUÉ* WAS HELD IN A HOUSE REEK-
ing with history: In the winter of 1798, Napoleon, who had not yet
conquered the world, declared himself in need of a country seat. A
graceful country house on the outskirts of Paris had caught his eye. It
was called Château Belmaison. The house was in a very sad state of
disrepair, but Napoleon saw possibilities. Still, he hesitated. His star
was ascendant, but he felt he could simply not afford the property on
his paltry military salary.

Josephine disagreed. In the unusually cold April of that year
1799, while France's new First Consul and his army were busy killing Arabs and conquering Egypt, Madame Bonaparte bought the estate by incurring a debt of three hundred thousand francs. Knowing her penurious husband would be angry with her, she began at
once to decorate it in an inexpensive manner, a style that would
surely please him.

Napoleon worshipped at mighty Caesar's throne, so she imagined
a blend of the neoclassical and the warlike: a space where Caesar
himself would feel at home. She hired the architects and designers
Percier and Fontaine. Together, they created the exquisite Roman-
themed Belmaison. The house was smashing and was immediately
imitated and widely copied throughout Europe.

Red (the color of Imperial Rome) was used throughout the
house. The walls of the library were covered with Roman red fabric.
A black-and-gold balustrade with lions' heads joined doors topped
with eagles. On the ceiling, fabric was draped to form a tent shape.
Napoleon loved it, and so did Luca. But the seventeenth-century
château would pass through many hands over the centuries before
he would acquire it.

After Napoleon's exile and death on the remote island of St. Helena, Belmaison was a historic site, open to the public. Millions passed through its rooms, the French citizens among them touched by a wistful longing for grander days. Dreaming of *La Gloire.*

The property eventually fell on hard times. It stood empty for many years, sunk in gloom, forgotten. Luca, riding on horseback to meet his mistress one afternoon, had spied it through the trees. When he learned of its storied history, he made a cash offer for the estate, sight unseen. It was accepted. When news broke that the famous Belmaison had been acquired at great expense by the current French minister of Foreign Trade, Napoleon's self-styled heir apparent, Luca, an alarm sounded. It was still echoing down the long halls of the Elysée Palace.

Many in government still regarded this Corsican upstart as a grave threat to the status quo. But Paris the city went into giddy paroxysms of social and political anticipation. Rumors swept the capital. A new Bonaparte was on the rise. Could gilded days of glory be far behind?

The *bal masqué* was the first party of any consequence at Luca's new residence. More than 250 guests received engraved invitations honoring the latest recipient of the Légion d'Honneur. The invitations called for First Empire period costumes. A state dinner would be served, with an early-nineteenth-century menu. A full orchestra would provide music for the waltz, the quadrille, the sautese, and la boulangere.

Until he got too warm, Luca wore a costume replicating Napoleon's coronation finery, including a faux ermine cape. Madame Li, no stranger to the art of disguise, came dressed in a ball gown as the tiny Empress Josephine. The sultan of Oman appeared dressed as a captain of the Barbary pirates. None of the three costumes were too far wide of the mark.

Shortly after nine, Luca slipped away for an hour. He had gone quickly to his study to take a call on his secure line. The call was from Beijing and he'd been expecting it. He spoke in whispered tones with the general secretary of the Central Communist Party for more than twenty minutes. His closest aide-de-camp, Captain Chamouton, emerged from a secret anteroom just as Bonaparte was hanging up. "It will be done precisely as you have ordered, sir," he heard the next leader of France say, just before he replaced the receiver.

Thus, the rumors of the power behind the throne began.

At the stroke of ten, a small squad of helmeted dragoons made a grand entrance onto the parquet of the dance floor. The waltz sputtered to a stop. The captain read an edict aloud to much twittering and amusement. He stated that the "Emperor Wishes to Consult with the Captain of Barbary Pirates at his Earliest Convenience."

The sultan of Oman, the guest of honor, dressed as a Barbary buccaneer, laughed, bowed to his partner. He sheathed his tin scimitar, doffed his jeweled turban, and the dragoons formed up around him. He was marched off the floor to the great delight of the ladies peeking from behind their peacock-feathered fans at the handsome Arabian pirate.

Waiting impatiently for the sultan's arrival, sitting at his beloved emperor's desk in his red library, Luca fingered a small golden snuffbox once used in a failed attempt to poison Napoleon in this very room. It was a reminder to be ever vigilant. These were dangerous times, and he was about to take dangerous measures. But he would survive, and he would lead his people to Glory. It started tonight. It started now.

"You wished to see me, Your Majesty?" the dashing sultan said, somewhat foolishly. The time for this nonsense was on the dance floor, not in Napoleon's library. The sultan was plainly in his cups.

"Mind your manners and take off your hat, Captain," Luca said to him with a thin smile. "You're in my house. And sit down. You're unsteady."

"I think I'll have a little touch of that brandy, if you don't mind," the Arab said to Chamouton. Luca nodded his assent and the captain poured. His hand was shaking. He was no longer a young man. He longed for his bed.

"*A votre santé,*" the sultan said, raising his snifter to Bonaparte. "To your very good health, my new friend."

Luca replied, raising his cigar, "We all hang by the same thread, do we not?"

The sultan didn't like the sound of that. He was still just sober enough to hear the subtle tone of threat in his host's voice.

"There is a problem?" the Arab said.

"An opportunity," Luca said, getting to his feet so that he would tower over the Arab.

"Always a frightening word in the mouths of diplomats, my dear friend," the sultan said.

Luca smiled. "I was afraid you had been 'over-Châteaued.' But I see the grape has not dulled your senses. This opportunity is only frightening if you are weak. If you fail to see the merit of what I am about to propose."

"Go on, go on," the Arab said, after draining his glass and looking to Chamouton for a refill. "I'm not stupid. I assumed you had invited me to Paris for some reason other than to hang another bauble around my neck."

"Tomorrow morning at precisely ten o'clock, the Légion d'Honneur ceremony will take place. Immediately following that event, you and I shall hold a joint press conference, Your Excellency. All the media will be present. You, Your Highness, are going to announce that you are inviting France to come to your nation's aid in a time of great turmoil in your country—"

"Turmoil? There is no—"

"Let me finish. A turmoil caused by certain extremist factions infiltrating north across the border from Yemen. Causing unrest and dissent amongst your people. Foreigners who would undermine you and bring your government down. Since your government consists of you, and you alone, you O mighty Sultan, are taking these unilateral measures to protect your sovereignty."

"What measures?" the man said, aghast. Beneath his silk turban, his face was turning purple.

"The very wise and sensible measure of coming here to France and asking for my help. Protection. You have asked me to send French troops into the capital city of Muscat. And to the oilfields, naturally. We must ensure the continued flow of oil at all costs."

"It's insane! I won't have any part of this!" He got up from his chair and stumbled back a few steps before Chamouton caught him in his arms.

"I am afraid you have no choice in the matter, Excellency. You have met my dear comrade, Madame Li?"

"Who?" the Arab said, gasping for breath. Chamouton now had his revolver pressed firmly to the back of his skull.

A small Oriental woman trailing yards of golden satin emerged from the shadows behind Napoleon's desk.

"Bonsoir, messieurs," the woman trilled.

"Better known to you as the Empress Josephine, Excellency."

"Madame Li?" the sultan said. "Who—who is—"

Madame Li, still dressed in Josephine's gala finery and jewels, quickly crossed the room and stood before the terrified Arab. It did not help the sultan's state of mind when the woman whipped off the bejeweled wig and smiled up at him bareheaded. Madame Li was clearly a man, and the dragons tattooed on his bald pate caused fresh terror to shine in the sultan's eyes.

"I am Madame Li," Hu Xu said. He opened the tiny sequined evening bag he'd carried to the ball and withdrew a small scalpel. The Arab recoiled, but was held fast by Chamouton.

"You have two choices, Excellency," Luca said. He was now sitting on the edge of his desk, enjoying his cigar and the unfolding drama. "One, take the opportunity I present you. Invite our troops and navy into Oman. Two—"

"What opportunity?" the Arab ruler screamed.

"The opportunity of continued health and happiness for you and your entire family." Luca smiled. "Nothing will change for you. Nothing. You will still have your palaces, your fleet of Rolls-Royces, your jets, and your yachts."

"But when I look out the palace windows in my capital of Muscat, I will see French uniforms."

"Exactly."

"And the oil?"

"We have a very thirsty customer to the east, O mighty Sultan. I will be richer than you in the not too distant future."

"The Chinese."

"Think what you will."

"And if I simply expose this outrage?" The man was gathering control, all traces of inebriation vanished. "Go before the cameras and denounce you for what you are? A liar! A thief! A murdering—"

"I have considered that possibility. You are an old man. Your own life, I'm sure, means little to you," Luca said, his voice dripping with cool irony. "But the lives of family? Friends?"

"What are you saying? Allah be blessed, if you harm them, I will—"

"You will what? What can you do, my dear Sultan? For the moment, listen. Then you can decide."

"Tell this man to let me go. And tell this bizarre creature to put the knife away. I will listen."

"Very well," Bonaparte said, nodding at both Chamouton and Hu Xu, who stepped aside. "You have a national museum, my dear friend. Once a fortress of some historic importance. On the island of Masara. Is this correct?"

"Fort Mahoud," the sultan said, a tremor marking his voice. "It was once Field Marshal Erwin Rommel's headquarters."

"Ah, that's the place. Your entire family is there, now, Excellency. Wives. Children, grandchildren. Some members of your palace staff from Muscat. Since your departure from Oman, they have been under my protection. Do not worry. My men in Oman will protect your beloved family from the terrorists who would harm them."

"But there are no terrorists in my country," the sultan said, all the air going out of him. "My people are at peace with the world."

Bonaparte smiled as if at a child. "No man is at peace with the world, Your Highness. Surely you have heard of the growing threat of the Christian right-wing militia outside the capital? The Yemeni forces coming up from the south? Yes, the Sultanate of Oman is in grave danger."

"My God," the sultan said, lowering his head. He'd been a fool. Vanity had dulled his instincts about this man. He had been blinded by the glittering prospect of the Légion d'Honneur, a prize he openly belittled but had long coveted.

"And as of this moment you are under my protection as well," Luca Bonaparte said, smiling. "For the time being. Immediately following your speech and a press conference, you will be flown secretly to Oman to rejoin your family."

"As prisoners in an island fortress."

"Only temporary, I assure you. Once systems are in place to redirect Oman's oil production, restrictions upon you and your family will ease considerably."

"I should like to sit down. Perhaps to have another brandy."

"Please. Let me pour it for you, Excellency," Luca said, taking a seat opposite his newly converted ally. "Let us now speak of opportunity. You are aware of a quotation, perhaps, one of my personal favorites? It begins: 'There is a tide in the affairs of men—' "

The sultan stared into the amber depths of his glass, his eyes glistening, thinking of his beloved family, now all held hostage by this madman. Then, he looked up and stared at Bonaparte.

The Arab began, " 'There is a tide in the affairs of men, which, taken at the flood, leads on to fortune . . . Omitted—' "

"Omitted," Bonaparte continued, " 'All the voyage of their life is bound in shallows, and in miseries . . .' "

The sultan finished for him, his old eyes gleaming, " 'And we must take the current when it serves, or lose our ventures.' "

"Well done! Tomorrow morning, we must take the current, my friend! The world is changing before your eyes! A flood tide that leads on to fortune! Now, I suggest you retire upstairs and get some sleep while I will return to my guests. I will say that you were tired. In the morning, wearing your new trinket, you will inform the world of your wise decision from the Salon Napoleon at the Elysée Palace," Luca said. "Do we understand each other?"

"I'm afraid we do."

"Good! There is one remaining thing. Very important."

"Tell me, for God's sake, what more I can do for you."

"You go before the cameras at ten-twenty. Afterward, I want you to invite Prime Minister Honfleur to go for a walk. A private discussion, tête-à-tête, most important, you will tell him. Do not allow him to refuse. You will take him for a stroll along the private road just on the north side of the Elysée. Do you know it? Closed to all traffic."

"Yes. I have walked with him there before."

"Tell him anything you wish. Bait the hook. Tell him you have certain reservations about me. That will be all you need to say. He will leap at that. Do you understand?"

"Yes."

"After exactly twenty paces, you must find some excuse to distance yourself from him. A particular flowerbed catches your attention. Make some excuse. Get away from him. Quickly. Someone will be watching."

"That someone will be me," Hu Xu said from his chair in the shadows.

Chapter Twenty-three

Hawkesmoor

THE CLOCK SITTING ON THE MANTEL STRUCK ELEVEN TIMES, and Hawke looked up from his book. Rain beat against the tall windows opposite his chair and the distant rumble of thunder could be heard rolling across the countryside. It was a quiet Sunday night at home and all was reasonably well. Picking up the telephone twice, he had started to dial Ambrose's number, then put the receiver down. It wouldn't do to fret over him. He was a big boy and he was sleeping with a pistol under his pillow these days.

Hawke had gone to bed with a book at ten, intending on doing some homework. It was a big, thick thing called, reasonably enough, *China*. A modern political history by someone named Chan, no relation to Charlie by the tone of the first few chapters. He dozed off, fitfully, for a quarter of an hour or so, couldn't sleep for some reason or other, and so wandered downstairs to the library, fishing for something else to read. He decided on *Riddle of the Sands*, one of his boyhood favorites, a novel written by Erskine Childers in 1903. It was about two young Englishmen on a sailing holiday in Germany who—

"Sorry to bother you, m'lord," Pelham said in his ethereal way, appearing magically in the doorway. "Someone wishes to see you, sir."

"See me? Really? I didn't hear the door." Hell, it was Sunday night. Steaming rain. Who in hell would be out mucking about on a night like this?

"She didn't come to the door, sir. She rapped on the pantry window."

Hawke put down his book. She? That was better. But it still seemed improbable.

"Pelham, have you been nipping at the sherry?"

The man didn't dignify that riposte with a retort. Or vice versa,

Hawke wasn't sure which was which. "She says it's rather urgent, your lordship. She seems to be—in distress—and I admitted her to the kitchen. Her car broke down and she's in a hurry to get somewhere. Gave her a cup of tea, sir."

"All right, old thing, tell her I'll be right with her. As you can see, I'm in my pajamas. I'll just run upstairs and put something on. How odd. Knocked on the window?"

"Yes, sir."

"Pelham?"

"Sir?"

"This mystery woman. What does she look like?"

"Wet, m'lord. Soaked to the bone. But quite beautiful in an exotic way, if I may say so, sir. She bears an extraordinary resemblance to a film star I saw last Sunday afternoon at the Bexleyheath Cineworld. An Oriental lady, sir."

"Jet."

"Beg your pardon, sir?"

"That's her name. I'll be right down. You might bring her in here, by the fire. Offer her some brandy, if you don't mind."

"Indeed, sir."

Hawke bounded up the stairs. The woman had figured prominently in his dreams ever since his return to England from the Côte d'Azur. In some, she was a good girl. In others bad. He supposed the truth was somewhere in between. Ah, well. Gave her his number at the office and hadn't heard from her since. Thought that was the end of it. Clearly, it wasn't. She'd somehow tracked him down. Something was urgent enough to warrant this nocturnal excursion into the heart of darkness. Car had broken down? Surely she could do better than that.

Still, he did have a few rather fond memories.

Five minutes later he was descending the staircase in a pair of faded jeans and a black pullover with the sleeves yanked up to his elbows. "Jet," he called out when he was halfway down, "I'll be right with you. I just have to speak to someone in the kitchen."

No reply from inside the library, and the door had been left open only the slightest crack. He caught a whiff of Gauloise cigarette smoke, however, and knew she was in there waiting for him. Fascinating. He strode across the center hallway and headed for the butler's pantry where Pelham would be closing up shop for the night.

"Pelham, what is her story? Did she say anything?"

"She thanked me profusely for the offer of brandy but said she would prefer a whisky, sir."

"That's all?"

"I'm afraid so, sir. As I mentioned, she appears highly strung. Perhaps you could drive her to her destination."

"No other hints of any sort? Nothing at all?"

"No, sir."

"Nothing for it, then. I'll enter the ring unarmed."

"As you wish, sir."

"Goodnight then, old soul. Trudge ever upward and onward in pursuit of your dreams. Don't wait up on my account. The lady and I are old friends, you see. We may sit up half the night recounting with unbridled joy the many shared adventures of yore."

Pelham looked at him for a moment, his face unreadable as always. He dissolved away.

"Goodnight, m'lord," Pelham said, over his shoulder, drifting upward.

"Yes. It's the sleep of innocents for you, Plummie, my lad."

Hawke smiled at his retreating back. "Plummie" was his boyhood name for his old friend. Hadn't thought of it in years. He turned round, headed across the black-and-white marble floors of the dining room and toward the library. Pulling open the door, he saw her in ivory profile, staring into the fire. It was Jet, all right. She was perched on the edge of the large sofa, an overstuffed monstrosity covered in pale blue satin.

She looked quite as beautiful as he remembered. Pelham had taken her rainwear. Her damp hair, now dyed platinum blond, was slicked back and she was wearing a turquoise cowl top over tight-fitting yellow pants. A black raw silk shawl was draped round her bare white shoulders. Not at all dressed for the weather, but that, he remembered, was her style.

"Hello," Hawke said. "I see you've got a drink."

"Yes." It was hardly the warm expression of gratitude one might expect on a night like this.

"You don't seem happy to see me. Pity, when you've come all this way. I'm sorry about Cannes."

He was trying to be light, but to tell the truth he was uneasy. Suddenly suspicious. He wasn't at all sure of her motive for being here. Had he really offended her so horribly? Perhaps he could have forewarned her he wouldn't be able to spend the night at the Carlton. Quick had seen her watching him from the balcony. Perhaps—oh, hell! If he smoked, he could have lit a cigarette now. Tamped down his pipe. Done something with his bloody hands.

"You are sorry? That's surprising." Her voice was flat. "What on earth do you have to be sorry about? You're alive."

"I mean—leaving so quickly."

"Leaving? Cannes?" she said, looking at him with a most curious expression. "You were on a mission, after all."

"Right. I'm glad you understand that. I assumed when I saw you up on my balcony that—well, then, I think I'll fix myself a drink. A martini should do it."

He went to the drinks table and unstoppered the decanter of vodka. Poured two fingers into a tumbler and added ice cubes. Normally, he drank rum. But he felt a martini coming on.

"You're not surprised to see me?" she said, reaching into her bag. Her hair was gleaming in the firelight.

"I am, actually."

"I didn't think anyone would let me in. My idea was to lure you outside. I assumed you'd call the police. You're not as clever as I've been led to believe."

"Not let you inside? I'm not that cold-hearted. A woman out in the rain on a night like this." He turned to face her. He'd been more than accommodating. He wouldn't suffer this kind of rudeness from anyone, no matter how beautiful.

"Tell me something. Why have you come here?"

"I thought it was the simplest option. I believe in the direct approach. Save you all the trouble of looking for me."

"You flatter yourself. I haven't been looking for you."

She laughed. "Don't be ridiculous. You've got half of Scotland Yard on my trail."

"What? Good God, woman, what kind of a man do you think—"

"My father sent me, Lord Hawke. He wanted me to give you this."

Hawke was so stunned at the sudden appearance of the gun that she almost got him. In that brief paralysis of incomprehension, she fired once, twice, the silencer deadening the sound to a spitting noise, and the paneling just above his head splintered, wood and plaster spraying all around him. He hurled himself sideways and hit the floor. Then he was up and lunging for the blue sofa. It was the only cover available.

The woman turned to raise the gun again, tugging furiously at it. The silencer had caught in her shawl.

Hawke was on his feet, circling round the sofa.

"What exactly is this about?" he said.

"This is about Harry Brock. You remember him."

"You're crazy, woman. Put the bloody gun down. Now."

"You think you can thwart my father's will, Hawke. You fucking Brits and Americans." She was scuttling behind the desk, trying to keep it between them and buy herself a few precious seconds.

"Your father? What the hell has he got to do with this?"

"You have crossed the Yangtze one too many times."

"Ah, that's it."

Hawke used this time to snatch up a small gilded chair. He raised it above his head and moved forward.

"Drop it," he said, but at that instant she got the damn gun free and pointed it at his head. He crashed the chair down, caught the side of her head, saw a flash of light and felt a blinding pain in his temple. He grabbed her by the shoulders and tried to spin her round. She twisted away. God, she was strong! He managed to catch one wrist and clamp it firmly, aiming the gun away from either of them. She stood there, spitting at him, hissing something in Chinese, and he took aim and high-kicked at the gun hand. The pistol sailed away.

Her lips peeled back from her clenched teeth and a slow scream of frustration seemed to drain what was left in the woman. She relaxed her muscles, let it all go.

"I'm going to release your arm, now. Do you promise to be a good girl and behave?"

His head was throbbing and warm sticky fluid of a certain familiar shade was running into his eye. He felt unsteady but he wasn't going to die anytime soon.

"Get out," he said, holding his hand fast to the wound to stanch the bleeding. "You're mad! Get out of my bloody house."

Hawke bent to pick up her gun and put it in his pocket.

They were both breathing hard. Neither spoke. Hawke felt dizzy, unsteady.

"I said, leave," Hawke said. Suddenly, it was very important that he get off his feet. Lie down somewhere. He couldn't do that until Jet left his house. She was truly deranged. She might kill him if he passed out.

"Look. I've no intention of calling the police. I'm sorry about Cannes. I was in a bit of a rush that night. I may have been a little abrupt. I apologize. Now, just please go."

She looked at him, trying to control her breathing.

"I've no idea what you're talking about," she said, walking to the doorway. "You are the one who is insane."

"Me?"

"You have me confused with someone, Lord Hawke. My sister, Jet."

"But—"

"You haven't seen the last of me. My sister's heart got in the way. So my father sent the heartless one."

He barely heard this last. A red veil was coming down over his eyes. Not blood, that was outside. This was inside. His brain wasn't processing new information. A few seconds later, he heard the muffled sound of the front door slamming shut. No car started. Either she'd walked from town or someone was waiting at the end of the drive.

"You forgot your raincoat," he said to the empty room. Then he fell down lengthwise on the blue sofa and passed out.

He came to with the phone in his hand, the voice at the other end saying weakly, "Yes? Who's there? This is Sergeant Smithers—the police station—who's calling, please?"

He woke, or regained consciousness, sometime before dawn. The tall windows opposite were still black. The lights in the library sconces were still burning brightly. He managed to get to his feet and stagger over to the desk. He collapsed into the chair he hadn't broken. His memory of the moments before he passed out were still fuzzy. He picked up the phone and speed-dialed Quick.

Listening to the line ring at the other end, he noticed the front of his sweater was matted with thick blood. It had soaked his jeans and was in his moccasins, too. How much blood was in the human body? Oh, right. Ten pints. He didn't think he'd lost quite that much.

"Quick," a voice said.

"Tommy, it's me," Alex said.

"Yes, sir. How are you, sir?"

"Bloodied but unbowed. Is Stokely still aboard?"

"Aye-aye, sir. He's gone to bed, though."

"Put me through to his stateroom."

"Right away. You take care, sir. You don't sound all that great."

Stoke, God bless him, picked up on the first ring.

"Hey, bossman."

"Stoke, listen carefully. You said you met Jet aboard the von Draxis yacht."

"I did."

"She was hurt. You brought her back to my boat and put her in sickbay."

"All true."

"Have you heard from von Draxis?"

"Heard he wants me dead is all."

"When did Jet leave? Did she fly out of Nice?"

"Leave? She didn't leave."

"She didn't leave."

"No, boss. She didn't leave."

"She didn't fly to London."

"She most definitely did not fly to London."

"Where is she now?"

"In her stateroom, I guess. Girl hasn't left there since the doc let her out of sickbay two days ago."

"She's in her room. Now. Aboard *Blackhawke*."

"Right. Just like I said. You okay, bossman? You don't sound all that great."

"Everybody says that. When was the last time you saw her?"

"I dunno. About ten, eleven o'clock, maybe. I peeked my head in the door to say nighty-night on my way down here."

"And she was in her bed."

"In her bed, reading a book. You want to know which book?"

"Stoke, look at your watch."

"Yeah. I'm looking at it—"

"I want you to remember this precise moment in time. You can tell everybody that this is the exact moment when Alex Hawke lost his bloody mind."

Chapter Twenty-four

Paris

EARLY NEXT MORNING, MADAME LI SASHAYED DAINTILY OUT onto the pavement beneath the covered entrance of the Hotel George V, smiling at the bellmen in their crimson uniforms. He already enjoyed a reputation for tipping heavily and often; and the resulting bowing and scraping everywhere he went was joyous to behold. He was wearing a black Chanel suit and carrying his custom umbrella. On his head, a wide-brimmed black silk hat with veil. Dangling from his shoulder, his new bright-red Kelly bag. It was the largest one Hermès made and just the right size for all Madame's essentials, the shopgirl had said.

Oh, how right she was! Everything fit perfectly inside! But, my, wasn't it heavy? Modern life had gotten so complicated. His necessities weighed almost ten pounds!

The petite Chinese delegate made his way to the rue du Faubourg Saint-Honoré. He quickly strode past the street's glittering array of haute couture emporiums and jewels sparkling in every window. Directly across the street, the colorful windows of Christian Lacroix. And then the ultramodern shops of Yves St. Laurent, and then Valentino, and—no matter. He tripped right past them all without so much as a glance in the windows.

No time to shop. He was a woman on a mission.

At number 76, rue du Faubourg Saint-Honoré, just a brisk walk from his hotel, he arrived at his destination. This was Sotheby's, Paris, a bastion of Old World style and elegance. Auctioneer to kings. And to not a few old queens like himself, he giggled. He paused a moment and looked up at the exterior facade, then at the edifice just across the narrow street. The wistful smile he wore belied a busy mind. He was getting his line-of-sight bearings. Directly across the street from

Sotheby's, though he pretended not to notice, was the main entrance to the Elysée Palace. This was the ancient seat of government in France.

He was not surprised to see the flurry of activity at the gate. Beyond the large black iron gates of the Elysée, a huge cobblestoned courtyard was visible. Many black cars were parked inside, many more official vehicles were lined outside, waiting to get in. Police and palace guards were everywhere, examining identification cards, inspecting vehicles both visually and with bomb dogs. Video uplink trucks parked along the curb. France 2, CNN, and Fox News. There was a huge press conference going on inside the Elysée. Rumors were flying.

The sultan of Oman was set to stun the world in exactly twenty-six minutes. Having just received the prestigious Légion d'Honneur, he was going to announce that his country was inviting French troops into the capital city of Muscat, a drastic measure intended to put down an insurgency supported by the People's Republic of Yemen against his government. Prime Minister Honfleur would then declare that France was proud to come to the aid of her old and valuable friend.

He glanced at his Cartier tank watch. Almost ten. In fact, the sultan was probably making his way to the podium just about now. He walked through Sotheby's door and made his way slowly to the reception desk. Two or three staffers were there, and he picked the one who looked most eager. An attractive boy, very well dressed, arranging catalogs for the upcoming show. He'd picked one up yesterday and enjoyed it immensely. The catalog, not the boy.

"May I help you, madame?" the boy said as he approached and put his small, gloved hands on the glass counter.

"Yes, you may," he said with a small smile. "I'm interested in purchasing a few items. Before they come up at auction this evening."

"*Mais oui, mais oui.* Which items are you interested in, madame?"

"The Maria Callas collection."

"Splendid. Callas. What a voice, what a marvelous woman. Her *Rigoletto* is still the standard. A soprano for the ages. You know, she died here in Paris in 1977. The Greek, Onassis, broke her heart when he married Mrs. Kennedy. You've seen our beautiful catalog, I take it? Magnificent jewels."

"Lovely."

"And, precisely which pieces is madame interested in purchasing?"

"All of them."

"All of them?" The boy, a young Louis Jourdan, was taken aback but manfully determined to hide it. "The entire collection?"

"Yes. All of it."

"Ah. I see. Well, in that case, let me just ring up to our director of fine jewels, madame. Monsieur Hubert Vedrine. Would you like to take a seat for a few moments? I'm sure Monsieur Vedrine will be right down." The boy's hand was trembling as he picked up the phone.

"Splendid," he said. He turned away to look through the window, humming a few bars from *Gigi*. He'd been singing "Thank Heaven for Little Girls" all morning long. His Maurice Chevalier had been re-alistic enough to startle the elevator operator at the George V out of his gloomy torpor.

"Your name, *s'il vous plaît*?" the boy inquired.

"Madame Li."

"Of the Chinese delegation? You are here for the afternoon Mid-dle East conference?" He nodded discreetly in the direction of the palace across the street.

"*Mais oui, monsieur*. Clever boy! How ever did you guess?"

Ten minutes later, having taken the private elevator situated behind Reception up to the third floor in the company of Monsieur Vedrine, he was seated across a lovely Directoire desk from the Sotheby's di-rector. Like Li himself, the man was small and exquisitely attired. Starched white Charvet shirt and matching tie, navy thee-piece suit. He had a pencil-line mustache and heavily lidded soft green eyes. Their knees were almost touching under the desk and every now and then he would feel subtle pressure against his right knee. The man was actually flirting with him, he was sure of it. Men were such ani-mals. Vedrine had even locked the door.

He had trays of magnificent jewelry stacked by his right hand. He would carefully remove a piece and place it on a black pillow just in front of Li, the facets brilliantly illuminated by a flexible halogen light. Madame Li was examining a ruby and diamond bracelet.

"Her favorite piece," Hubert said. "Cushion-shaped rubies and baguette diamonds. Callas had a marvellous eye."

"And deep pockets until Jackie O came along. How much, Hubert?" He found it amusing that they were already on a first-name basis.

"This piece, I would estimate one hundred thousand U.S. dollars. More or less. But this is the gem of the collection, if you'll excuse my humor. A pair of ruby and diamond earclips, mounted by Cartier, once owned by the duchess of Windsor and—"

"I'll take it." He looked at his watch.

"Which one?"

"All of them. At the pre-auction price."

"*Parfaitement*, madame!"

"Will you take a check?" he asked, bending over to get to the bag at his feet.

"Certainly. A quick call to your bank, madame. To verify the funds. And then we should be delighted."

Instead of the bag, he chose the umbrella. Still hidden behind the desk, he quickly removed a nearly invisible plastic protector from the sharpened tip. He could see Hubert from the waist down. His knees were apart and his shiny little shoes were bouncing up and down with excitement over the impending sale of the complete Maria Callas collection.

He drove the umbrella tip deep inside Hubert's groin. The dioxin-tipped steel point found the artery. It was only a matter of seconds. The dosage was ten times that used on Ukrainian opposition leader Yevchenko in fall 2004. Yevchenko had been a failed Te-Wu experiment in collaboration with the Ukrainian secret police. He had lived. Poor little Hubert would not.

Hubert fell backward in his chair, expelling a whuff of air, and then he was around the desk and on the man, his hand clamped over his mouth. Hubert had gone instantly into shock, as expected, and his pulse was racing. Madame Li waited for the poison to take effect, watching the sweep second hand of his new watch. He'd found that if the surprise was wholly unexpected and sufficiently brutal, they seldom made much noise. The little man went slack and Madame Li got up quickly and returned to his bag.

He removed the rifle and quickly assembled it, taking great pride and pleasure in the doing. The matte black weapon was Austrian, a Steyr, 7.62mm, with a lightweight polymer stock, and most suitable for effective engagement of targets up to fifteen hundred feet or less. The Scout Tactical model also had a low-magnification scope—only 2.5X but ideal for quick target acquisition at short and medium distances. It was a lovely toy and perfect for the occasion. Chosen with care by those who do care.

Checking to ensure that Hubert had expired (he had), Madame Li moved to the window. He'd noticed the old-fashioned window sashes earlier and the book lying on the sill, obviously used to prop up the window whenever Hubert felt warm. It was a feeling he was rapidly losing now, but Madame Li would be gone long before the corpse had gone cold. The carefully planned escape route assumed a damaged elevator. The service stairway led to a door on a back alley. The confusion of a prearranged bomb would ensure he was out and window shopping before anyone made it to the fourth floor.

He lifted the window three feet off the sill. It stayed there. The private street alongside the palace was empty.

At the near end of the deserted street, just below on the rue du Faubourg Saint-Honoré, a cordon of uniformed tactical police. The far end of the street, which led in the direction of the Champs Elysées, disappeared into the trees of the palace gardens. He found it fascinating that the French president and his guests took walks along such a route. Luca Bonaparte, buying some bauble for his current mistress, had stood not long ago at this very window, and had seen Queen Elizabeth strolling her spaniels unaccompanied by security. And it had given him a very good idea.

Madame Li pulled a cell phone from his red bag and turned it on. The signal bars came right up to strength.

At half past ten, two men, one large and jovial, one hunched over and apprehensive, appeared at a side door to the palace. They paused and acknowledged the police and a small crowd of citizens who'd gathered to gawk at all the hubbub. Even without the scope, Madame Li could see the Sultan of Oman's terrified expression. And the confident glow of the prime minister of France, Honfleur. The tall, sleek Frenchman, who towered over the sheik, then put his left hand on the Arab's shoulder and steered him up the empty street. Half of the police on the line watched their progress intently.

The other half now turned in place to face the street, their faces swiveling side to side. Periodically, their eyes would rise to check the windows of the storefronts opposite. Madame Li stayed far enough away from the window so as to be in shadow. From his vantage point, he could see an ice cream truck, its bell chiming, rolling slowly up the street. The truck rolled to a stop in the street just below the director's window. The driver got out and vanished into the crowd.

It was time.

He punched the number that Bonaparte had given into the phone. Star-one-seven-eight-nine. Just before he hit "send," the significance of the number 1789 dawned on him. Of course! The year of France's great Revolution. He smiled and thumbed the green send button.

Boom, he said softly, just before the explosion rocked the street and the nearby buildings.

The walls of Mr. Sotheby's building shook and the windows on the ground floor exploded inward. Everyone in Reception was probably dead. Madame Li, raising his rifle, stepped to the window. On the street below, chaos. Flames erupted from the black and twisted hulk of the ice cream truck and thick black smoke smelling of burned fuel, plastic, and other less pleasant things rose upward. The small crowd and the cordon of police were down, dead or wounded in the street, but Madame Li had his right eye pressed to the rubber eyepiece of the scope and he had eyes only for Honfleur.

The prime minister was frozen in place. Through the scope you could see the fear and panic in his eyes. The sultan, surely sensing what was actually happening here, dove to the pavement.

Madame Li squeezed the Steyr's trigger and fired. The round literally blew the Frenchman's head off. And opened the floodgates of what some French historians would later term the Second Terror.

Chapter Twenty-five

Hampstead Heath

"GENTLEMAN FOR YOU, MR. CONGREVE," MAY PURVIS SAID, coming out into the garden. It was the early morning following Hawke's near-death experience and Ambrose was sitting outside in the bright sunshine. He had a good picture going. It was a study of the crabapple tree that stood outside his kitchen window. It was not in flower now, but Ambrose was dabbing on scads of pink and white blossoms anyway, clouds of them. His artistic philosophy was simple: Paint things the way they *should* look.

It's not the truth, but what you believe to be the truth that is important in art. That was his opinion, anyway. Never let the truth get in the way of a good painting. Or a good story, for that matter.

Like his great hero Winston Churchill, Ambrose Congreve used the very delicate art of watercolor not only for self-expression but also as a meditative medium. A release from all his worldly cares. He had slipped into the trance. The Zone. He had not heard the front-door bell.

"Whom shall we say is calling, Mrs. Purvis?" he asked, trying to mask his irritation at the intrusion. His housekeeper had been filling her basket with apples for a cobbler she was making for his pudding. This simple act had inspired his painting.

He was making good progress and any interruption was unwelcome. At any rate, he certainly wasn't expecting anyone at his door this early on a Sunday morning. It simply wasn't done. It wasn't civilized. It wasn't—

"It would be his lordship, sir. Lord Hawke."

"Ah! Splendid!" A visit from Alex was another matter. Ambrose had been dying to show off his new digs. "Would you just bring him out here to the garden? See if he wants anything. Tea. Coffee, perhaps."

"I should certainly expect he wants something, sir. He's—"

"Eggs. Or, on second thought, lemons."

"Lemons?"

"He eats lemons."

"Sir! Lord Hawke is on the telephone!"

"Good lord! Well, why didn't you say so in the first place?"

Mrs. Purvis shook her head and returned to the kitchen. Ambrose, muttering, went round the far side of the house, through the rose garden, and entered by the exterior door to his study. He grabbed his pipe, plopped down into his worn leather chair, and picked up the receiver.

"Hullo, Alex," he said into the phone.

"Ambrose. What are you doing for lunch?"

"Painting it."

"Well, drop that. You need to meet me at Harry's at one."

"You sound—stressed."

"Someone tried to kill me last night. Failed miserably. I'll fill you in over a plate of Harry's spaghetti. Meanwhile, Brick Kelly is back in town. He wants to meet with us. Urgently."

"Us?"

"He specifically asked that you be there. You've read the Paris Deuxième case file I gave you?"

"I have."

"So. Your crystalline logic and supernatural powers of deduction. What do they tell you?"

"Riddled with discrepancies. Pages missing. Erasures. An unsolved murder needs solving. I suppose I could drive the Morgan into town."

"Brilliant. See you at one."

"Wait! Who tried to kill you? You can't let me just hang out to—"

"A tout à l'heure, mon ami," Hawke said and rang off.

Harry's Bar is one of London's better-kept secrets. It's a private club and there's no name on the door, which may account for its lack of notoriety. Congreve was shown by a gentleman in black tie to a quiet table in the rear of the front room. Harry's walls were washed pale yellow and hung with framed vintage cartoons from *The New Yorker* magazine. Sounded odd, but the effect was cheery and cozy nonetheless. Approaching, he saw Alex and Kelly huddled deep in conversation. He was sure that Kelly had reserved the surrounding tables as well and that, if anyone showed up to be seated nearby, they were armed employees of the United States government.

"Ambrose!" Kelly said, getting to his feet and shaking Congreve's hand. "Hawkeye and I were just speaking of you."

The tall, slender man had a quiet, gracious, slightly rumpled manner. There was a lot of steel behind that honeyed Jeffersonian demeanor, Ambrose knew, but Brick Kelly was damned if he'd let it show through.

"Hello, Brick," Ambrose said, taking the man's hand. "I've just heard on the radio about the French prime minister. Honfleur. Another assassination at the top of the French government. It's all over the news. Good lord."

"Yes, it's all getting very dicey. International consternation of this kind could easily lead to war. Anyway, I'm so glad you could come. We'll speak of it at lunch. You can be of great help in this matter, Ambrose."

"Greetings, Constable Congreve," Hawke said, smiling and shaking his hand. "And, how did you and your beloved Lemony Snicket perform on the highways and byways this morning?"

"Lemony Snicket?"

"Your new automobile."

"I have dubbed it the Yellow Peril, as you well know, Alex, and it performed splendidly. A magnificent machine. What on earth has happened to your head?"

The maître d' pulled out the one empty chair and Congreve sat. Hawke was breezily indifferent to the fact that he had a white gauze bandage swaddled round his head. Only Hawke could manage to make the whole affair look faintly piratical. All he needed was an eye patch.

"I was just telling Brick," Hawke said. "Amazing thing. An acquaintance of mine tried to snuff me last night. Took one to the temple. Superficial, but it knocked me silly. I'll have a nice scar, according to the doctor who sewed me up. Bloody female came into my house under false pretenses and pulled a gun. Damn near killed me."

"She missed," Kelly said by way of explanation to Congreve. "I'm trying to find out why."

"I hit her first. With a chair. Spoilt her aim, but she nicked me. She conceded the match and left before I could ring the local constabulary." It wasn't quite true; he'd thrown her out after taking the gun. And he could not remember whether or not he'd called the police. He'd meant to, he was sufficiently alarmed, but in his woozy state he wasn't sure he'd gotten round to it. Still, Hawke didn't want to be seen as softhearted in this particular company.

"You hit a woman with a chair?" Ambrose said.

"Yes, I did. And I'm proud of it," Hawke said.

"Some old flame of yours? Is she a stalker?" Brick asked.

Hawke said, "She is if she comes back. Right now she's simply mad as a hatter. By the way, Constable, she's Chinese. We are both being stalked by Oriental ladies with a view to a kill."

"Does this thinly veiled coincidence raise a question in your mind, Alex?" Ambrose said, sipping from his water goblet and opening his menu. He was famished.

"Yes," Hawke said. "Mere coincidence, do you think?"

"I think not. Perhaps they are sisters. Twin sisters."

"Sisters. There's a thought. I seem to recall something about— never mind, I've lost it."

"Sisters. Yes. Even twins," Ambrose said. "Evil twins, one might say. One trying to kill you, the other, me. Be careful, Alex. I have a very bad feeling about all this. We're all suffering from some kind of China Syndrome, in my opinion."

"Just the subject young Brick and I were getting round to," Hawke said. "You'll be interested to hear what Brick has to say on the subject of our inscrutable Chinese friends."

"Try me," Congreve said, "as soon as we've ordered a beverage."

Kelly signaled to one of the hovering waiters and drinks orders were given. No one seemed to be having a cocktail, so Ambrose quietly ordered a Bloody Bull while no one was looking. No celery stick or olives or anything that smacked of booze, he whispered in the waiter's ear. The whole world might have ceased to drink at luncheon, but that didn't mean one had to act the sheep and follow the flock. Ambrose Congreve had long decided he would remain steadfast in his habits, albeit quiet about it.

The director made a tent of his fingers, looked at each of them over it with his keen blue eyes, and said, "Let me tell you what's going on in this little world of ours. We have, I'm very sad to say, a rapidly deteriorating situation. America's position in this thing is extremely perilous. In short, China, using this new French regime for cover, is about to make a grab for America's most precious commodity. It could easily push us right to the brink."

"War?" Congreve said, and Kelly nodded gravely.

"It certainly may come to that, if we're not very smart about it. It's a bit complicated, Chief Inspector."

Hawke said, "Let's start with France, Brick. In addition to the latest assassination, I heard on the television this morning that France is considering sending troops, lots of them, into Oman. At the express invitation of the sultan. Who, by the way, disappeared from the face of the earth just after the announcement."

"What?" Ambrose said. "That sounds like an invasion to me."

"It's not an invasion when you're invited in by the host country," Kelly replied. "But, I don't buy it. Neither does the president. I think somebody, namely this madman Bonaparte, put a gun to the sultan's head. I can't prove it, of course. That's where you two come in."

"I think the bloody French have finally lost their minds completely," Ambrose said. "It's outrageous!"

Kelly stared at Congreve for a few long moments before he spoke. There was a softness in his eyes that was remarkable.

"We Americans have a long and complicated relationship with France," Kelly said with his trademark diplomacy, lowering his voice even further. "The secretary of state has likened it to two hundred years of marriage counseling."

"It hasn't worked," Hawke said, sipping his water. "Somebody better call Raoul Felder."

"Who?" said Ambrose.

"Famous American divorce lawyer," Hawke said, smiling at Brick.

"First things first, Alex," Brick said. "Bonaparte has disappeared the sultan. And his family. We need to find him and get the truth out of him. End this charade before France invades. Save them from themselves, if we can."

"You want me to find out where the sultan is."

"Exactly. We think Boney has stashed him somewhere. Someplace remote, I imagine. Your job is to find him and get the truth out of him. America has its hands full in the Gulf right now. Iraq, Iran,

Syria. We can't be seen as having any involvement with this. So, you can't—"

"I've been down this road, Brick. I know how it works."

Kelly nodded and said, "I assume—do you two know about the submarine disaster off Sri Lanka?"

"What happened, Brick?" Hawke asked, suddenly grave.

"It happened last evening. The USS *Jimmy Carter*. One of our *Seawolf* class of attack subs. The most heavily armed sub ever built and our premier spy sub. Designed for Naval Special Warfare and as a test platform for some radical new submarine espionage technology. She had the ability to tap undersea cables and eavesdrop on the communications passing through them."

"And?" Hawke said.

"Down with all hands."

"Good lord. Accidental?" Congreve said.

"God knows at this point. There were a few garbled transmissions from the sub and then we lost all radio and sonar contact. But right before she disappeared, she was being tracked by an Agosta-B, that new-generation French sub France is trying to peddle to Pakistan."

"So what happened down there, Brick?" Alex asked.

"Typical cat-and-mouse stuff. Happens all the time. No weapons were fired. And to their credit, the French are actually aiding in the search. It's possible it was a tragic accident. But, with the mood in Washington right now—it's tense."

The drinks arrived and the director stopped talking while the waiter served them. After taking a sip of his cocktail, Congreve resumed the conversation.

"Those poor lads," he said, raising his glass. "And they've all got mothers. I must say that what simply astounds me is the unmitigated chutzpah of these sodding French. Here they are, throwing their weight around like a superpower, taking potshots at Alex here—somebody should smack them good, I say."

"I'll volunteer for that assignment," Hawke said, not smiling.

"You already have, Alex," Kelly said. "Finding out where the sultan is and getting the truth out of him is a good start."

Kelly was silent for a moment, looking at both of them and collecting his thoughts. "You've nailed the issue. France needs a wake-up call. And fast. But, we can't smack them, as you say, without putting the whole damned world at risk."

"Why not?" Congreve asked.

"Very simple, actually. In a word, China."

"I've been thinking about this, Brick," Hawke said.

"Please," Brick said, and motioned for him to continue.

"The French abandoned the EU because they were sick and tired of being lumped in with the 'old Europe.' They're psychically tortured by decades of political impotency—so they're using the Chinese to reassert themselves. Provide some nuclear and economic muscle, you might say. That is pretty much it, at least as I see it."

Brick nodded. "Exactly. Fifty years of America and the Soviets hogging the limelight has been extremely tough on France's national ego. But this new relationship with China, it's more complicated, more—symbiotic than that, Alex. These two feed off of each other. But China is in the driver's seat. A surging China is using a resurgent France to further the global interests of each."

"It's simple, isn't it?" Congreve said. "China wants oil, France wants power. Voilà!"

Brick said, "Yes, Ambrose, and if they succeed at this game, America will have to go to war to protect her vital interests in the Gulf."

"France is riding the tiger," Hawke said. "And tigers bite."

"Yes," Brick said. "France, however, may be just an unwitting pawn in this game. Ready to be sacrificed by China at the earliest opportunity. But, meanwhile, just as you say, Alex, France has gotten tired of sitting on the sidelines. They've got the spotlight now and that's just where they want to be."

"And China stays in the shadows, right where she wants to be," Hawke agreed.

"Yes. There's a desperate power struggle going on in Paris right now. The attempt on Bonaparte's life two days ago, the assassination of the French prime minister yesterday. I think it all leads back to Beijing. Right back to the top of the Chinese Communist Party. To the Forbidden City and to the premier's powerful Hong Kong stooge, General Sun-yat Moon."

Congreve was startled. "The CCP took out Honfleur? Good lord, man, why?"

"To pave the way for their *enfant terrible*, Bonaparte."

"What are the details, Brick?" Hawke asked.

"We can't prove anything yet," Kelly said. "But we think a Chinese agent, working for Moon, murdered the director of Sotheby's in his office overlooking the Elysée Palace. Then she shot Honfleur with a sniper rifle from the dead director's office windows. The sultan of Oman, luckily, was not wounded in the attack."

"You said 'she' murdered the director. The assassin was a woman?"

"Yes. A woman carrying Chinese diplomatic credentials, as a matter of fact. She slipped away in the confusion."

"Well, hell," Hawke said, looking directly at Congreve. "Chinese female assassins seem to have arrived on our shores in droves. Brick, do you have a witness who can identify her?"

"Yes. A man working Sotheby's Paris reception desk survived the bomb blast in the street seconds before the assassination. He provided a detailed description of the killer. The woman was in her seventies, well-dressed in French couture, shopping for very expensive jewelry. She was escorted up to the director's office for a private viewing, where she killed him with some kind of poison-tipped weapon. Drove it into his groin, I might add."

"Lovely," Congreve said, wincing. "Was she carrying an umbrella, by any chance?"

"Good point," Kelly said, smiling at Ambrose.

"Weapon of mass deduction," Hawke said, patting Ambrose on the shoulder.

"Too kind," Ambrose said, and took a sip of his drink.

Hawke massaged the slight stubble on his chin. "Where was Luca Bonaparte during all this bloody excitement?"

"You mean the brand spanking new prime minister of France? In his brand spanking new office at the Elysée. Handling the press furor over France's imminent incursion into Oman."

"The French press is furious?" Congreve asked, a wry smile on his face.

"Are you joking? The French press is ecstatic. *Paris Soir* ran a headline saying 'France Is on the March!' It's the rest of the world who take a dim view of this invasion. France says they were 'invited' in by the sultan. To suppress a radical insurgency. My guys think Bonaparte leaned on the sultan. A physical threat to him or his family, or perhaps some kind of blackmail. Nothing else makes any sense."

"I'll find him, Brick," Hawke said.

"Yes. But, this is very strictly off the record. You're going NOC on this one, old boy. As I said, the United States simply cannot afford to be seen as meddling in French or Arab affairs right now."

"NOC?" Ambrose asked.

"Not on Consular," Hawke said to Congreve. "No records. It means if I get caught you don't have to worry about funeral arrangements."

"Ah."

"Since the president was reelected," Brick said, "the administration has been in a full fence-mending mode with our European allies. We very much hope to solve this quietly."

"But I can meddle," Hawke said. "Quietly."

"You certainly can. You're a Brit, after all. You have three or four hundred years of bad blood with the French. I want you to meddle to your heart's content."

"I love to meddle, too," Ambrose said. "I was born to meddle."

Kelly smiled. "I was just coming to you, Chief Inspector. Bonaparte is, to all appearances, invulnerable. Right now, he's viewed as the modern savior of France. Hell, he's the new Napoleon. Napoleon's brains, charm, and charisma. But he's dirty, Ambrose."

"Money? Haven't they all been on the take for years? Saddam and Elf Acquitaine and all that rotten business. Doesn't seem to have made one whistle's worth of difference to any of their careers."

"I think Luca Bonaparte coerced Oman into this invasion. China needs oil and oil means money. Huge amounts. He knows everybody. Hell, he was the Foreign Trade minister. And there are far too many rumors around that he murdered his own father when he was fifteen years old. We're going after him on both counts. If we're lucky, and you two succeed, we've got a chance to bring him down without a shot."

"Do you have any new proof of this murder?" Ambrose asked.

"Not yet. That's where you come in. You've read the file. It's a thirty-year-old homicide, still unsolved on the Paris Deuxième's books. It seems likely that Luca was a boyhood bagman for the Union Corse back in Corsica. We think he made his bones by killing his father. And we think the American Mob, which was battling with the Corse in those days, was somehow involved."

"I think I see where you're going. If you can prove that, you might bring him down quickly and with a minimum of international fuss," Ambrose said. "People don't forgive patricide easily."

"That's the idea. We've just uncovered some old French Sûreté case notes. Apparently, two American mobsters were involved in the murder. My case officer in New York believes she has identified two possible suspects. Both quite elderly, but still alive. Possibly residing in New York City."

"When do I start?" Congreve asked, literally rubbing his hands together. "Nothing like a foreign intrigue to take one's mind off troubles at home."

"I've got you on a military transport leaving RAF Uxbridge at noon tomorrow. Arriving in New York in time for supper. Does that work?"

"Splendidly."

"Good. Now you, Alex, how soon can you be ready to travel?"

"First thing in the morning."

"Good. I'm chairing an emergency Gulf States sitrep briefing aboard the USS *Lincoln* at thirteen hundred hours tomorrow. I'd like you to be there. There's an operation still in the planning stages at Langley. An idea Brock had. A good one."

"We're flying out to the *Lincoln* together?"

"No, I'm going out early. You're going to like this. I've lined up a new Joint Strike Force airplane that needs strenuous exercise. I'm talking about the F-35, Alex."

"What?"

"You heard right, Hawkeye," Brick said, smiling. He knew Hawke was crazy to get back in the air. A friend of Brick Kelly's at Britain's Ministry of Defense had told him weeks ago that Lockheed-Martin was looking for a few top British fighter jocks with Harrier VTOL combat experience. They were needed to evaluate the new jet intended to replace the Royal Navy's Sea Harrier FA2.

Alex's face lit up. "The F-35? Never even heard of it."

"Not surprised. It so happens I've landed you an extremely early prototype of the new U.S.-U.K. Joint Strike Fighter. Built in the States by Lockheed-Martin. The most advanced supersonic single-seater in the air. The latest STOVL technology. Apparently, the thing can come to a complete stop in midair. Yours for the duration of this operation, if you don't crack it up. You can practice your night traps. Maybe even your shooting, if you get lucky."

"Shooting?"

"After you download your impressions of the F-35 to the Pratt & Whitney engineers, you're headed to the Gulf. We're implementing Operation Deny Flight, a no-fly zone over northern Oman. You'll hear all about it on the *Lincoln*. And get briefed on what I have in mind for you and Brock."

"Brock? What's he got to do with this?"

"He's going to help you track down the sultan. Let's order some food, shall we?"

Yours for the duration!

Hawke went through the motions of ordering and eating Harry's renowned pasta, but all he could think about was the fact that the navy (probably with a little push from his friend Brick) was putting him back in the saddle. And not some Barney Rubble fighter like he flew in the Gulf War, either. No, a single-seat supersonic stealth fighter just off the drawing board.

Good lord, a man could fly straight to heaven with an airplane like that.

Chapter Twenty-six

Aboard Blackhawke

"DOC SAYS YOU CAN GO HOME," STOKE CALLED DOWN TO JET. She was standing a deck below him, leaning against the portside rail and smoking a cigarette. He watched her from above, saw her gazing out at her home away from home, the giant German yacht *Valkyrie*. The boat still lay at anchor about a half mile away. You had to wonder what the girl was thinking, lost in that cloud of blue smoke, not even hearing what he said, seemed like, zoned.

Stoke had emerged from his stateroom, coming out on the deck to perform his morning ritual: yoga and tai chi exercises and his old SEAL warmup routine. He was wearing his usual outfit, black Viet PJs and the U.S. Army Sniper School T-shirt that Sarge had given him a couple of years ago down in Cuba. The one that said, "You can run, but you'll only die tired." Loved that shirt.

He spaced his bare feet to the width of his shoulders, sucked down a lungful of air, placed his palms together before his face, and saluted the lazy old sun eight or nine times. The sharp iodine bite of the sea air felt good so deep down in his air bags. *Bonjour*, world! Speak to me! The rocky green coastline of Cap d'Antibes was sparkling on this fine morning, whirling birds, big white villas, and sandy beaches below the thick seaside forests. More huge yachts floating at anchor than you could shake a stick at.

After his workout, he used a towel to mop his face and torso and trotted down the curving steel and mahogany stairway leading below. He joined Jet at the rail, giving her plenty of space. He guessed he was still a little fragrant after a couple hundred ab crunches.

"Hey, you," he said.

"Hey, you," she said back, staring out to sea.

"Doc says you're okay."

"That's nice to know."

"Oh. She's in that mood. Okay, great."

Jet was wearing a black-and-gold silk robe that used to belong to Vicky, Stoke thought. Trousseau stuff. Alex had bought it for her in India or Burma somewhere. The idea of Jet wearing it now made him a little queasy, but it probably wasn't a good time to bring it up. Hawke had called. Jet and Stoke needed to have a little talk about the future.

"If you want to go home," Stoke said, "you can. Is all I'm saying. Go home. Stay aboard *Blackhawke*. Either way, the man says it's cool."

Certainly what Stoke would like to do was stay aboard a big yacht on the Riviera. Hell, who wouldn't? The beds were soft, the food was sensational, the morning sun was bright on the water, dancing gold coins on the surface, and white seagulls and terns were diving overhead. Made him kind of hate to leave.

But Hawke had called from the carrier *Lincoln* early this morning, round six. Brought him up to speed on the big CIA briefing out there. He wanted to know all about Jet. How she was doing. What Stoke thought about her. And her German boyfriend, von Draxis. One thing led to another and Stoke suddenly found himself with a brand new mission in life. Boss wanted him to go to Germany. Seemed that CIA guy, Harry Brock, the one they'd snatched off the *Star*, was doing a lot of talking now.

One of the things he talked about was some kind of French-German-Chinese operation. Something code-named Leviathan that originated in Germany. Von Draxis had a heavy hand in it, the boss said. Hawke wanted Stoke to go check out this von Draxis character a little more. Dig, poke, rattle the hometown cages in old Deutschland.

After what the man had done to Jet, that cage, Stoke couldn't think of anything more fun than rattling von Draxis's own cages some more. If it ain't fun, stop. One of Stoke's favorite mottoes.

Last time Stokely had had any real fun at all was down in the Florida Keys. That was a couple of years ago, back when he and Ross Sutherland were chasing that Cuban bad boy Scissorhands and his badass Cigarette boat to hell and gone along the Mosquito Coast of South Florida. Heat 'n Skeet, the SEALs had called that part of the

Keys. That's where Vicky's murderer was running when they'd caught up with him. They caught him all right and stuck his ass in the ground for good on a place called No-Name Island.

"So, what do you think," Stoke said. "See, I'm going to Germany. I could drop you off somewhere. Not that boat over there. That boat is definitely bad for your health, girl."

Jet lit another smoke off the red coal of the old one. Her third since he'd been watching. Girl needed a new program. He had an idea for one that might do her some good.

She said, thinking about it, "Is Schatzi still aboard over there?"

"Der Führer? Hell no, girl, Schatzi's long gone. He left in his big Nazi-black helicopter last night. Winging his way back to his Berlin *flughafen."*

Jet was no longer surprised at the things Stoke knew about Schatzi or the comings and goings aboard the big German yacht. He'd told her a little bit about *Blackhawke's* snooping capabilities. Didn't mention the ship's Aegis Defense System or Towed Array Sonar or any of that stuff. Just told her about how their commo center could eavesdrop on any radio or cell transmission within a radius of twenty miles or so. Triangulate the location, too, though he didn't mention that part.

"So, I could go get my things."

"Yeah, you probably could. What kind of things?" Stoke asked.

"Jewelry. A few clothes. Things I need."

"An acetylene torch so you can hop in and out of bed."

"That's actually funny," she said, coughing up some smoke.

"Thanks. You got a house, Jet?"

"A flat in Paris."

"How about the baron?"

"What do you mean?"

"Where does he live mostly? Good old Schatzi, the lion tamer."

"I don't live with him, if that's what you mean."

"You're not that crazy."

"Are you sure?"

"I'm leaning that way. Where does he live, Jet? I need to know."

"He has houses all over Germany. There is a large one in Berlin. On Friedrichstrasse. Number 7. He also has a secret mountain château in Bad Reichenhall. Huge. A *schloss.* That's 'castle' in Bavarian."

"That's helpful. Thanks."

"Are you going to kill him? Blow him up?"

"How can I? You're in love with the guy, remember?"

She laughed, making a raw sound. "Love? I was young. A somewhat exotic Chinese girl in Berlin trying to get into films. My background was—interesting to him. I'd just started working for the Chinese secret police. He was a successful film producer then. He cast me."

"Happens all the time."

"An escape from my crazy family."

"Have you got a sister, Jet?"

"That's an odd question, isn't it, Mr. Jones?"

"Humor me."

"There's a twin sister. Bianca. We aren't close. Why do you ask?"

"Humor me again."

"She still works for my father. Te-Wu agent. I've no idea where she is. They don't tell me anymore. Tell me about Alex Hawke."

"What about him?"

"What is he like? As a man?"

"Grit clean through."

Girl had no reply to that, just sucked the cigarette coal down to her fingertips and flicked it, jammed another one in the corner of her mouth, and lit up again.

"I like him. Tough outside. Soft inside," Jet said.

Stoke looked at her and asked, "Okay, now you tell me about von Draxis. Why'd he beat you up, Jet? Something to do with Alex Hawke?"

"I'm going back to *Valkyrie*."

"I figured that. They even got a syndrome named for that. Battered Movie Star Syndrome."

"You don't understand. I just want to get my things."

"Good call. Sarge will get someone to run you over there whenever you ready."

"Thank you."

"Don't mention it. You're all torn apart, girl. Hell, you don't know what you want. Mixed loyalties. That's dangerous. I don't let dangerous women get too near Alex. He's been hurt enough."

"He can handle himself."

"Yeah. Normally. Boy pretty much sealed himself up when his wife was murdered. But he likes you, too, for some unknown reason."

"Ridiculous. He doesn't even know me."

"No, it ain't. I like you, too, Jet. Don't trust you worth a damn, but I like you."

"When can I leave all this love?"

"Right now. Listen, Jet. Tell me something before you go. Why did your little pal Schatzi invite my boss to that party?"

"Spice up his guest list? Hawke is famous. He keeps his name out of the papers, but certain people know about him anyway. Schatzi likes to surround himself with famous people."

"Wrong answer. Hawke makes people like Schatzi nervous. Hell, he makes me nervous sometimes and I'm his best friend. One of 'em, anyway. What Schatzi likes is to beat up women. He beat you up, girl! You let him down somehow, didn't you? Was it the green-eyed monster? You and Alex Hawke got a little too close for comfort, that it?"

Jet sucked hard on her cigarette, burning it down to the filter. She looked up at Stokely, smiled, and then flicked the dead butt into the water. A symbolic gesture, they called it.

"Maybe," she said.

"No more maybe. Tell me what all this is about, Jet."

"I was supposed to find out why Hawke was in Cannes."

"Did you?"

"Yes."

"Did your job. So why'd Schatzi get so mad at you?"

"I was disobedient. My orders were to alert my colleague aboard the *Star of Shanghai* if I determined a hostage rescue was in play. I— hesitated. Hawke presented a clear threat and I did nothing."

"What colleague?"

"My subordinate officer was aboard the *Star* with the prisoner. He took responsibility for reacquiring the American agent in Morocco. And returning him safely from France to Hong Kong. He and I work for the Te-Wu. Chinese secret police. I hold the rank of captain."

"Your job to stop Alex, Cap?"

"My job was to kill him. I failed. I'd say my career at this point is pretty much over. Assuming I survive, I have no idea what to do next."

"Kill him how?"

"With this," Jet said, and reached inside the high slit in the silk robe. She pulled out a nasty little gun she must have had strapped to the inside of her thigh.

"You going to not kill me same way you didn't kill Alex Hawke?" Stoke asked, "Are you? Captain?"

Jet held the gun up, loosely pointed at Stokely's left eye. Her gun hand drifted out over the rail for a second, and the pistol fell thirty feet or so to the water. It made a faint splash. More symbolism, Stoke thought, looking at her hard now.

"Jet, this may turn out to be the worst idea I ever had in my whole life. How'd you like a free trip to Germany? All expenses paid."

"You going, too?"

"Absolutely."

"What a pair we'd make. What makes you think I won't betray you?"

"Observed behavior. Love makes people do crazy things. You just changed sides, girl, even though you don't know it yet."

Girl didn't reply and Stoke took that as a yes.

"We got to make one stop first. Pick up your stuff aboard *Valkyrie*. Also, I may need to talk to my friend Admiral Bruno again. How well do you two get along?"

"Bruno has seen every one of my pictures twenty times."

"Does he like you enough to keep his mouth shut?"

"He worships the ground I will walk on in future lifetimes."

"Good. Call Bruno up. Be nice. Tell him you'd like to come back. Like, early this evening. Would he go for that?"

"Yes."

"You think you could occupy his mind for twenty minutes?"

"I think I could."

"Okay. We go soon as it's dark. I like to swim at night."

Half an hour after the sun went down, Jet was aboard *Valkyrie*, finding new and different ways to distract Bruno without letting him anywhere near her. Stoke, in his old SEAL gear, was treading water about two hundred yards from the yacht's bow. He looked at his dive watch. Jet was down in her stateroom by now, collecting her stuff and making goo-goo eyes at fat little Bruno. She had promised Stoke she'd keep him occupied for ten minutes minimum. Stoke thought that should about do it.

He'd dropped Jet off at the starboard-side boarding float. Then he'd gunned the Zodiac out of sight of anybody paying attention on board *Valkyrie*, zigzagging through all the anchored yachts. He found a good spot, threw a small Danforth anchor over the side, and paid out enough line to keep the inflatable hidden behind a big Feadship. Then he slipped over the side and swam the last thousand yards about ten feet below the surface.

When he got to the huge German yacht's bow, he dove deeper, following the hull aft a few feet, inspecting the length of it for camera placement. He saw the first one, mounted in a clear housing suspended from the keel. The lens was moving slowly toward him. The new underwater video surveillance cameras made even the old-fashioned stuff a little tricky. He counted six cameras in all, two fore and aft, two amidships on either side of the keel housing.

That was weird. There was no keel. Maybe it was retracted inside the hull.

He paused for a few seconds, memorizing the different camera cycles while running his fingers along some odd protrusions on the hull. Through-hull fittings. A hairline seam in the steel. And some kind of retracting hatch, it looked like. Big enough to drive a truck through when it was open. What the hell? He swam then, kicking hard and fast, zigzagging through the oscillating cameras, until he reached the sternmost section of the hull. Two cameras remained, outboard of the massive bronze screws.

No divers had splashed. Good sign. His Draeger rebreathing apparatus meant no bubbles were visible on the surface. So he drove his flippers harder, swam through the two aft cameras while they were still both cycling outboard, and then hung in the water off the stern and simply allowed buoyancy to take him up. He surfaced just off the wide stern platform that ran the width of the beam.

This was the area they used for launching sailboards and Jet Skis and other equipment. Empty. Except for one bald-headed guy in a white jumpsuit who emerged through a small door in the hull. The guy stepped out to the edge of the platform and whipped out his willy. What?

Oh, yeah. Drain the lizard. While the bald guy took his pee off the stern, Stoke swam a few silent strokes to the far end of the platform and pulled himself up onto the teak deck.

The guy, still with a good stream going, turned around and looked at the recently arrived monster from the Blue Lagoon. Stoke had seen VC and NVA regs in Nam simply faint dead away at the sight of him appearing suddenly in his SEAL shit on a dark night. This guy didn't faint or do anything much at all.

"How you doing?" Stoke said, getting to his feet. "Water was getting a little warm off the stern."

"What the—"

"Shh. I ain't supposed to be here. Private property."

Stoke saw the guy had a lipmike and was about to use it. He covered the distance between them in one millisecond and smothered the man's mouth with his gloved hand. When he felt teeth biting through the rubber glove, he shut the guy down with two fingers into the neck, collapsing the carotid artery. He put one hand on the unconscious man's chest to hold him up and quickly patted him down. He didn't normally swim with guns, but one might come in handy tonight.

No guns on the guy. Just a glass vial of pills and some kind of weird instrument in a black metal barrel that looked like a very high-tech fountain pen. He'd seen one like it before but couldn't place it. Stuck both items in his waterproof dive bag just for fun. He rolled the guy over the edge into the water and looked back at the narrow through-hull door. There was a keypad beside it, but he wouldn't be needing any entry codes right now. The guy'd figured on a quick squirt so he'd left it open. Mistake.

He stepped inside and was surprised to find himself in a small elevator. He hit the lowest button and it started to move, down and forward. He imagined the thing was on an angled track, running down the keel. Good. Real good. He was very curious about this part of the boat that was so boring nobody needed to see it.

When he stepped out, he was disappointed. He hadn't any idea of what to expect, some kind of Dr. No running around with goggles on his head, maybe, dials and big glass static lightning balls, maybe. But not nothing at all, which was what he found down in the bilges. A huge black space, empty, except for some serious hydraulic machinery. It was mounted above the keel housing that rose from the shiny steel waffle-plated decks.

Having nothing better to do, he walked over to check it out. Below the boat, underwater, he'd noticed the keel was retracted. Which made sense in such shallow water. You needed the keel down only when you were sailing. Otherwise, you kept it stowed right here, winched up inside the hull.

What didn't make sense was that somebody would remove the keel altogether. There was just a big housing, with waves lapping down inside. The twelve-foot-high housing would keep the water out, even if she was heeled hard over. But, still. Stoke had the very strong feeling he was seeing something here that he wasn't supposed to see. Problem being, all he saw was nothing.

The dank oily space reminded him of something he'd seen as a kid. Couldn't place it. Then he did. The bomb bay of a B-52. There were some metal shavings on the floor, like something had been sheared off when the keel was coming out or going in. He bent and picked up a handful. That's when the barrel-shaped thing in his pocket started clicking rapidly. What the hell?

Click-click-click-click-click.

Hell, it was a dosimeter. Measured radiation. He pulled the guard's little glass vial out of his bag and looked at it carefully. Iodine pills. Yeah, okay, iodine. For radiation sickness. Interesting.

He'd have to ask the baron about all this interesting shit next time they got together over some cold Liebfraumilch at his secret villa up in sunny Bavaria.

His big *schloss*.

Chapter Twenty-seven

Gloucestershire

"YOU HAVE HIDDEN TALENTS, AMBROSE CONGREVE," DIANA Mars said. The other guests had departed, leaving the two of them alone for a moment. She had just unwrapped his gift and they had moved outside to the stone flag terrace overlooking the parterre. Beyond the formal garden, the dusky green countryside rolled in a gentle succession of rounded hills down to the silvery ribbon of the Thames.

"Well, it's just a study," Congreve said of the watercolor he'd fussed over endlessly.

"Don't be ridiculous. It's quite good. In fact, it's perfectly lovely. What is prettier than a crabapple in bloom?"

It was dusk, and thin veiled fingers of fog slid over the distant river and into the black trees that crowded the banks. She had surprised him with the invitation to late tea at Brixden House. Called out of the blue, she did, as he was sitting by his solitary library window thinking abstract thoughts and staring at the phone. For some reason, just at that very moment, he realized he had been thinking of Diana Mars. Yes, he certainly had been, he thought as he picked up the telephone and heard her voice.

It was one of those odd little chip shots to the green that the universe is capable of making now and then.

Ambrose had accepted the invitation immediately, realizing just how badly he wanted to see Diana before he left for New York. All business, of course—he needed to apprise her of Scotland Yard's latest thinking in the missing butler case. Sutherland had just given him a new report. But also, he wanted to give her the picture he'd painted of the crabapple that stood outside his kitchen. He'd asked Mrs. Purvis to wrap it in some old Christmas paper he kept folded for just such emergencies. She'd done it, but she hadn't seemed too thrilled about it, for some reason. Women were such curious creatures.

Vexing.

"Ambrose Congreve," Diana had said when they were still standing in her parlor by the window. She'd just opened the picture and she was tracing his signature at the bottom of the watercolor with her delicate white finger. "The name sounds like some sweet old soul in a floppy hat out tending his rosebushes on a rainy spring morning."

"It does?"

"Yes."

"I wonder, shall we step outside for some air?" asked Ambrose, who desperately needed some himself. This floppy-hatted cove she imagined was hardly the robust picture he wished her to have of him. He'd just have to throw more color into the next picture. Perhaps an action scene. A trout rising or a salmon leaping. That might do it.

They moved a bit farther out across the flagstones, near the ornately carved balustrade that overlooked the darkening woods below.

"I have a garden, you know, Diana. Oh, nothing like this, of course. A few dahlias. I'll be at Chelsea this year. With a hybrid I've got high hopes for. If I could only think of a name for it."

Damn it. He was only digging his hole deeper. What on earth was wrong with him?

"I've heard your house is charming, Ambrose." She took his hand and squeezed it briefly before letting go. It sent such a shock rocketing through the system that numbness started traveling up his arm. He scrambled for a reply before the charge could fry his brain completely.

"Really?" he managed to croak out before his jaw could lock up. "From whom?"

"Oh, friends of friends. Friends who know you."

"Really? Who—?"

Ambrose had started to ask which friends and then hesitated. He felt a strange wave, a heady mixture of flattery and confusion wash over him. She was asking around about him, was she? And she was bold enough to admit it. He plowed ahead, willing himself to stay on his feet. He would look ridiculous staggering over to the stone ledge and tumbling arse-over-teakettle into the boxwoods below.

"I say, Diana. You've been an awfully good sport about all this China Doll business. And now that Sutherland and I are off to New York for a week or so, I wonder—are you quite sure you don't want my chaps from the Yard on the property any longer? Sutherland would be delighted with the assignment. I worry about you, to tell the truth. Out here in the country, all alone."

Diana patted his arm in what was meant to be a reassuring gesture.

"All alone? Hardly. One of the blessings my dear husband left me with is hot and cold running servants. Besides, I think you've scared them off, whoever they were. At the window that night. I don't think they were expecting anyone to shoot back."

"Well, I'm not at all sure that is the case. There has been a subsequent incident, which I shall describe to you in some detail. I wonder, has any staff seen hide or hair of your former butler? Oakshott?"

"Not since Scotland Yard was here to question everyone. Poof. I never even had the pleasure of firing him. Why?"

"It seems that last night someone tried to kill my dear friend Alex Hawke."

"Lord Hawke? I don't know him, certainly, but . . . how?"

"A woman. Talked her way into his house. Some ruse or other about car trouble. Pulled a gun and shot him at point-blank range. She missed, but it was a close thing. He was wounded."

"Do you have any idea who she was?"

"Yes. Chinese, actually. Perhaps the twin sister of a woman he met in the South of France. I think it was our friend Bianca Moon paid him a visit."

"Not really?"

"It's the only explanation that makes any sense," Congreve said, tamping down some fresh Peterson's blend into his bowl. "I believe our Bianca and her sister and Mr. Oakshott are somehow complicit in the attempts on my life and Hawke's. All working in tandem, as it were." He was on his own turf now, the solid platform of an investigation, and feeling much less dizzy. He fired up the meerschaum and tried to appear stern and reflective. Floppy hat, indeed.

"What do you really think, Chief Inspector?" Diana asked, after a few long moments had passed. "About all this nonsense?"

"I'll tell you what I think. Would you like to stroll down to the river? There's still enough light left in the sky to walk down and return before dark."

"Lovely idea," she said, looking up. Her eyes were dewy in the fading light.

He got yet another high-voltage shock when he lightly took her hand as they descended the slippery stone steps to the parterre. It was as if she had electrical currents surging through her veins instead of blood like any normal woman. He took a deep breath and hung on, trying to get both of them to the bottom of the mossy steps without breaking any bones. What on earth had gotten into him lately? Buying that yellow Morgan and racing around the glen like a lad on a bender. Not to mention these positively electrifying feelings where Diana Mars was concerned.

It was all most peculiar, he thought, strolling by her side.

Midlife crisis? He supposed he was old enough. Diet? Mrs. Purvis was trying to make him go organic. Lately, she'd been serving something called "free range chicken." Here, he had drawn the line. "Mrs. Purvis," he told her quite sternly, "if a man wishes to eat chicken, do you think he would wish to consume a chicken that has recently been, as you tell me, 'ranging free'? Some wild capon, capering about over hill and dale, wholly unsupervised? No! I think not, Mrs. Purvis! If Ambrose Congreve is to eat chicken, he bloody well wants to know where his chicken has been! Every minute of every day!"

Eating contaminated chickens, then? Or had he simply lost his mind? Perhaps he should consult one of those top brain specialists while he was in New York. Yes. A wise move before he went completely off the rails. And another thing. He had to see to Diana's protection whilst he was gone. He'd speak to Sutherland about it, put that worthy fellow in charge of looking after her.

The ornamental garden was laid out in a formal pattern marked with low evergreen hedges of razor-sharp boxwoods. Now, the loamy beds they bordered were empty, but freshly turned earth indicated the gardeners had been preparing to fill them with annuals. They strolled through the maze of hedges and emerged on the slope that led down to the Thames. The gauzy yellow disc of the sun hung in a banded purplish haze above the horizon.

The view was quite beautiful, and Ambrose stole a glance at Diana. She caught him looking and cut her eyes away. He noticed, however, that she did not remove her hand from his as they walked down toward the river. Miraculously, he found his vocal cords still reasonably operational and he continued his narrative in clear, bell-like tones.

"To continue, Diana. As you well know, I was running a spy at the French embassy. My cousin. He turns out to have been a double agent, working for the Chinese. He disappears without a trace. We learn that a Chinese woman of your acquaintance, assuredly involved in espionage, is responsible. Within that same approximate time frame, Alex Hawke snatches an American agent from a Chinese vessel moored in French territorial waters. And then—good lord, what's the matter with that man?"

"What man?"

"Down there, on the path."

A large man was making his way toward them, loping up the hillside pathway and calling out to them, his hands cupped around his mouth. His shouted words were lost in the wind. But Ambrose believed he had clearly made out the word "drowned."

"It's my head gardener, Pordage. Poor old soul, he'll have a heart attack running up this hill."

"Diana, listen," Congreve said, wanting to shield her from the once seen, never forgotten sight and smell of a submerged corpse, "there's some kind of trouble down there. I'll run down and meet Pordage. Perhaps you should go back up and notify the—"

She'd kicked off her shoes and was flying down the hill toward the river ahead of him.

"He says they've found a body!" she cried over her shoulder.

Chapter Twenty-eight

Paris

THE DATE WAS NOT ACCIDENTAL. IT WAS THE FOURTEENTH of July. Bastille Day. History records that it was on this very day, in the year 1789, that the citizenry of Paris had stormed the Bastille Prison and brought about the surrender of King Louis XVI. Violence had erupted throughout the country. Following the "Terror," many French nobles and men long accustomed to privilege in government, fearing for their lives and their ill-gotten fortunes, had fled abroad.

Those who remained in Paris found themselves, usually with but a semblance of a trial, trudging up the blood-soaked steps to the guillotine. With each thunk of the heavy blade, the *ancien régime* saw that their collective necks were stretched thinner and thinner. The old guard quickly realized that it was no match for the new nation's twin passions, Liberty and Equality, and took to their heels. That was the eighteenth century. The twenty-first had brought new, more volatile passions to old Europe and what the dailies heralded as the New France.

Once again, a lot of heads were on the chopping block.

A flat-screen television monitor, sitting atop a gilded ormolu desk in a corner of the French prime minister's office, showed a live feed of the wild melee now occurring at Orly and Charles de Gaulle airports and at the train and bus stations of Paris. Chaos. At one of the bridges across the Seine, a sea of flashing blue lights and the red beacons of emergency vehicles. Smoke was curling from a burned-out tank and many overturned automobiles.

At daybreak, CRS riot police, one of the groups still loyal to President Bocquet, had clashed with a mob of Bonapartists on the Pont Neuf. Seventeen banner-carrying citizens belonging to an Anglo-American society had died when the exploding tear-gas pellets and a hail of rubber bullets failed to stop their advance toward a protest rally near the Elysée Palace. The now-smoldering tank had opened fire and killed a dozen rioting students before three heroic youths clambered aboard and dropped Molotov cocktails down the opened hatch.

Bonaparte was not watching these disturbing images on the monitor; he had eyes only for the restive crowd gathering beneath his windows. He had his head bent forward and his hands clasped behind his back in the familiar ancestral pose.

"Those who ignore the lessons of history are doomed to repeat them," Luca Bonaparte said softly, quoting Santayana to no one in particular.

The quotation was not lost, however, on his companion.

Bonaparte and a very well-dressed black gentleman stood before an array of tall windows overlooking the palace's large interior courtyard. A narrow bar of sunlight sharply bisected Luca's face; his eyes shone with battle fire. His somewhat cruel mouth was in shadow. In the courtyard and in the surrounding streets below, a seething mob heaved and surged over the cobblestones.

The euphoric horde had been growing all morning, in both size and volume. New estimates were coming into the newly named prime minister's quarters every half hour. The latest aide to enter Bonaparte's gilded offices had calculated the crowd's strength in this arrondissement alone at more than one hundred thousand electrified Frenchmen.

"*Vive le France!*" the masses shouted. "*Vive le roi, vive Bonaparte!*"

"They want a king," the elegant black man observed.

"They shall have an emperor," Bonaparte said.

This was the dream that had lain restive in his mind since the mock battles of boyhood. Luca's lips curled into a wry smile as he lifted his gaze from this amorphous human mass to the sunlit palace wing on the opposite side of the courtyard. There, behind windows much like his own, he could almost make out the shadowy figure of Bocquet himself.

Unquestionably, the current president of France was staring at the selfsame scene below with a growing sense of horror. Luca raised an ornate brass spyglass, bequeathed to this office by Napoleon himself, to his eye.

He twisted the ring and brought the optics into crystalline focus.

"Monsieur le President Bocquet and I share a similar view of this situation," he said to the little black man. "Albeit our reactions to it may not be quite the same."

His companion chuckled appreciatively, his eyes glittering behind his gold pince-nez glasses.

"Everything in life depends on your point of view, My Liege," the man said in his deep new voice. The bone-rattling chuckle, like the nappy white wig, was an essential part of his new disguise.

Bonaparte smiled in appreciation of the Chinaman's bon mot.

After the successful completion of the Sotheby's affair, Hu Xu had shed Madame Li forever. In her place, a foppish African diamond merchant from the Côte d'Ivoire. This smart white-haired gentleman with the startlingly white teeth and the coal-black face had a polished manner and was impeccably dressed. He wore a well-tailored light grey woolen three-piece suit, a patterned red Hermès tie, and mirror-polished black wingtip shoes. A gold watch chain spanned his little belly. And his voice had miraculously dropped from a clipped soprano to a broad basso profundo.

Earlier that morning, the reigning president of France, Guy Bocquet, had appeared on his balcony. Weaned on decades of the adulation of the French populace, he had been shocked at the reaction to his appearance at the balustrade. Sensing the brittle mood of the mob, he had wisely stepped back inside. He hurriedly conferred with his closest political and military advisors. Something must be done. Bocquet could feel his city, his country, his dominion, veering out of control.

And his lifelong friend Honfleur's corpse was hardly cold!

The mood everywhere inside this presidential wing of the Elysée was understandably tense. At 6:00 A.M., Bocquet had ceased taking Bonaparte's telephone calls. The last one Bonaparte had made attempted to reassure the president of his new prime minister's unflagging support at this extremely difficult moment in history. Did the president wish him to step out onto his own balcony and attempt to pacify the mob? In the face of this dripping transparency, Bocquet had hung up without a word. He had then called upon his generals, some present and others by telephone, and ordered Bonaparte arrested.

One of the generals present, Lebouitillier, had swiftly but discreetly disappeared from the suite of rooms and down a long corridor. In a forgotten cloakroom that he frequently used for the purpose, the general whipped out his mobile phone. He was put straight through to Prime Minister Bonaparte and informed him of Bocquet's orders.

"On what charge?" Luca demanded of General Charles Lebouitillier, the loyal (to him) commander of the Ville de Paris Defense Corps.

"Sedition, Excellency," the general said. "Also, suspicion of murder."

"Of whom?" Bonaparte asked. It was not a facetious question. He had murdered, or caused to be murdered, many men in the last few months. The president himself was complicit in some of those crimes. Thus his need for clarification before responding.

"Your predecessor, Excellency. The late prime minister Honfleur."

"I see. Is Bocquet still planning to address the cameras at noon?"

"Yes, sir, he is."

"Two hours. Very well. Slip back into his office. Assure him that plans are well under way for my immediate arrest and imprisonment. Tell him he still has the general army, air force, and the media. How soon will your division be here at the palace?"

"My Third Armored Division left HQ for the palace ten minutes ago. Another division has already begun forming up at the bridges. They will reinforce CRS riot police already in place. A large mob is heading down the Boul St. Mich, ripping up cobblestones and looting. I estimate they should arrive at the bridge in fifteen minutes, Prime Minister."

"Tell me about this mob."

"Led by that damned fool L'Espalier. Carrying banners, huge Chinese puppets with your face on them, shouting treason and murder, that it was you killed their beloved Honfleur. Calling for your head, Prime Minister."

"Any sign of violence from this insurrectionist mob and your men are to fire upon them without mercy. A rebellion must be put down at all costs. For the well-being of the state. You understand me, General?"

"Certainly, sir."

"However, I must make it clear to you that this latest writ to preserve the peace with armed force comes directly from the hand of the president himself. I hold the original copy with his signature in my hand. Convey this to all: It is the president alone who has ordered you to fire on our own people. Not me. I want the media to know that the president has not consulted me in this matter. And that, time and again, I have registered my fervent opposition to murdering our citizens. I am a man of the people. Any questions at all?"

"None, sir. God bless you. *Vive le France.*"

"Good. Keep me posted. *Vive le France.*"

Luca turned to the Chinaman. "I will save this country if I have to kill every damn citizen to do it," he said.

"Spoken like a true visionary," Hu Xu replied without a trace of irony. "There'll be no blood on your hands, Excellency. Bocquet will do it for you. His cannons will send them running to you for salvation."

Luca laughed. He'd developed something approaching affection for the little madman. He said, "Well, are you ready to play your next role on the world stage, my friend?"

Hu Xu bowed slightly from the waist. "Give me but a minute, Highness," he said, and turned away.

He opened the alligator valise he had carried into the office ten minutes earlier. In it were all his worldly possessions at the moment, including, in a black mesh cage, a medium-sized brown rat gnawing with spiky little teeth on a hunk of bone. At Sotheby's, he had sliced off one of Hubert's fingers as a treat for his pet. He took the rat from his cage and cradled him in one arm, stroking the sharp ridge of his slick back. Hu Xu looked up at Luca, beaming.

"Would you hold my little kamikaze a second, while I prepare his harness? His name is Chou, by the way."

"Hold that disgusting animal? Good God, no," Luca said, "are you insane?"

It was a moot point and Hu Xu let it go. "All right, back in your cage, *mon petite* Chou," he said, putting the oily creature back inside. Out of the valise came a small wooden spool mounted on a tiny leather harness of his own design. The harness was adjustable, with Velcro fasteners, and looked to be a good fit for the rat Chou. On the spool, about one hundred feet of ceramic wire with a thin gel coating. The wire was clad with rubbery, plasticized C4 explosives. "Bomb wire" was a creation perfected by the labs aboard the Hong Kong headquarters of General Moon.

The idea of the rat belonged to Hu Xu.

He carefully unfolded an old blueprint, an elevation and schematic of the Elysée Palace done at the time of the last restoration. The section he needed was heavily marked with red pencil. It showed a small anteroom just off the Salon Napoleon where even now cameras were being set up for Bocquet's address to the nation. It was Bocquet's standing practice of many years to sit alone at a simple wooden table in the small room and read his prepared remarks aloud, one final time, before entering the grand salon.

"We have two hours," Bonaparte said, looking at his watch.

"This shouldn't take long," Hu Xu said, stripping off his jacket, waistcoat, and tie. He removed a white coverall from his case and stepped into it. He yanked up the plastic zipper and then placed the flat blue hat of the palace Maintenance brigade on his head. Luca opened a locked drawer and snatched up a high-level security badge with Hu Xu's blackened face and signature already laminated in place. In addition, he gave the Chinaman a special security authorization from the president's office in the event that the man was challenged at any point during his mission.

Hu Xu slid the laminated ID card into its sleeve on his breast pocket. He wasn't expecting to be challenged, but he'd spent an hour in front of his mirror practicing the sort of outraged gutter French that would send anyone who bothered him scurrying for cover. He placed the hungry rat, Chou, into a smaller case, the one Maintenance used for tools and other standard equipment.

"You can keep the bag," Hu Xu said, handing Bonaparte the alligator-skinned valise. "It's a good one. Well. I leave you to your destiny."

"*Au revoir et bonne chance,* Master Hu Xu," Luca said, taking the man's offered hand. "We shall work together again. For the glory of our two nations."

Ten minutes later, Hu Xu was alone in the anteroom off the salon. Eight leather chairs stood around a heavy writing table in the center of the room. He had locked both doors from the inside. In the excitement gripping the palace, his passage through the hallways had gone wholly unnoticed. He knelt in one corner, behind a large settee, and used a small hacksaw to cut through the baseboard of the wall. He then punched a fist-sized hole in the plaster with a ball hammer. Fetid air escaped. He now had access to the wall's interior. He stuck his hand inside and determined that his blueprints were correct: There was a good three inches of space between the walls.

"Be patient," he whispered to the rat, Chou, "your moment of glory is coming."

In the courtyard beyond the small room's ground-floor windows, he could hear the mob chanting Bonaparte's name. One side singing his praises, the other cursing his name, they were united only by a common loathing for America. There was a rising hysterical note in the chorale he hadn't heard earlier. Well, it was certainly out of his hands now. As he neared his exit, Fate was taking the stage.

With any luck at all, someone would pull a gun and shoot a palace guard. Then President Bocquet's troops would open fire on the mob. At that point, Luca Bonaparte would step in front of the guns himself. A single raised hand would silence them. Bonaparte would ride to glory on the shoulders of the people, the savior and hope of all France.

A new and glorious beginning.

That was the plan, anyway. Hmm. He crawled around the table to the opposite side of the room and made a fresh hole of the same dimension there. He then withdrew a foil-wrapped block of Roquefort cheese from the tool kit. Unwrapping it, inhaling its fragrant aroma, he placed the cheese on the dusty floorboards inside the wall. He then tacked the baseboard back into place and used a bit of sawdust in a brown shoe-polish base to hide any trace of his alterations. He rocked back on his haunches and admired his work. Perfect.

"Hungry?" he asked the rat. He already knew the answer. He had been starving him for forty-eight hours.

Scurrying over to his original hole, where Chou waited impatiently in his cage, he took out the spool of C4, ran off a foot or two, and tacked the bitter end to the wooden floor just inside the opening. Next, he clipped a detonator to the wire and set it to receive a radio signal rather than one from the default mode, a digital timer.

All that remained was to strap Chou into his little harness.

"Ah, my pretty one," he said soothingly as he took the rat out of his cage. "Your time to shine at last has come." The rat was one of several that Hu Xu had mission-trained for just such work in China. His technique of using rats to run explosive lines behind walls, under floors, and over ceilings was in its infancy. Hu Xu was using the assassination of the president of France as an early test bed of the protocol. It was a singular measure of his confidence in his abilities.

General Moon was deeply interested in the success of this mission, naturally. China's plans and the meeting of its long-term energy needs depended in large measure on the succession of Bonaparte to the office of president of France. Although Hu Xu was supremely confident, he had chosen the rat that had demonstrated the most courage and ability to overcome unseen obstacles once it left his sight. Chou had been first in her class. She had arrived from Hong Kong by diplomatic courier just the night before. Chou could smell the cheese on his fingers and nipped greedily at them, drawing a bit of blood. Tsk-tsk, he said to the rat, soothing her.

He secured the Velcro straps under Chou's belly. The rat's tiny claws were snickering on the polished hardwood floor, desperately trying to gain purchase. Chou now had the scent of the Roquefort wafting through the walls from the far side of the room. Nothing would stop her now.

She would literally go through walls to achieve her objective.

Hu Xu placed the squirming rat inside the hole. The animal paused on its haunches, pawing the air, sniffing the dank odors within the ancient walls, her wet black nose held high and twitching feverishly. Then, she rocketed away with a hum of wire, the spool on her back spinning furiously as the C4 unwound. The rodent raced through the dark, compacted rubble of centuries in search of her supper.

"*Pauvre petite* Chou," he whispered to himself. Poor thing. The rodent would soon be suffering grievous constriction and spasms in her circulatory system. He had spiked the cheese with just enough rat poison to kill a small dog. Don't want her retracing her steps now, do we?

No. Covered in soot, dust, and debris, the rat finally reached her target. She ripped the foil aside and began gnawing furiously at the pungent supper, wolfing down the pride of Roquefort. Her spool was empty. A hundred feet of high-velocity explosive wire now encircled the room. There was enough plastique C4 in these walls to bring down a good-sized building.

Chou expired on the spot.

The assassin carefully replaced the last bit of baseboard and meticulously erased any trace of his alterations. Only then did he look at the new Tank watch on his wrist. It had taken him only twelve minutes to set the "rat trap," as he called his new technique. Hu Xu unzipped and stepped out of his coveralls and doffed his hat. Returning that wardrobe to the tool case, he stood and straightened his tie, inspecting himself in a large gilt mirror.

His blackface needed a little touch-up, which he did, but otherwise this new being he inhabited would serve him well for a day or two in London. He'd booked a suite at the Dorchester, a luxurious hotel he found conveniently located just across Park Lane from Hyde Park. Because General Moon's daughter had failed yet another assignment, he had an appointment with a certain Lord Alexander Hawke. This British gentleman, codenamed "Pirate."

And so to England!

When he unlocked the ornate anteroom door and stepped outside into the corridor, it was as if he had boarded a sinking ship loaded to the gunwales with human rats. He wrinkled his nose in disgust. The stink of panic was upon the place. Diplomats and secretaries, staffers and military personnel, all running through the palace halls, whispering into their cradled mobile phones and into each other's ears in a rising cacophony of fear:

What is the president going to say to the cameras?

Is Bocquet to step down? There are riots in Toulon!

And what of Bonaparte? He says we are weeks away from sending troops into Oman? Are we no better than the fucking Americans?

Hu Xu turned a corner into a wide corridor and swam upstream in the onrushing river of bureaucrats. Here were more shouts than whispers:

Who will stop the carnage in the street?

We're on the brink, I tell you! A second Revolution!

Can you get me on a plane? How should I know!
Any fucking plane, you idiot!
MON DIEU!
Après moi, le grand déluge, Hu Xu whispered to himself.

The cowards, chewing pencils and dropping papers, scurrying by with their nervous, frightened eyes, didn't even notice him.

He made his way down a narrow set of stairs leading to a vestibule and a small side door. This was the very door to the side street used by the late unlamented Honfleur and the sultan of Oman only yesterday. When last seen around midnight, the once-mighty sultan was still alive. But he had been bound and gagged, loaded into the back of a limousine, and was on his way to the airport. A small chartered jet would return him to Oman. There, he would be secreted away, a prisoner in his own palace.

Just as he was being bundled into the car, Madame Li had bent and kissed him on the lips. Poor old dear. He looked so frightened.

Stepping lightly out into the street in his highly polished shoes, the elegant black gentleman motioned to a big black Peugeot idling on the opposite curb. The liveried driver, one of General Moon's Te-Wu policemen in Paris, smiled his recognition as he swung open the rear door. Hu Xu entered and they slipped into the heavy traffic, honking its panic.

"*Vive la Nouvelle Napoleon!*" the Chinese driver said over his shoulder as he placed a flashing blue light on the dashboard.

"Screw Napoleon," Hu Xu replied with a laugh. "*Vive les Chinois!*"

Hu Xu relaxed back into the leather seat. The assassin had the satisfied and reverent air of one who had successfully completed his mission and learned much from his sojourn. The savior of France was in fact an inspiration. Before this trip, Hu Xu's god had been Moon. Now, there were two all-powerful deities whirling in his heavens. Two giants would soon be standing astride the world. On their shoulders, a chameleon whispering evil deeds in their ears.

Two hours later, as Hu Xu stood on the tarmac beside the small Citation V that would ferry him to England, his mobile silently vibrated. He flipped it open and said, "Yes?"

"Is there cheese in the trap?" a voice asked in Chinese. It was the general's PR man, Major Tony Tang. The man in the grey flannel suit.

"Indeed there is."

"Spring it."

"As you wish, Major."

"One more thing. Developments in London mean your presence is no longer required there. Your appointment with the Lord of the Manor is postponed, unfortunately. There is a problem at the New York office. An unfortunate blemish on Monsieur Bonaparte's record that needs to be erased immediately. I'm afraid you shall have to fire two of his former employees. Terminate them as quickly as possible. Bianca will explain it all to you when you arrive in New York."

"Bianca is no longer with our London office?"

"It was Bianca who discovered the CIA's sudden interest in the two old employees. She will contact you when you arrive in New York," Tang said, and hung up.

Hu Xu looked at his phone, savoring the moment, and once more keyed in the talismanic number. History, once reminded of this number, would never again forget it.

One . . . seven . . . eight . . . nine . . .

Send.

Chapter Twenty-nine

The Cotswolds

"WHO FOUND HIM?" CONGREVE ASKED THE HEAD GAR-
dener, Jeremy Pordage. Mr. Pordage was a stout, wheezy fellow. His
cheeks were flushed bright red and he smelled faintly and not un-
pleasantly of manure. Panting mightily, he produced a pleasant two-
toned whistle as he inhaled and exhaled. He placed a rough red hand
over his heart as if to calm it, and Ambrose was startled at the sheer
size of the hand. The mud-caked fingers were horny, twisted and
gnarled like the roots of an old elm.

Diana stood right behind the man, peering round his shoulder.
She was striving mightily to give the impression of not staring at
the thing hung up in the river. Death is absolute, Congreve had long
observed, but there is nothing more dead than a floater. He raised
his eyes to escape the sight. On the farther bank, timid willows
stepped daintily down to the stream. They seemed to be testing the
ochre waters with their delicate wands before fully deciding to take
root.

The body was hanging face-down underwater, near the edge of
the muddy riverbank. The head had fouled in the crook of a partially
submerged tree. The arms and legs were dangling down, animated by
the swirling current. A grey hand broke the surface of the water, then
slid back down into the murk. A second gardener, a sturdy boy of
about ten or twelve, was standing atop the half-rotted and uprooted
trunk, trying to pull the body ashore without falling in himself.

"The boy and me, we did, sir," old Pordage said. "Found him just as
you see him, we did. Here, Graham, use this. I'll help you haul him
out." Pordage handed the boy his long-handled rake. After a few tries,
using the rake as a gaff, the boy was able to hook the corpse under
one arm and pull it away from the fallen tree. The head popped free

and bobbed to the surface, the face grotesquely swollen, slick and grey with fat rubber lips.

"It's Henry," Ambrose whispered to himself, although he was not entirely sure.

Pordage and the boy stood impassive. After the excitement of discovery, the corpse seemed of no more consequence than the perpetual forest deadwood that needed clearing.

"Oh!" Diana said, and then she was silent.

"I'm Chief Inspector Congreve, Scotland Yard," Ambrose said quietly to the gardener. Old Pordage gravely nodded his white head and took Congreve's measure. The dead were not impressive, but policemen were.

"I know well enough who you are, sir," he said, lifting his cap. "Honored to meet you. The boy there is my grandson, Graham. He's a groundsman, now."

"Hello, Graham," Congreve said to the boy, who was now looking at him, making his own appraisal. Graham Pordage had his gumboots planted firmly on either side of the old stump and was grappling with the body, carefully working the corpse in close to the bank. The victim was not a large man, Congreve could see now. Medium height, slender. Expensive shoes.

"Are you really a policeman, sir?" the boy asked, over his shoulder. He had a grasp on the head and torso, the body face-down, almost halfway up the steep muddy bank. Just then the boy lost his tenuous grip and the corpse slipped back under.

"I am indeed," Ambrose said.

"Scotland Yard, Graham," the grandfather added as he bent to help his grandson with his awkward burden. They had him firmly now, half in, half out of the water.

"Mr. Pordage, think back for a moment, please. To that instant when you first observed this body. Before you disturbed the scene in any way. Did you see any signs of a struggle here? Were there any tracks here along the bank? Footprints? Tire treads in the woods?"

"None at all, Inspector. We believe this gentleman must have floated downstream. Snagged up in that fallen tree there maybe sometime late this afternoon. We were by this way twice before. Once at noon, and once again around four o'clock, and there was nary a body in sight then, sir."

"No trace of blood anywhere, I don't suppose."

"None that I could make out, sir. Getting on dark already when we first spotted him. We were just trying to free him up when we saw you and her ladyship up there on the hill."

"Don't put him on the ground," Diana said, seemingly unperturbed by the sight of the dead man. She quickly shed her oiled all-weather coat and spread it on the mucky ground. When she was finished, Pordage and his son carefully lay the body face-up upon it. The clothes were sodden, and water and other, possibly less pleasant fluids gushed out of his trouser legs and the sleeves of his macintosh. The face was grey, the eyelids swollen horribly shut, the mouth gaping open and full of leaves, twigs, and irregular teeth.

"It's Henry, Diana," Ambrose said, with all the emotion of one who has seen Monday follow Sunday.

He had his penlight out and was playing it about the skull. Thin strands of dark reddish hair were plastered to the chalky pate. Bright orange wisps they would be in the light of day. Ambrose put one knee in the muck and gently peeled the eyelids back, first the left, then the right. He bent forward with his penlight, shining the thin beam directly into the fish-dead eyes. Then he picked up the left hand, the fingers wrinkled by immersion, and held it for a second, then let it drop to the ground.

"Hmm," he said, getting back to his feet.

"What does that mean, hmm?" Diana Mars asked.

"Nothing much. Extremities are rigid. Rigor mortis. Left eye is normal, right eye is completely dilated."

"And what does that mean, Ambrose?"

"Blunt force trauma. An unseen blow to the head, I would say, based on the complete lack of defensive wounds to the hands. We'll see what the forensic lads have to say. We should go up and call immediately, Lady Mars. Now, Mr. Pordage, I would ask that you and your grandson remain here with the body until the police arrive. It shouldn't be long. I'm sure they'll have more questions for you. The SOCOs, those are the Scene of Crime officers, will interview both of you in some detail. Please try not to leave out anything, no matter how seemingly insignificant."

"I'll certainly do my very best, sir."

"That's all anyone can ask."

"He's a relative of yours, sir?"

"My cousin. How did you know?"

"You said, 'It's Henry,' sir. Everybody on the place has been asked about Henry Bulling. Shown his picture. Didn't recognize him, myself. I'm sorry for your loss, Inspector."

Ambrose thanked him, took Diana's arm, and turned to go.

He had a thought and it stopped him dead in his tracks.

"One more thing, if you don't mind, Mr. Pordage?"

"Certainly not, sir."

"You haven't by any chance seen her ladyship's former butler, Oakshott, about, have you? I mean, since your chance pub encounter at the Feathers?"

"No, sir, I have not seen hide nor hair of that gentleman."

"I seen him, sir," Graham Pordage suddenly said. "I seen Mr. Oakshott. Just this very morning."

"You did?" Ambrose said, turning to the boy.

"What's that?" his grandfather said, his face reddening with anger. "You never said a word, boy."

"I didn't, Grand, and I am most truly sorry now that—that—that we found that body."

"Why didn't you tell your grandfather you had seen Oakshott, Graham?" Diana Mars asked, looking at the boy evenly. "You certainly knew the police were looking all over Gloucestershire for him, didn't you, child?"

" 'Cause I wasn't at all sure it was him, ma'am, is the reason. And he was always kind to me, he was, Oakshott. When he was in service, I mean. Before he became a murderer."

Ambrose said to the boy, "What makes you now think Oakshott's a murderer?"

"I think it was Mr. Oakshott killed that dead man right there, sir."

"I see. This is a very serious charge. You're accusing a man of murder, Graham. There's nothing to be afraid of, but you must tell me precisely what happened. Starting with exactly what you saw this morning."

"Well, that's the thing, sir. I didn't see him, to be honest."

"You did not see him?"

"No, sir. And that is—I mean, which is why I was afraid to say that—I had seen him. I didn't. I heard him, is what happened, sir."

"You heard him. Where? How?"

"I was havin' me morning tea as usual, I was, sir. Under Cobble Bridge, the old footbridge is where I like to have it. About a mile upstream from here. A half mile beyond Spring Cottage. Beans on toast, sir, and my cuppa. Isn't that right, Grand?"

"Aye, he does. That's the truth."

"Go on," Ambrose said.

"I guess I drifted off a bit, sir. The sun was barely up and I hadn't quite awoked. That's when I heard 'em. Footsteps over me head. And two men shoutin'. One was shoutin'. The other, not so much."

"What were they shouting about?"

"Couldn't rightly say, sir, could I? The one, I thought I recognized his voice as that of the gentleman formerly in service, Mr. Oakshott, he was telling this other bloke, whose voice I did not recognize, that it was all his fault. That he ought to kill him for what he done. That he ought to blow his brains out. The other one, I could tell he was sore afraid. Then—"

"Then, what?"

"They was fightin' right above me head, sir. Terrible struggle, wasn't it? Both of 'em not sayin' anythin', just grunting and hitting. I put me hand over me mouth so they wouldn't hear my breathin' so hard, sir, I was so afraid. Then one a'them, he must have thrown something in the river. There was a splash, right about in the middle where the current is strongest. That's when the one ran off, sir. I heard him crashing into the woods. T'other one, Mr. Oakshott, he chased after him and I ran off the other way, sir."

"Was it a gun? That went in the river?" Congreve asked.

"I couldn't rightly say, sir."

"And you kept this all to yourself all day long?" Ambrose asked.

"Aye. I didn't want Mr. Oakshott to come to any trouble on my account. And I was afraid I'd seen something bad, sir."

"You did, Graham," Ambrose said. "And the Yard will be grateful if you can—"

"Oh," Diana cried.

There was an awful noise as something shifted inside the corpse and a large bubble of thin grey gruel appeared on Henry Bulling's lips, popped, and trickled from the side of his mouth.

Diana clung to Ambrose and he put his arm around her shoulders. She was trembling.

"There, there, Diana," he said, patting her upper arm.

This time when he touched Diana Mars he didn't feel any electric shocks or a frightening frisson.

He felt only softness and warmth.

Chapter Thirty

Aboard the USS Lincoln

"HELL OF AN AIRPLANE," THE NEW AND IMPROVED CIA MAN Harry Brock said, squinting his brown eyes in the midafternoon sun. The wind was out of the northeast and ripping whitecaps from the crests. Large ocean swells of clear turquoise water were heaving the broad steel deck fore and aft. Brock and Alex Hawke were standing on the USS *Lincoln*'s flight deck along with a group of sailors, fellow admirers who'd come up on deck to take a look at the future.

The experimental stealth fighter had drawn a crowd as soon as Hawke touched down six hours earlier. The F-35 Strike Fighter would soon complement or replace all the U.S. Navy F/A18 Super Hornets it now shared the carrier deck with. And, pending further development and the rigorous assessment of many more former U.K. combat aviators like Hawke, the Royal Navy would shortly be flying F-35s instead of the Sea Harriers.

The plane Hawke had landed on the *Abraham Lincoln*'s flight deck early that morning was simply the most advanced piece of flying machinery on earth. Capable of speeds approaching Mach 3, the single-seat supersonic fighter could also stop in midair. Literally, as Hawke had learned to his delight on his flight out from RAF Uxbridge. Fighter jocks liked this feature. It meant that when you hit the brakes in a dogfight, your pursuer rocketed past you to become your prey in a nanosecond. Confused the living hell out of them before they died.

The supercarrier USS *Abraham Lincoln* (CVN 72) was the flagship of the *Lincoln* Carrier Strike Group currently on station in the Indian Ocean. At 660,000 tons, with four and a half acres of flight deck, and in excess of six thousand men and women on board, it took two nuclear reactors generating a half-million horsepower to move her at battle speeds through the water. The good news was, once her reactors were topped off she was good for fifteen to twenty years without stopping for gas.

On orders from the navy's Seventh Fleet, the *Lincoln* was now proceeding from a port visit in Hong Kong, steaming due west at flank speed some two hundred miles southwest of Sri Lanka. Neither Hawke nor Brock had been made privy to her ultimate destination; of course, they were only aboard for the emergency powwow recently hosted by the *Lincoln's* new skipper, Admiral George Blaine Howell, and CIA director Brick Kelly. It had been a long meeting, full of bad news and frightening scenarios.

Hawke had been asked a question by Howell toward the end. "Commander Hawke," the admiral said, "you've been very quiet during this briefing. You've seen all the projections, all the war-gaming, all the scenarios. The buildup of Chinese troops in the Gulf. I'd like to know what you think the navy's strategy for dealing with this goddamn Chinese situation ought to be."

"I think there's only one long-term strategy for dealing with the Chinese Communist Party, Admiral Howell."

"And what might that be, Commander?"

"We win, they lose."

Howell had looked at him for a second and then a smile broke across his face.

"I think Commander Hawke has pretty well summed up my feelings as well, gentlemen. Any further comments? No? Thank you, everyone. Dismissed."

Another bloody meeting, blessedly, over. Afterward, as the smoke cleared, Brock had ambled over to the corner where Hawke and Director Brickhouse Kelly were huddled in serious conversation. Brock waited at a discreet distance until the talk was over, then approached Hawke. He asked if he minded if Harry followed him down to Flight Ops. There were a number of things they needed to discuss, he said.

Brock wanted to see the plane, and he wanted to thank Hawke personally for snatching him from the Chinese. And the director had told Brock the night before he would be working with the Brit on an extremely sensitive mission in the Gulf. First, Hawke was to test the new no-fly zone the Americans had in place over Omani airspace:

Operation Deny Flight. Then he was to link up with Brock on the ground.

This was an operation authorized by Hawke's old flame Conch. Consuelo de los Reyes was the American secretary of state. She and Alex had a complicated past. It involved an on-again-off-again romance that just wouldn't seem to die. For now, the best word to describe their relationship was comatose. Hawke had made a serious mistake. He'd gone running to Conch when his wife had been murdered. Deliberately or not, she'd misunderstood his intention. He'd only been looking for a port to weather the storm. She'd thought the mooring was to be permanent.

Now, after long months of tears and bickering, their relationship was back on a business footing.

De los Reyes had picked up hard intel from an asset inside the Muscat embassy. She'd learned that the sultan had been smuggled back into Oman and was possibly still alive although held hostage. Conch had decided that Hawke and Brock were to lead the small task force that would slip into Oman and gather hard intelligence on the sultan's possible whereabouts. It was a straightforward assignment. Find him, get him out, get him in front of a camera speaking the truth about Bonaparte's ruse. To discredit the Frenchman would go a long way toward resolving the current crisis without a war.

Oman is widely reputed to be one of the most inhospitable places on earth. Hawke was hardly surprised to learn Conch was sending him there. But, Brock? What the hell did she have against him? Brock was apparently headed straight to Oman, catching a ride aboard one of the Agency's Citations. He would coordinate Kelly's CIA operatives now moving from Saudi Arabia into Oman. Locate the sultan. Then he and Hawke would have to get him out.

Hawke had barely recognized Harry Brock. It had been well over two weeks since he'd last seen him. His eyes were clear. The shaggy hair and beard had been shorn, and Brock looked tanned and very fit. Part of his recovery had clearly taken place in the weight room. The broken, drugged, and wasted prisoner Hawke had found in the filthy storeroom aboard the *Star* was gone.

"Holy Jesus," Brock now said, staring at the jet fighter. "Thing looks like the tip of a spear. Most beautiful damn airplane I've ever seen."

"Yeah," Hawke said. He couldn't take his eyes off the airplane either. Viewed from any angle it was a powerful work of engineering art. He was anxious for the techs who'd flown out to the carrier from Pratt & Whitney Europe to complete their work so he could climb back into that seat and light the monster up again.

One of the techies had found a glitch with the F-35's STOVL nozzle while Hawke was in Admiral Howell's briefing. Part of the new propulsion system was a nozzle that directed exhaust gases for short takeoff and vertical landing capability. The STOVL system was working beautifully when Hawke took off in England and also when he had landed. But brand new fighters were full of surprises.

The techs had fixed that particular glitch, the Pratt & Whitney rep had told him, but they were still checking and rechecking the entire aircraft. A discernible glitch often hid an indiscernible glitch. The obsessive tech squad's exhaustive inspection was understandable. Hell, it was a fifty-million-dollar airplane. And, although it had been in development for ten years, the lift fan and propulsion system was still in P&W's System Development and Demonstration Phase. Translation: It had taken the better part of a decade and they'd got a lot of the bugs out. But maybe not all of them.

Hawke had already completed his own preflight inspection. But right now, at least ten guys were crawling all over his airplane. He was supposed to be airborne in thirty minutes. His next stop was an airfield in Italy where U.S. and U.K. representatives of the Joint Strike Force fighter project were waiting to debrief him. From there, he had just learned in the briefing, he would be flying the plane to Oman.

"You some kind of test pilot, Hawke?" Brock asked.

"I guess I am now. Used to be an ordinary fighter jock."

"Is that an upgrade or a downgrade?"

"Beats me. But it's some ride."

"Bat out of hell, huh? Christ, it looks like one."

"More interesting than fast. The damn thing has a mind of its own. Practically flies itself."

"What do you mean?"

"Hard to explain. That airplane takes advice, not orders. It's always one step ahead. You even think about something, the plane does it. You think, Okay, I'll pull the nose up fifteen degrees, right? Sorry. Airplane's already done that."

"Just don't think about crashing," Brock said with a wry smile.

"Never crosses my mind."

"Good. We got a lot of work to do in the next few weeks, you and me."

"Right. My new partner. The director just told me. Whose mind did that wicked idea spring forth from?"

"Don't look at me, sir. I'm just a lowly field wonk."

"Just because I saved your life doesn't mean I have to dance with you."

Brock laughed. "Somebody at Langley thinks we're good casting is all I can tell you, Hawke. Listen, I gotta ask you this. You think we'll go to war with China? Is that where we're headed?"

Hawke looked at the American carefully and considered his heavily loaded question. He liked the man well enough, and he'd just learned he was going to be working with him; at some point he had to trust him. But he hardly knew the guy. Brick Kelly had told him Brock was mean and clean. The CIA docs had finally determined that the Chinese hadn't planted any bugs in his brain. They'd eliminated the Manchurian Candidate scenario completely.

Agent Harry Brock, Brick said, knew more about what the hell was going on inside China than anyone else at Langley. The intel he'd gathered during six months inside her borders was one of the key reasons so much brass had gathered here on the *Lincoln*. Because of what Brock had been able to learn, the current mood in Washington and London was more than a little tense. As a result, everybody in both capitals was tiptoeing around, walking on eggshells these days. Times like this, you wanted to watch every word you said.

So Hawke said, "I think they're testing our resolve. What do you think, Brock?"

Over the American's shoulder, Hawke saw crew disconnecting the external power lines that ran across the deck to the gleaming F-35. It was a hopeful sign he'd be airborne shortly.

Brock said, "Hell, Hawke, I think we're back in the nuclear soup is what I think."

Hawke just looked at him.

Brock shook his head as if trying to clear the cobwebs. He was edgy. Hawke was edgy. Hell, everybody was. According to everything the two men had heard in the last three hours, the whole bloody world was going to hell in a handbasket. It looked like a return to the bad old days of a nuclear standoff and mutually assured destruction. Yesterday, a huge bomb had blown the French president Guy Bocquet sky high along with one whole wing of the Elysée Palace. France was teetering on the brink of revolution.

The last thing they'd seen in the briefing room was French television video of cheering throngs held back by police cordons as Bonaparte rode up the Champs Elysées on a big white stallion. Kind of picture you didn't forget.

The new French government, now firmly in Bonaparte's hands, had just announced it was seriously considering the sultan of Oman's invitation. Many in France viewed this as an invasion of a sovereign Gulf state, but no one dared say such things openly anymore. Oman was a small nation of some three million souls that had had a long and important relationship with both Britain and America. But the leadership of France was claiming they'd been "invited" into Oman by the reigning sultan, the British-educated Aji Abbas.

The clip of the missing sultan's press conference ran endlessly on France 2 television. In it, the sultan claimed French troops were desperately needed to quell a radical insurgency supported by the People's Democratic Republic of Yemen.

Kelly wasn't buying it. Nor was the American president. It was, they both believed, a French fabrication backed by Chinese muscle. The sultan had disappeared shortly after his speech. The United States had Omani intel indicating that the sultan's family was under house arrest in a former seaside fortress on the coast of Oman. Why? The Americans knew the men holding them there were French secret service and military abetted by a large number of Chinese "technical advisors." In any case, Hawke was fairly certain neither his country nor the Americans would just stand idly by and let France invade Oman.

There was now a French diplomatic mission in the capital of Muscat ironing out the logistics of the impending French deployment. And sat photos depicted a squadron of French Mirage fighters parked on the ramp at Oman's Muscat Airfield.

As of this morning, Oman still honored an understanding to allow the United States to use port and air base facilities. Hawke's first F-35 mission was to test that understanding. He was to enter Omani airspace unannounced and land at Muscat International. See if anybody tried to shoot him down. Meet briefly with airport authorities and then get the hell out of there and report what he'd seen. Both America and Britain, who still imported Oman's oil, had a vested interest in the tiny country's sovereignty. Economically, politically, and morally.

It should come as a surprise to no one that the *Lincoln* Carrier Strike Group was now headed for the Indian Ocean. From there, it was an easy move north into the Gulf of Oman. The interesting part would come when they encountered the Chinese fleet, now en route to join forces with the French.

"Commander Hawke," a young naval aviator said, saluting him. Late twenties, he wore a fore-and-aft khaki hat cocked over one eye, a lieutenant's silver bars glinting in the sun.

"Yes?"

"I've been instructed by the JSF chief technical officer to inform you that your aircraft tech check is complete, sir. She's certified airworthy and she's all yours. I've got to say I'm just a little bit jealous, sir."

"I'm jealous of myself," Hawke said.

Hawke saluted and turned back to Brock.

He said, "See you in Oman, Harry. Wine, women, and song."

"Something like that, I'm sure," Brock said, laughing. "Hey, Hawke, hold up. I forgot something."

"Yeah?"

"I have to say this and I mean it. Wasn't for you, I wouldn't be standing here. Or anywhere else, for that matter."

"Just doing my job, Brock," Hawke said, smiling at him.

Hostage rescue, the gift that kept on giving. He turned and made for his plane. As he climbed the boarding ladder up to the cockpit and dropped his helmet bag down in the seat he heard a few "at-taboys" and "give 'em hells" lobbed in his direction from the crew-men standing around his plane. He paused, then, frowning, he climbed aboard.

So word was already out. They knew he was headed to the Gulf, and maybe to Oman, Hawke thought, irritated. Who the hell had leaked that info? He leaned down, checking to see that the safety pins were properly installed in the ejection seat. Christ. Less than half an hour after the meeting, word from the top-secret briefing had probably spread through half the ship. Wasn't even a record, he thought, buckling up. He took a deep breath and settled in, care-fully letting his eye rove over the booted-up color cockpit displays, landing-gear handle, wing-position lever, and fuel-dump switches.

In the first Gulf War, Hawke had seen combat action rumors spread stem to stern on the HMS *Ark Royal* in five minutes. He leaned his helmet back against the headrest and closed his eyes for a moment. Another bloody crisis in the Gulf. Only this time it wasn't some tinpot Arab dictator and his amazing disappearing army that needed taking out.

No. This time the stakes were bloody enormous. And here, now, was where it would start. Let's say the French didn't honor the Americans' new no-fly zone over Oman, Operation Deny Flight. Let's say the French scrambled that squadron of Mirages he'd seen in the intel photos. For argument's sake, let's say he, Hawke, or some other fighter jock shot down a French Mirage or two. France naturally goes ballistic. The world would then be headed down a very bad road indeed.

Because France was only the tip. China was the iceberg.

That's the whole point, he realized. Right now, France had them boxed in pretty well. The no-fly zone would up the ante. Ipso facto, as soon as France raises a stink over the loss of a fighter or two over Oman, her new ally China climbs into the ring. Then the really big bear starts flexing its muscles. Demands Britain and America back off. Leave France and her adventures in the Gulf alone. Now the West is staring down the barrel of the first real global nuclear con-frontation since JFK stared down Nikita Khrushchev over the Cuban missiles way back in 1962.

Save the horrific regional conflagrations, a half century of relative world peace and stability was about to go up in flames. Oman would be the line in the sand. If China did indeed step into this on the French side, as every last man in that briefing room had believed she would, then you were looking deep into the yawning black abyss.

How to step back from the edge? According to Brick Kelly, the linchpin in the whole damn mess was this new Bonaparte. The way Hawke and Kelly read the man, for all his delusions of grandeur, he was just a pawn. Still, he had to be taken out, and fast. In New York, at this very moment, Ambrose was searching for a way to do it. With eyewitness testimony to a homicide and a warrant in hand, Interpol could storm the Elysée Palace and arrest Bonaparte for the murder of his father.

And then there were the Germans. Stoke was now in Germany. His job was to determine what role they played in this mess. France and Germany, Hawke knew, were trying to create a "United States of Europe" to achieve some economic, political, and military parity with the West. Baron von Draxis had a role in this, but what was it?

If anyone knew, it was the lovely Jet. Right now, according to Stoke, she was cooperative, even helpful. Stoke had convinced himself she could be trusted. Hawke's gut told him Stoke was right. Still, he wasn't absloutely sure. After all, her twin sister, Bianca, had tried to kill him. Ambrose had the best men at the Yard combing the country for her. Maybe when it came to Jet and Bianca, blood was still thicker than water.

Another worry, he thought, casting his eye over the instrument panel.

And all of this was a mere preamble to dealing with the bad boys in Beijing. It was simple, really. They had to find a way to stop this godawful mess before it ever got to the nuclear tipping point.

More Chinese troops in the Gulf joining the ones already in Sudan? Her tankers in the Red Sea? Her forces controlling the Strait of Hormuz? Dominating the world's oil supply? It just wasn't going to happen. At least not on President Jack McAtee's watch. As long as McAtee was in the White House the Gulf States would be off-limits to the Chinese. Hawke had heard him say as much at a private dinner in D.C. two months ago.

Well, Alex Hawke thought, trying to stretch his lanky frame

within the confines of the F-35's snug seat, if the world was about to go up in smoke, at least he'd have the damndest front-row seat money could buy.

He reached forward and initiated the sequence that would start the powerful Rolls-Royce engine.

Time for a cat-shot.

Chapter Thirty-one

The Bavarian Alps

"MOUNTAIN CLIMBING'S JUST LIKE SMIRNOFF," STOKE SAID to Jet, trying to make her smile for the first time all morning.

"What?"

"Leaves you breathless."

She didn't get it. She was tired, panting, her feet hurt, and it was all his fault.

"Yeah, breathtaking up here, ain't it?" Stoke said and filled his lungs with pure alpine air. He and Jet had just climbed up another steep rocky rise through the trees. He decided to stop and let her get her wind back. They were standing on an outcropping of rock overlooking something called the Obersalzburg.

He was having the time of his life. Whole damn countryside was beautiful. Even the dirt. The ground, even up here at this elevation, was soft underfoot. Spongy, Stoke thought you'd call it. Light was filtering down through the tall trees onto a soft bed of pine needles and the air was cool and clean. He looked up. There were noisy black birds, jackdaws, riding the currents above the swaying treetops.

Surprise, surprise. He liked Germany. It was pretty.

What he'd seen of it on the way to Salzburg, anyway, whizzing by his window in the dark on the midnight train down from Berlin. Now, in the last couple of hours of climbing, he'd been seeing little white stone villages and green farmland spread out far below. Salzburg, where they'd spent last night, was some twenty klicks to the north. You could still see it in the clear distance. Beautiful. All around him, towering above the thick green forests, were the jagged slate-grey peaks of snow-capped ranges. He pulled his map out of his knapsack and identified them as the Untersberg and Waltzmann mountains. To the southwest, sparkling blue in the sun, was a pretty lake he'd like to see one day, the Konigsee.

"Just smell that," Stoke said. "Christmas."

"What the devil are you talking about, Stokely?"

"Christmas trees? Am I right?"

Jet rolled her eyes at him and walked off to stand by herself. She bent from the waist, putting her hands on her knees for support, and took deep breaths. Girl smoked way too much and she was a little out of shape. He'd have to work with her on that. Especially now that they were telling everybody in Germany that he was her personal trainer. It was a good cover story. Jet had thought of it. Told him how to act the role. One thing the girl could do was act. No, wait. He didn't want to go there.

In fact, Jet was one hell of an actress. And that, he had to admit, was the scariest part about this whole damn trip. Climbing mountains was easy. Figuring out whose side Jet was really on was tough. Just when you thought you had her pegged, wham. You'd see something in those eyes that didn't seem right.

Stoke, former SEAL and New York City cop, hadn't done a whole lot of actual mountain climbing himself. But he had to say that after this morning's experience he had a feeling he'd be pretty damn good at it. How hard could it be? He'd read a book, something about being up in thin air. Maybe thin up on Everest, but the air wasn't all that thin right here in Obersalzburg, and they were plenty high up.

"Look at that," he said, looking up from his map to a huge snow-capped mountain rising in the distance above the treeline.

"Look at what?" Jet said, lighting up.

"Over there. That's the Zugspitze, or however you say it."

"Zoog-spits."

"Right. Zugspitze is almost ten thousand feet above sea level. Tallest mountain in Germany. Right about there is where the Bavarian Mountains meet the Tyrolese Mountains. Hell, girl, let's see a smile. We're in Germany now. We're almost there. It's all downhill from here."

"Don't talk about my life like that."

Girl was tired. Irritated. A little scared, even though she'd never admit it. Her father sounded like a pretty scary cat, all right. And now she'd crossed him, big time. Jet hadn't wanted to leave her fancy suite at the Adlon Hotel in Berlin in the middle of the night and catch the train to Salzburg. Too bad. There was a chance they'd been made and Stoke had a lot of digging to do before he dealt with Baron von Draxis on a personal basis.

What happened was, he'd seen the two Arnolds in the lobby of their hotel in Berlin. They had their backs to him, standing at the check-in talking to the receptionist, when he'd come back all sweaty from his evening run. He was on his way to the elevator when he spotted them. Kept his head down. Just kept walking and they hadn't seen him. Maybe. Ah-nold and Ah-nold, he called them. The two blond goons from *Valkyrie*, who provided muscle for von Draxis.

Still. Kind of odd, wasn't it? The two of them checking into the most expensive hotel in Berlin. What was that all about?

Stoke had a theory. He'd developed it in Vietnam in order to stay alive. Things that didn't make sense at first always made perfect sense if you just stopped and thought about them a second. But sometimes you can't stop, so you got to go with your instincts if you want to keep breathing.

He went right to his room and got on the phone. First he called Jet's suite, woke her up. Told her he was booking two seats on the midnight train to Salzburg. They had to leave the hotel now. By the service elevator. She wasn't happy. Even though it was her idea that they should check out Schatzi's secret Bavarian hideaway.

He was learning about Jet. She wasn't too big on hiking or mountain climbing or staying in dumpy little guesthouses like where they'd gone after arriving in Salzburg. Didn't like her room or her bed. Didn't like the mattress. Didn't like the pillow. Didn't like breakfast. Didn't even seem to like the Christmas trees all that much. Probably didn't even celebrate Christmas in China, come to think of it, so he'd give her a pass on that one.

He handed her the canteen and she tilted it back, the muscles in her throat going up and down. Thirsty girl.

Stoke pulled his black wool sweater over his head and tied the arms around his waist. It was getting a little warm up here as the sun rose over the Alps. They had been in the mountains for about six hours now. An hour before sunup, they'd slipped out of the small *gasthaus* deep in the woods above Salzburg. He felt great. He'd liked his bed and his pillow. Slept like a baby under the soft eiderdown thing they used instead of blankets. He'd knocked on Jet's door at 4:00 A.M. and again at four-thirty. Give her credit; she was standing tall at five.

Not happy, but awake and dressed.

He figured his only real problem was the drowned guard on *Valkyrie*. But to be realistic about it, it wasn't much of a problem. Nobody had seen Stoke aboard. Guy was taking a leak and fell overboard. Happened all the time. Biggest cause of death on boats was guys pissing over the side and falling overboard. He'd read that somewhere. So. Baron von Draxis probably wasn't really expecting his former girlfriend and a giant black guy tracking his ass all over Germany. Still, seeing the two Arnolds in the Adlon lobby bugged him sufficiently for him to bust a move.

He'd finally reached Alex on board the USS *Lincoln*. Hawke was in a bad mood, too. He'd been cooped up in some briefing for about twelve hours and not happy about it. The man still wasn't all that crazy about the idea of Stoke bringing Jet to Germany. Stoke had pointed out that she could speak German and could be a big help digging around in Schatzi's life. Plus, Stoke told Hawke, he thought she was in love with his ass.

Hawke said, yeah, okay, but she was also a Chinese secret police captain who had at one time considered killing him. Stoke said he didn't want to argue. He'd keep an eye on her. And anyway, Hawke sounded like he was a little preoccupied with getting his ass the hell off the *Lincoln* and trying to prevent World War III.

Few things in particular Hawke told Stoke to dig into: One, what the hell was *Tempelhof*? The Chinese general who had recaptured Brock had said the word "Tempelhof" like it was some big deal. Hell, it was an old airport in Berlin, everybody knew that. But Brock had no idea what the hell Tempelhof had to do with all this. Find out. Two, were the bloody Germans involved with the French—and how? Third thing. What was the von Draxis connection exactly? The baron was certainly tied to both the frogs and the Chinese. But, how?

Stoke said he was on the case and hung up.

"How much further?" Jet asked, handing him back the canteen. Empty. She was hot and tired and thirsty but he was having a hard time feeling sorry for her. She knew what to expect on this trip.

She'd said there were no roads to the place. Inaccessible by automobile. She said you had to take a helicopter to get there. Stoke had said choppers tended to attract unwanted attention. He said they'd have to walk. They could pretend to be hikers. She agreed. Now she obviously wasn't so sure she should have. He told her the good news. According to what he saw on the map, they had only a mile to go. He said mostly downhill but that was a stretch.

Half an hour later, sticky with perspiration, he was standing in a sunny clearing on the side of a thickly wooded hill. At the base of the postcard mountain stood a very large Hansel and Gretel–type house. A Tyrolean château, he supposed you called it, built up against the sheer face of the rock. A narrow winding path of crushed pebbles disappeared around one side of the house and into the woods to the east. On the west side, a grassy clearing big enough to accommodate a chopper. The grass had that fresh smell and look of having been cut recently. Maybe they kept it cut. Or maybe they were expecting company. The big, black Nazi helicopter, for instance.

The first floor was white stucco with big red-shuttered windows. The top three floors were dark and wood-sided with balconies railed with white flower boxes on all four sides. Red geraniums filled the boxes on every floor. Stones had been laid on the wide overhanging roof. Hold the wooden shingles down in the high winds, Stoke guessed.

"Is that it?" he asked Jet.

"That's it," she said, holding on to his forearm while she bent and massaged her sore ankle.

It certainly didn't look like a billionaire's mountain getaway to him. Looked like something Snow White might have lived in after she got married and had a bunch of rugrats. It looked like a fairy-tale house. But maybe that was the whole idea.

"I thought you said he had a big *schloss*," Stoke said, trying not to laugh.

"I've tried to explain this. The castle is hidden inside the mountain behind the house," Jet said. "This charming little guesthouse is just there for appearances. It's a false front hiding the secret entrance."

"Pretty damn realistic, though," Stoke said. "Now, I get it. Zum Wilden Hund. Did I say that right?"

"No."

She pronounced it correctly but Stoke was damned if he could tell much difference from the way he said it and the way she said it. German was such a weird-ass language anyway. No matter what you said in German it sounded like you were going to rip someone's throat out. *Ich liebe dich*. Translation: I love you. Sounds like: I'd like to eat your nuts for supper.

"Let's go say hello to Frau Wienerwald," Stoke said. This was the woman who ran the baron's phony *gasthaus* and from what he could gather from Jet, she was the kind of innkeeper who ate any small children who got lost in the woods.

"Winterwald," Jet said. "Trust me, she won't think it's funny if you get it wrong. She's the official gatekeeper to Schatzi-World."

"This whole damn country feels like Disneyland," Stoke said.

"It isn't," Jet said.

Chapter Thirty-two

The Indian Ocean

HAWKE HAD HAD HIS FIGHTER PILOT'S BREAKFAST—TWO AS-
pirin, a cup of coffee, and a puke—and headed for his airplane. Engines spooling up. Green jackets, purple jackets, yellow jackets, the
color-coded crewmen ranging over the broad flight deck. The swarm
of F/A18 Super Hornets, just arrived from the *Nimitz*, loaded and
lethal, still, looking prematurely antiquated by the presence of the
sleek, sculpted, single-seat F-35 in their hive.

And, too, there were the young aviators gawking lovingly at his
plane. Kids who never ever wanted to do a damn thing in this world
but fly airplanes. See if they had the stuff, ace.

Turn inside the other guy, turn your damn plane inside out if you
had to, pulling nine or ten g's and close as billy-be-damned to a suicidal red-out, all the blood rushing from your brain to your extremities. Get on some faceless boy's six, unleash a Sidewinder and blow
his punk ass out of the sky.

Yeah. Rain death and destruction down on invisible strangers and
then fly home to a warm bunk on a big boat with a few thousand
other guys. Get drunk and fight with your fists and sleep it off in the
brig. Shed friends, shed wives, shed family. Even shed a few tears
maybe when it was all over, when even the great shooting match in
the sky was finally over.

All for what, hotshot? Hawke thought.

Honor? Danger? Death? Glory?

Who the hell knew?

It was a stupid question, anyway, Hawke told himself as he reached
forward to adjust his suddenly squawking radio. Because the only pilots who would ever really know the one, true answer were dead.

"That really you down there, Hawkeye?" Alex heard a familiar voice say in his headset.

"Roger, sir, it's me all right," Hawke replied, tightening his harness. Girding my loins, he thought, and smiled.

"Well, I'll be damned, it shore as hell is him! Look at this, boys, Captain Hawke's flying himself a real bona-fide airplane this time!"

It was the *Lincoln's* new air boss. A crusty old bird named Joe Daly. Lately arrived from the *Kennedy*, where the American jocks called him the Iron Duke. Hawke recognized Daly's droll twang from his own brief sojourn aboard the American carrier *Big John*. Alex had caused a bit of consternation on board when he'd landed his little seaplane on the carrier three years ago. This was at a critical moment during what he'd come to call his personal Cuban crisis. Irritation was more like it. For some reason, he and the Iron Duke just hadn't clicked. Checking his fuel, he heard a crackle in his phones and the Duke was back.

"Last time I saw you, Hawkeye, you were flying that little toy airplane of yours. Built it yourself out of tinfoil and rubber bands. Took you four or five passes to get that dang Tinkertoy down on my deck. What'd you call that thing?"

"*Kittyhawke*, sir. Finest airplane in the sky."

"You're bleeping nuts, boy. Get your ass off my deck."

Hawke laughed. He followed the taxi director's hand signals and moved the plane the last few feet into the catapult shuttle of cat number 1. Flaps and slats to takeoff, he merely sat and watched. A green-jacketed crewman instantly knelt on the deck and attached the towbar connecting his nose gear to the shuttle in the slot. Get ready for the cat-shot.

"It was actually only two passes, as I recall, sir," Hawke said, craning his head around for one last look at the *Lincoln*. "Third time's the charm. I see you got yourself a new boat."

"Yeah, well, the cream rises to the top in this man's navy, Hawkeye. You sure you know how to fly that damn thing?"

"We'll find out soon enough, I guess." Hawke noticed that the hand on the control stick was shaking a bit. Adrenaline. Had to be. C'mon, boys, hook me up. He wasn't scared of the monster, he told himself. He was just excited about what a carrier launch would be like in this thing. Right. He was just shaking a little because he was ready to light the candle.

C'mon, Momma, now light the candle 'cause you know your poppa is too hot to handle . . .

"Okay, Hawkeye, you are number two for launch," the Iron Duke said in his phones. "You, uh, you might want to let that Super Hornet there in front of you get airborne before you push any unfamiliar buttons. Sound good to you?"

"Aye, aye, sir, sounds good to me," Hawke said, grinning from ear to ear. Single seat. Single engine. Supersonic.

Nowhere to go but up.

But there was a problem with the aircraft in front of him. Hawke forced himself to sit tight in his cockpit and wait for the tugs to pull the disabled fighter off the cat and put him in its place. The process seemed to take from here to eternity.

"Hawkeye, you are number one to go," the Iron Duke said after a few long minutes.

"Roger. Number one to go. Onward and upward, sir."

The jet blast deflector rose up from the deck behind him.

His hand went to the throttles. Oil pressure and hydraulics okay. He waggled the stick and checked the movement of the horizontal stabilizers. He could see the "shooter," the catapult officer down in the little domed control pod that protruded just above the deck. He was getting the cat ready. Clouds of white steam were rising from the slot beneath Hawke's airplane.

The shooter was monitoring the pressure building up in the cat cylinders. The combined pent-up force of the steam behind the catapult shuttle and the enormous thrust of his Rolls-Royce–built engine was about to hurl him into the sky. It was definitely time to fly.

Hawke wound it up, gave the salute, and waited for the launch.

One heartbeat, two heartbeats later, he felt the thunk as the shooter eased the shuttle into position with the hydraulic piston. He shoved the throttle forward and the big engine came up nicely: rpm, exhaust gas temp, fuel flow. Looks good. The cat fired. The big plane shuddered like some living thing and started to go.

Then . . . nothing.

He was moving down the deck all right, but there was no acceleration. Christ! He pulled the power and stood on the brakes. Somehow, he had to shut it down. Where the hell was that bloody computer when he really needed it? It was supposed to anticipate his every need. Surely it must have seen this nightmare coming!

Two seconds later, his heart pounding, he found himself teetering over the leading edge of the flight deck. The air boss was saying something very calm and soothing in his earphones but the big fighter was rocking right on the edge with every deep rolling wave, every sickening movement of the ship. He reached over to blow the canopy. He had to get the hell out, now, while he was still alive. Too late to eject? Maybe not, if—

"Stay in the cockpit, Hawkeye," the air boss said, as if reading his thoughts. "We are going to hitch you to a tug—we, uh—"

"Uh, roger. She's rocking and rolling pretty badly out here. You might want to . . ."

"Yeah, yeah, I know . . . shit . . . I've got several crew trying to hold your tail down now, sir. We need to, uh, need to change your aircraft's center of gravity until we've got you safely hooked up to the tug."

"Well, that's a real good idea but—"

"Goddamnit! Stay in the cockpit!"

"Roger. I'm not going anywhere."

"Almost got you hooked up, Hawkeye. Holy shit. Gimme a second here and—"

"Hey—bad—watch out for—"

A huge swell rocked the ship.

Over he went, the aircraft falling toward the water below.

As it fell, the F-35 rolled sideways. Hawke could now see the ship's massive bow plowing through the water. He didn't know which was worse . . . seeing the water coming up at him . . . or seeing the knife-edge of the carrier bow slicing through the water toward him.

Bloody hell. He should have ejected. Now he'd be strapped in and run over by the bloody ship. He felt the gorge rise in his throat. He hit the water. Hard. And saw the terrifying sight of the towering bow slicing toward his tiny aircraft. He was directly in its path.

He didn't even have time to close his eyes.

He knew he was dead as soon as he heard the terrible sound, an awful snap. The ship's bow severed his airplane, broke it in two. Only he wasn't dead. He was tumbling end over end, slamming into something just above him. The bottom of the carrier. He felt like he was in a jeep going a hundred miles an hour on a washboard road.

But he was still alive. He remained sealed inside his cockpit module. It seemed intact. The bow must have hit the plane just aft of him, just forward of his wings. The water was so clear! He could see all of the carrier's bottom as he was bounced and bobbed along. He could see and feel every bob and hit every time he slammed up against the ship's massive bottom. Every time he hit, big chunks of his cockpit's Plexiglas canopy were gouged out by the barnacles on the carrier's hull.

But still it held.

Then his world flipped violently upside-down and his seat rocketed forward. He was slammed into the Plexiglas and he was sure he was going right through the canopy, going to shoot right out of the jet. Somehow, his oxygen mask got shoved aside. Shards from something cut his face, sheeting it in blood. His vision blurred. But miraculously the canopy held. His mind raced, clawing at survival. Training and temperament shifted his mind into disaster reflex, his brain trying to figure out what was happening and what to do about it. Total time compression. What seemed like a minute was a second.

The bolt that held his ejection seat to the floor had failed. That was it. That's why, when his nose went down, his seat shot along the railing and his helmet and seatback had almost broken through the canopy. At that moment, the nose was jerked upward by unseen forces and the seat slid back down the railing to the floor. Good. Much better. He could swivel his head now. And his neck wasn't broken.

He was thinking then that he might just make it out of this bitched-up mess alive. That feeling was short-lived. Terror struck him again when a truly horrifying sound filled his world.

The screws.

A loud, deep-pitched whine, rapidly growing closer. The sound was deafening. Overpowering.

Oh, shit.

He could see them vaguely now, hanging down below the hull, way back at the stern. There were four of them and they were coming up fast, the cruel blades all but invisible inside whirling clouds, a maelstrom of white water.

He was aware of fear then. The real thing. It was a fear that he had never even guessed at. He supposed it was just that bloody high-pitched noise triggering all those mental pictures of a particularly bad way to go. Whatever it was, it was working. Inside the hurtling cockpit, Alex Hawke was well and truly afraid.

There were four massive bronze propellers, each of them over twenty feet across and weighing thirty tons. Four whirling, knife-edged blades, biting and slicing the water. Each screw was mounted to a long shaft, which was connected to a steam turbine powered by one of two nuclear reactors. The ship's propulsion system generated a half-million horsepower. Each screw was now turning at over two thousand rpm.

Surging toward those four meat-grinders, Hawke had at last discovered the true meaning of fear. It didn't creep up and touch your neck with icy fingers. It exploded inside your brain. And made everything numb. He was shivering violently. He clenched his jaw shut to stop his teeth from chattering.

Alex Hawke's battered capsule was bouncing along, slicing off spiky chunks of barnacle, heading straight toward them. He could see more clearly how he was going to die now. He visualized being chewed up and spat out in countless pieces even now as he felt a sudden surge of speed bringing him closer and closer to the churning propellers.

If the noise was intolerable, the view was terrifying. The water amidships was still amazingly clear and as he got closer to the stern he could see the huge billowing clouds of minuscule bubbles, could see the four vortexes the giant screws created, four huge vacuums sucking him aft at a tremendous rate of speed.

And he was still accelerating.

He wanted his eyes open now for this last bit. Wanted to see everything. He wanted to stare down the fear as he sped toward his very certain death. He could see the wicked curved blades of each screw in perfect detail as he hurtled headlong into the vortex.

He forced his eyes to stay wide open.

He was in the relentless grip of the outboard screw. It was happening. He was entering the roiling pipeline to death. He started spinning now, now that he was in the tube. The vibration and the noise blotted out everything but the looming knife-edges of the whirling blades. The screw seemed to have slowed a fraction, but perhaps it was just his imagination. All in slow motion now.

He strained against the harness, trying to see it coming. The gaps between the blades were much larger from this angle. But not wide enough with the pod at this forty-five-degree attitude. What if he could get weight suddenly forward? Hope surged. He might even slip through if he could somehow get his nose down—wait—the seat pin was out—the weight of the ejection seat slamming forward again just might be enough to—he grabbed the handles on either side of the cockpit and yanked himself forward with as much force as he could generate.

It was one last utterly desperate gamble and he might just kill himself doing it. But if the nose was angling downward as he passed between two of the blades, perhaps gravity and hydrodynamics would be on his side. He was no physicist, no expert on wave mechanics, but what the bloody hell, he—

The seat shot ahead on the rails and he slammed once more into the leading edge of the canopy. His helmet took the brunt of the impact again. He heard a loud pop, the sound of the helmet splitting or maybe the canopy. No water, though. Just fresh sheets of warm blood that drenched his face. He couldn't see. He thought he felt the nose dip a fraction before merciful blackness descended and surrounded him.

Disoriented and rolling violently in the screw's wake, he regained consciousness and suddenly saw the orange sun bouncing on the horizon.

Somehow, he was still alive.

He wiped some blood from his eyes and noticed that he was bobbing violently on the ocean's surface. The forces tossing him about came from the backwash of the *Lincoln*'s four giant meat grinders. He could see the looming stern of the carrier moving away from him. His heart was pounding against his ribs with such force he felt the bloody organ might rip away from his chest wall. He knew he had to do something to get out of the capsule but he couldn't control his shaking hands. He tried several times to blow the canopy but he just didn't seem to have the necessary coordination to do it. Until his third try.

He blew the canopy.

And realized very quickly he'd made a very serious mistake. The cockpit capsule immediately began flooding with water. Seawater rose instantly above his knees. It kept rising, slopping around, quickly filling the cockpit. Since the nose had the most air to displace, the capsule nosed over. It submerged and immediately began to sink. He was going straight down fast. He tugged furiously at his harness, clawed at it, shredding his fingertips.

At about thirty or forty feet beneath the surface, his fingers ripped at the buckles one last time and he managed to wrench himself free. He wriggled out of the harness, kicked away from what little remained of his lost aircraft, and started clawing his way to the surface.

Breaking the water, he heard a loud thumping noise above and saw a big Sea King helicopter blotting out the sky overhead. One rescue swimmer, already in the water, was paddling furiously toward him. Another stood poised in the open hatch. The downdraft was making the waves worse and Hawke went under, swallowing a pint or two of seawater. He felt the crewman yanking upward on his flight suit. A few seconds later, he was sputtering on the surface again, only to be blindsided by another crashing wave.

"Christ, sir," the swimmer shouted at him above the chopper's roar, somehow looping a line over his head and getting it down over his shoulders. "We almost lost you when she swamped!"

"Yeah, I know!"

"Are you crazy, sir? Why the hell did you blow your canopy?"

Hawke spat out the last saltwater he could summon up from his burning pipes, then wrenched his head around and smiled. His savior was just a kid, couldn't be much more than twenty years old. The cinch tightened over Hawke's chest and he was jerked upward, slowly at first, toward the hovering Sea King.

"Never blow the canopy!" the kid shouted again.

"Next time this happens," Hawke shouted down to the kid, "I'll try to remember not to do that!"

Chapter Thirty-three

New York City

AMBROSE CONGREVE ARRIVED AT 21 WEST FIFTY-SECOND Street in a sunny mood. Why not? He was dining at the "21" club, his favorite watering hole in all of New York. The leisurely stroll down Fifth Avenue in the warm twilight had been delightful. He had suitable accommodations, having been satisfactorily installed in a nice corner room at the Carlyle up on Seventy-sixth and Madison. Plenty of cozy chintz and overstuffed furniture. And there'd been a huge arrangement of hydrangeas waiting in his room when he'd checked in that afternoon.

The scented blue envelope from the Park Avenue florists, now safely tucked inside his waistcoat pocket, would have to wait. He knew who it was from and that was sufficient.

He was saving the card. He envisioned ordering an ice-cold martini and then reading her words while standing at the bar waiting for his dinner companion. He was deliberately early. He wanted time to savor Diana's note laced with gin.

"Good evening, Mr. Congreve," the debonair gentleman standing at the entrance to the dining room said. He offered his hand as Ambrose entered the familiar room, chockablock with model boats, aircraft, and sports memorabilia hung from the ceiling. "It's good to have you back with us again."

Congreve shook the man's hand warmly. Bruce Snyder, as far as he was concerned, was the heart and soul of the legendary old speakeasy. A tall and good-looking chap with slicked-back hair and impeccable tailoring, Bruce managed to combine an elegant New York sophistication with an easygoing manner that was part and parcel of his Oklahoma upbringing.

Still, Snyder was the keeper of the flame in this very clubby atmosphere; the arbiter of social stratification within these hallowed walls. It was he who decided whether you were seated at one of the cherished banquettes in the front room or banished to Siberia behind the bar. But Ambrose knew that, unlike many in his position, Snyder was a good man who wore his mantle of power lightly and with genuine bonhomie.

"I'm meeting someone, Bruce," Congreve said. "I'm a little early. And thirsty. I thought I might have something cold and clear at the bar first."

"Good idea. I've saved the banquette table in the corner whenever you're ready," Snyder said. "Business or pleasure bring you to New York this trip, Chief Inspector?"

"Both. Two items are on my personal menu this evening, Bruce. Your delicious lobster and that tough old bird Mariucci. A sort of 'Surf and Turf,' I suppose one might say."

"He's not so tough." Snyder laughed. "Matter of fact, he was in with his granddaughter just the other night. Her birthday."

"Moochie didn't shoot out the candles?"

Snyder laughed again and walked with him toward the bar. "We make him check his six-shooter at the door. Just give me a shout when you're ready to sit down."

Ambrose ordered a very dry Bombay Sapphire straight up and pulled the small pale blue envelope from his pocket. It was the same shade as the hydrangeas that Diana had sent to the Carlyle. He noticed that his hands were trembling. His martini arrived magically and he put the envelope down, feeling like he needed a drink before he opened it. He really was losing it, he thought—just going starkers and—

A large beefy hand was on his shoulder.

"Hiya, sailor, first time in New York?"

Known as Moochie to his many pals in the metropolis and by less cordial monikers by the many villains he'd sent upriver, Detective Captain John Mariucci had collaborated with Ambrose very successfully on a couple of cases. All ancient history now. Moochie was somewhere north of five feet tall, a barrel-shaped individual with a full black mustache and skin the color of sun-bleached terra-cotta. His neatly trimmed black hair was shot through with grey now, but instead of aging him, it seemed to smooth out some of the rough edges.

Ambrose slipped Diana's card back into his waistcoat and shook the man's hand, trying not to wince at the pain. Moochie had the strongest grip of any man he knew outside of Stokely Jones, but Stokely, at least, knew how to keep his under control.

He turned to the bartender. "Two more just like this, please, and send them over to our table."

"Okay, Chief," Mariucci said after they'd been seated and he'd swallowed the top half of his drink, "Let's skip the chase and cut right to the outcome. We'll renew our acquaintance later. What are you doing in my town and how the hell can I help you do it? Women, a table at Rao's, what are we talking here?"

Ambrose smiled and sipped the delicious gin. "Ever hear of a chap named Napoleon Bonaparte?" he asked.

"Yeah, I think that rings a bell. Short little guy, French, as I remember. Always had his hand inside his jacket like he was going for his frigging piece."

"That's the bird, all right."

"He giving you a hard time, Chief Inspector?"

"In a manner of speaking, yes, he is."

"I'll kick his ass."

"That's why we're here."

"Talk to me, Ambrose, but let's order a steak first. My treat, by the way, you paid last time I was in London." Ambrose didn't argue about the menu or the tab. He was on Moochie's turf and he knew better. Mariucci signaled to a hovering waiter and informed him that they didn't need menus, just food. "Two New York strip steaks, rare, French fries, and two Sunset salads with Lorenzo dressing."

"You want the steak and the chicken?" the waiter asked, scribbling on his pad. It wasn't a problem, nothing was a problem, he just wanted to make sure he'd understood.

"I'm hungry, what can I tell you? Too much food, though, you're right. So, hold the chicken in the Sunsets, and just bring the lettuce and cabbage part."

"Very good, sir."

Mariucci sat back against the banquette and surveyed the room. It was full of glamorous semifamous and famous faces and Ambrose was sure the seasoned captain could put names to most all of them. Then he looked at Congreve and said, "France has gone crazy, right?

Fuck is wrong with those people? They forget a little beach resort called Normandy? Jesus. Speaking of France, you still wearing yellow socks all the time?"

"Certainly."

"Show me."

Ambrose stuck his foot out beneath the table and hitched up this trouser leg. He was wearing black Peale wing-tipped loafers and his signature yellow cable-stitched socks from Loro Piano. Mariucci shook his head and frowned. He and Ambrose had never seen eye to eye when it came to gentlemen's attire.

"You are a total and complete piece of work, you know that? Now, you were saying about Napoleon?"

"He had a son. Not many people know that."

"I'm one of those people."

"The point is that there's a line coming down through history from the emperor. A man named Luca Bonaparte, one of Napoleon's direct descendants, is the reason I'm here."

"Oh, yeah. The new head of France or some shit like that."

"That's my boy. He's creating very serious problems for your country and mine."

"In that case, he's a dead man. You want some wine?"

"It goes without saying."

"I'll get us a nice Barolo. Or a Barbaresco. Any wine that starts with 'B' is good Italian wine. I told you that before, right? Tell me more about this Bonaparte guy."

"He murdered his father. In Paris, thirty-five-odd years ago. Langley stumbled on an old Deuxième file when digging into Bonaparte's past. You'll see it later, I checked it with my hat. I'm actually here at the specific request of your CIA director, Patrick Kelly."

"So you knew I got promoted?"

"I did not. What exalted status do you now occupy?"

"You said CIA is all. I'm now the Senior NYPD guy on the Federal Anti-Terrorist Advisory Council. ATAC. Which makes me sort of a half-assed fed myself. But with command of all the active-duty cops. Where in Paris did this murder occur?"

"At Napoleon's Tomb in 1970."

"Any witnesses?"

"Yes. At least two. A fellow named Ben Sangster. And his business associate, a chap by the name of Joe Bonanno. Both Americans."

"You gotta be shitting me."

"I assure you, Mooch, that is the furthest thing from my mind."

"Benny Sangster and Joey Bones, sure. I oughta know those two birds, I sent 'em both up. But I do recall at the trial some crap about them working a job in Paris. Something with the Union Corse. You know much about them?"

"A little. You can read much more in the file."

"Tell me what you know about the Corse."

"The French Mafia. Brutal, even older than the Unione Siciliano. Started in Corsica, birthplace of Napoleon, as you know. Back in the sixties and seventies, the Corse syndicate had extensive operations right here on the East Coast, mostly smuggling and drug operations. They sometimes worked as tools for European corporations, rather like the Yakuza does for Japanese businesses. The Corse is the only Mafia organization with a political agenda."

"Political?"

"Yes. They funded and organized terrorist actions against non-Euro corporations. That's where my boy Bonaparte first made a name for himself. Back then, the American families had a turf war going with them."

"I see."

Congreve said, "Are Sangster and Bonanno still incarcerated?"

"Incinerated for all I frigging know. I think they got ten to fifteen, something like that. Took a little time-out up at Attica. They're probably out, far as I know."

"I'd very much like to speak with both of them."

"And when exactly would you like to have this little chat?"

"You think you can find them?"

"I can find anybody, Ambrose. Except Hoffa. Him I can't fucking find to save my ass. Doesn't mean I won't find him, however. Lemme go make a call. When would it be convenient for you to interview these two jailbirds?"

"Tonight would be ideal."

"So there's really some kind of crisis looming?"

"Always, Captain," Ambrose said, "History, as H. G. Wells once remarked, is always a race between education and catastrophe. Right now, catastrophe appears to be ahead by a furlong."

Mariucci just looked at him, a smile in his eyes before he spoke. "I'll make the call. Shouldn't take five minutes. And don't touch your steak until I get back, either. As Mrs. Mariucci of Brooklyn once remarked, 'It ain't polite.' "

The Bide-a-Wee Rest Home was on a dark side street off a major thoroughfare called Queens Boulevard. It was a squat three-story building with peeling stucco walls and a steeply pitched wood-shingled roof in need of repair. Congreve and Captain Mariucci had left the uniformed officer sitting behind the wheel of the brand-new Chevy Impala cruiser. They'd parked half a block away and walked. The captain's idea, and a good one.

"Play your cards right, Ambrose, and you, too, can end up here," the captain said as they made their way up the cracked and heaving pavement of the rest home.

"Depressing old pile, isn't it? It's mob run, did you say?"

"Yeah. Lot of grizzly goombahs in diapers playing pinochle and rehashing the good old days. Hey, you wanna hear a funny joke?"

"Why not?"

"These two ninety-nine-year-old geezers are sitting in their rockers on the front porch of a joint just like this, see, and one says to the other one, he says, 'Paisano, let me get this straight. Was it you or your brother that was killed at Anzio in World War II?' "

"Quite good." Ambrose laughed. He climbed the sagging steps and the captain was right behind him.

"Pisser, ain't it? Okay, who's doing the talking at the door? You or me?"

"It's my investigation, I believe," Ambrose said, and rapped on the cracked and peeling front door. There were a few lights on downstairs and one or two on the second floor. A window tucked up under the eave was dark. After a moment, a large man in green scrubs appeared at the door. He opened it, but just barely.

"Good evening, sir," Ambrose said, holding up his credentials. "I'm Chief Inspector Ambrose Congreve of Scotland Yard. And this is

Captain Mariucci of the New York Police Department. May we come in?"

"What's this all about?" the man said, closing the door a fraction.

"I'll tell you when we're inside," Congreve replied, shoving the door open and stepping over the threshold. The captain followed him inside and the three of them stood in a small hallway under the pale yellow light of a dusty ceiling fixture.

"What you want?" the man said. "I ain't done nothin'. I'm just the orderly here."

"What's your name?" Mariucci asked.

"I'm Lavon, sir. Lavon Greene."

"Is there a manager on the premises, Mr. Greene?" Ambrose asked.

"He don't sleep here. He leaves at eleven and goes home. I'm just the night man."

"I see. Where is his office?"

"Down the hall there. Last door on the left."

"And the files for all the—patients? Are they kept in that office?"

"Yes, sir."

"You have a resident here by the name of Ben Sangster?"

"Yes, sir, there is. He's upstairs now. Sound asleep."

"Good. Captain Mariucci is going to get his file for me. You're going to show me to Mr. Sangster's room."

"Yes, sir, right this way. Mr. Ben's on the top floor. Only one up there. He's asleep, though, like I said. He takes his meds at six. Man is lights out after that. He don't wake up till orange juice."

"Captain," Ambrose said, "I'm going to accompany this very nice gentleman upstairs and look in on Mr. Sangster. Won't you join us once you've retrieved his file from the office?"

"Certainly, Chief Inspector," Mariucci said with a mock bow, "I'll get on that right away, sir." He ambled off down the dingy hallway, mumbling something under his breath. Lavon pointed to a narrow staircase across the hall and Ambrose started up ahead of him, taking the steps two at a time.

"Is this his room?" Ambrose asked when they'd reached the top floor.

"Yes, sir."

"After you," Congreve said, and let the big man open the door and enter ahead of him.

A sharp coppery smell assaulted Congreve's twitching nose. He knew what he would find even as he reached for the light switch beside the door. There was fresh blood in this room. A lot of it. He turned on the light.

"Oh, lord Jesus," the orderly said. "Oh, sweet Jesus, how did this—"

Ambrose looked at Lavon Greene and said, "This man was alive when you last saw him?"

"Yes, sir! He—"

"The last time you saw him was when you administered his medication. You gave him his medication at what time?"

"Six. Six o'clock, is what I'm saying. Same time every day. Oh, my lord."

"You're absolutely sure he was alive at six o'clock this evening?"

"Alive as you or me. Yes, sir. He was."

"And you haven't heard anything since then? No noise? No shouts or cries?"

"No, sir."

"I believe you. That bloody pillow on the floor was held over his face. Could one of your patients have done this?"

"No, sir. Ain't none of 'em got the strength to cut a man's head half off."

"Has anyone besides you and the manager been in this house tonight?"

"Just the dish man."

"Dish man? A cook?"

"No, sir. Man who came to fix the dish on the roof."

"Ah, that dish. What time was this?"

"Around seven, I guess. Everybody who ain't bedridden was down in the lounge watching the TV and suddenly the picture went out. Man showed up here about ten minutes later said he was here to fix the dish. Had to go up on the roof, he said."

"What did he look like?"

"He was a little guy. Big smile on his face. A Chinaman."

"A Chinaman. That's very interesting. I want you to go downstairs right now and ask Captain Mariucci to come up here immediately. Can you do that, Mr. Greene? Run down there, now."

"Ain't nothing like this ever happened here before this. Never."

"Go."

The late Benny Sangster lay faceup in his blood-soaked bed. His throat had been slashed down to the spinal column and the wound was gaping like a second red mouth under his chin. Approaching the bed, Congreve could see the blood was partially congealed. That's when the second wound caught his eye.

There was also a gash in the center of the chest. In Ambrose's experience, this meant organs had been removed. From the size and location of the wound, he would guess the heart.

Someone had known Congreve was coming to New York and why. That someone had beaten him to the punch, had gotten to Benny Sangster before Ambrose could. Congreve heard Mariucci's heavy tread racing up the stairs.

"Captain!" Congreve shouted over his shoulder, "Where the bloody hell is Coney Island?"

"What are you, a tourist? It's in Brooklyn, for crissakes. The southernmost—Aw, shit," Captain Mariucci said. He was standing in the doorway staring at what was left of Benny Sangster.

"Joe Bones is next," Congreve said, "Let's go."

"He's next, all right," the captain said, "and whoever did Benny here is thinking the same goddamn thing. Let's get outta here."

Traffic was light for a Friday night. The uniform had the Impala cruiser doing at least one hundred on the Belt Parkway, weaving in and out of the lanes.

"He's a cannibal," Ambrose remarked, gazing out the window at the blur of Brooklyn.

"What? Who is?" Mariucci said.

"The killer. The Chinaman who murdered Sangster."

"Fuck you talking about, Ambrose?"

"Eating the heart of one's enemy. An act of psychological brutality. The killer ate Sangster's heart. At least he removed it. Assuming it would be cumbersome to transport, especially if he's planning a second murder tonight, I believe he ate it while standing over the corpse."

"Jesus."

"The Chinese are not as squeamish as we are, Captain."

"You saying this is understandable behavior?"

"I'm saying the taboo against cannibalism is weaker there than it is in the West. In wartime, many starving Chinese acquired a taste for human flesh. And there are many stories of workers in morgues or crematoriums slicing off the buttocks or breasts of female corpses and taking them home for supper. Stuffing for dumplings, you see."

"Can you stop? Please?" Mariucci begged. "Now!"

The uniform up front turned around. "Here?" he asked, dumbfounded.

"Not you, him," Mariucci said.

At Exit 6, the cop driving the cruiser went up on two wheels taking the turn. He then went south on Cropsey Avenue, taking that all the way down to Surf. At the corner of Surf and West Tenth Street, he screeched to a halt and the captain and the Scotland Yard man scrambled out of the backseat.

Joe Bones, Mariucci had learned tonight, worked at Coney now. Ever since his retirement from family-related activities, he'd been the night man at the Wheel. Since it was a Friday night and not quite midnight, Mariucci figured his best chance of finding Joey was at Coney. The rides closed at midnight, so he was probably still here. He'd got on his cell and called in the homicide as they ran down the stairs of the rest home. The meat wagon was already en route to Bide-a-Wee. He figured Lavon wasn't going anywhere. The big man was still standing over the corpse and weeping when they ran out of the room.

Chapter Thirty-four

Bad Reichenbach

FRAU IRMA WORE JACKBOOTS UNDER HER LONG BLACK skirt, Stoke was pretty sure. Shiny black ones, right up to her chubby, pink little knees. She wasn't the prettiest girl in Bavaria. She had her wispy grey-blonde hair pinned up in two big doughnuts on each side of her head. She had a square, flat face with a beaky nose right in the middle of it. She wore some kind of heavy white face powder, although she was already quite white enough, in Stoke's humble opinion. She had a short, compact body, and one good thing you could say about her, she looked very strong for a woman.

"Zo," Irma said to Jet, looking down at her registration book, "we had no idea you were coming."

"We're hiking," Jet said, repeating what she'd already said twice when they were still standing outside, hot and thirsty in the blazing sun at the front door. The Frau was obviously very surprised to see Jet without her boyfriend the baron. And when Jet had introduced Stokely Jones as her personal trainer, she'd looked at him as if he were some giant alien specimen of another life-form. Stoke had smiled and said *Guten Tag*, but she didn't seem to understand his German too well. GOO-ten TOG. Had to work on that one.

"Ach. Hiking," Frau Irma Winterwald said, but not in a warm, welcoming way. The way she said it, Stoke thought maybe hiking was strictly prohibited in these mountains. The *gasthaus*, Zum Wilden Hund, was a little spooky inside. Thick velvet drapes kept out most of the sunlight. The carved furniture was heavy and dark and there were a lot of shaggy heads with beady glass eyes mounted high up on the walls. Dead stags and deer and bears all staring down at the huge man in hiking shorts as if it were him who should be up on the wall and not them.

The guest house, Stoke decided, was a Bavarian version of the Bates Motel.

Another weird thing was the music. There was very loud piano music coming from a great big grand piano at the far end of the room. The guy playing, Herr Winterwald, was too old to be Irma's husband so Stoke figured it must be her father. He was blind and wore dark glasses and a dark green felt jacket with buttons made out of bone. His white hair stuck straight out from his head as if he were permanently undergoing electrocution. The music he was now playing sounded like new-wave Nazi marching tunes, if there was any such thing.

Irma noticed Stoke staring at the guy and said, "He is a genius, no?"

"Yes," Stoke said, "I mean, no."

"Zo," Irma was saying, "It will just be for the one night, *ja*?"

"One night," Jet said with her best actress smile.

"*Und, ein Zimmer*? You will need only one room?" the frau was looking not at Jet but at Stoke when she said this. She gave him her most suggestive look. Lascivious was the word. Stoke gave her his biggest smile and held up two fingers.

"No," Jet said, "We will need two rooms, Frau Winterwald." Stoke could tell it was taking all of Jet's considerable acting skills not to jump over the counter and rip this ugly toad of a woman's head right off. You can tell when two women don't like each other much. It's not pretty.

"*Zo, zwei Zimmer*. One for Fräulein Jet, *und* one for Mr.—"

"Jones," Stoke said and she wrote it down with her big fat ink pen. Real ink, Stoke noticed. These people didn't mess around.

"Jones," she repeated, drawing the word out as she wrote it. "Such an American name, *ja*?"

"I'm an American," Stoke said, shrugging his shoulders. Jet gave him a quick wink.

"*Zo, alles gut*. No luggage at all?" Irma asked. She stood on tiptoes and peered over the desk as if luggage was about to magically appear. She had fishy eyes, Stoke noticed, man-eating fish eyes.

"No luggage," Jet said.

"*Still* no luggage," Stoke said, unable to stop himself.

"*Und*, tell me, how is Baron von Draxis, dear girl? We have not seen him much since the skiing is over," Irma said. "Have we, Viktor?"

Viktor shook his head and kept playing his piano. It suddenly hit Stoke who he looked like. Albert Einstein. Just goes to show you that a bad haircut can make anyone look dumb.

"He is very well," Jet said. "He and I have been traveling in the Mediterranean aboard *Valkyrie*. You've heard perhaps, Frau Winterwald, that Baron von Draxis and I are getting married in September?"

It was a very different Frau Irma Winterwald who looked up and answered that question. *"Nein,* my child, I had no idea! How splendid! I am delighted for you, dear girl. He is the most marvelous man! And so rich! What a catch, you lucky girl! Would you and your friend like to have lunch in the garden?"

They ate in a fenced-in garden on the sunny side of the house. Frau Irma, now a smiling, benevolent creature, brought them each a glass of cold white wine with their menus. Stoke ordered the Wiener schnitzel since it was the only thing he recognized and he thought he liked it. Jet, no surprise, ordered a green salad, and Frau Winterwald bowed and scraped her way back inside the house. You could hear Viktor banging out his neo-Nazi marching tunes even out here in the garden.

"Irma La Not So Douce," Stoke whispered to Jet after she'd disappeared back inside.

Jet smiled. "Yes. That old bitch has always hated me. I think we're okay, though. You did well."

"I'm great as long as I don't talk. You know what's funny? They've got one page of food on this menu and thirty pages of wine list."

"You should see the wine cellar," Jet said, looking at him carefully. "Maybe tonight when they've gone to bed."

"I knew there had to be a reason you brought me here," Stoke said, smiling at her. "Other than the hospitality."

"She reads to him after supper. They usually go to sleep at ten," Jet said. "I've brought a little something to put in their tea. I'll make sure they're out and knock on your door sometime after midnight."

"They don't keep the cellar locked?"

"I know where she hides the key."

It was sometime after two in the morning when Stoke and Jet descended into the funky-smelling gloom of the *gasthaus* cellar. The steps leading down from Frau Irma's kitchen were old worn stone and slippery, and he had to hold Jet's arm to get them down without falling. He had the little Swiss army flashlight he'd put in his knapsack and he kept it aimed at Jet's feet so she didn't slip.

On the wall at the bottom of the steps was an iron fixture with a candle, and Stoke found a box of matches on the shelf under it. He lit the candle and took a look around. He'd never seen so much wine in his life. The little room they were in had shelves up to the ceiling full of dusty bottles and there were corridors leading off in every direction, both walls lined with shelves full of wine.

"Schatzi's pride and joy," Jet said. "The largest collection of pre-war Bordeaux in Germany. Come on, it's this way."

"How come you know about all this stuff?"

"We came here. A lot. To ski. What you're about to see is Schatzi's favorite getaway after the boat. Like I said, the *gasthaus* is just a front. Only about five people know this place even exists. Believe me."

"Show me the money."

Stoke gave her the flashlight and followed her down the long dark corridor on the right. They came to a dead-end, a small circular room with an old oak table with two chairs pulled up to it in the center of the stone floor. There was a candle standing in the center and Stoke lit it. A large leatherbound book lay on the table. Jet sat down and opened it, flipping through the gold-edged pages, running down the entries scrawled there in red ink with a ballpoint pen.

"What's that?" Stoke asked.

"Wine registry. You have to sign out every case with this pen. These case numbers here in the margin are the key." Jet was adding and subtracting a series of numbers in the palm of her hand. Stoke noticed she was writing down only the last digit of the last seven entries.

"Key to what?"

"I'll show you," she said and closed the book. She stood up and said, "Help me shove this table out of the way."

They moved the table to one side. There was a loose stone in the floor where the table had stood. Jet pulled a small penknife from her pocket as she knelt to the floor. She inserted the tip of the blade in the crack on one side of the stone and pried it up. Stoke aimed the flashlight at the square hole revealed in the floor. There was a black steel panel with a digital readout window and a keypad. Jet looked at the numbers written on her palm and they appeared on the readout as she entered all seven. She pressed another button and the numbers began to flash.

"They change the code every week," Jet said. "It's a good system."

"Flawless," Stoke said as the wall of bottles started to rattle and shake, "Obviously."

Then the whole floor-to-ceiling wall of wine began to sink into the floor. Behind it was a stainless-steel wall. Set into the steel wall was a burnished bronze elevator door.

"I get it. He keeps the really, *really* good wine on another floor, am I right?" Stoke said.

"Pretty good," Jet said, looking up at him and smiling.

They stood quietly and watched the last shelf of priceless wine disappear into the floor. Despite his own worries, and Hawke's misgivings about Jet, he knew now he'd never have gotten this far without her.

"Okay," Jet said. "We're almost in."

She placed her right hand flat against a matte black panel to the right of the doors. A bar of red light passed under her hand as the biometric scanner read her palm. Instantly, a small light above the panel began flashing green. Stoke could hear a faint rumble and knew an elevator car was descending behind the steel doors. It took the cab a long time to get down to their level.

Stoke suddenly saw the whole thing.

"This elevator shaft goes up inside the mountain right behind the guesthouse, doesn't it?" he said. Jet nodded.

"Welcome to the Schloss Reichenbach," Jet said as the doors slid silently open. "One of the most secure and exquisite private residences in the Alps."

"Cool," Stoke said.

They rode up in silence. The interior walls of the elevator were lined with highly polished brass. Stoke looked up. There was a strange light fixture in the ceiling, a bronze eagle with spread wings holding an illuminated glass globe in its claws. It took ten minutes to get to the top of the mountain. When the cab stopped the doors slid open he and Jet stepped out into the most awesome space he'd ever seen.

"Glorious, isn't it?" Jet said, studying his face.

"I can't talk," Stoke said.

Stoke simply stood there, taking it all in. They must have been at six or seven thousand feet. One whole wall opposite them was a massive stretch of curving glass. Beyond, a series of moonlit snow-capped mountains marched off into the distance under a black and starry sky. A massive chandelier hung from the peak of the soaring ceiling above them. Jet touched the button that illuminated it.

There was very little furniture in the room. No rugs or carpet on the floors, just vast areas of polished wood in various intricate inlaid designs. A few low leather chairs were arranged around a great open-hearth stone fireplace to Stoke's left. Above the carved mantel hung a large oil portrait. Two men on horseback in the snow, high up in these mountains. Even from a distance, Stoke recognized one of the two men as von Draxis. He was wearing some kind of funky uniform. Very heroic-type painting.

"Who's the other guy?" he asked Jet, moving toward the fireplace to get a better look.

"That's Luca Bonaparte," she said. "Schatzi's best friend."

"Bonaparte, huh? So that's him. I should have guessed by the way he's got his hand stuck inside his overcoat. Well, I'll be darned. Wow. What's that neat outfit Schatzi's wearing?"

"Alpenkorps. The uniform of the German Alpine Corps. World War II vintage. He has quite a collection of military uniforms at Tempelhof."

"There's that word again. What's Tempelhof? You mean the airport?"

"The old aerodrome at Berlin. Designed by Albert Speer and built around 1937. A huge crescent building about five kilometers long. After Hitler conquered the world it was going to be the continent of Germania's main airport. A few years ago, the city of Berlin was going to tear it down but Schatzi bought it out from under their noses. It now houses all of the von Draxis corporate offices and shipbuilding and aircraft design studios."

"Is that right? Germania. That's what he planned to call the world, huh? I never knew that."

A single crescent-shaped table with one chair stood facing the great window. On its highly polished surface stood only a black and white photograph in a large silver frame and the model of an old three-masted sailing ship. The hull was some kind of black stone and the sails were all made of ivory so thin you could see starlight right through them.

"So this is his desk?" Stoke said, approaching a semicircular table of walnut with carved eagles for legs. Behind the desk and the curving glass wall, the top of the world unfolded and rolled out below.

"Yes. Sit in the chair."

"You don't think he'd mind?"

"I'm sure he would. Go ahead."

Stoke did as she said. Sitting here, it was hard not to feel like the man who owned the world. It was a very uncomfortable sensation.

"Who's that in the silver frame? Daddy?"

"Kaiser Wilhelm."

"You don't say. My, my, my. Isn't that something?" Stoke placed both of his hands palm-down on the desk and spread his fingers, quiet for a few seconds, just thinking about the whole thing. After a few long moments he looked up at her and said, "Tell me, Jet. What exactly does your boyfriend do for a living?"

"He's a shipbuilder. The most successful and powerful in Germany. His family has been in the business for four centuries. The Krupp family built the guns. The von Draxis dynasty built the ships that carried the guns across the sea. The family shipyard in Wilhelmshaven is where they built the *Graf Spee*."

"Right. Germany's ultimate pocket battleship. The Brits cornered her down in Uruguay, right? It took three Royal Navy ships to sink her."

"The Brits didn't sink her, Stokely. Hitler ordered her scuttled in the Montevideo harbor. To prevent the British from learning the secrets of von Draxis's construction and Krupp's experimental weapons systems. The *Graf Spee* was designed and built by Schatzi's grandfather, Konrad, for the Kriegsmarine. Launched in 1937."

"Kriegsmarine, huh? Does our little Schatzi still build boats for the German navy?"

"Not so much now."

"German navy hasn't got the big-bucks budgets it used to have. So, what kind of boats does he build these days?"

"Come with me and I'll show you."

"Where are we going?"

"Schatzi's residence includes a marine design studio where the modelmakers first create what he creates and then do real-time simulations of sea trials. The boats are flawless before the real hulls ever splash."

"What's he building now?"

"The greatest ocean liner ever built."

"For Germany? Is he planning to put guns on this one?"

"No. He's building her for France."

"France. Isn't that some fascinating shit? France and Germany. I guess they finally decided to kiss and make up. Let's go take a look."

"Are you okay? You're acting funny."

"I feel good. This is just how I get when I'm impressed."

They had to pass through a number of interesting rooms to reach the studio. There was a dining room with a table long enough to seat a small town. They came to a door marked *Kriegsmarine* and entered a model room where Stokely could have spent a week. Beneath the domed ceiling painted to look like a stormy sky was a sea of glass cases. Each one contained exquisitely detailed models of ships the von Draxis family had designed or built for the German navy.

Stoke paused for a moment to admire a few of them. There were the massive battleships *Tirpitz* and *Bismarck*. But also Stoke's personal all-time favorite, the *Schnellboote*. It was arguably the fastest and best-designed PT boat ever built during World War II. Maybe ever.

A steel-and-bronze door with intricate carving barred the way to the next room. On it were depicted all the epic sea battles the Kriegsmarine had fought in the last few centuries. Stoke felt he was getting to know Schatzi better. And he was beginning to feel like Hawke's decision to send him to Germany had been a good one. He couldn't get the portrait over the fireplace out of his mind.

Jet worked her electronic magic with the door and they entered the test model studio. The ceiling was a glassed dome and stars twinkled high above their heads. Jet was reaching for the light switch when Stoke touched her arm and said, "Don't. Let's just leave it like this a minute."

He walked inside ahead of her. There was only one model in this room and it stood in the center of the inlaid marble floor. It was encased in a closed glass structure at least thirty feet in length and fifteen feet high. Inside was the most gorgeous ship Stoke had ever laid eyes on. The name of the giant ocean liner was on her stern in gold leaf.

Leviathan.

"*Leviathan?*" Stoke said.

"The sea beast," Jet said. "Biblical. It's Schatzi and Luca's idea of a joke."

"Got it," Stoke said, although he didn't. He guessed this new French monster was maybe half again as large as the world's current largest liner, the *Queen Mary 2*, built by Cunard. That would make her about fifteen hundred feet in length and about three hundred feet high. If Stoke had to guess her gross tonnage he'd put it at three hundred thousand. Jesus.

"It's a working model," Jet said, handing him a remote control pod.

"What do you mean, 'working'?"

"Everything works. Here, I'll show you." She pressed one button and the ship lit up from stem to stern with a thousand tiny interior and exterior lights along the entire length of her superstructure. The red and green running lights on either side of her bow were as big as golf balls. She hit another button and the tiny anchors started to drop.

"Holy shit," Stoke said. The thing was truly beautiful.

"That's nothing. Watch this," Jet said. She hit a button and the interior of the glass case began filling with clear blue water illuminated from below. It rapidly rose up the walls of the case until it reached *Leviathan*'s waterline.

"You can simulate all kinds of sea conditions," Jet said, "There are wave paddles hidden at the bottom of the case. And sensors throughout the tank to monitor the parameters of wave action on the hull. Want to see a Force Five gale? A tsunami? Seas of fifty feet?"

"Not right now."

"Would you like me to start her engines?"

"Yes, that I would like to see," Stoke said, transfixed as Jet fingered the remote. There were propulsion pods hung from the stern. As she pushed the joystick, the pods revolved 360 degrees and the minature bronze props began spinning, creating whorls of white water around them.

"There you go. Four propulsion pods. She carries two fixed, and two azimuthing. This model is an exact replica of the real thing, down to the most minute detail."

"What's that big bulge in the keel? Weird looking."

"That? Bulb keel. Lowers the VCG. The vertical center of gravity."

"You know a lot about this stuff, Jet."

"Enough."

"How come she doesn't have any smokestacks?"

"That's an easy one. She's nuclear."

"Holy shit," Stoke said, "Nuclear? An ocean liner?"

"Hmm."

"Is the baron actually building this thing?"

"Oh, she's already built. Her maiden voyage is coming up soon. She's sailing from Le Havre to New York."

"Le Havre," Stoke said, "That's in France, isn't it? I'd like to be at that launching. But first I think we ought to go back to Berlin and poke our noses around that Tempelhof aerodrome. Do it at night like this, you know, so nobody will bother us."

"Hmm," Jet said, looking at her watch. "Look, it's getting late. We'd better get down the mountain and back in our beds before we're missed."

"You ever read 'Hansel and Gretel'?" Stoke asked, "No? Just curious."

Chapter Thirty-five

Coney Island

"HE WON'T COME DOWN?" CAPTAIN MARIUCCI WAS ASKING the manager of the Wonder Wheel at Coney Island. "What do you mean he won't come down?" The captain was clenching his jaw in frustration. It seemed the semiretired mobster, a Mr. Joseph Bones, was alive but currently unavailable for questioning. Joey was holed up in one of the sixteen swinging cars at the very top of the world's tallest Ferris wheel.

"How can I say this better? I mean, he won't come down," Samuel Gumpertz said, running his hands through the imaginary hair on top of his head. He'd been studying the car where Joey was hiding through his binoculars. He'd gaze in frustration at all the unhappy customers standing around the old Wonder, and then he'd look back up at Joey. The Gumpertz family had been running the number-one attraction at Coney for the last three decades. But it was Sammy's baby. It was his show. This action, he had to admit, was a first.

His night man, Joey Bones, an old Mob guy who knew his carny shit backward and forward, was ordinarily a stand-up guy. But about an hour ago, what happened was Joey had flipped out about something, he wouldn't say what. So now, he was up at the top of the wheel holed up in one of the cars and there was no way on earth to get his skinny old ass down.

In addition to a growing crowd of very pissed-off paying customers, he also had this NYPD captain all over his ass. Him and his sidekick, this English cop from Scotland Yard looking like something out of an old Sherlock Holmes movie wearing a caped coat and one of those weird goddamn backward and forward caps on his head. Smoking a pipe, for chrissakes. Give me a frigging break with this shit.

"May I borrow those binoculars?" this English character Congreve asked Gumpertz.

"Why, certainly," Gumpertz replied, "My pleasure."

"Thanks so much."

"Don't mention it."

"I hate to interrupt this little tea party, Mr. Gumpertz," Captain Mariucci said, "But I'm only going to say this one more time. I want you to start up that goddamn Ferris wheel up and bring that man down. Okay? *Capisce?*"

"How many times I gotta explain this again, Captain? All right. One, Joey is an old goombah, you know. He's eighty-five. Set in his ways. He's stubborn. He don't like being told what to do by nobody. Two, he's my brother-in-law, all right? He's my wife Marie's brother, okay? Bottom line, anything happens to Joey up there, I'm dead meat. And, three, he did something funny to the frigging gearbox. So we can't turn the wheel. End of story."

Mariucci said, "Whatever he did to it, it ain't funny. Fix it."

"Fix it, he says."

"That's what I said, fix it."

"Would that I could, Captain, just fix it. You see that fat-assed guy in the machine shed now? That's my mechanic, Manny. What do you think he's doing in there right now? Jerking off? Playing canasta? No. He's trying to fix the frigging Ferris wheel. But there's a little problem, as I explained to you earlier. Joey did something to the mechanism before he went up; you see what I'm saying? He took something out of the machinery, I dunno. Something critical. A wheel, a gear, who the fuck knows."

"He stuck a fucking monkey wrench in the thing," the mechanic said. He had appeared in the shed's doorway, his face and T-shirt blackened with century-old grease from the machinery. The news on his face wasn't good.

"You see that," Gumpertz said, "a monkey wrench sounds about right."

"He jammed a big spanner in the main drive wheel," Manny said. "He stuck it in so the big wheel would only do one half a rotation. Then she'd lock up. Smart."

"Yeah, he's a frigging genius," Gumpertz said. "So pull the frigging spanner out, all right? Hey! It's Friday night! Hello? I got huddled masses coming out the friggin' wazoo here, and you're giving out progress reports. Get your ass back in there and pull that thing out of there. Could you do that for me, please?"

"Yeah, yeah, okay," the mechanic said, turning his back on them. "I'll give it another shot."

"Give it a shot? Do me a favor. Just do it. Jesus. I need this, right, Captain?"

A strong wet wind had suddenly come up, howling in off the Atlantic. The undersides of boiling black and purple clouds were painted bright yellow and red with the carnival glow of the midway below. Congreve stood with the borrowed binoculars observing the car with Joe Bones inside.

The swinging car rocked violently to and fro in the gusty easterly wind. To the east, a flash followed by a rumble of thunder. A big storm. Ambrose imagined the pendulum-like motion of the rocking car was enough to make even a strong man wish he were someplace else. And it hadn't even started to blow yet.

"Mr. Gumpertz," Congreve said, "Tell me again precisely what caused Mr. Bones to engineer his current predicament."

"Okay, look, here's what I know, Inspector. Something spooked him, okay? Earlier. About nine-thirty I think it was. He got a call in the ticket box. He came outside, offloaded the wheel, then put the chains up, closing down the ride. I said something like, 'Hey, asshole, what the fuck you think you're doing?' and he's like, 'Sammy, ya gotta help me, I'm in deep shit.' "

"But he didn't say what kind of trouble?"

"No. He didn't have to. Spend your whole life on the streets of Brooklyn, you know that look, believe me. He got the word on the phone. Somebody was coming to whack him."

"Did he say who called him?" the English detective asked.

"Yeah. He said it was his buddy Lavon over at the Bide-a-Wee rest home. Joey used to go over there all the time and watch ballgames with his old pal Benny Sangster."

At that moment, someone in the crowd screamed.

Congreve whirled about and saw a large woman in a black babushka pointing upward at another soaring attraction just across the midway from the Ferris wheel. It appeared to have been out of operation for many years. The blackened and twisted wreckage of the tall wrought-iron structure resembled the Eiffel Tower after a bad fire. The thing was enormous. It had to be almost three hundred feet tall. Congreve raised the binoculars to his eyes. A third of the way up, at about a hundred feet above the midway, a man in white coveralls was rapidly climbing the superstructure.

"Captain Mariucci," Congreve said, "I think we have a problem."

"What have you got?"

"Up there." Ambrose handed him the binoculars.

"Aw, shit. I don't believe this."

"What's going on, Captain?" Gumpertz asked, looking up.

"We're screwed, that's what's going on," the captain said. "You see that little guy all the way up there? He's going to climb high enough until he's got a clean shot at your employee Mr. Bones."

"You got any idea why they want to whack him?"

"He's the last witness in a thirty-year-old murder case Chief Inspector Congreve here and I happen to be investigating. And there ain't dick we can do about it at the moment."

"No shit?" Gumpertz said. "He never told me about that."

Mariucci was already on his phone and barking orders to the ATAC command. He needed backup, goddamnit. He needed a cherry-picker, he needed a chopper. Now.

"Mr. Gumpertz," Congreve said, taking the man by the arm and pulling him through the crowd, "what on earth is that thing?"

"That's the old Parachute Jump. Brooklyn's Eiffel Tower, we used to call it in the old Dreamland days. She was built back in 1939 for the World's Fair. Out of service, as you can see. For about thirty years. Piece of rusted junk that could fall down at any minute, but you should have seen it in the glory days."

"No elevator, I don't suppose."

"Elevator? You kidding me? Nah, the only route up the Chute is the one that maniac is taking. Question. Why don't you just shoot the bastard?"

"I'm sure the captain is trying to arrange that as we speak. A helicopter with a sharpshooter would be helpful. The question, to be sure, is time."

"Haven't you got a gun?"

"Not on me, no."

"Look at that little guy go! Climbs like a frigging monkey."

"A skillful display."

"You guys didn't exactly come prepared, did you?"

"Not for this. Good God, where is that bleeding helicopter?"

A woman in a black raincoat stood slightly apart from the crowd now gathered at the base of the Parachute Jump. She had a paper cone of fluffy pink cotton candy in her left hand. She let the spun sugar melt on her tongue as she watched the madman's ascent of the tower. The sagging fences around the base were hung with faded signs depicting a skull and crossbones and the word DANGER. Decades of salt air and neglect had made the derelict iron structure dangerous indeed. Four park security men were still arguing about who should climb up and bring the man down before he got too high. No one had yet volunteered.

A low murmur of approval greeted the climber's virtuosity every few feet. He moved upward with a grace and agility that hardly seemed human. And strength. With powerful strokes, he pulled himself upward from girder to girder and he danced from beam to beam with amazing speed. It appeared that he would be successful reaching the summit as long as he didn't slip. Or as long as one of the rusted iron girders did not give way beneath his feet.

The wind had come up, and with it, a sharp ozone bite to the air. It had begun to rain, softly at first, and then sheets of it. Lightning filled the black sky above the tower. The woman held her breath when she saw a flash of it etch the Chinaman's silhouette against the sky. He appeared to lose his grip on a girder. He stood on the beam, arms pinwheeling, his body swaying. Finally, through some miracle, he was able to regain his balance.

He continued upward.

Once Joe Bones was dead, she and Hu Xu would go after the Englishman. The Scotland Yard detective named Ambrose Congreve. He was somewhere here in New York City. With Congreve and the two American witnesses dead, maybe her father's confidence would finally be restored. Since childhood, Bianca's sister, Jet, had been the darling, his perfect angel. How *could* Father love Jet more?

She saw a door opening and she was going to use it. Jet had betrayed their father. Major Tang said she was sleeping with the enemy.

Bianca saw her chance. She'd kick the fucking drugs. Kick all the stupid, stupid men who abused her out of her bed. And, one day, one day soon, she'd kick her treacherous sister right out of her father's heart.

Bianca threw her head all the way back and let the pelting rain strike her full in the face, relishing the sting of the slanting raindrops.

Bianca Moon thought she might finally find the one thing she'd been searching for these last twenty-seven years.

Redemption in her father's eyes.

And, of course, love.

Chapter Thirty-six

Gulf of Oman

"JOHNNIE BLACK, YOU GOT A BOGEY APPROACHING, TWENTY-five miles out." Alex Hawke couldn't believe his ears. He thought he'd had enough airborne excitement in the last few days to last a lifetime. The "incident," as it was now referred to, aboard the USS *Lincoln*, was one of those memories that was not going to fade rapidly. For two days, the mere act of waking up in the *Lincoln* sickbay had come as something of a surprise.

What's this? Still here, old fellow?

Yes. Bruised (his neck and right shoulder were a lovely shade of violet from slamming into the canopy when his seat broke loose) and battered, but still here. With a brand-new airplane from Aviano in Italy. And now, Archangel, the American AWACS plane directing Operation Deny Flight, the still-dewy no-fly zone over northern Oman, was warning him that a bogey, a French Mirage F1, was fast approaching him.

He craned his head around inside the bubble-shaped canopy of the F-16 Fighting Falcon and radioed his wingman. "Jim Beam, Jim Beam, this is Johnnie Black." The American pilot, whose name was Lieutenant Jim Hedges, was floating just off his starboard wingtip. "You got this guy?"

"Uh, roger that, Johnnie Black. I have him at heading two-seven-oh, maintaining twenty-five thousand feet at four hundred knots. We're doing low to high, is that right, sir?"

"Affirm. We are doing low to high, Jim Beam," Hawke said.

Low to high meant he wanted his wingman to go low and look for more bad guys while he alone climbed upstairs to confront the single known enemy. He had his reasons for this but he had been ordered not to share them with his American wingman. He was sure Hedges thought this whole mission was a crock, but there was nothing he could do about that right now.

He had taken off that morning at 0600 hours from Aviano Air Base in Italy, en route to Saudi Arabia for a fuel stop and a briefing. Ultimately, he was headed to Oman. He'd been ordered to test the new no-fly zone firsthand and report what he found to Kelly. And, meet up with Harry Brock at a small coastal village called Ras al Hadd and discuss the number-two reason he was going to Oman. First job, get the sultan and his family out of French hands.

There was a complete mission briefing in his flight bag. Aerial acrobatics and hostage rescue, his two favorite things in all the world.

The rescue sounded simple enough on paper; Hawke and Brock were supposed to determine if it was feasible to snatch the sultan and his family. If it was, do it posthaste. They were believed to be held captive in a seaside fortress on a small island called Masara, just a mile off the coast of Oman. The CIA had boots on the ground in Oman now. Their last humint assessment had indicated the beleaguered sultan had also been moved to the island.

Hawke's F-16 was the number-two jet in a four-plane formation destined for an American air base high in the western mountains of Saudi Arabia called Taif. Taif Air Base, situated at forty-eight hundred feet, was conveniently located about a two-hour drive from Jeddah. It was the home of the United States Military Training Mission to the Kingdom of Saudi Arabia. You don't hear much about them. This is a group that liked to stay out of the news.

USMTM in Saudi was a highly classified joint training mission under the command of Headquarters, United States Central Command (USCENTCOM) at MacDill AFB, Florida. Hawke, who frequently worked very closely with the Departments of Defense and State, and was privy to not a few secrets himself, knew that the tiny Taif Air Base was where the CIA and the American Department of Defense were coordinating and preparing for any eventuality arising from a possible French invasion of Oman. American personnel at Taif Air Base also flew support missions with the F-15s the Saudi RSAF had bought from the United States. The Royal Saudi Air Force squadrons flew out of the air base at Riyadh.

At Taif, in a sweltering Quonset hut, Hawke was briefed on Operation Deny Flight, the no-fly zone now being established over

Oman. Two of the fighters who'd accompanied him from Aviano were staying on the ground in Saudi Arabia. They had other plans. He'd be flying a two-plane with Hedges for the balance of the short flight from Saudi Arabia to its neighboring state, Oman. During the briefing, his aircraft was refueled.

Hawke was flying a loaner, an F-16 Fighting Falcon, reluctantly relinquished to his care by the grouchy four-star commanding the Sixteenth Air Force, and the Thirty-first Fighter Wing headquartered at Aviano, Italy. Hawke was quick to forgive the general his grudging generosity. The general had a lot on his mind lately.

The Sixteenth Air Force's area of interest includes NATO's southern lines of communications, waterway chokepoints to half the world's shipping, the crossroads of Islam and Christianity, and some of the world's major oil-producing countries. This vast piece of real estate was home to dramatically increased levels of political, ethnic, religious, and economic tension and the Sixteenth Air Force had been very busy lately. One particular chokepoint had everyone in the command center at Aviano's attention right now: the Strait of Hormuz at the northern tip of Oman.

Talk about a strategic stranglehold. Most of the world's petroleum was shipped through the narrow stretch of water separating Oman and its glowering neighbor Iran. Hence, the no-fly zone to keep out anybody who had no official business there.

Hawke could understand why the four-star had been a little grouchy when he learned one of his airplanes was being loaned out. Especially when he'd been told the name of the recipient of his largesse. Commander Alexander Hawke, the British aviator involved in the "incident" with the brand-new F-35 aboard the *Lincoln*. Knowing the military as he did, Hawke understood precisely what was going on. He knew that, although it had been determined conclusively that the mishap was due strictly to catapult malfunction and not plane or pilot error, a certain stigma had attached itself to his name and it would follow him around until all the navy flyboys ceased to be interested in him any longer.

He also knew that, unfortunately, there would be questions about the F-35 for a while. Ill-founded questions, Hawke knew, and he had assured the American aeronautical engineers who had grilled him mercilessly on the ground at Aviano that the plane had performed flawlessly. According to his instruments, everything had been perfect when he had throttled up for launch. As he told them, he couldn't reasonably expect the aircraft's computers to pick up the problems with the bloody catapult.

Would he fly an F-35 again if he got a chance, they asked, as Hawke headed for the door. In a heartbeat, he'd said.

"Okay, Johnnie Black, bogey is at twenty miles and lining up beak-to-beak," the AWACS officer flying high above him said.

"What flag?"

"Armée d'Air. French Air Force. Check your offset, sir."

Well, Hawke thought, there you have it. The bloody French had gone completely round the bend. Challenging the American no-fly zone was all the proof anyone needed that Bonaparte was wholly insane. Find out if they'll shoot, Brick had said to Hawke. He was about to do just that.

"Roger, Archangel," Hawke said, "Executing offset. Vertical offset minimum of five thousand, roger?"

"Affirmative. That's a good number, sir. No more than that."

"Maintain vertical offset at five thousand," Hawke said, "Johnnie Black."

For some reason, the Americans were giving whisky call signs to all Operation Deny Flight aircraft. He supposed the British whisky appellation he'd been given, "Johnnie Black," was some kind of USAF humor. Hawke drank only rum, but Johnnie Walker Black was damn good whisky and if he had to have— Uh oh.

"Uh, Johnnie Black, climb and maintain three-five-oh, over."

"Johnnie Black climb and maintain three-five-oh."

Hawke had been so busy with radar, weapons systems, radio, and the vivid memory of his recently aborted career as a test pilot, he'd barely registered the AWACS warning. He got busy fast.

"Roger that," Hawke said, scanning his canopy for shapes that might suddenly get much larger as he and the bogey converged. He knew he would see the guy going from not really moving in the canopy, to suddenly starting to shift. The F-16 was equipped with the most sophisticated weapons systems, avionics, navigation, and electronic countermeasures that money could buy. But any good fighter jock got a whole lot of information about a bogey's speed and heading by carefully observing how the tiny target plane grew and shrank and moved against his canopy.

If the bogey got bigger and bigger without changing relative position, it meant you were about to experience the once-in-a-lifetime thrill of a midair collision.

But, if the other guy got bigger, and drifted from one area of the canopy to another, like this guy was doing, it meant he was in a turn. The secret to staying alive up here was the ability to instantly grasp the "picture" of the two combatants' relative positions and react accordingly. Without thinking. Right now, the bogey was moving fast in the canopy, meaning the two jets were starting to pass each other.

"Turn right, Johnnie Black," Hawke heard in his headset. He was already doing that. With his left hand, he hit the afterburner. Hawke was pulling nine g's in the turn. Blood was trying to leave his head in a hurry and go to his feet, but he strained his muscles against the pressure suit so the red-out didn't happen. The two jets were turning away from each other, each making a circle in the sky. It was a two-circle fight now. Each pilot was hoping to outrun the enemy plane and end up behind him. On his six, they called it. Sometimes referred to as "Position A."

"Good work, Johnnie Black," Archangel said suddenly. "Get your nose lower."

"Roger." Hawke eased his nose down. Making any turn going downhill added power, since gravity added to the plane's energy. Hawke now turned toward the enemy plane, trying to make this a "one-circle" fight. He wanted to get inside the bogey's turn circle so he could get off a quick shot from behind. He knew he was taking a chance. If you overshoot, the hunter ends up prey, out in front of the bogey. If you slow too quickly, you have only a fleeting shot and then you wind up on the defensive.

The two opposing aircraft were sliding, slipping, and zooming through the air. There are only two kinds of aircraft in the sky. Killers and targets. Johnnie Black and the French Mirage testing the American no-fly zone were in the deadly process of sorting out who was who.

"Uh, Johnnie Black," Archangel said, "what exactly are your intentions, sir?"

"Roll out, get the burner cooking, go for turn circle energy," Hawke replied.

"What speed?"

"Four hundred knots."

"Okay, roger. Don't get beyond five hundred knots, sir. We're not trying to pick a fight here, sir. We, uh, we—we're still setting up shop here."

Hawke grinned. *Not trying to pick a fight?* Why the hell else would they be there? Hawke fired up his air-to-air radar and pinged the opposing fighter. As soon as the ping hit him, the Mirage went into violent defensive maneuvers and Hawke dove down after him. They were now both in a circling spin toward the ground. Each pilot was hoping to take advantage of a split-second mistake by the other guy. He was at twenty thousand feet and the whole of the Gulf of Oman lay below him. He caught his first glimpse of the Strait of Hormuz.

From this altitude, it wasn't hard to grasp the strategic importance.

He had the bogey locked up, and a warning signal sounded in the cockpit as he armed his AMRAAM radar missiles. The new Aim-120s under his wings were the latest thing. Air-launched aerial intercept missiles employing active radar target tracking. They were capable of speeds of Mach 4 and provided capability against single and multiple targets in all environments. The bogey beneath him, now spinning earthward like a pinwheel, was already dead. He just didn't know it yet.

"Johnnie Black, veer off! Veer off!" Archangel shouted in his phones.

"Repeat?" Hawke said, his voice incredulous, his right hand poised in midair. "I have this bogey locked up! You want me to disengage?"

"Affirmative, affirmative. Disengage! Do not shoot! Veer off now, sir."

"What the bloody hell is going on? Somebody want to tell me?" he said, letting anger and frustration creep into his voice.

"This is not a shooting war, Johnnie Black."

"It isn't? Then there's some serious lack of—what the hell kind of war are you boys fighting?"

"Right now it's strictly a pushing and shoving war, sir."

"Pushing and shoving."

"That's affirmative. Until further orders."

"Roger, Archangel," Hawke said, simultaneously calming himself down and peeling away. "Seems to have been a serious lack of communication somewhere along the line, Archangel."

"Roger that, Johnnie Black. We apologize, sir. We, uh—were not informed you were coming. We, uh, oh shit!"

There was a muffled boom below and Hawke flipped his plane left and saw what had caused it. The French Mirage F1 jet had augured into the side of a mountain. Licks of orange fire and thick black smoke were curling up from the crash site. The pilot's evasive maneuver was sound but he'd gone too deep. Or rather, Hawke thought, he'd been pushed and shoved too deep. Another pilot who'd run out of luck and experience at precisely the same moment.

"Looks like the other guy blinked," Hawke said. "Too bad."

"Roger that, Johnnie Black. You've certainly made our day a helluva lot more interesting. Sorry about the misunderstanding. We'll definitely make the evening news tonight. Have a lovely day, sir."

"Johnnie Black proceeding to Seeb International, Oman."

Hawke rolled the jet right and came to a new heading. He could see the capital city of Muscat dead ahead. Jim Beam floated up on his left side. Hedges looked over at him, shaking his head. He was sure the American AWACS pilot thought he was crazy for going after the Mirage as aggressively as he had. But the French pilot was testing the waters. And Kelly had asked him to be as realistic as possible when he tested the waters himself. If Langley wanted a realistic assessment of Operation Deny Flight's performance, then by God he was going to give them one.

The CIA wanted to find out exactly what the French pilots would do if challenged. Now they knew. Maybe this wasn't a shooting war, not yet anyway. But all that might change radically and soon. A lot depended on what Johnnie Black found on the ground in Oman.

So far, if you didn't count the little contretemps in Cannes a few weeks ago, not a single shot had been fired in this war. But each side had now lost one airplane. Only one side had lost a pilot.

So far.

Chapter Thirty-seven

Bad Reichenbach

STOKE HEARD THE PIANO TINKLING AS HE AND JET CLIMBED the slippery steps up from the cellar. Something deep and stirring in a minor key. Viktor was in great form, but it was four o'clock in the morning. What the hell was he doing awake? Jet said she had dumped enough of her potion into their teapots to put both him and Frau Irma out for a week.

"Is she in there, too?" Jet whispered. Viktor was banging out some heavy chords and Stoke didn't think their whispers could be overheard. Jet was standing behind Stoke in the darkened kitchen doorway, both of them looking out into the living room. Flickering light and shadows were dancing on the ceiling and walls. Pairs of beady glass animal eyes were gleaming all around the room, staring down from the walls. Candles?

Yeah, Viktor had all the candles on the piano lit up for his moonlight sonata or whatever the hell he was playing now. Sure as hell wasn't Ray Charles. Viktor's setup looked like Liberace the way he had the heavy black lid of the piano propped up and the big silver candelabra lighting up the keyboard as he raised his hands up high before bringing them down on the ivories. Tinkle, tinkle, boom.

"Don't see her. I think it's just him," Stoke said in her ear.

"Good. If we can slip past him and up the stairs to our rooms it would save us a lot of trouble. But you can't make a sound. His sense of hearing is phenomenal."

"Yeah? How come he plays such awful shit all the time?"

"Good question."

"And, why the candles? He's blind."

"Smell," Jet said. "He loves the smell."

"Aromatherapy. It's everywhere. Ready?"

Viktor was banging on the left side of the keyboard now, building up to his big climax. Jet squeezed his arm.

"Hurry. We must get to the stairs before this song ends. Go."

They were halfway across the room when the music stopped, Viktor's hands frozen in air above the keyboard. His head swiveled in Stoke's direction.

"*Guten Morgen, Herr Jones,*" Viktor said after the last mournful note had faded away. "*Wie gehts?*"

"Pretty good, Viktor. How you doing, buddy?" Stoke said, wondering how on earth the man had heard him crossing the room in the middle of all that damn racket.

"Zo. You are a somnambulist, *nicht wahr?*"

"A what?"

"A sleepwalker."

"Yeah, that's right, Viktor. I'm seeing somebody about it but, man, nothing seems to work. It's a problem. Listen, you don't know any Ray Charles, do you?"

"*Was?*"

He stood there looking at the guy sitting at his piano. With the candlelight gleaming in the lenses of his dark glasses and his wild Einstein hairdo, Viktor looked like a demented eighty-year-old Bavarian rock star. Had he heard Jet, too? Maybe not. Girl moved like a tiger stalking something in the bush. She was frozen in place and watching Viktor like a cat. Stoke looked at her and put a finger to his lips. Then he motioned to her to continue padding over to the staircase while he engaged their host in conversation.

Stoke's plan had been for the two of them to be packed up and out of here before Frau Irma and Viktor woke up in the morning. He'd leave a note and a lot of cash to cover their expenses. Down in the wine cellar, they'd carefully replaced the wine registry book and put the cellar table back just like they'd found it. He figured since the baron still had no idea where they were, no sense having Frau Irma calling him up and raising a lot of questions in his mind. He was also pretty sure he and Jet had given the two Arnolds the slip at the Adlon in Berlin.

Jet had flashed an okay sign and started to creep toward the staircase on tiptoe. Girl moved like a big cat who—

The explosive sound of the big weapon firing was so unexpected and so loud in the stillness of the dark room that Stoke almost came out of his shoes. He saw Jet hit the floor, hard, and roll up into a ball. Couldn't tell if she was hit or what. He looked at Viktor and saw the smoke seeping from the muzzle of the gun in his hand, still aimed at where Jet had been. An old gun, some kind of funky machine gun, but it seemed to work okay. Now, Viktor swiveled on his piano bench and aimed the gun directly at Stokely. He was resting his shooting arm on top of the piano.

There was a second explosion as Stoke made a move toward the heavy desk to his left. The round buzzed by his head and slapped into the stone wall, just missing a big old woolly grizzly's gleaming chompers.

"Don't move," Viktor said, "I warn you." So, he spoke English, too. Boy was full of surprises tonight.

"Take it easy, Viktor, I'm not going anywhere," Stoke said, inching sideways toward the desk. He'd considered simply diving over the piano and taking the old Kraut out. But he was watching Jet out of the corner of his eye. She was crawling silently on her belly toward the piano. No blood that he could see anywhere on her. She didn't seem to be hurt. Good.

"I said, don't move!" Viktor said.

"Easy does it, Viktor. Let me ask you, what kind of gun is that?"

"*Das ist ein Schmeisser*! A Schmeisser machine pistol. The best gun the Reich has ever produced."

"It's cool. I like it."

"Zo, the *Amerikaner*, Mr. Jones. Enjoy your tour of Schloss Reichenbach, *mein Herr*?" Viktor asked him. The way he said it, his little grin, and the way his voice rose up at the end of the sentences, you could tell this was his idea of sarcasm and humor. His voice was scratchy like some old newsreel from World War II.

"Well, I didn't get to see all that much of—"

"*Das ist verboten*!" he screamed. "Strictly forbidden!" He pointed the business end of the old Wehrmacht machine pistol directly at Stoke's heart. It was pumping pretty hard at the moment. Stoke wondered if Viktor's overdeveloped ears could hear it.

"Your heart is beating very fast, Herr Jones. You are scared, no?"

"Jesus. Not that much."

"I have orders from Baron von Draxis to shoot anyone who tries to gain entry to *der Schloss.*"

"Well, good. I've already been up there once, so you can scratch me off the list of folks to shoot. What a view, up there, Viktor. You ought to charge admission," Stoke said. "Make you a fortune."

"*Der Schloss* is off-limits to the guests," Viktor said. "I told you. Strictly *verboten.*"

"*Verboten,* huh? Well, how about that? Nobody told me. Hey, Viktor, let me ask you another question. What'd you do? Go get that laser eye surgery while I was up there taking the *Schloss* tour?"

"Eyes? I see with my ears, Herr Jones. You should wear soft-soled shoes."

"You see with your ears? Unbelievable. Okay, Viktor, how many fingers I'm holding up right now?"

"*Was?*" Viktor said. "*Nicht verstehen.*"

Stoke had figured his fingers joke was pretty funny but Viktor didn't seem all that amused. If he lived to be a hundred, Stoke thought, he'd never understand the German sense of humor. Jet was in range of the piano now, and she was up on the balls of her feet, palms on the floor, in a crouch. She had a plan and Stoke could see it was a good one. He even saw a way to help her out.

He'd seen a heavy glass paperweight on the desktop behind him. A snowy alpine village inside. Stoke carefully reached behind his back, crabbed his fingers across the desktop until they brushed up against the baseball-sized globe. He palmed it, liking the heft. He considered just beaning Viktor with it, then decided on a better plan.

"Who's that?" Stoke said suddenly.

"Who?" Viktor instinctively responded.

"Over there," Stoke said, "Look! Another somnambulist."

He hurled the glass ball at the mirror over the fireplace. The glass shattered and Viktor rose up off the stool, leaned forward across the opened piano and fired the Schmeisser at the sound of breaking glass. He got off a short burst of useless rounds but by then Jet was already in the air, flying toward the piano.

She came out of her tuck, did at least one midair somersault, and landed with both feet on the raised piano top. The heavy wooden lid slammed down hard on Viktor's head and shoulders, smashing his face down against the taut wires. The whole top half of his body was now trapped inside the piano case, Jet's weight keeping the lid down.

Jet stood atop the Steinway, smiling at Stoke.

"Crouching tiger," she said. "Never fails."

"Damn, girl, that was pretty good. Bruce Lee, eat your heart out good. You ever make a kung fu movie?"

From inside the piano came a low moan. Viktor was still alive anyway, but just barely, and Stoke didn't really feel like giving him first aid right now. He pried the Schmeisser from his clenched fingers just for good measure. Good souvenir. Plus, he wasn't remotely interested in that horror movie ending where the dead guy raises up and shoots your ass while you're going out the door with the girl.

"You know what," he said to Jet, "let's do the early checkout thing. Do they have that here, you think?"

"Good idea. Where to next?"

"You said *Leviathan* was designed at this Tempelhof in Berlin, right?"

"Yes."

"Ever been there?"

"Countless times."

"How's the security?"

"I think I could get us inside. Getting out alive would naturally be up to you."

"Yeah. We'll go check it out. Let's pack up and vamoose."

At the top of the stairs, they separated. He sent Jet along to her room to pack up since he knew she'd take longer. He continued up the stairs leading to the top floor. He thought it would be a real good idea to check on Frau Irma. He couldn't imagine how she'd been able to sleep through all the commotion downstairs.

He entered the dark bedroom, pausing at the door to listen for snoring. Nothing. There was a funky smell in the room, but nothing he could put his finger on. The east windows were beginning to cast a faint grey light into the room. He could make out a lumpy shape lying in the middle of the four-poster bed. She was out all right, not moving a muscle. Jet must have administered some serious sleepy-time tea. He walked over to the bed and looked down at her.

He switched on the lamp by the bed. The shade was draped in a silk scarf that bathed the whole scene in soft red light.

Sleeping like a baby. A very ugly baby. Stoke had to say he finally understood that old expression "a face only a mother could love." Her hooded yellow eyes, those man-eating fish eyes, were closed, praise God, and her long grey hair was down, splayed out on the pillow in thick, greasy strands. Stoke had to say it looked better up in buns. Her lips were pulled back from her teeth in a kind of grin and there was a little dried spit on her chin. She was very still. He bent down to see if she was breathing.

In the lamplight, her face looked yellow, as if all the blood had drained out of it. He reached down and put his hand on her powdery cheek. It was very cold and he quickly pressed two fingers to her carotid artery. Nada. There was another star in the skies over Germany tonight. The lovely Frau Irma Winterwald was dead. Jet had maybe accidentally overloaded her teapot with deadly nightshade. He'd have to ask her about that. Girl was getting frisky.

Stoke switched off the lamp. He hoped like hell Frau Irma was going to have herself a closed-casket funeral. Just for the undertaker's sake if nobody else's. She hadn't looked all that good when she was breathing, but at least she had some color in her cheeks. Dead, she was a train wreck. You don't want something like that lying around your funeral parlor in plain sight. Bad for business.

He looked up from the corpse and saw Jet standing in the door-way. She'd changed clothes. She was wearing a hooded parka and had a knapsack dangling from her shoulder.

"You killed her?" Stoke said.

"Yes."

"Can I ask you why?"

"Self-protection, obviously, but I loathed that old woman. Any-way, we are almost finished with the Germans now."

"Finished? What's that supposed to mean, 'finished'?"

"It's complicated. I'll explain on the way to Berlin. Let's go. Have you looked out the window lately?"

"Hey, look at that. Wow. In summertime, no less," Stoke said, moving to the window.

"Right. It's snowing like crazy," she said, walking over to take another look. Visibility was down to zero. A white-out.

Stokely said, "We've got to get out of this house, Jet. Now. We can't afford to get snowed in up here."

"Because?"

"Because maybe you can't hear it, girl, but there's a great big clock ticking and it's getting louder by the second."

Chapter Thirty-eight

Ras al Hadd

HARRY BROCK WAS WAITING FOR HAWKE OUTSIDE THE dusty little cantina in the coastal village of Ras al Hadd. The squat, unpainted tourist café had two large windows on a second floor overlooking the sea. The drive south along the coast road from Muscat had taken almost three brutal hours. According to his handheld GPS, it continued in much the same fashion for another thousand kilometers or so, south along the coast to the town of Salalah.

Of course, he couldn't confirm that on any map. Maps were forbidden in Oman. It was intended to confuse the sultan's enemies but it worked pretty well for his friends, too.

Hawke parked the brand-new Toyota Land Cruiser they'd given him under a dusty pomegranate tree. It was the only tree he'd seen in the last hour. He drained the last of the water they'd provided and stuck his face right into the stream of icy air coming out of the center console. As he reluctantly switched off the ignition and opened the door on the blast furnace that was Oman in summer, Harry Brock strolled around the corner of the building.

Despite the intense heat and dust, Brock appeared fresh and cheerful. He wore the beginnings of a new beard, a clean white T-shirt, a pair of worn khakis, and a brown felt hat that had seen better days tilted back on his head. Hawke kept expecting him to say "Aw, shucks," or something similar, but he never did.

"Welcome to Oman," Brock said, shaking Hawke's hand as he climbed out of the Toyota.

"Is that yours?" Hawke said, eyeing the Royal Enfield motorcycle parked by the side of the building. It was a Bullet 350, black, a legendary bike among the cognoscenti.

"Yeah," Brock said, "I just picked it up yesterday in Muscat. With these so-called roads, I thought maybe a bike was a good idea."

Whatever else could be said about Harry Brock, he had excellent taste in motorcycles.

"Nice place," Hawke told Brock, looking around at the bleak and sunblistered location. The restaurant, which for some mysterious reason was named the Al-Kous Whisper, was surrounded by a low garden wall of rough-hewn stone. There was a carved wooden portal through which you entered this little Shangri-la in the desert.

"Isn't it? Ras al Hadd is considered one of Oman's garden spots."

"Because it's got a tree," Hawke said.

"Bingo."

So far, from what Alex had seen of the benighted countryside, Oman didn't have a lot of garden spots. It looked like Mars in the off-season. Reddish, stony ground, baked dry. Desolate riverbeds, cracked and empty. Abandoned villages hanging from the terraced mountainsides. Dead scenery, he thought, driving through the un-remittingly hostile environment.

The unprepossing Al-Kous Whisper was clearly reserved for tourists. Omanis weren't allowed to drink alcohol, and he wasn't even sure whether they were allowed to eat. No hootch, no maps. It was a very strict country. The sultan ran a tight ship. The Al-Kous had a flat roof and was built of concrete block. There were a few houses scattered nearby, looking abandoned and empty. These were older buildings constructed of wood and palm thatch.

Omanis clearly didn't believe in renovation or gentrification. When a town got old, they simply packed up and left. En masse. The townspeople moved further into the mountains or the desert and built a new town.

They passed through the portal into the withered garden. There was an old well just outside the restaurant and someone had left a noisy goat tied to it. Harry patted the dehydrated creature on the head as they walked past it up the path of crushed stone.

"Four stars in the *Zagat*," Brock said to Hawke, swatting at the buzzing flies and sidestepping dogshit. "Amazing wine cellar. They've apparently got a specialty dish the chef prepares, sautéed lightly in a sort of pine nut sauce, that is out of this world. Fresh goat, so they say. Isn't that right, little fella?"

"Is it always this bloody hot?" Hawke said, mounting the mercifully covered steps and ignoring both Brock and the goat. He was tired and thirsty. He hated dry heat and he felt as if he were being roasted alive in the sun. The white linen shirt he was wearing was plastered to his skin. He was tempted to have his meeting with Brock in the Toyota with the AC blasting. Would have, in fact, but he was hungry, too.

"Oman is actually the hottest place on earth," Brock said. "No lie. Pretty mild right now, though. At eight this morning it was 120 in the shade."

"But there is no shade."

"Bingo."

Harry followed Hawke through the open door. It was dark and cool inside, comparatively speaking. It was also empty, which was good. He was sure Brock had scoped the place out pretty well before suggesting it as a rendezvous. The two men mounted the narrow stairway and took an empty table by one of the open windows on the second floor. Brock ordered two cold beers. It was a local brew called Gulf and it was nonalcoholic. According to Harry it was liquid and it was cold and that was good enough.

A timid, giggling girl in a black chador delivered the beer. There were only two employees, the girl waiting tables and an old man behind the bar. The man was more sensibly dressed in the manner of most of the male population. Loose white garments and a turban. Like most Omanis Hawke had seen since touching down at Seeb International, he was on his cell phone.

The fact that Brock seemed unconcerned about this meant the proprietor was probably already on Harry's payroll. Boots on the ground, the CIA called it.

Brock rocked his chair back on two legs and smiled at Hawke. "You look like shit," he said, lacing his fingers behind his head.

"Thanks," Hawke replied, studying the flimsy mimeographed menu. He opened his bottle and took a swig of beer. "I bet you say that to all the boys."

"If I hadn't seen it with my own eyes, I wouldn't have believed it."

"Believed what?"

"Oh, come on."

"What the bloody hell are you talking about, Brock?"

Hawke didn't bother to hide his irritation. He knew Brock would bring up the incident as soon as they met. He supposed he'd have to tell him about it sometime, but not now. His aching and bruised body had been jammed into a cramped cockpit all day and every bone in his body ached. If the sadist who designed the F-16 seat were ever allowed to design prison furniture for Camp X-Ray at Guantanamo, the hue and cry from the world media would be deafening.

What Hawke did not need at the moment was an American with a sense of humor. But Brock wouldn't let go.

"Your little mishap on the *Lincoln*?"

"You mean the *incident*," Hawke said, and cut his angry eyes to the window.

"Yeah."

"It could have been worse."

"How's that?"

Hawke said, "Old pilots say it's better to die than to look bad, but it is possible to do both."

Brock thought about that a second, saw the hard cast of Hawke's eyes, and decided to shut up.

Neither man said anything else for a few minutes. They sat and sipped their pseudobeer in silence, both of them looking out the window. Hawke imagined Brock was probably having the same misgivings about this mission that he was. These things were all about team. This team had been thrown together without their knowledge or consent. They'd been asked, told, to conduct a critically important operation. Like most hostage rescue ops, it promised to be very dangerous. And they were going in blind. Neither man knew what to make of the other. Hawke knew why he'd been chosen. He was pretty good at this stuff.

What he still didn't know was why the hell Kelly had chosen Harry Brock.

Hawke sipped his beer and stared morosely out the window, trying to adjust to his new environment. A bloody wasteland. A school bus went by, jouncing along the rocky road, a cloud of dust trailing behind it. There were curtains in all the windows and they were tightly drawn. So the little boys outside couldn't see the little girls inside. Or vice-versa. He was sure someone could offer a good explanation for this bizarre custom, but to Hawke it just seemed unnatural and cruel.

I am definitely the stranger in the strange land, he thought, suspiciously eyeing the goat tied to the well. He'd never eaten goat. He wasn't about to start now. Goats were bad luck. There was a reason why when things in the military went to hell they called it a goat-fuck. The shy girl in the black chador returned for their order. Brock ordered lamb kebobs. He ordered the fish and rice. The nondescript CIA briefing book lay on the table unopened. Hawke didn't have the energy to break the seal.

"Somebody's meeting us here in about twenty minutes," Brock finally said. He opened the brief and started flipping through the pages.

"Yeah? Who might that be?"

"A friend of the family. Name's Ahmed. Great guy. You'll like him."

"A friend of whose family? Yours?"

"The sultan's."

"Two more boots on the ground."

"Bingo."

"That's convenient," Hawke said, trying to be pleasant, "Where'd you bump into him?"

"Let's just say we've done business before. He's the one who found me the Enfield. Name's Ahmed Badur. He is wired in this country, I gotta tell you."

"Is he the one who's going to help us find the sultan and his family?"

"Bingo," Brock said.

"If you say that word again, I'm going to kill you," Hawke told him.

At that moment, hot, exhausted, and miserable as he was, he almost meant it. Yeah, he'd cracked up a very expensive airplane. Until he was completely cleared of pilot error, there was going to be a little black cloud following him around. But it wasn't his fault, goddamnit. And he wasn't going to spend the rest of his life taking heat for it. From anybody.

Hawke added, "And guess what, Brock. Because you're a NOC? I'm going to get away with it."

"Listen, pal, you might be a big effing whoop in jolly old England, but—"

A loud ah-oogah sound from the street below broke the moment between the two of them. Hawke looked out of the window and was surprised to see a 1927 Rolls-Royce Silver Ghost arriving in a billow of dust. On the louvered bonnet behind the famous "Flying Lady" atop the radiator was a small triangular pennant. Orange, white, and green, the national flag of the Kingdom of Oman.

When the dust had finally settled, a nattily dressed man with slicked-back black hair, a full black mustache, and gold aviator sunglasses was revealed, sitting behind the wheel of the open car. He turned and grinned up at Hawke, who was looking at him through the window. He was wearing Western clothing, a white linen suit. He looked, Hawke thought, like a tango instructor.

"I suppose that's your friend," Hawke said, watching the man climb out of the old Roller.

"That's him."

"Why is everyone in this bloody country named Ahmed?"

"Not everyone. Only about 80 percent."

"Nice car."

"The sultan gave it to him. Prince Charles gave it to the sultan after he and Diana paid a state visit. They're old buddies."

"I like your chap's low-key, understated approach to espionage," Hawke said. "Exactly what's required in a covert operation like this one."

"Look, Hawke. Everybody in Oman knows this guy. He was the sultan's right-hand man for two decades, the go-to guy at the palace. He's a living legend around here. What would be noticed is if he arrived on a camel or crept up to the back door in full desert camo."

"I'll try to keep that in mind," Hawke said as the man entered the upstairs room and approached their table.

"Sit down, Ahmed, and say hello to Alex Hawke," said Brock.

"A great pleasure," Ahmed said, his wide smile revealing two gleaming rows of perfectly spaced white teeth. He bowed formally from the waist. "I have heard of you, Lord Hawke. The Prince of Wales speaks most—"

Harry looked up. "Wait. *Lord* Hawke? Is that what he just called you?"

"Drop it, Brock," Hawke said, "I don't use the title."

"Yeah, but still. I had no idea—"

"Mr. Badur," Alex said, ignoring Brock and motioning to the man in white to sit down. "Thanks for coming. I assume Mr. Brock has already told you why we're here."

"He has indeed. Britain and America are old friends of Oman. And of Sultan Aji Abbas as well. You two men are here on a most important mission. Vital to our country."

Hawke looked at the man and decided that, appearances and conveyances to the contrary, he was a chap who might be trusted. Hawke said, "I am here as a private citizen, Ahmed. But Mr. Brock and I will do whatever it takes to resolve this crisis. Our first order of business is to rescue the sultan's family."

"Yes. Please. This, we must do immediately."

"Who is holding them? Troops?"

"Scum. French mercenaries. In the country illegally. They slipped ashore at night at Masara. A French submarine was spotted off that coast that morning. I have informants on the island who say they are all ex-Legionnaire washouts who do this kind of thing for a living."

"How many of them?"

"Thirty-some-odd. But not under French command. A Chinese officer arrived here on a diplomatic mission two weeks ago. Along with his military aides-de-camp."

"Do you know his name?"

"Yes. Major Tony Tang."

"Does this Major Tang stay in one place? Frequently, hostages are moved about."

"They have not been moved since they were placed under the protection of the French at the fortress. Don't worry, your lordship. I know where they are at all times. I have a man in the kitchen, you see."

"Tell me about the location, please, Ahmed."

"It is a medieval fort on the island of Masara, sir. The fortress was originally built in the thirteenth century for strategic purposes. It guards the southern approach to the Strait of Hormuz. It is built into a bluff overlooking the sea. It is called Fort Mahoud and it is historic indeed. In late 1940 or so, Field Marshal Rommel himself chose it as his temporary headquarters while he was planning his relief of the Italians in North Africa."

"Rommel? I had no idea," Hawke said. He had studied Rommel at war college and found the brilliant and complex man fascinating.

"Yes. He made many modifications to the physical plant, naturally. Implemented much-needed reconstruction and modernization. In 1941, when the Desert Fox left to join his Afrika Korps in Libya, he left behind a great fortress indeed. And, a small Wehrmacht garrison as well. The Nazis remained there on the rock until the Allies finally drove them off near the end of the war."

"And exactly how did the Allies do that?" Hawke asked. "Drive them off."

"Bombed the living hell out of them, sir. From the air and sea."

"That works for me," Brock said.

"Bomb the living hell out of the sultan's family?" Hawke asked Brock, his blue eyes unwavering.

"It was the only way to do it, as you will both soon see," Ahmed said.

"Then what happened?" Hawke asked.

"There was much damage, and after the war, the fort was pretty much forgotten. About twenty years ago, His Highness decided to turn the fortress into a national museum. A showcase for new generations to see the glories of Oman's past. I am an architect by training. I was chosen by His Highness as the designer and curator. I have with me many sets of plans for the fort. Even those Rommel left behind. And my own plans for the museum I built. It has not changed much since I completed the work some twenty years ago."

Hawke was encouraged by this access to the plans. "Good. Could be a fairly simple snatch, then. Let's find a fisherman willing to take us out there and go have a look."

"Have no false impressions, your lordship," Ahmed said, rolling the plans out on the table. Brock put beer bottles at two corners to hold them down. "It will not be simple at all."

"Tell me why," Hawke said, turning over an old exterior elevation of the fort, being careful not to tear it. "We just have to get the sultan and his wife out. And a few children."

"You have put your finger on the problem, sir."

"What problem?"

"The sultan has more than one wife, sir."

"How many? Two? Three?"

"Over twenty of them when last I counted, sir."

Hawke looked at Brock. *"Twenty women?"*

Brock grinned, looking at Hawke.

"Doesn't sound like a simple snatch to me, your lordship," he said.

Chapter Thirty-nine

Coney Island

LIGHTNING SIZZLED ALL AROUND THE OLD AMUSEMENT park. Every second or two, the bizarre skyline of rocket towers and roller coasters was etched in stark relief against the dark sky. Congreve stood in the blinding rain, bathed in flashing blue lights, wiping the water from his eyes. The English detective looked through the binoculars for the umpteenth time, silently praying that one of these jagged bolts would strike the great whacking tower atop which the Chinaman now clung for dear life.

Most noncivilians present were convinced that as soon as this driving rain and wind let up, the Chinaman would remove his weapon from the haversack on his back and start shooting. From his angle, at the very top of the Parachute Jump, it would be like shooting fish in a barrel. He would be able to see almost straight down into the swinging car where Joe Bones cowered. Now, thank God, it was all the assassin could do just to hold on. Congreve knew how he felt. He, too, was holding on, but his frustration was mounting with every added second of uncertainty.

Above his head, the rumble of thunder was preempted by the booming thump-thump-thump of the ATAC and NYPD helicopters hovering over the park. Most had their brilliant bluish white spotlights trained on the swinging car at the top of the Ferris wheel. A single black ATAC Sikorskey chopper under the ground command of Captain Mariucci was now hovering directly above the tower. The chopper trained its beam on the tiny man in white.

Also aboard was a medical retrieval team. And an ATAC sniper who stood braced in the open bay. He had his sniper rifle zeroed on the Chinaman's heart. His finger was on the trigger but he didn't dare pull it. He had orders not to.

He couldn't fire because of the extraordinary political situation on the ground below him. Nor could his brethren in the circling NYPD helicopters. It wasn't for lack of muzzles aimed in his direction that the man on the tower was still alive. There were plenty of guns trained on him. It was because an impasse had been reached in the raging turf battle between city, state, and federal law enforcement units. So, everyone just stood at the base of the tower and looked up at the Chinaman in the spotlight, clinging to the Parachute Drop.

Except for Captain Mariucci, who was stomping around, splashing furiously in the puddles and demanding to know who the hell was in charge here. It was a good question.

Amazingly enough, in Ambrose Congreve's view, the sharpshooters on both sides of the law enforcement equation had been ordered to hold their fire. This was the crux of the argument. The man on the tower was trespassing, correct. He was a suspect in a homicide that had just occurred in Queens, yes. He was armed, yes, maybe, but you couldn't prove it. Who knew why he was up there? And he hadn't threatened or shot at anyone. Who knew?

An NYPD commander had just told Mariucci that, for all he knew at the moment, the guy had permits to carry a concealed weapon from the freaking FBI. At this point, who knew? Maybe it wasn't even a gun in that case on his back! Maybe it was an umbrella! Or a nine iron!

"What? What did you just say?" Mariucci screamed. He put his hand over the mouthpiece and looked at Congreve, his face contorted with disbelieving rage. "You won't believe what this lunatic just said to me."

"What did he say?" Congreve asked.

"He said, and I quote, 'Suppose we shoot this guy and when we scrape him up off the sidewalk we find out he's some wacko Chinese rock climber on holiday who's just getting in a little practice,' close quote."

Who knew, indeed?

Congreve and Mariucci, at least, were equally convinced of one thing. This was the Chinaman who had only hours ago stood over Benny Sangster and ingested his heart while the old mobster slowly bled out on his bed. Motive? It could only be that certain members of the French government had heard somebody was poking around inside a thirty-year-old murder case. So they sent a Chinese assassin to rub out the only two remaining eyewitnesses save the murderer himself.

That, at least, was the case the captain was making to the powers that be at One Police Plaza at this very moment. That, and the indisputable fact that it was an urgent matter of national security.

But Mariucci couldn't prove any of it standing down here on the ground in the pouring rain.

More red and blue lights flashed across Congreve's face as Ladder Company 103 arrived on the scene. The massive hook and ladder fire engine came rolling to a stop on the midway, just at the base of the Ferris wheel. Immediately, firemen leaped off the truck and converged on the controls at the rear. There was a huge extension ladder mounted on a turntable. The fireman operating the ladder began raising it.

As the ladder ascended into the rain-whipped sky, Ambrose Congreve had, as was his wont, an idea.

It took a few minutes, but he finally managed to get his friend the irate NYPD captain to stop screaming into the phone and discuss the situation like a reasonable facsimile of a normal human being.

"What am I going to do?" a still livid Mariucci said to Ambrose, snapping his phone shut. "I'll tell you what I'm going to do. I'm going to get one of my guys here to volunteer to go up that frigging ladder and get Joey out of the frigging car. That's what I'm going to do. Because, despite the mass of chaos and confusion you see on the ground and in the frigging air, I am in charge here, goddamnit."

"The Chinaman will shoot as soon as your man starts up the ladder," Ambrose said in a deliberately soothing voice.

"Exactly! Now, you're thinking, Inspector. You're right, he will! And, as soon as he even *looks* like he's going to shoot, blammo, my sharpshooter takes him out like fucking dumplings in a box. *Capisce?*"

"A clever way out of the current stalemate, perhaps."

"Thank you."

"But you're putting your man's life in grave danger."

"Really? I didn't think of that. Good point. Now that I do, you're absolutely right. But, gosh darn it, that's just the way we do things here in New York City, Inspector. So, if you'll excuse me a second—"

"I may have a less risky solution."

"Really? How interesting? May I ask what is it?"

Congreve stepped back and looked from the top of the tower to the tip of the ladder, his brow wrinkled with concentration.

"Extend the ladder to its full height," Congreve said. "Swing it around hard. Don't be shy. Just be careful you don't accidentally slam the ladder into the top of the parachute tower when you're bringing it around."

"What did you just say?" Mariucci said, looking up at him, and then the ladder, through squinty eyes.

"When you swing that ladder into position, be careful."

"Yeah. I see what you mean about the ladder. Naturally, we got to be very, very careful when we move it. We wouldn't want to hit the tower or nothing."

"Definitely not. The Chinaman might fall off if you did that."

"Accidentally."

"Exactly."

"He could get badly hurt. Even die."

"Surely the latter."

"Would you excuse me for a moment, Inspector Congreve? I would like to go over and have a quiet word with the fire chief of Ladder Company 103 over there. Name's Bellew. Old friend of mine. No one in this very unfortunate turf battle has seen fit to inform him of the risks the man on the tower poses to our national security. I think I should do that, don't you?"

"I certainly do."

Ten minutes later, he was back.

"He's going to do it."

"Good for him."

"What do you mean? Of course he's going to do it. I told him the whole story. He's a great American. Okay, here we go. Watch this."

The turntable atop the fire engine began to rotate. The ladder, fully extended, began to move toward the tower in a great sweeping arc.

"You think this will work?" Mariucci whispered.

"I do. I wouldn't have suggested it otherwise."

"How come you look so worried?"

"I must say I hadn't considered the fact that you would have to involve your friend Chief Bellew."

"What do you mean?"

"Repercussions. The law of unintended consequences. There will in all probability be an investigation into the 'accident' that is about to occur. Chief Bellew may face serious questions about his role."

"Serious questions? He's faced a whole shitload worse than that, Inspector. That's a terrorist up on that tower. The tower's going down, and he's going with it. Poetic justice, right?"

"I suppose it is."

"Inspector Congreve, listen to me. The New York Fire Department *alone* lost 343 of the bravest men in the world one very shitty day in September. It's a day we'd all like to forget. But we won't. We're all in the antiterrorist business now. Every last one of us."

"He's doing the right thing. So are you. I'd like you to keep your job, though."

"If I lose my job over this—look, it's getting close—if I lose my job over this one, Inspector, I—"

"Yes?"

"I guarantee you I will leave the NYPD just like I arrived."

"And how is that?"

"Fired with enthusiasm."

"Oh, my God, look!" someone shouted. In the confusion, a few civilians had managed to evade the posted police and duck under the police tape strung up to cordon off the midway. It was mostly teenagers and younger children, but there were a few adults as well.

A cry went up from the small crowd when it became obvious what was going to happen. The heavy steel-reinforced aluminum ladder was moving fairly rapidly. Congreve thought it might just lop the top of the rotted tower clean off. But what happened was, it didn't. The ladder slammed into the tower with a resounding clang that shuddered down the rungs from above. But the ladder had stopped dead upon impact with the iron structure. And when it had stopped, the Chinaman was still there.

The crowd below, in its ignorance, cheered.

When the ladder reversed direction away from the tower, the crowd breathed a collective sigh of relief. Only to cry out again when they saw that the ladder was swinging once more toward the tower. And this time, it was moving very, very quickly indeed.

"See what I mean about my guys?" Mariucci said. "New York City doesn't forgive and it doesn't forget."

Ambrose couldn't muster a reply. He was simply transfixed by the sight of the Chinaman's death struggle at the top of the tower. He couldn't go any higher. And he knew what was waiting for him at the bottom.

Chapter Forty

Bavaria

"I FORGOT SOMETHING," STOKE SAID, TRYING TO CATCH HIS breath. They'd been climbing in deep snow for nearly an hour. The sun was barely up. The boughs of the high-altitude pines were heavy with new snow already starting to melt. Last night's freakish storm had eased up to flurries, and you could see bright blue sky behind the clouds. It was going to be a beautiful day. But that didn't help Stoke's mood much. It was still bitingly cold and heavy slogging. He looked at Jet and tried to fake a smile.

"I'm sorry, Jet, we got to go back down to the damn hotel."

"What did you just say?"

"We have to go back down."

"I cannot believe this," Jet said, ripping her goggles off and flinging them into the snow.

"I can't believe you!" Stoke said. "Here I save your ass and—"

"You saved me? I'm the one who took out Viktor when—"

"No, I meant the other time when—you know—back on Schatzi's yacht. That cage thing."

"Jesus, Stoke."

Jet was not a happy camper. Slogging through heavy snow up a steep mountainside in the dark and cold didn't appeal to some women. But it had to be done. They'd left in a hurry. Stoke had pointed out that before their deaths either Viktor or Irma could have put in a call to von Draxis. It could have easily happened while Jet was giving Stoke the tour of Schloss Reichenbach. There was obviously no way to know. But you had to assume it was a possibility. So it had made sense for them to vacate immediately before they were trapped in the *gasthaus* by the snowstorm.

Jet agreed. The good news was the storm was probably keeping all aircraft grounded. Von Draxis wouldn't be able to put a chopper in the air. But, Jet told Stokely, there was a strong likelihood von Draxis would already have men with their descriptions posted at the local train and bus stations. Yeah, Stoke said, they would have to go back the way they came. On foot. Over the mountains to Salzburg. There, they could rest and then catch the first *Schnellzug* smoking to Berlin.

Snow was rare this time of year. But, at this elevation, it was not at all unheard of. So, before bidding fond adieu to the late Viktor and Irma, he and Jet had turned the house upside-down. They'd rummaged through all the drawers and closets and found enough snow gear and parkas to get them back to Salzburg. But, at the last minute, Jet had handed Stoke two long skinny sticks with leather straps on them and told him to put them on. Stoke looked at her like she was crazy.

In that way, Jet had learned that Stokely didn't know how to ski cross-country. So, now, they were making the trek using snowshoes. It wasn't his fault, she'd told him, that it had snowed. Or that he didn't know how to ski, or any of that. No, no, none of it was his fault, but she sure as hell acted like it was. All of it. All the way.

"You've got to be kidding me," Jet now said, calmer, brushing wet snow from her eyes and stamping her feet. "You *forgot* something?"

"I wish I was kidding. I hate these damn shoes. How's anybody supposed to walk around with tennis racquets strapped to his feet? It's not natural."

"All right, Stokely. What did you forget?"

"Oh, the damn guest register, that's all."

"The guest register! Shit! I can't believe it!"

"I know, I know. Like leaving a signed confession at a murder scene. Really stupid."

"Not you, me! How could I have forgotten that?"

"You don't blame me?"

"Hell no. It's on me. Serious lapse of professional concentration on my part. I was so worried about the storm closing in that—you're right. We have to go back. Let's get going. I apologize."

"All right, then," Stoke said. Smiling, he began following the fresh path she'd made in the snow, happier than hell to be out of the doghouse. Also, he had to admit her being the lead dog made the view much better and the going much easier. He was beginning to understand why Alex Hawke, despite his misgivings about the woman, had told Stoke to take good care of her.

After half an hour of picking their way carefully back down the mountain, they came through the pines to a rocky ridge. The site overlooked a bowl-shaped valley, dazzling white with snow. To the left lay a jewel of a lake, a deep, sparkling blue. Beyond the valley was the treeline where the serious trees grew. Great big towering conifers, draped in snow, soaring sixty or seventy feet into the sky. The blue sky and water, the green trees, the white snow. It was so pretty, like a fairy tale, Stoke could hardly stand it.

"Let's hold up a sec, catch our breath," Stoke said, looking around at the view. A minute ago, he thought he'd heard something. Like a faint buzz. He held his breath and listened. Now, it was gone.

"Good idea," Jet said.

"Hey, what's that?"

"What?"

"Back there behind us. Just coming over the mountains. Little black dot in the sky. See it?"

"No."

"Well, I do. Let's get across this valley as fast as we can. Once we reach the treeline we'll be all right. C'mon. Hurry!"

Stoke took off, running as fast as he was able in the damn snowshoes. Stoke was fast—in another life he'd been professionally employed as a running back—but Jet kept up with him.

"What is it?" she said, crunching the snow right behind him.

"A helicopter," Stoke said. "Maybe just a coincidence, but we can't afford to take that chance."

"Right."

"Hey, am I holding you up?" He'd heard her coming up fast behind him.

"A little."

"Go on ahead then, girl. I'll catch up with you at the guesthouse. If that's who I think it is up there behind us, we can't afford to have them find the bodies and our names in the guestbook. They'll get on the chopper radio and we can forget about ever making it to Berlin. Go!"

She raced ahead. Stoke couldn't stop looking over his shoulder at the little black dot that kept getting bigger and bigger in the sky. He could hear it clearly now, too. Kind of a high droning noise. He'd been trying to convince himself that maybe he was lucky. Maybe it was just a Bavarian Mountain Rescue helo, out for a spin. Looking for lost campers. But Stoke had a saying about these kinds of feelings: "Luck is for losers."

He took the snowshoes off, Velcroed them to his backpack, and started plowing through the snow in just his boots. He thought it seemed a little faster. But he was still way behind Jet. She was already into the woods. Girl ran like a deer, even in snowshoes. Anyway, he could still make it to the treeline before the chopper got close enough to see him. Leastways, he thought he could. He ran even harder.

Out of breath, he dove headlong into the woods and lay panting on the ground. The buzz got louder. He got to his knees, remaining crouched between two evergreens in the scrub to watch the oncoming helicopter. It had clearly descended to a lower altitude. He kept hoping for a course change. That would make their lives a whole lot simpler. But it wasn't happening. The chopper was on a direct heading for the *gasthaus*.

The damn thing flew on, dropping below the far rim of the big white bowl he'd just crossed, flying right down on the deck and headed straight for him. The thing was flying in out of the sun, juking this way and that, hotshot stuff. A pilot with attitude.

Suddenly the pilot banked hard left, swung around, and flew even lower. They were examining the fresh tracks in the snow. Satisfied, the pilot pivoted and got the big bird back on course. His heading would take him right over Stoke's head to the helipad at Zum Wilden Hund.

Stoke looked up at the chopper as its skids barely cleared the trees, roaring over his head. It was black, all right, just like the one he'd seen in the South of France. Had the same letters, VDI, painted in bright scarlet red on the sleek flanks and the belly below the cockpit. Only now Stoke knew what those letters stood for. Von Draxis Industries. Stoke scrambled to his feet and started running through the dark woods as fast as he could. He wanted to get to Jet first.

He didn't.

When he got to the *gasthaus* and the clearing in the woods, the chopper was on the pad, the sagging rotor still whirling listlessly. Nobody remained inside the helicopter that he could see from this distance. There were fresh tracks in the snow all around the bird. Stoke, guessing by the deep depressions in the snow, made it to be two crew, the pilot and one passenger. There were some other tracks around the skids, too, as if an animal had been there earlier. A fox maybe. Or, judging by the tracks, maybe a big wolf.

The house was quiet. There were long carrot-shaped icicles hanging down off the roof, dripping in the warm sunshine. Jet was nowhere in sight. Keeping the helicopter between him and the *gasthaus,* he moved quickly to the nearside of the chopper. Leaning against the fuselage, he spent one minute trying to get some more frigid air into his lungs. When this thing was over, he was going to go someplace warm and get his ass in serious shape. This heavy-breathing shit was for beginners. Yeah. He'd go to Miami, Key Biscayne, see his true love by the sea. The beautiful Fancha. Hell, yeah, he would.

His fingers were numb with cold. He banged his arms to his sides to get the blood flowing. He slipped out of the backpack, let it drop softly to the snow. He fumbled with the flap but finally got it open. No sounds coming from inside the house. He pulled Viktor's Schmeisser out of the bag and slung it on his shoulder. He had the feeling that this was the gun the old boy had carried during the war. Back in the day when he was a handsome young Alpenkorps officer. And Irma was a semibeautiful *Fräulein* just busting out of her dirndl. Damn, he thought, looking at the Schmeisser machine pistol in his hand, should have given the gun to Jet.

Running for the house in a low crouch, he heard Jet cry out. A warning? No. Worse. Pain. Have to be some scary shit going on inside to make that girl cry out in pain. Been there, felt that.

He ran up the six steps leading to the front door, not worrying now about how much noise he was making busting icicles. The door was slightly ajar. He pushed it open with his left hand, stepped inside, entering the room sideways to present less of a target, and low, with the lethal-looking Schmeisser out in front of him. *I'm home!*

He swept the room left to right. Empty, except for poor old Viktor, who was still slumped over at his silent piano with his hands on the keyboard. Viktor, his head smashed sideways under the piano lid, had a little icicle of blood hanging from the tip of his nose. It was cold as an igloo inside.

He and Jet had shut the furnace down in the hope of preserving the proprietor and his daughter until somebody found them up here. Now he could see his breath as he moved quietly through the living room. The little red leather guestbook was on the reception counter right where he'd last seen it. Thinking that he was just crazy enough to forget it again, he picked it up and jammed it into one of the side pockets of his parka.

He heard noises coming from the very rear of the house. That would be the kitchen. That would account for why nobody had seen or heard him coming.

He moved as quietly as he could along the empty hallway leading to the rear of the *gasthaus*. At the end, sunshine poured into the hall. The kitchen door was open. Two male voices shouting angrily in German. And a low menacing growl. What the hell could make that kind of noise? He kept going until he got to the door and peeked inside.

The kitchen was large and sunny with pretty red-and-white checked curtains on all the windows. He couldn't see anybody at first, had to step softly around the big wood-burning stove that was blocking his—

Christ. It was the two Arnolds. They were wearing black VDI Security uniforms that bore a frightening resemblance to the old SS outfits Stoke had seen Nazis wearing in the movies.

They hadn't heard him. Their backs were to him and they were both talking at once, shouting in German, stepping on each other's lines.

Stoke knew just enough vocabulary to know they'd found the two bodies and they were really pissed off about it. *"Tod! Tod!"* Dead! Dead! The Arnold on the left had a stubby little automatic. The Arnold on the right had one end of a steel chain leash in his hand. The fabric of his uniform, stretched tight across his big shoulders, was about to rip wide open. He was struggling to control a vicious, snarling animal that looked like it could rip his arm right out of his shoulder socket.

At the other end of Arnold's shiny leash was a huge black Doberman pinscher, just dying to sink his teeth into Jet, who was on the floor in the corner. Blood was trickling out of her mouth and running down her chin. Otherwise, she looked okay. The Doberman was rearing on his hind legs, straining at the chain, his paws scratching at the air, his head whipping back and forth, loopy white saliva flying from his snapping jaws in all directions. Stoke figured it was high time to put an end to all this melodrama.

"Ah-nold's in the kitchen with Dinah . . ."

He sang just that much of his old favorite and the Arnold on the left swung on him, bringing the muzzle of his gun up as he spun.

"Was ist los?" the blond guy said, and Stoke put one in his forehead. He crumpled to the floor, spraying bullets that luckily didn't hit anyone except some little gnomes up on a shelf.

"Remember me?" he said to the remaining Arnold, who was staring at him with his mouth wide open. "The *Valkyrie* party?" Stoke added, helpfully. "The big black guy, remember?"

"Was gibt hier?" That was the best the poor guy could do under the circumstances. Stoke raised the Schmeisser. The guy's eyes went wide. He had no desire to join his fraternal twin pumping blood for a living on the floor. Not to mention his own sidearm was securely snapped inside a leather holster that didn't allow for the quick-draw approach.

"Here's the problem, Arnold," Stoke said. "I shoot you, the dog eats her. See what I'm saying? So maybe I'll shoot your dog and *then* shoot you, okay? Sound good?"

Arnold said something that was probably unprintable in German. Stoke ground the Schmeisser's v-and-blade gunsight into his right ear and said, "Call him off now or you and your dog die."

"Don't shoot the dog, Stoke," Jet said.

"What?"

"Tell him to release the dog."

"Are you completely nuts?"

"Just do it."

"Maybe you're suicidal, but he isn't going to let this dog go long as I got my gun in his ear."

"Then take the leash away from him with your other hand, Stoke. Then you've got control of the dog and him."

"Okay. That sounds more like it. You heard her, Arnold. I'm going to take the dog now. You just be cool and nobody gets his head venti-lated."

As a precaution, Stoke ground the gun barrel deeper into the German's ear canal while he unwound the dog leash from his hand and wrapped it around his own. Instantly, the barking and snarling animal attempted to rip Stoke's arm from the socket. He was getting jerked around so badly by the lunging Doberman it was hard to keep the Schmeisser aimed at Arnold's head. It wouldn't take Arnold long to figure out that now was his chance.

"All right, I got the dog. Now what?"

"Just let him go, Stoke," Jet said. "It's okay."

"Jet, seriously, have you lost your mind?"

"She's my dog, Stoke."

"Your dog."

"Right. Her name is Blondi. She's just happy to see me, aren't you, girl?"

"Your funeral," Stoke said and dropped the chain. He was all out of argument with the woman. The big dog bounded across the floor and, instead of going for her jugular, immediately began lathering Jet's cheeks and forehead with wet sloppy kisses.

"Good dog, Blondi," Jet said, patting his head and nuzzling her cheek against the dog's neck. She put both arms around Blondi's neck and hugged the big Doberman to her.

"You believe this?" Stoke asked Arnold, the two of them standing there looking down at her.

"Not really," Arnold said in surprisingly good English.

"Schatzi gave her to me when she was a puppy," Jet said. "Didn't he, baby? Right? Who's my buddy?"

Stoke and Arnold just looked at each other.

"Hey, Arnold," Stoke said, "You think I could fit in your uniform?"

Arnold looked at him.

"Little tight across the shoulders, maybe?" Stoke said. "What do you think?"

Chapter Forty-one

Gulf of Oman

CACIQUE ROLLED HEAVILY IN THE SIX-FOOT SEAS. THE SIXTY-four-foot trawler, under the command of Captain Ali al-Houri, had seen better days. Her old diesel was moody. Temperamental. But Brock's new sidekick Ahmed had assured Hawke that she was at least seaworthy enough for their current purposes: a surveillance circumnavigation of the island of Masara and a closeup look at Fort Mahoud itself.

Ahmed had found and chartered the old trawler for them, assuring them that she normally did a milk run along the coast from Ras al Hadd down to Salalah. The theory was that since she'd frequented these waters for years, no one on the island or the mainland would pay her any mind. With a checklist prepared and supplemented by Brock, he'd made sure she was properly provisioned.

Properly, in Brock's parlance, included weapons, explosives, experimental optical equipment, hi-res digital video and still cameras with telescopic lenses, a dozen SEAL scuba rigs, a bottle of Gosling's Black Seal for Hawke, and a case of Budweiser for Brock.

Between the wily Ahmed and the well-connected Brock, it seemed, anything on earth was attainable. Watching the supplies arrive on board, Hawke imagined that if he told Ahmed he simply could not proceed with the hostage rescue until he had the original of van Gogh's *Sunflowers* under his arm, the framed painting would appear a few hours later.

As it was, a brand-new U.S. Navy SDV minisubmarine was hidden under an old tarp, lashed to blocks on the stern. The SDV, a Swimmer Delivery Vehicle developed by the navy for the SEALs, had been just part of the shipment arriving at Muscat on a Hercules C-130 the night before.

At the moment, *Cacique* was steering a northeasterly course along the Masara Bank, a good fishing spot lying roughly a mile off the eastern coast of the island of Masara. They were doing a leisurely eight knots in the rough seas. Hawke had been outside at the port rail with his high-powered Zeiss binoculars for the last hour. Finally, he'd grown weary of reconnoitering endless miles of bleak grey rock being pounded by heavy waves and stowed both the Sony video camera and the Zeiss Ikons.

The sun was already dipping below the yardarm of the stubby mast for'ard of the pilothouse. The only thing of interest Hawke had seen all afternoon was a herd of green turtles and a small blue fishing boat chugging along towing a string of white dinghies behind her. He'd counted ten of them bobbing along like baby ducks behind their mother. It was something he'd not seen in any other part of the world.

Hawke and Brock sat inside the pilothouse at a small table strewn with maps, satellite photos, and thermal-imaging photos of the island and Fort Mahoud itself. A dedicated U.S. bird launched six hours ago had shot the Oman recon photos Hawke was looking at now. The mood inside the pilothouse was grim. It had rapidly become obvious to both men that their early plan of getting the hostages out by air would be well nigh impossible.

Ahmed, having grown weary of the endless strategizing, had wandered out onto the afterdeck and found himself a comfortable patch of precious shade. Despite all the pitching and rolling, he was now lounging in one of the old-fashioned steamer chairs lined up along the stern rail. His chair was carefully aligned amidships for minimum yaw, facing aft. He was reading a ten-year-old copy of *Architectural Digest*, happily flipping through the pages. He seemed to have decided that, since he was going to be living aboard this old tub for a few days, he might as well make himself as comfortable as possible.

The desolate island of Masara lay just off their port beam, bleak and, so far, uninhabited. It was basically little more than a large rocky outcropping situated a few miles off, and lying parallel to, the coast of Oman. So far, the only island residents Hawke had observed were massive flocks of white flamingos. Ahmed had told him that morning that the bird-watching in the afternoon would be spectacular. Oman was the central corridor in the migratory pathway of thousands of exotic birds journeying between Asia and Africa.

Hawke had thanked him for this very useful information but said that he was far more interested in whirlybirds at the present moment. He was searching for some place, hidden from the spy cams above, where he might put a chopper on the ground. A wide spit of sand revealed at low tide might even be sufficient. Hell, anything remotely flat would do.

So far, nothing. No smooth hilltops, no elevated plateaus, no roads. Hawke saw nothing remotely resembling a place to set even a small bird down. Nor did the surveillance photos reveal any flat surfaces within or atop the fortress that looked large enough to accommodate a helicopter.

Finally, there were no large interior courtyards, a thing that Hawke had been hoping for. He concluded there was simply no place to land aircraft of any kind on Masara. This "simple snatch," as Brock had come to call the mission, would clearly have to be accomplished from the sea. Getting this job done was, to all appearances, going to be an extremely difficult proposition.

Somehow, he and Brock had to figure out how to storm this bloody fortress, subdue a few dozen French mercenaries, rescue the sultan and his harem, and get them safely back out to *Cacique*. And they had forty-eight hours to figure it out. Brick Kelly had called Alex on the sat phone earlier in the day. He said events were moving very rapidly in Washington and London. The president and the British prime minister had just issued a joint statement saying that any invasion of Oman by any foreign government would have serious consequences.

"Don't let us get to that point, Alex," Brick had said before he hung up. "And don't get caught. Brock's already a no-name NOC. As you well know, you're an honorary one. The U.S. has no dog in this fight. Got it?"

Hawke now looked over at the man standing at the old-fashioned wooden wheel, feet planted wide apart, eyes peeled for shoals.

"Captain, how do they get supplies out to this island? Food and drink for the museum staffers, I mean?"

"Please call me Ali, sir," the captain said, smiling back at Hawke.

"All right, Ali, tell me about the supply situation."

"There is a long steel dock, sir. Built into the rocks just below the fort. Where the daily tourist ferries tie up. The supply ship, she comes once a week. She ties up there, too."

"A supply ship," Hawke said, "Same day each week?"

"Yes, sir. Comes every Saturday night around nine. Day after tomorrow. Just like clockwork, sir."

"Very helpful, thank you."

"In about fifteen minutes we'll be rounding Point Mala, sir. Then you'll be able to see our beautiful fort in 3-D living color."

Hawke had taken an immediate liking to the *Cacique*'s skipper. He'd already decided he could trust him. Years of exposure to sun and salt air had weathered his skin to a fine, nutty brown. He was a good-looking fellow, in his midforties perhaps, with thick black hair just going grey. His large brown eyes were sad and watchful above the jutting nose. He had strong white teeth and a mouth that, while smiling at the moment, could easily harden into a fierce line when the shooting started.

Hawke had sized the captain up as both a steadfast friend and a merciless enemy. He was glad to have him aboard.

"Here's our problem," he now said to Brock, tapping his index finger on a faded drawing appended to a larger elevation of the fort.

"The twin towers," Brock said with only a trace of irony.

"Right. Standing guard over the only entrance in the entire structure, according to Ahmed. Look here. These steps leading up from the sea to the entrance. I have them rising fifty feet above sea level, leading up to this main gate. The only way in or out. If I were Rommel, I would have put heavy machine guns in those towers. High-rise pillboxes. I would imagine the Chinaman in charge has done the same."

"No way inside from the rear?" Brock asked.

"No. The rear of the fort is built right into the bluff facing the sea. Surrounded on three sides by solid rock. Whoever built this bloody castle was thinking ahead."

"We can't sneak up behind them, we can't land on their roof. Looks to me like we've got to go up the front steps and knock on the front door."

"With the towers providing overlapping fields of fire."

"Turning anyone attempting to mount the steps into hamburger."

"And any approaching vessel to scrap iron. Sounds exciting, doesn't it, Harry?"

The captain turned away from the wheel.

"All right, Commander, you can see the fort just coming into view on our port bow!" Ali said. "I won't be able to get any closer or slow down, I'm afraid. Otherwise it will look like we're looking."

"Let's go see this thing," Hawke said.

He and Brock got up from the table and quickly moved outside onto the afterdeck. Ahmed put down his magazine and looked up as if pleasantly surprised by all the commotion. "Hate to disturb your studies, old fellow," Hawke said. "Apparently Fort Mahoud just hove into view."

The three men ran for'ard and stood at the rail on the port bow. Hawke and Brock both had their glasses trained on Point Mala. Gulls and terns whirled about above the towering waves that hammered the ragged and rocky shoreline. The air was misty along that point of land, and it was difficult to see much from this distance.

Hawke found himself watching with not a little apprehension as *Cacique* plowed through the deep, rolling waves and bits and pieces of the fort became more and more visible. They had the thing almost abeam now, and as soon as this huge wave receded, he'd have a much better idea of what he was up against.

Hawke was both thrilled and appalled by what he saw. Fort Mahoud was far more forbidding in reality than on paper. Huge waves continously smashed against its battlements and retreated. It stood there as it had for centuries, back against the sheer-faced wall, impregnable and unassailable.

It was as magnificent an example of military architecture as he'd ever seen. The fortress was built of whitish stone that seemed to gleam in the late-afternoon sun. It was battlemented, crenellated, and towered. The most imposing aspect was the looming, perfectly circular towers facing the sea. He could see the wide steps now, leading up to the large arch of the gate. It appeared to be a massive iron-barred affair that was raised or lowered from within the fort.

"See that gate?" he said to Brock standing beside him.

"Oh, yeah. I was just checking it out. I got one word for you. Semtex."

"Yes. Assuming there is still someone alive at the top of the steps to set the charges."

"I guess we can forget about coming down that cliff face."

"I guess so," Hawke said.

Fort Mahoud had been purposefully designed and built with its back hard up against a sheer perpendicular wall of reddish rock. The rock face swept up smoothly above the fort, with neither a crevasse nor a crack to be seen, for a good five hundred feet up to the top. Any thought of a nighttime abseil down that vertical cliff face was now clearly seen to be impossible. It was obvious that the only possible approach was the suicide steps leading up from the sea.

"Is this as close as we can get?" Brock asked.

"It won't get any better closer up," Hawke said. "What do you think, Irontail?"

Brock looked at him. "What did you call me?"

"I got it from the director. He says bullets bounce off your butt. So, what do you think?"

"Okay, how do you like your news?"

"Straight up."

"Reminds me a little bit of Normandy in a funny, bad, way," Brock said with a wry smile. "All we have to do is make it to the beach alive and then, completely exposed, dodge a few bullets going up fifty feet of steps, scale two sixty-foot-high towers and overpower the guards up there, take out a couple of their heavy machine guns, blast our way through an iron gate, kill a few dozen heavily armed ex–French Legionnaires and some Chinese characters, and then get twenty women and god knows how many children safely off this island."

"I'm sorry," Hawke said, "I wasn't listening. What did you say, Brock?"

"I said, all we have to do is—"

"Hold on a second," Hawke said. He'd been scanning the steel dock built into the rock on either side of the staircase. Now, he quickly swung his glasses a few degrees back to the left and froze. He'd seen something there a few seconds ago, during a break in the waves. Now it had disappeared underwater. An anomaly in the rock, perhaps, just above the waterline. He started moving the glasses in tiny increments farther to the left. The binoculars froze once more.

"What have you got, Hawke?" Brock said, raising his binoculars. "You see something I don't see?"

"Ahmed, take a look at this, will you?" Hawke said, handing the man at his left the Zeiss glasses. "Left of the staircase. About four or five meters. Almost invisible. Tucked up under the dock."

"Ah, yes, I see it."

"What is it? It looks like some kind of small crescent-shaped opening in the rock."

"It leads to the powder magazine."

For the first time all day, the sun came out on Alex Hawke's face. "The powder magazine?"

"Yes, sir. For wartime purposes. So forces on the mainland could resupply the garrison. They could secretly ferry stores inside the fort during a siege. During the night. Powder and ammunition."

"Strange, I didn't notice it on any of the plans I saw."

"You won't see it anywhere."

"And why is that, exactly?" Brock said, newfound optimism in his voice. He raised his glasses and found the near-invisible tunnel again.

"A military secret, Mr. Brock. If the fortress plans unfortunately fell into enemy hands . . . well, you could easily see what a disaster that would be, sir, if your enemy discovered a tunnel leading directly inside the fort to the powder magazine. Field Marshal Rommel had it sealed up for just such a reason in early 1941. I myself had it reopened when I restored Fort Mahoud to original specifications. Frankly, I'd forgotten all about it. It's not on the tour."

"That's good news," Hawke said, "Do you think our Chinese friends are aware of it?"

"I very much doubt it. It's only a bit of chance that you yourself saw it. It is only visible from the sea at a certain precise angle. And even then, the chances of ever seeing it are minute."

"Why?"

"The entrance is completely below sea level most of the time. Only at dead low tide, like we have right now, for a short time, is it visible and accessible."

"Feel like a swim?" Hawke asked Brock, a wide grin on his face.

"A swim?" Brock hadn't told Hawke this, but he was something of a landlubber. Unlike his lordship, who seemed in his element at sea, Harry Brock longed for the feel of good old shifting sand beneath his feet. Compared to Hawke, he was Ahab the A-rab, the Sheik of the Burning Sands.

"We'll wait until dark. Then swim over there and check out this very serendipitous chink in the armor."

"Yeah," Brock said, his expression grim. "Thank God for serendipitous chinks."

"Ever hear of an outfit called 'Thunder and Lightning'?" Hawke asked.

"Hell yes. Everybody in the community has. Legendary. Fitz McCoy and Charlie Rainwater. Seriously bad boys. Bunch of kick-ass mercs based out of Martinique, right? Some old fort with a fancy French name."

"Right. They call it Fort Whupass now."

Brock laughed. "You know those guys?"

"We shared some special moments in Cuba a few years ago. When Fidel went on vacation and his generals took over. It got noisy. We all got along pretty well."

"Still have their number?" Brock said, a big smile on his face.

"No, but my buddy Stokely Jones does. Maybe I'll give old Stoke a call."

"Yeah. Considering what we've got here, I think that's a real good idea."

Chapter Forty-two

Coney Island

"WHAT'S HE GOING TO DO?" MARIUCCI SAID, "A FUCKING swan dive?"

Congreve thought perhaps that was exactly what the Chinaman had in mind. His position was precarious. The second swipe of the ladder had crumpled the entire top section of the tower. The aircraft warning light formerly at the tower's pinnacle was now dangling by tangled wires, sparking and snapping just above the killer's head. The rotted black crossbeam he was standing on was sagging dangerously in the middle. It looked as if it could give way at any moment. The crowds below were swooning in anticipation. It was all faintly ghoulish, Ambrose thought, but he couldn't turn away.

"I'll be right back," the captain said, "I think they're about to get the Ferris wheel moving."

Mariucci had no need of seeing another jumper. Congreve imagined he'd seen enough falling bodies for a lifetime on that cruel day in September.

The captain squeezed the top of Ambrose's arm gently and disappeared into the maze of police, fire personnel, television news crews, and their respective vehicles, all parked willy-nilly wherever they had come to a stop. The midway was now jammed with useless emergency equipment and mobbed with people who had no business being there. All massed between the two opposing attractions and all looking up into the sky.

They stood with their eyes riveted on the drama unfolding a hundred feet up. Light rain was still falling. The beams from spotlights on the ground and mounted on the hovering helicopters looked like solid columns of light.

All were trained on the little man in white coveralls. He had his back to the crowd. His arms were stretched above his head, hands clinging to the beam above. He hadn't moved in ten minutes. His audience was rapt, transfixed.

For those fortunate enough to have binoculars, the only thing missing was the expression on the man's face as he unslung the haversack from his right shoulder and let it fall. It hit a beam or two going down, bounced once or twice, and dropped out of sight.

"Jump!" some civilian screamed. It seemed not everyone in the crowd was rooting for the Chinaman. Some of them even laughed out loud. "Turn around so we can see you!" a woman cried out.

As if in response to the crowd's demands, the man could be seen to loosen his two-handed death grip on the skewed beam just above his head. He pried the fingers of one hand loose and slowly released the beam with that hand. He deftly turned ninety degrees, so that he was facing parallel to the beam. His grace and economy of movement, Congreve had to say, were those of a champion gymnast. An Olympian performance.

He paused and took a deep breath, or so it seemed, and then released the other hand. He gently lowered both arms to his side and stood unassisted on the narrow beam. It was a feat of balance to be admired, and some in the crowd showed their appreciation with applause as if he were a circus artist. This was Coney Island, after all.

The man then moved his feet slowly, tiny steps, turning carefully around so that he was now facing the midway.

"I can't look!" a woman cried out, but she did.

The Chinaman raised his arms straight out from his side holding them poised like a high diver at shoulder height. After a long moment, he folded both arms across his chest and lowered his head. The crowd was stone silent now. Waiting. Many of them rubbing their eyes with the strain and the rainwater in them as they stared without blinking at a man surely about to plunge to his death.

Behind them, the colored lights of the Ferris wheel had illuminated once more and the big wheel started revolving slowly. No one even noticed, not even Ambrose Congreve, but Joey Bones was coming back to earth.

The Chinaman didn't jump. He put his arms to his sides and lowered his head. He seemed to hang there for a second. Then he simply leaned out into space and pitched forward off the beam. He fell head-first, arms tightly held against his side, legs held firmly together, toes pointed. By diving in this way, Congreve estimated, he was able to increase his velocity from the normal speed of a falling object to approximately two hundred miles per hour. Terminal velocity.

Terminal being the operative word.

Ambrose watched him fall, feeling a wave of nausea wash over him.

You could almost see him accelerate.

At the last fraction of a second, he tucked up into a tight ball.

The crowd screamed. It was terrifying and riveting to watch a human being fall to his death. It took all of two seconds for him to hit the ground.

The Chinaman was dead. But he had gone out with a certain style, nonetheless, and Congreve found that interesting. Ambrose turned away and saw that the Ferris wheel was indeed turning. Joey Bones's car was now at the bottom. You could tell because that's where all the lights and news cameras were trained now.

Because of the tall fence, few people, mostly policemen and ATAC team members gathered inside the fence surrounding the tower, actually saw the man hit the ground. But the sound of a falling body hitting concrete from great height was not one anyone there that night would ever forget.

Nor was the sight of him sitting bolt upright on the cracked stone, his shattered legs sticking straight out from his erect, shattered body. From the back, he looked almost normal. Except that his shoulders were far, far too narrow. And his head rested right atop them, no neck to support it. From the front, those who dared to look at the corpse saw a face from a nightmare, its features rearranged in a surreal fashion, one eye below his nose, the mouth a vertical slit.

"Chief Inspector," a uniformed policeman at Ambrose's elbow said, "could you come with me, please? Captain Mariucci is asking for you. He's inside the Ferris wheel car with the victim."

"Victim?" Congreve said, his heart skipping a beat. After all this, he couldn't believe they'd now lost their sole remaining eyewitness.

"Yes, sir. It's urgent. Follow me, sir," the young cop said, and Ambrose did as he asked. When they finally got to the other side of the midway, Ambrose saw that one of the EMS vehicles was now backed up to the wooden ramp leading up to the Ferris wheel entrance. The back doors were flung open, the engine was running, and the rooftop lights were flashing. It didn't look good.

Congreve found Captain Mariucci and the two EMS responders from the ambulance inside the car. The two medical technicians were frantically administering assistance to a human skeleton lying on the metal floor between two opposing bench seats. He looked to be breathing, just barely, and the technician was standing by with oxygen. The stark features of Joey Bones's drawn face were writ with pain. His skin was white as marble and coated in a thin sheen of greasy sweat.

"What happened?" Congreve asked Mariucci. The captain was down on his knees beside the man, bending over him, cradling his head in one hand, and Ambrose joined him there, kneeling on the floor.

"It's bad, Ambrose. He broke his back. Lungs filling up with fluid. Maybe a coronary. They can't move him."

"What happened?"

"I guess he fell when it started down, landed the wrong way on the edge of the seat. Or maybe he was on his feet when a gust of wind hit the car."

"Is he able to talk?" Ambrose asked.

"Barely. These guys are saying he probably won't make it back to King's County Hospital. They're just getting ready to blast him with morphine. If you want to talk to him, this is probably it."

Congreve nodded and bent closer to the old man's ear.

"Joe? How are you doing? My name is Ambrose Congreve. I'm a friend of Captain Mariucci's."

"Moochie—he's the one who sent me away to college, y'know," Joe Bones said with a tight grin. His voice was raw and barely audible.

"Joe," Ambrose said softly, "I want to talk to you about Paris. Do you understand?"

"Off the record?"

"Off the record."

Joe took a few shallow breaths. "Yeah. Tell me about Benny, first," Joe whispered. "Did they get to Benny, too?"

"Naw, Benny's fine, Joey," Mariucci said. "He'll be by to see you tomorrow in the hospital. Bring you some pretty flowers."

"Good," Joe rasped. "That's good. They didn't get him, huh? Rat bastards."

"Joe, this is important," Ambrose said. "You could possibly save a lot of lives, certainly a lot of trouble, if you can help me."

"Hey, listen, you're talking to Joey Bones, right? The man. Go ahead."

"Joey, you were in France thirty-five years ago. Paris. What were you doing there?"

"A beef with the Union Corse. That was the Mob in France, see. They was trying to move in on us over here. We—wanted to hit one of their own—on their turf . . ."

"Where, Joe," Congreve said. "Where in Paris?"

"Napoleon's Tomb. Yeah."

Congreve looked up at Mariucci and the two men nodded. "You were there?"

"Yeah. Me and Benny both . . . but, you gotta know something, Mr.—uh—"

"Inspector Congreve."

"Congreve? Funny name. I ain't no button man, Inspector. I was just a soldier. A lowly shylock. I never clipped nobody."

"I'm sure."

"But that night was supposed to be the hit. Benny's crew had the contract to pop this guy. The Corse was getting big on the East Coast, and we wanted to send 'em a message. At the last minute, Benny took me along for the ride, said maybe I could make my bones, you know? I was just a middle-aged punk kid, a *cugine*. A fuckin' nobody . . ."

Congreve tipped some water from a cup into the man's mouth.

"Who was the hit, Joe?" Mariucci asked. He was scribbling furiously in his notebook.

"Guy name of Bonaparte. Emile, I think. A Corse button man who'd pissed off somebody. Some Commie Brigade, whatever the fuck it was. Weird, we found out later he'd fucked up a job or something. Some internal shit over there, but the Commies wanted him burned, too. The really weird thing was his own k-kid—his kid was in on it . . ."

"Who was that? What was this kid's name?"

"The big French guy. You know. On the news. The guy that's trying to whack me and Benny, that's who. Luca Bonaparte. The bigshot pol over there. That French fuck knows what really happened, see. And now he don't want me and Benny talking about it, I guess. We're like inconvenient."

"How'd you find out somebody was trying to whack you, Joey?" Mariucci said.

"People called me. My goombah Vinnie at the deli. Said some foreign broad was asking around about me. Chinese. Japanese. I dunno. Vinnie said it sounded like she was coming to break my balls and feed 'em to me one piece at a time. And then, Lavon—"

"Excuse me, Captain," one of the EMS men said. "We have to give this man some oxygen. He really shouldn't be talking like this."

"Can you give us one minute?" Mariucci said, looking plaintively at the technician.

"Yeah, sure, Captain," he said. "I understand."

"Joe, how are you holding up? Okay?" Congreve asked the dying man.

"Yeah, sure. I ain't going anywhere. Tough as nails. I fooled that little Chinese bastard on the tower, didn't I? Sonafabitch thought he could fuck with me. Is he dead?"

"He's dead, all right," Mariucci said. "Believe me."

"Good."

"What happened at the tomb, Joe?" Ambrose said. "Tell me about that night in Paris."

"Like I say, the guy's kid was in on it. Whoever ordered the hit from their side, the Corse, they wanted the kid there. So, we played along, you know. What the hell. Crazy frogs."

"What next, Joe?"

"We had the guy, the hit, up against a rail or something. Right over the friggin' tomb of Napoleon. Benny gave me the piece and told me to do it. You know, make my bones. But—but then—"

"Then, what? What happened, Joe?" Ambrose said, staring into the man's eyes.

"I don't feel so good," Joe said, his eyelids fluttering. "Feels like something's wrong with my, uh—"

"Okay, Captain, I think that's it," the EMS guy said. "We need to administer—"

"Gimme a second, here. Please." Mariucci said, holding up his hand with the forefinger extended. "This is very important. One second."

"Joe," Ambrose said, "Did you kill Emile Bonaparte in Paris that night?"

"Naw. I didn't kill him. I couldn't do it, see? God as my witness. We was in a cathedral, f'crissakes. A house of God. I couldn't kill nobody in a cathedral. I'm a Catholic, Inspector. I couldn't kill nobody. I ain't proud of it, but I never did."

"Who did kill Emile Bonaparte, Joe?" Congreve said. "Tell me, please. Did Benny do it?"

Joey Bones closed his eyes and for a terrible second, Congreve thought they'd lost him.

"The kid," he whispered.

"The victim's son?"

"Yeah."

"Keep talking, Joey," Mariucci said, "You can do it."

"The kid did it," Joe whispered through parched lips. "See, when he saw my hand shaking, that I wasn't gonna shoot, this kid Luca grabbed the piece right out of my hand and shot his old man right in the heart. Never seen anything like it. His own father!"

"Luca Bonaparte murdered his own father," Mariucci said, looking Joe Bones in the eye. "In Paris, in 1970."

"Saw it with my own eyes," Joe said. "Got no reason to lie no more."

"Thank you, Joey," Ambrose said, looking up at Mariucci, his face flooded with relief.

"Yeah, Joey, you did good, *paisano*," Mariucci said.

The captain flipped his notebook shut and put it inside his jacket. Ambrose had what he'd come to New York for. They could both use a drink.

Joey lifted his bony arm and placed his hand on the captain's shoulder. "You got something else, Joe?" the captain asked.

"When we, uh, got h-home from P-Paris," Joey Bones said, his voice rattling with effort, "Benny kinda let it get around on the street that it was me who'd whacked the guy. Why not, right? Who would know? Nobody in the neighborhood ever messed with me after that. I was a made man, you understand? I was Joey Bones!"

It was very quiet in the car. Just the patter of soft rain on the tin rooftop.

"You did good, Joey," Mariucci said.

But Joey was already gone.

As they emerged from the car into the glare of the TV lights, Mariucci paused, squinting, and said to Congreve, "Who the hell is that?"

"Who?" Ambrose said.

"Over there. Edge of the crowd. There's a woman in a black raincoat staring right at you. See her?"

"Where?"

"Never mind. She's gone."

Chapter Forty-three

Berlin

THEY WAITED UNTIL DARKNESS FELL AND THE MOON ROSE over the snowcapped mountains. Then they flew. Jet was wrapped in a blanket, sound asleep on a bench seat behind the pilot. She'd put another blanket on the floor for Blondi. Arnold was flying. Stoke sat in the copilot's seat to his right, now wearing Arnold's muscleman black VDI uniform, a perfect fit if a little tight across the shoulders. They were headed almost due north, destination Berlin. The moon was full, just rising over the ragged peak of the Weissspitze at nine thousand feet.

"You do know how to fly this thing, right, Arnold?" Stoke had said to him as they trudged through knee-deep snow from the Zum Wilden Hund out to the black chopper on the pad. It was a specially modified Super Lynx helo that had once belonged to the German navy. Stoke noticed AIM missile brackets mounted under the belly between the skids and asked about them. The Lynx formerly flew antisubmarine warfare missions for NATO.

"Yes," Arnold said, "I know how to fly it."

"Good. Then we got the right Arnold."

Twenty minutes into the flight, Stoke leaned over in his copilot's seat, pressed his face against the cool Perspex, and stared down thoughtfully at the endless white ground. At this altitude, basically zero, give or take a foot or two, you had a pretty good sensation of speed. They were skimming across snow-covered fields, brushing the tops of the tall pines, and jinking and juking around any small hill that got in their way. There was a whole lot to be said for the fun factor, flying below the radar across Europe. Stoke concentrated on their little moon-shadow zipping along on the sparkling snow just beneath them.

"What's that up ahead?" Stoke asked Arnold.

"Czechoslovakia," Arnold said.

"Let's try not to hit it."

Sometimes, Arnold would get so low down, the Lynx and its darting shadow almost kissed. Catch a skid and you're *not* sitting on top of the world, Stoke thought, and looked at his watch. If they could stay down on the deck and maintain this speed without cracking up, they'd touch down at Tempelhof well before midnight. It was nice and warm in the cockpit. It had been a long day. Stoke let his head fall back across the seat and closed his eyes.

"Put it down just there," Jet said to Arnold, waking him from some dream of swaying palms and convertibles and his beautiful Fancha climbing out of a turquoise pool dripping wet and naked as the day she was born. Soon as all this was over, first-class ticket nonstop to Miami.

The black helo was approaching the LZ low and dark, no landing lights outside; inside, the cockpit was lit only by a dim red glow from the instrument panel. Stealth chopper. He hoped. Heavy armed resistance at this point would be a problem. He had only the Schmeisser and a few mags of ammo he'd been able to scrounge up going through drawers at the *gasthaus*. Jet had the dead Arnold's automatic and two spare mags.

They approached Tempelhof low and from the rear, away from the entrance where the guards were stationed. Here, boxy apartment complexes and warehouses would hide their approach from the guards at the entrance on the far side of the field. Arnold dropped down below the rooftops. He flew between the buildings, along a narrow deserted street that dead-ended at the fence line. They rose slightly and almost clipped the fence. A darkened helo, coming in low, a hush kit to dampen the engine noise, hell, they had a pretty good chance to arrive unannounced.

He wasn't sure what they'd find on the ground, but as they crossed the perimeter and flared up for a landing, he sure as hell felt like they were going into the belly of the beast.

They set down on a very remote part of the airfield, in the moon-shadow of a rusty hangar that looked like it hadn't seen much use since "Operation Vittles," the American airlift that began in 1945. There was a high perimeter wall all around the field, topped with concertina wire, and probably guarded by remote sensors. In the far distance stood an illuminated complex, the huge semicircular building that housed Von Draxis Industries.

Stoke swung his cockpit door open and was met with a blast of cold air. It felt good, woke him up. So did the snarling hellhound that leaped up out of the darkness behind him and flew bare-fanged across his chest and out the open door. Doing his mental weapons check, minding his own business, he'd clean forgot about Blondi. The Doberman might even the odds up a little bit. Maybe a lot.

"She had to go," Jet said by way of explanation.

"Okay, Arnold," Stoke said, cocking the Schmeisser, "shut this bird down and sit tight. We're going to get out, stretch our legs, and figure out what to do next."

"We know exactly what to do next," Jet said. "Let's get moving."

Stoke smiled at Arnold. "Like the lady said, we know exactly what to do next. Let's get moving."

There was an old wooden sign above the door with the faded word *Steinhoffer* painted on it. Name of a Luftwaffe ace jet-set. The doors were locked. Stoke kept the machine pistol on Arnold and Blondi straining on her leash while Jet unlocked the padlocks on the rusty corrugated hangar doors. The fact that she had a key to this old building was mildly surprising but Stoke kept his mouth shut. They were on her turf now. When a woman had a plan, you had to be prepared to zip your lip and go with it. It had taken him nearly half a century to figure that out.

Jet got the lock open and pushed back the sliding doors. The hangar was empty except for the gleaming black car.

"Stokely," Jet said, "there's a tool shop at the rear. Get some duct tape and immobilize him. Use a lot. We might be a couple of hours. I'll take Blondi."

"You heard the lady," Stoke said to Arnold. He handed the leash to Jet. "Let's go get you taped up."

Ten minutes later, having secured Arnold to a heavy wooden workbench that was bolted to a wall, he was back. Jet was squatting on her knees beside the car, talking to Blondi in German. Telling the Doberman the plan, Stoke assumed. He was pretty sure he'd be next to find out what it was.

"That's some car," he said to Jet. And it was. It was maybe the most beautiful machine he'd ever seen. Glinting black in the moonlight that filtered through the skylight, it looked like a high-tech space-ship. "What is it?"

"Mercedes SLR," Jet said. "Built in England by McLaren. It's basically a Formula One race car you can drive on the street. Six hundred eighteen horsepower, top speed of over 320 kilometers per hour."

"This is your car?" Stoke said.

"Schatzi gave it to me when he got bored with it."

"And you keep it out here?"

"If I kept it at my apartment, it would get stolen. I don't use it that much. This is probably the safest place in Berlin."

Stoke was puzzling over the English license plate mounted on the rear. Four letters. SPQR.

"SPQR," he said. "What's that stand for?"

"It's an acronym. It stands for *Senatus Populusque Romanus.* Which means the 'Senate and People of Rome.' Schatzi is a big fan of Caesar. Might help you understand who you're up against."

"I'll take all the help I can get, Jet," Stoke said. He didn't ask her why the Q got left out in translation.

"Get in. We'll put Blondi in the back."

Jet thumbed the remote in her hand. "Mind your head," she said, "the doors swing up not out. Gullwing, like the old 300SL. Load, Blondi!"

Stoke climbed in and buckled his belt. The car was so low and sleek, he was amazed there was enough room for someone his size. He looked over at Jet and saw she was adjusting a pair of night-vision goggles over her eyes.

"I take it out on the Autobahn late at night," Jet said, "No traffic. I run three hundred kilometers per hour flat out with the lights off. No *Polizei.*"

"Anybody saw you, they'd think it was a UFO."

The supercharged V-8 roared to life, a beautiful exhaust note burbling from the sidepipes. Jet let it idle for a few seconds, then blipped the accelerator. Just the sound of the thing inside the hangar was enough to push Stoke back in his seat. Then she engaged first gear, popped the clutch, and hit it. The tires lit up and they rocketed forward, went sideways out onto the tarmac, no lights, the rear wheels screeching and smoking.

It didn't take long to get across the field. Runways built of ballast stone were ideal for cars like Jet's. Stoke didn't even look over at the speedometer. There was a large square building adjacent to the main structure. Jet seemed be headed in that direction but it was pretty blurry outside so Stoke wasn't sure.

"Don't seem to be a whole lot of guards around," Stoke said.

"The main entrance is where all the guards are. That's the only way in or out. They're not expecting company tonight, either. VDI Security is still waiting for a report on us from Zum Wilden Hund, remember? Besides, nobody really knows what goes on here."

"What does go on here?"

"You'll see."

Tempelhof itself, the main building, looked like something you might have seen in ancient Rome only much, much bigger. "Impressive architecture," Stoke said as they sped closer.

"Neoclassical. Albert Speer was Hitler's personal architect," Jet said, "no small plans."

Jet slowed to below a hundred and used a remote to open a door in the secondary building that was coming up fast. It looked like they were going to go right inside doing about eighty.

"What's this building?" Stoke said, gripping the door handle with his right hand.

"Underground parking," Jet said, tapping the brakes and spinning the wheel. Once they were inside the doors she stood on the brakes and put the wheel hard over. The SLR did a tight three-sixty on the polished cement floor. Jet put it in first and started up again in the direction of a tunnel marked *Eingang.*

"Four levels," she said, pushing the NVG goggles up to the top of her head. "We're going all the way down to Level Four. Corkscrew turns. Hold on."

"I'm beginning to see what Alex Hawke sees in you."

"Alex Hawke hasn't seen anything yet," Jet said. But she was smiling when she said it.

After they'd parked and locked up the Mercedes, Jet led him back to an anonymous grey door tucked inside an alcove. A door you'd never find unless you knew it was there.

"*Wilkommen* to the *Unterwelt*," Jet said, pulling the rusted steel door open.

"Welcome to what?"

"The Underworld."

Chapter Forty-four

Gulf of Oman

"YOU LOOK UNHAPPY," HAWKE SAID TO HARRY BROCK. THEY were standing on the trawler's stern in the dark. All the ship's lights were doused. Ahmed was helping them get suited up in wetsuits and high-tech SEAL gear. The equipment included German Draegers, "re-breathers," that purified and recirculated their oxygen so no tell-tale bubbles marked their progress on the surface. Now that night had fallen, Hawke was reasonably sure the recon mission could be carried out unseen and unnoticed.

Harry was upset they weren't using the Swimmer Delivery Vehicle he'd procured from the Navy. And he hadn't found it amusing when Hawke had said, "Don't you think that's a bit of overkill, Irontail? We're just doing a light recon. We can swim it."

The sun had set and the moon had risen while the darkened trawler *Cacique* poked along the northern tip of the island, looking for a suitable mooring on the rocky coast.

Cacique had to be sufficiently near the island for the two men to swim to Fort Mahoud's entrance and back. But the trawler also had to be anchored somewhere out of sight, away from any prying eyes at the fort. After his recent experience aboard the *Star of Shanghai*, Hawke had a new rule of thumb when it came to unexpectedly dropping in on new friends. Always assume you're expected, no matter what they tell you.

They'd managed a pretty good spot. The anchorage was tucked inside a deepwater cove just west of Point Arras on the northwest side of the island. Hawke figured it was maybe a half-mile swim out around the rocky point and then south two thousand yards to the fort's entrance. The trawler would be invisible in the cove, even from atop the twin towers. He told Ali to drop anchor. Ahmed had brought up the equipment, recently arrived from the United States, from below.

"You okay?" Hawke asked.

"Yeah." Brock was struggling with his regulator. "I'm no fucking water baby, that's all, Your Lordship. Why do you think I went to all the trouble to get the goddamn SDV, for chrissakes."

Hawke smiled and looked at Brock, now smearing night camo paint on his face. "Stay close to Papa. You'll be all right."

"Mr. Hawke, sir! Mr. Brock!" Captain Ali al-Houri was at the rail just above their heads.

"Yes?"

"A message just came in over the wire, sir. Urgent. A speech on the radio. I've got the shortwave tuned in to BBC, sir! It's starting in a few minutes, sir."

"We'll be right there." Hawke slipped off his tank and flippers. So did Brock, who seemed grateful for the reprieve, however temporary.

The old trawler wasn't large enough to have a real radio room. The commo equipment was all in the main saloon, sitting on a book-crowded shelf over the nav station. When Hawke came inside the darkened room, Ali was seated at the tiny station, twisting the knob on the ancient Grundig receiver, looking for the strongest signal. They all pulled chairs from the round dining table and gathered around the radio. It was quite homey, Hawke thought.

"Somebody at Langley sent you a fax?" Brock asked Hawke, who held the flimsy two-page message in his hand, reading it in the dim light. Brock wasn't accustomed to seeing an archaic fax machine used for the transmission of coded messages from highly sophisticated intelligence agencies.

"Your boss at Langley. He didn't sign it, naturally, but that's who this is from."

"What's he got to say?"

"Seems the new president of France is about to make a radio address to the nation. The Elysée only announced it an hour ago. According to this, Kelly believes Monsieur Bonaparte's got some serious problems. Basically, he's trying to put down an insurrection. He's got the army and the navy with him, but the populace is up in arms about the assassinations and the impending invasion of Oman. The remnants of Honfleur's old government are on the attack, too."

"What the hell happened to *liberté, égalité, fraternité?*"

"According to Brick, the turmoil is a result of French bloggers having a feeding frenzy. They're all over the chat rooms, accusing Bonaparte and his boys of selling France to the highest bidder. Namely, your little pals in China."

"God bless Al Gore for inventing the Internet."

"Right—hold on—here he is now . . ."

"—and, live now from Paris on BBC One, World Radio Tonight, this is Robert Markham. . . . President Bonaparte has entered this very uneasy room here at the Elysée Palace. The Salon Napoleon III, with its gilded columns and eagles symbolizing the Empire, is a hectic scene tonight. Bonaparte, resplendent in a military uniform, is shaking hands with some of his highest-ranking military officers . . . smiling . . . I must say he seems very relaxed this evening . . . the question on everyone's mind is, can he hold on to the seat of power now that he's got it? He's stepping up to the microphone . . . BBC One will provide simultaneous translation of his remarks . . . here is the new president of France."

There was a burst of static, and then President Bonaparte spoke.

"Good evening. A few short weeks ago, during my tragically short period as your new prime minister, I made my first appeal to France. I asked for perseverance during turmoil and I asked for courage on the road ahead.

"Tonight, as your new president, my voice is firmer. The tragic deaths of Prime Minister Honfleur and our beloved president Bocquet at the hands of France's enemies will be avenged. France will recover. Look around you! Thanks in part to my new foreign trade policies, factories across the country are already humming. Wages are up, production is up, unemployment is down. But many Frenchmen won't believe it. To them I say, 'You have short memories!'

"Believe me, this is no time to engage in bitterness or reprisals . . . or give way to despair. You have not been sold, abandoned, or betrayed. Not to Germany, not to China, not to any country. Those who say so are lying . . . and throwing you into the arms of the Anglo-American fascists, capitalist warmongers whose greatest fear is the economic and military power of a resurgent France.

"Yes, we may suffer in the coming weeks. Our troops are headed into battle. We will liberate the brave people of Oman from the tyranny of terror. It will not be easy. I need your trust at this hour. The trust of your hearts and minds. I need your wisdom and patience. Those attributes you will attain only under my leadership. None but those who forget our history, or those enemies of our unity with our new allies, will seek to destroy us.

"Remember, you are citizens of an old and glorious nation. I speak to you tonight as the proud descendant of Napoleon, the emperor who restored honor and glory to France . . . and in his name, a name that echoes still down the corridors of history . . . citizens of France, in the name of Napoleon Bonaparte, I ask you to put down your arms!

"Forget your anger, your tears. Give me your trust. All for one, and one for all. I, Bonaparte, am that one. And, together with you, I promise that I will protect you from the forces of evil. That one day soon we shall emerge from the dark of the old century . . . and into the light of the new. Thank you very much. *Vive la France!*"

"Guy can talk," Brock said as the captain reached up to shut off the radio.

"He's a megalomaniac who wants to be emperor of Europe," Hawke said, getting to his feet. "A megalomaniac who needs stopping. Let's go swimming, Mr. Brock."

Twenty minutes later, roughly five hundred yards offshore, a head popped out of the sea. It was encased in a half-head ballistic helmet, matte black, with a communication headset and night-vision goggles on a flip-up mount. What little of the face remained visible was smeared black with greasepaint. Ragged clouds scurried by the moon and the surface was choppy. Alex Hawke flipped down his goggles and trod water as he studied the target and fortifications, confident he would not be seen from the towers.

"You survived," Hawke said into his boom mike as a second head joined him on the surface.

"Just trying to keep up, boss," he heard in his earpiece.

Hawke said, "Okay, Brock. Simple mission. Reconnoiter, identify, infiltrate, mark it, and get the hell out. Right?"

"Sounds good."

"But for a small problem, it is," Hawke now told Brock. "Take a look. A new arrival."

Brock swung himself around and saw what Hawke was talking about. There was a cutter now moored along the steel dock to the right of the entry steps. A large patrol boat with a French tricolor hanging off her stern. Twin 40mm guns on her fore and after decks. He could make out crewmen on the bow and stern, casting off lines. A powerful spotlight on the bridge was illuminated. She was headed out.

"Problem," Hawke said. "If she turns left and heads north around the point, it's trouble. She'll find *Cacique* and probably board her. Even if we started swimming right now, we'd never make it back in time to warn Ali and Ahmed."

"So let's hope she turns right and heads south."

"Let's hope. Even if she goes south and around the island the long way, we'll have to make this quick. Assuming she patrols at an average of five knots, she can circumnavigate Masara in less than an hour. We need to do this recon and be back aboard *Cacique* and under way before that or we've got a new set of problems."

"Let's go," Brock said and submerged. Hawke followed immediately and saw the little clouds of phosporescence trailing behind Brock's flippers. He swam easily up alongside the American and gave him a thumbs-up. If he'd been worried about Brock earlier, he now saw those fears as perhaps unfounded. In fact, the man was doing fine. He was, Hawke reminded himself, a tough, thorough, hard-bitten professional field agent who'd survived capture and torture at the hands of the most vicious secret police on the planet.

He'd been hand-picked by the chairman of the Joint Chiefs to go into China alone.

Who knew what else was on his resume? In the great Kingdom of Spookdom, Brick Kelly had assured him, Harry Brock was a crown prince. Harry had walked the walk, Hawke knew. He just hadn't swum the swim.

Five minutes later, Hawke held up his hand, signaling Brock to stop. They were hanging twenty feet below the surface, a few hundred yards from the docks, and the sound of the patrol boat's twin screws was rapidly growing louder. She was headed straight for them.

The underwater sound was, for Hawke, a most unpleasant reminder of the incident aboard the USS *Lincoln*. The two men hung in the water and watched the patrol boat approach and slide overhead. The underside of the fifty-foot hull was clearly visible as it passed above. Both watched intently, instinctively holding their breath despite the re-breathers. If she made a left turn north toward Point Arras, they had serious problems.

Captain Ali and Ahmed would be caught completely unawares. They were both clever and resourceful men, but what plausible and speedy explanation could be offered for *Cacique's* presence in the little cove so near the fort? And if they were suddenly boarded by armed French sailors, would one of them have the presence of mind to quickly duck below and hide or remove any incriminating evidence of documents and equipment? It wasn't likely that there would be time.

The two men in the water breathed a sigh of relief. The patrol boat had turned right and away from *Cacique*. She was steaming south along the coast. Still, they had less than an hour to complete their mission and get back to the boat. They swam for the fort.

"Shit," Brock whispered under his breath as they broke the surface simultaneously.

"Now what?"

They had surfaced as planned under the steel dock. No one had seen or shot at them. But the water was thick with jellyfish. Hawke himself could feel a few stinging welts rising across his cheek and the back of his neck. Portuguese man-of-wars. A few more of these electrifying stings could send a man into a state of shock. He decided not to tell Brock about that part.

"One of them get to you, Harry?" Hawke asked.

"Yeah. Damn it."

"When you get back to the boat, rub some of your own piss on the welts. It'll take the sting away."

"What?"

"Trust me. I think the opening is just below me. I can feel it with my flipper."

"Yeah, I feel it, too."

"Go. I'll mark the spot and catch up inside."

"Kick ass. Loot and shoot."

"Kick ass? No, Harry, we—"

Brock had disappeared below the surface. Hawke took out his assault knife and carved three horizontal slashes in the barnacles on the piling. The entrance below was now clearly marked but out of sight on the inside of the piling. He checked his stainless-steel watch. This was mean high tide. At dead low, a few hours from now, the opening in the rock would be large enough to accommodate a lighter full of men and ammo. Or an outbound vessel loaded with rescued hostages.

Then, as the tide came back in, the opening would disappear. The timing on this operation was going to very interesting.

Hawke dove down, used his knife again to mark the entrance with three slashes just above the arch, and swam inside.

He and Brock were not heavily armed. Hawke himself carried only a compass, a plumb line, and a depth gauge in addition to his knife. They weren't here to kick ass, Hawke was thinking as he swam toward the phosphorescence that marked Brock's rapid progress inside the tunnel. No. They were here to run away and fight another day.

Namely, tomorrow. That's when Stokely would arrive. Along with his deadly friends from Martinique, the antiterrorist team known as Thunder and Lightning. Tonight's objective was solely to reconnoiter the powder magazine and find a safe way inside the fortress. To figure out precisely how to kick ass when they came back. And get the women and children out safely.

Loot and shoot? That's what Harry had said.

Hawke swam faster.

A loose cannon was one thing. But a loose cannon without a cannon was another matter entirely. Hawke made another mental note: Keep an eye on Harry.

Chapter Forty-five

Die Unterwelt

THE TUNNEL WAS DANK AND CLAUSTROPHOBIC. THE STONE walls were cold to the touch, wet. The ground beneath Stoke's boots felt like loose shale, pockmarked with puddles. Jet led the way with a small halogen light from the SLR's emergency roadside kit. Blondi ran ahead, sniffing the ground. Every fifty feet or so there was an alcove with an exit door. All the doors were painted the same faded luminous green. These exits to nowhere still glowed faintly in the dark, a century after they had been installed.

There were exposed pipes and pneumatic tubes running overhead. Strange egg-shaped lanterns were mounted on rusted steel frames attached to the walls, every twenty feet or so. Now and then you'd see hand-cranked ventilators beneath the egg lamps. Stoke stopped a second and tried one. It made a creaking sound, but it turned and he could feel a slight suction from the grate. Still operable, Jet said. They'd been installed in World War I. Their purpose was to thwart any lethal gases an enemy might unleash in the tunnels.

There was, Stoke learned, an extensive network of bunkers and abandoned tunnels beneath the Tempelhof airfield. All were laid with small-gauge railroad track. Smaller tunnels like this one led off to a vast system of bunkers beneath the city of Berlin. And connected with even larger tunnels that could actually accomodate automobile traffic.

"During the war," Jet said, her words bouncing off the dripping stone walls, "Goering used his big Mercedes staff car to commute out here in secret. Every day, he was driven out from his Luftwaffe headquarters on Wilhelm Strasse in Berlin. This tunnel is seven kilometers long."

"Yeah? What about these smaller tunnels?" Stoke asked.

"They loop around the entire field. During the war, electric trams ferried ammunition and supplies out to the squadrons. Luftwaffe Junkers and Messerschmitt crews used trams to get out to their aircraft. The idea was to keep as much human activity as possible below ground and away from the eyes of Allied bombardiers."

"These tracks look new."

"They are. There's a tram station about five hundred yards ahead. New high-speed trams. That's how I get out to my car."

"Where's the third rail? For the electric trams, I mean."

"They're not electric now. Levitation. Antigravity propulsion."

"Get out of town."

"You'll see for yourself if we have time. When the Allied bombers came, these tunnels and bunkers were used as bomb shelters by millions of Berliners. I imagine you could barely feel the tremors down here."

"Must have been great," Stoke said.

After they'd been walking along the tracks for about five minutes, Jet paused at one of the unmarked green doors. "This is it," she said.

"How do you know?"

"Trust me. Where's Blondi? *Kommen Sie hier! Schnell!*"

She pushed the green door open and they went inside, Blondi trailing happily behind.

The walls of the large room were lined with triple-bunk beds. In the center of the room, what looked like an operating table. In a corner stood an old toilet. More hand-cranked ventilators. Over the door, in chipped and peeling paint, was the word *Wehenzimmer.* Stoke paused to look at the sign.

"This was one of the labor rooms for pregnant women," Jet said. "There were shops, hospitals, breweries, everything you'd need down here in the *Unterwelt.* Come on, we're almost there."

"Where?"

"This route is Schatzi's escape hatch. He showed me once. It leads indirectly to his private office. He can get out in a hurry if he has to."

"Why does he need an escape hatch?"

"If I were your girlfriend, wouldn't you want an escape hatch?"

"Good point."

At the end of the narrow hall, another room. A *Weinstube,* looked like, with a dark oak bar and a modern glassed-in wine cellar.

Schatzi's after-hours hangout. Behind the bar, there was a nondescript wooden door with a modern elevator hidden behind it. Jet placed her hand on a biometric print scanner set into the wall and the doors parted, disappearing back into the walls. They rode in silence all the way to the top.

Once they came to a stop, Jet pressed a numerical keypad and the door slid open on another world. White walls, gleaming marble floors, high ceilings, and lots of glass. Even at night, the space was full of light.

"*Überwelt,*" Stoke said.

Jet laughed. "Good one," she said, "You know more German than you let on. Come on. His office is just down this way."

They walked along the gently curving white hallway. There was magnificent art, massive canvases, and heroic sculpture lining both walls, but Stoke didn't take time to admire it. He knew he was getting close to something. Whatever her reasons, and he still had his private suspicions, Jet was taking him to it. Her shifting loyalties were troublesome. Alex Hawke had gone along with his idea of bringing her to Germany. So far, that had been the right decision. He wouldn't be here without her.

The white hall dead-ended in a glass-walled atrium that soared five or six stories high. It was some kind of reception room with an oval desk and a few leather sofas and chairs. On the opposite wall was a pair of stainless-steel doors flanked by a sculpted pair of golden eagles standing about thirty feet high.

"Schatzi's got a thing for eagles," Stoke said, crossing the atrium to the massive doors. To his left, visible through the floor-to-ceiling glass wall, the moonlit airfield was spread out before him. The margins of the criss-crossing runways were lit with faintly glowing blue lights set low to the ground. It was beautiful, and mercifully free of command cars and half-tracks full of guys in black with machine guns.

"Caesar had a thing for eagles. So did Napoleon. So does Schatzi." Jet leaned into what looked like a fish-eye lens set behind black glass in the wall.

"What's that?" Stoke said.

"Facial thermography. Identifies the characteristic heat patterns of the face. Over sixty-five thousand different temperature points, believe it or not."

"I'd believe pretty much anything at this point."

"Far greater accuracy than fingerprints. Can't trick it with facial hair or even cosmetic surgery. Only way you can beat a thermograph is with alcohol."

"You been drinking? Looks like you beat it."

The doors parted, disappearing back into the walls. "No. He just forgot to lock my face out. Probably figured he'd never see it again."

Beyond the doors, Stoke saw another stark white room, smaller, but with equally spectacular views of the field. Schatzi's office was filled with moonlight and more grandiose art. The white marble floor was covered with a large Oriental rug. Very cozy. The entire wall behind the German tycoon's desk was a Mercator projection map of the world painted on glass. On the desk itself, a gleaming model of a flying saucer.

"Guess he didn't change the locks," Stoke said as he walked over to the ornate carved desk. He picked up the model saucer and turned it over.

"No, he's not that stupid. He changed them. But that keypad in the elevator allows you to enter a code to override all the locks in this part of the building. He forgot to change that code. And to delete my print from the print scanner."

"Forgot he showed his girlfriend the escape hatch, too. Hey, Jet, is Schatzi building flying saucers here?"

"That's the new disc prototype. The Messerschmitt ME-1. The Germans were working on antigravity flying discs in 1944, so it's not exactly new technology. The idea is that an electrogravitational field can be created by a fast-rotating superconductive disc. Schatzi's just picking up where they left off. So is Boeing, by the way, but they don't talk about it."

"No shit? Who's the fat guy in the painting?"

"Hermann Goering. Founder of the Luftwaffe. This was his old office." Jet hit a button that illuminated the wall-sized map.

Every square mile of Europe, Asia, and Africa was the same color blue. GERMANIA was splashed across the map in bright red foot-high letters. An old vision of a new world. A vision that died hard. And took an unthinkable number of people with it. Standing in this room, you got a definite feeling of bad déjà vu.

"Deutschland über alles," Stoke said.

"That was the general idea."

"Jet," Stoke said, looking at her carefully. "You didn't bring me all this way to look at Nazi maps and flying saucers."

"No, I did not. Listen to me. Almost everything you and Hawke need to know right now is in this room. Three years' worth of *Leviathan* correspondence, detailed project design drawings, financial records, everything. This keycard opens the desk. It also opens all those file cabinets along the wall."

"Leviathan? Harry Brock mentioned that. What is it?"

"The sea beast." Jet opened the center drawer of the desk and took out a black leather folder embossed with a gold crown. "Start with this file. Good luck."

"Good luck?" Stoke said, peeking inside the file. "Where are you going?"

"I'm going home, Stoke. I thought about it the whole time we were flying. I've had all the betrayal and treachery I can stomach for a while. I've done what I could to help you and your friend Alex Hawke. You're on your own now, I'm leaving." She called to Blondi and headed for the door. "I'm going to sleep for a few days. Don't forget to lock up."

"Wait a damn minute, Jet. How do I know what to take? Half this stuff is in Chinese. You just can't walk out now and say—good luck!"

"I can't?"

She and Blondi were halfway across the atrium when he caught her.

"Jet, hold up. You said, almost everything I need is here. What else is there?"

"I have no idea. I'm just a cop, remember? But I can promise you this, that if my father, Luca Bonaparte, and von Draxis have a hand in it, it's something very, very bad. Whatever it is, you'll figure it out, Stoke. You're a smart guy. If you want to talk at some point, call this number in Hong Kong. Maybe I'll feel different about helping you then."

She started to say something else, then stopped herself. She handed him a card with her name engraved on it and beneath that a handwritten number. "A friend of mine will answer. She'll tell you how to find me. Good-bye, Stoke."

She went up on her tiptoes and kissed him on the cheek.

"Thanks, Stoke," she said. "For saving my ass."

Stoke watched Jet and Blondi disappear around the curving wall and then walked over to the glass overlooking the field. There was a faint red line glimmering on the eastern horizon. He figured it would take an hour to sort through everything in the office. Take whatever looked interesting. He'd love to take a look at the plans for *Valkyrie*. See what was up with that missing keel. With any luck, he and Arnold could be airborne before dawn.

Then he'd go find Alex Hawke down in Oman.

A few minutes later, he was still at the window, thinking about Jet's kiss. Was it a "see you later" kiss? Or a "good-bye, dumbass" kiss? He couldn't help thinking about what a perfect trap she could have led him into. Man shot dead while stealing secret documents on private property. Hell, it was true.

A moment later, he heard a muffled roar out on the runway. It was the black SLR. She had her night-vision goggles on all right, had the lights out, nearly invisible, a fast-moving blur streaking along the blue-lit runway at more than two hundred miles an hour. She was headed for the main gate. If they had any brains, the VDI guards would just put the damn gate up and to hell with it. One thing he knew for sure about Jet now. She sure as hell wasn't going to stop for anything.

Or, anybody.

Had to get moving now, and be quick about it. He'd just seen an urgent text message on his PDA from Alex Hawke. He was in Oman and he needed help bad and he needed it now. He turned from the window.

Time to loot. And maybe, shoot.

Chapter Forty-six

New York City

AMBROSE CONGREVE WAS A LIGHT SLEEPER. THE SOUND OF sirens and garbage trucks on the streets of old New York nudged him awake at 5:00 A.M. He dozed fitfully for an hour or two, then, through sheer force of will, woke himself up. He slipped out of his warm bed and into his leather slippers and robe. He stretched and yawned and briefly considered jumping right back in bed. No, he was hungry. Ravenous. Small wonder. It was nearly tea back in London.

He fumbled for the bedside phone and rang room service. Yes, two eggs over easy, toast, a pot of black coffee and some fresh-squeezed grapefruit juice. Thirty minutes? Thanks very much.

He gently replaced the receiver in its cradle. Turned on the bedside lamp. Ouch. It was bright. A sensation one might describe as severe pain bloomed somewhere behind his eyeballs. What on earth was the matter? He was a vigorous chap long accustomed to rising at the crack of nine. Ah, yes. Jet lag. Two days in New York and he was still suffering mightily. True, he and Captain Mariucci had stopped off for a nightcap, but—ouch. His head was banging.

Jet lag and—well, truth be told, he was a bit hung over. A wee touch of the Irish flu, to be perfectly honest about the thing. He had only a vague memory of going to bed in the first place.

After their midnight thrills at Coney Island, Congreve and Mariucci had fallen victim to consecutive nightcaps in Bemelman's Bar, an establishment just off the Carlyle lobby downstairs.

"One and done," Mariucci said when the cruiser braked to a halt outside the Madison Avenue bar entrance. One? Neither man knew the meaning of the word one when it came to adult potables. Yes, cold, wet, and exhilarated by their stunning success in the dark heart of Brooklyn, the two old chums had succumbed to the siren call of Mr. Bemelman's bar.

The colorful and storied bar at that hour had been very nearly deserted. They chose the chocolate brown leather banquette beneath Ambrose's favorite scene, an enchanting depiction of picnicking rabbits. After reviewing the evening's macabre events, they had come to Joey Bones's poignant last moments on the floor of the Ferris wheel car.

"Hell of a thing, Ambrose," Mariucci said, draining the last of his third Gin-Gin Mule, "Seeing him go out like that."

"Didn't know Joe, obviously," Ambrose agreed, sipping his delicious Macallan's. "Still, I must confess I rather hated to see the old boy exit this mortal coil. I quite liked him during our brief acquaintance."

"Well, you got your deathbed confession, Chief Inspector. Now what? Storm the beaches of France again? Take Paris? What?"

"The president of France is almost certainly a cold-blooded murderer. We now have eyewitness testimony to a murder. Interpol and the Yard will issue warrants and we'll journey to Paris and take him into custody."

"Simple as that, huh?"

"No one said it would be easy. He won't give up without a horrific fight."

"What's this 'we' crap? I ain't going to Paris. I got my hands full right here in River City."

"In that case, I suppose I shall have to take sole credit for the collar of the century, Captain," Ambrose said. Looking at his watch, he rose somewhat unsteadily to his feet. He thanked Mariucci profusely for his help and then bade the good captain a very good night indeed. Or, at least, that's the way he seemed to recall his leave-taking.

Ambrose hadn't even dared look at the clock when he'd switched out the light and climbed into bed. He didn't want to know. He supposed he'd had two or three hours of sleep. In that time, he'd had a remarkable dream. The lovely Diana Mars had the starring role.

She was in some kind of danger. His cousin Bulling was slinking about, stalking her. No, no, it was that butler, Oakshott. He shook his head. Couldn't remember anything more. He hoped Sutherland was keeping a watchful eye on her in his absence. He worried about her. No, he missed her.

Now, feeling as if he were moving underwater, he padded across the room to one of the corner windows. His slippers made slapping noises on his heels. A watery grey light was leaking through a crack in the draperies. Pulling the heavy chintz aside, he looked out at the city below. The skies were indeed grey, though the storms of the previous evening had abated, leaving only a soft rain to swirl against the window.

His mission was satisfactorily concluded. He'd call Kelly and Hawke and give them the details. Then he'd book himself on the evening BA flight to Heathrow. That left him with a free day in New York to spend any way he wished. Perhaps he'd stroll over to the Met. There was an exhibit of the drawings of Peter Paul Rubens he was keen on seeing and that would be a lovely way to spend—

The telephone jangled. He crossed the room and picked it up.

"Hullo?"

"Is that you, Ambrose?"

"Diana?"

"Yes."

"You sound like you're just next door."

"I am, almost. I'm at the Colony Club on Park Avenue."

"You're in New York?"

"Arrived late last night."

"Good heavens. You're here. Are you quite all right?"

"Of course I'm all right. It's just that—"

"Just that what, Diana?"

"Detective Sutherland thought it a good idea for me to go on holiday. To get away from England for a time."

"Why? Did something happen?"

"Well, it was nothing really. Someone got into the house. The night before last. About three in the morning. I heard a noise and called the number you and the detectives gave me."

"Yes? Go on, go on."

"Well, there are police on the property, as you know. They came at a run. But someone was right at my bedroom door. It was locked obviously, but the—the knob was turning and—"

"Good lord."

"Yes. One hopes. At any rate, I got my trusty shooting iron from under the bed and went to the door. I gave fair warning. I said, 'I've been waiting all my life to do this,' and opened fire. It was quite marvelous."

"Did you hit anything?"

"Well, the door, certainly."

"I mean—did you shoot anyone?"

"No, unfortunately. He, or she, was gone by the time the coppers got there. No blood on the carpet, so I suppose I missed. I was disappointed, frankly. The nerve of someone to—"

"Thank God you're safe."

"Safe as houses, I suppose. What are you doing today?"

"Me? Well, I've a few phone calls to make. My trip's been a great success. I can't wait to tell you about it. And then—well, I was thinking of popping over to the Met. Been ages since I've had a good look round. There's a good Rubens show on if you'd like to join me?"

"Oh. I can't, I'm afraid."

"Ah, well. Perhaps another—"

"Ambrose, the reason I called is this. I've been invited out to the Hamptons for a few days. My dear friends the Barkers. Jock and Susan. They're from Cleveland. He was America's ambassador to Canada during the Reagan years. I told Su-Su I was coming to New York and—"

"Yes?"

"Well, I was wondering if you might not like to come along?"

"Come along."

"Yes. They've a lovely old place on Gin Lane. Right on the ocean. I'm sure they'd be delighted if you came. Men of your brilliant attractions are rather at a premium at house parties in Southampton. I promise you shan't have to play croquet or swim or do anything that might bring on physical prostration."

"I don't object to physical exertion. I play golf. I just don't swim well."

"Well. They've got oodles of room."

"Oodles."

"Please say yes. Jock has sent his car for me. I could have the driver stop at the Carlyle and pick you up."

"What time?"

"Oh. Shall we say eleven?"

"It sounds wonderful."

"See you then. What fun!"

"Oh, Diana, before you go—thank you very much indeed for the lovely flowers. I'm looking at them now."

"Well, I thought they'd be cheery."

"They certainly are. Well. Good-bye."

"Bye."

Ambrose hung up and sat down for a moment on the edge of the bed, a rather large smile on his face. The whisky clouds had lifted, the gin mists had cleared, and the old brain was ticking over quite nicely, thank you. Life was good again. He kicked off his slippers, scrunched his toes into the soft carpet, and clicked his bare heels together. Time to get moving if he was going to be packed and checked out by eleven. What to wear?

He stood and saw the small blue envelope on the floor, peeking out from beneath the dust ruffle. It was Diana's card. He'd intended to read her note at the bar at "21" and then again just before dropping off to sleep. It must have slipped unread from his hand. Now, he bent down, picked it up, and read her words:

My dearest Ambrose,

I never, till now, had a friend who could give me repose; all have disturbed me, and, whether for pleasure or pain, it was still disturbance.

But peace overflows from your heart into mine.

Diana

Chapter Forty-seven

Berlin

THE SMELL OF SMOKE. SOMEONE WAS IN THE HALL WITH him. Stoke froze, stopped breathing. Where? Somebody smoking cigarettes. Maybe ten, fifteen yards ahead. Stoke had the big leather satchel full of purloined documents in one hand and the Schmeisser machine pistol in the other. He raised the gun and listened. Just around the bend in the hallway, two men, guards most probably. He could hear them talking now, smell the smoke drifting back from their cigarettes. They must have just entered the hallway from one of the other elevator banks he'd passed on his way to Schatzi's office.

Clearly no hidden alarms had been sounded. The two Germans were laughing at something one of them had said. At least they were headed in the right direction, namely, away from him. He put the satchel down carefully and walked rapidly toward them on the balls of his feet, making no sound at all. There were two of them, all right, miniature versions of the Arnolds, wearing black uniforms identical to the one Stokely wore. Machine guns slung on their backs.

"Halt!" Stoke barked loudly when he was just ten feet behind them. *"Nicht rauchen!"*

The two guards stopped dead in their tracks.

"Nicht rauchen?" one of them said with a grin in his voice, apparently finding it funny. He started to turn around.

"Yeah, you heard me," Stoke said in English, jamming the muzzle of the Schmeisser between the guy's shoulder blades. "No smoking. New rule."

While they were thinking about that, he slung the machine pistol on his back, reached out with both hands, and slammed the two guards together, head-first. There was a sickening thud and the two men dropped to the floor, arms and legs akimbo, out cold.

"See what I'm saying?" Stoke said to the two unconscious guards at his feet. "Smoking is very bad for your ass."

He took their weapons, H&K MP 5 machine guns, and added them to the collection slung on his back. Then he went back and got the satchel. On the way, he saw the elevator he and Jet had used to come up from the *Unterwelt*. Clearly, Tempelhof was coming to life. It was time to get while the getting was good.

He took the elevator to the bottom level and passed quickly through the dismal rooms of the bunker. A minute or two later he was back in the tunnel. Left was the underground parking garage. Right had to be the trams. He turned right. The tunnel went from dark and dingy to bright and white up ahead. The tram station. He crept forward and took a peek.

There was a three-car train in the station. The cars were open, round and shiny white, and seemed to hover about a foot above the tracks. The station itself was all white tile, shiny and new. Two guards, helmeted and wearing full body armor, stood on the platform talking. Behind them, two sets of escalator stairs rose through the ceiling. Just like the A train, only much cleaner and without all that old-fashioned gravity shit to worry about.

"Morning, boys, how's it hanging?" Stoke said, striding right up to the platform, the Schmeisser flat down at his side.

"Was ist das?" the nearest one said, swinging around with his H&K coming up. When he saw Stoke's SDI uniform, he hesitated a beat too long, just like Stoke figured he would.

"Das ist the new guy," Stoke said, and squeezed the trigger.

He blew the guy off his feet with an accurate burst from the Schmeisser. The other guard must have said something very negative about Stoke into his headset because all of a sudden all the lights were flashing and alarms were sounding, including an electronic oogah horn that sounded like something from a U-boat during a crash dive.

Yeah, and here comes the cavalry to the rescue. They'd reversed the up escalator so all stairs were coming down. Guards on both sides, plus a bunch sliding down the wide stainless-steel middle part on their butts, firing in his general direction like kindergarten kids gone crazy. What saved him was, he was up against the platform edge now, only his bobbing head and shoulders visible from above. And he was moving. He was ducking and sprinting toward the train, pausing and firing a quick burst every few feet.

He'd strapped the satchel to his back. He had the Alpenkorps machine pistol in his right hand and an H&K in his left. He fired a second Schmeisser burst at the guard who'd sounded the alarm, putting him on the ground in a puddle of bright blood. With his left hand, he got off a long staccato riff, spraying the guys just coming off the escalator. It seemed to diminish their sense of urgency. Then he heard a new and disturbing noise above all the shooting and the shouting and alarms: the piercing sound of howling, growling Dobermans. Crazy animals, unlike Schatzi's storm troopers, who didn't flinch in the face of a little unfriendly machine-gun fire.

Shit.

Rounds were ripping up the tile around his head. Sharp chunks of ceramic stung his face. The dogs were bounding down the escalators behind the guards, even knocking some to the floor in their mad dash to chew Stokely into tiny pieces. He ducked completely below the platform edge and hauled ass for the lead car of the little Buck Rogers train. He hoped Buck had left the keys in the ignition.

Christ. Okay, that really hurt.

One dog had raced ahead of his brethren and was nipping at Stoke's heels. Got a piece of him, too. He stopped, pivoted, and swung the butt of the H&K at the salivating dog. He got lucky. A glancing blow to the head distracted the animal just long enough for him to haul himself up and into the lead car.

"You bite my ass again, I'm going to use the other end of this gun, *verstehen Sie*, Fido?"

He knew just enough German to know which was the "Go" button, a green one on the dash. He pushed it. There was an odd noise and a humming vibration as if a disc just beneath his feet was spooling up and spinning incredibly fast. Dogs were on either side of the car now, lunging and trying to get at him. He kicked out in both directions and sent two dogs flying back into the howling packs.

He felt a slug of hot lead whistle past his ear.

Distracted by the frenzied hounds, he'd let the storm troopers get too close. Rounds were sizzling over and around him. Ten or fifteen guys in black had leaped off the platform and were headed down the track toward him, filling the tunnel with lead. Funny thing was, bullets didn't seem to have much of an effect on the shiny white train cars. They just ricocheted off! What the hell was this thing made of?

The closest bad guy was maybe fifteen yards from the rear car. Stoke took him out with the Schmeisser and heard the most dreaded sound in close combat, the dry fire. Empty. He raised both of the H&Ks, firing at his pursuers, putting one boot up on the bench seat and leaning back against the instrument panel to brace himself. He must have hit reverse, because suddenly he was moving backward in the direction of his onrushing attackers!

Damn! He twisted around and looked to see what he'd hit. A simple lever. He'd pushed it down farther. This might work! The train accelerated supernaturally fast. But there was no sensation of speed in the cab. No g-forces slamming him backward. Weird. He watched the SDI uniforms panic and scatter wildly. He hit a couple and that was enough. Those who didn't take off back in the direction of the station flattened themselves against the walls or dove for either side of the track.

Now he pulled the lever up a bit and the A train seamlessly reversed directions. He pushed the lever forward and the train accelerated into the tunnel, whizzing by the men still flattened to the walls. He firewalled the throttle and the thing just flew. Hyperdrive, like that scene in *Star Wars*. Oddly enough, he still felt no jolt of speed.

Only explanation he could think of: If the machine created its own gravity field, then the normal rules of gravity didn't apply. Whoa.

Goddamn Germans were onto something here, he thought, gliding on air, leaving all the howling hounds and shell-shocked storm troopers in his dust. *Swoosh.* Man who had the brains and the money to put these things under New York City could be looking at some seriously positive cash flow.

He proceeded out in a great gentle loop, a white blur of station platforms to his right every few seconds, until he felt the tunnel begin to bend toward the left. Calculating speed and distance, and what he recalled of the above-ground geography, he figured he was getting to the far end of the field. That hangar where they'd stowed the helo had to be coming up. He slowed the train by backing down the lever a few notches. It instantly reached a speed where he could read the platform signs flashing by. *Udet, Voss, Richtofen . . . Lowen-hardt . . .* and, here it comes *. . . Steinhoffer.* Oh, yeah. He slowed to a crawl and stopped.

Home again, home again.

The platforms out here were much smaller. Maybe ten feet long, max. Only one car could access the platform at a time. But well-lit, and the white tile was brand-new. No escalator, just a simple iron stairway leading up to a closed door. Stoke took his bulging satchel and stepped off. He'd felt something familiar on his cheek, up his nose. A stale wind. Sweeping up from the dark tunnel ahead. Definitely funky. The kind of air forced ahead of a moving train.

He took one last look at his ride, the air-cushioned electra-glide Buck Rogers Special. Some damn train all right. Man. He took the stairs going up three at a time. A trainload of VDI troopers was on its way.

"What up, Arnold?" he asked the duct-taped prisoner inside *Stein-hoffer's* tool room. He located a small saw blade and went to work on Arnold's feet first.

"Mmmpf."

"Yeah, well, it took a little longer than I thought it would. Had us a big ass-kicking conference down in the Underworld subway station. I won, you'll be glad to know. How much fuel left in the helo?"

"Mmmpf!"

"That much, huh? Is that enough to get to Zurich, you think? Or not?"

"Mmmpf-mmmpf!"

"Chill your ass out, Arnold, be cool. What's your problem? You got control issues? I'm dancing as fast as I can here. Damn, you neo-Nazis are some seriously bossy individuals."

Chapter Forty-eight

Gulf of Oman

AN HOUR BEFORE DAYBREAK, TWO DAYS AFTER HAWKE AND Brock had gone for their swim. The decks were varnished with rain. There were patches of fog appearing and disappearing on the gently rolling surface of the pearl-grey sea. The old supply vessel, *Obaidallah*, was anchored in fifty feet of water just off a small village on the coast of Oman. To the northwest lay the old port city of Ghalat. To the east, slouching like a slumbering cat on the horizon, lay Masara Island. The good ship *Obaidallah*, loaded to the gunwales for this run, would make her weekly supply trip to Masara tonight.

Stoke had arrived from Berlin two days earlier. He'd met up with Fitz McCoy and Charlie Rainwater at Muscat airport, along with their team of mercenaries just flown in from Martinique. The supplies that had been loaded for this particular run were all of the non-potable, nonedible variety. The stores now stacked in the hold were the exploding kind: satchel charges, limpet mines, mortars, rocket-propelled grenades, and nine-millimeter ammunition. The transfer of supplies from one boat to another was taking place in the dark and in secret.

At midnight, the trawler *Cacique* slipped up along *Obaidallah*'s port side and offloaded the weapons, ammunition, and other sundry equipment Brock and Ahmed had been accumulating in Muscat during the past week. The most prized item: *Bruce*, a minisubmarine developed by the U.S. Navy for the SEALs.

It resembled nothing so much as a huge squared-off torpedo with a wide shark's smile painted on its nose. Now, the thirty-foot-long vessel remained on deck, covered with a heavy canvas tarp and lashed to the stern. This latest battery-powered vehicle was equipped with propulsion, navigation, communication, and auxiliary life support systems.

It was capable of delivering a squad of fully equipped combat swimmers and their cargo in fully flooded compartments to a mission site, loitering, and then retiring from the area while remaining completely submerged.

The *Obaidallah*, their new home at sea, had a brand-new captain and crew. The old team had been paid a month's wages and sent home grinning like cats to their families. Ali al-Houri, captain of *Cacique*, had temporarily relieved the *Obaidallah*'s regular captain, a darkly handsome young man named Abu. He had agreed to stay on. He would serve as first mate for this run since he was well known to the French out on the island.

Ali was down in the engine room with his first mate working on the diesel now. There'd been some problem with the fuel pumps. Ali and Abu told Fitz they were pretty sure they could fix it. Meanwhile, the clock was ticking. They had to go, and go tonight, one way or another.

Now, the sun was coming. And with it, the heat of day. Beneath the rolling purple ceiling of a low-hanging cloud bank, yellow light was leaking over the rim of the world. Hawke watched dawn's arrival through the open porthole, blinking back tears of fatigue. Ah yes, Hawke said to himself. Here it comes. It's morning again in Oman. Another crappy day just this side of paradise.

Hawke knew something his team did not.

Langley personnel on the ground in China had intercepted a red cell transmission out of Hong Kong. A communiqué from General Moon. The gist of it was, Kelly told Hawke, that the sultan was a dead man. If not already deceased, then soon. A courier had been dispatched from Hong Kong twelve hours ago with secret orders to murder Sultan Aji Abbas and his family.

Some bright boy in Beijing PRC headquarters had finally figured out that the sultan's services were no longer required. It was the thing Hawke and Kelly had most feared during the run-up to this operation. Now it was happening.

Now that Sultan Abbas had publicly invited French troops into Oman, his continued existence was pointless. Even, as the Chinese had now figured out, dangerous. China had to assume the United

States was looking for the sultan. If the United States succeeded and could actually locate him, the jig was up. The Americans would put him in front of a camera. He would proceed to denounce the French invasion and expose China's role in the operation. The ensuing flap would demolish any chance of covert success.

As if the mission Hawke and his men faced wasn't fraught with enough danger, the clock was now ticking. It was absolutely essential that they got to the sultan before the Chinese assassins did.

Below deck, five bearded and haggard men were seated around a battered wooden table in the dark, cramped space that passed for the main saloon. Even at this hour, with an ancient electric fan whirring away from its perch on a shelf, it was stifling below. Sweat stinks. So do Gauloise cigarettes. Two of the men were smoking heavily, all were drinking cold coffee out of tin cups, trying to stay awake. Maps, charts, diagrams, sat recon photos, and ashtrays littered the table.

All five were staring through bleary eyes at a crude handmade diagram Harry Brock had drawn of the underwater entrance and tunnels leading off from the powder magazine inside Fort Mahoud.

They'd been hard at it, formulating and rejecting and reformulating strategies, for a day and a half. A cherished hour here and there for sleep. It had been forty-eight very long hours since Hawke and Brock returned from the successful reconnaissance mission inside the fort. In that brief span of time, the world had changed.

The French navy was on the move. The *Charles de Gaulle* and *Foch* carrier battle groups had been repositioned to the Arabian Sea. Troopships were also en route, believed to be carrying an amphibious landing force of some forty thousand French infantry. It was rumored that, before the impending invasion of Oman, France's much-vaunted Mirage and Dassault Rafale fighters would once more challenge the Anglo-American no-fly zone currently being enforced in the northern skies over the Strait of Hormuz.

If it happened, this would be the first such challenge since a Mirage F1 had gone down during an encounter with an unknown British pilot during the early days of the crisis. The American no-fly zone had stirred the media pot even before the French plane went down. Now the mainstream media in the United States were having a field day, showing hourly updates on this "Second Front." Since no grisly murder trials or celebrity pedophiles were currently available, this unfolding drama in a place few in the world had ever even heard of would have to feed the beast with a billion eyes.

The downing of the Mirage over Oman had elicited a fierce hue and cry from the French press and diplomatic corps, demanding the as-yet-unnamed pilot be turned over to French authorities. That unnamed British pilot, now drinking cold coffee, didn't even know a French lynch mob wanted his head. Had he known, he would have been too busy to care.

Alex Hawke was one of the five men seated around the table in *Obaidallah*'s smoky and stifling saloon. The ship's radio, tuned to the BBC, was muttering in plummy tones on a shelf above the table. The news was uniformly bad. But no one was really listening anymore. There was too goddamn much to be done.

The gist of the thing, according to the BBC man now droning on, was this: China's foreign minister, Nien Chang, had just announced the commencement of joint naval exercises with the French. The two fleets would be conducting operations just outside the territorial waters of Taiwan. Through diplomatic channels, Washington and London had expressed their stern disapproval of such provocative actions. All this at a time of heightened anxieties over peace in the region. Taiwan, threatened, was a key pressure point in U.S.-China relations.

If there was to be a nuclear confrontation between the two superpowers, it would start on that island republic. A Chinese invasion of Taiwan, without an American response, would simply destroy U.S. credibility throughout the world. It was a classic Catch-22. Act, and you risked global war. Do nothing, and you risked total impotence.

The U.S. ambassador to China, the Honorable Barron Collier, had expressed the American concerns to the Chinese foreign minister in Beijing. So far, Ambassador Collier had received no reply.

"Turn that goddamn thing off," Harry Brock said, and someone did.

To say that the hopes of many in Washington and London were now riding on the shoulders of the five men here assembled was no exaggeration. It was hoped that, even at this late hour, an appearance by the sultan of Oman denouncing the French invasion of his sovereign territory might prevent a disastrous incursion. It was not just tiny Oman and the sovereignty of the Gulf States that was at stake. It was the very shaky planet itself.

Once the French were in and seized control of the oilfields, ports, refineries, platforms, and pipelines, they would be extremely difficult to remove. And once China had had her first taste of pure Omani crude, private reserve, it would be damn near impossible to wean her off it. Wargamers in the Pentagon and at NSA were still shaking their heads over this one.

A French invasion of Oman? Coupled with a simultaneous Chinese threat to Taiwan? Even the most prescient inside the Pentagon had not seen this little scenario coming. The allies were scrambling. Already, the United States and Britain were rapidly moving air and naval assets up from the rear. In Hawaii, shore leaves had been canceled. The Pacific Fleet had been called out on an emergency basis.

On point in this new theater of war, the good ship *Obaidallah*. A battered old barge that had no business being on top of the water. By all rights, she should have gone to the bottom decades ago.

Seated to Hawke's right in the saloon was Stokely Jones, recently arrived from a most successful mission in Germany. Even now, the documents he had obtained in Berlin were being examined at both Langley and NSA. CIA analysts were especially interested in the Chinese connection to the German megacorporation, Von Draxis Industries. Next to Jones, another American, Harry Brock.

To Hawke's left, two more recent arrivals: FitzHugh McCoy, a strapping Irishman, and Charlie Rainwater, a full-blooded Comanche Indian. McCoy and Rainwater, known affectionately in the worldwide antiterrorist community as Thunder and Lightning, headed up a loosely organized group of mercenaries. All were ex-Legionnaires, Ghurkas, Rangers, and battle-hardened soldiers of fortune.

It was safe to say that Rainwater and McCoy, whose motley band of eight warriors were now sleeping in *Cacique*'s crew quarters, constituted the best freelance hostage rescue team in the world.

Harry Brock and FitzHugh McCoy had taken an instant dislike to each other, Hawke noticed. Brock must have seen Hawke salute the little man on the dock. Which told Harry that Fitz was probably a Medal of Honor winner, since they were automatically entitled to salutes from anyone of any rank. Brock chose not to salute. Odd. But then Brock's behavior had been odd ever since they'd linked up in Oman. At night, running down his list of worries, Hawke kept thinking about Brick's *Manchurian Candidate* comment just after Harry Brock's rescue.

"What's your story?" Brock had said when Fitz first stepped aboard.

Fitz smiled and walked right up to the much bigger man. "Quick on the turn, fast and hard into battle. What's yours?"

Brock wisely didn't respond. But Hawke decided to watch him even more closely from now on.

"All right then," Fitz said, his thick brogue raw with fatigue and tobacco, "I know everybody's bloody hot and tired. But the more we sweat now, the less we bleed later. Let's take it from the top. One more time, boys. Then we all go get some bloody sleep. Stokely? You're up."

Stoke tilted his chair away from the table until it was perched on two back legs that threatened to give way any second. He looked at his old pal McCoy, old Five-By-Five, and smiled. Fitz grinned back. There was a bond between the two men that went back decades. It had been forged in the Delta swamplands.

"You want me to go through it all again, Five-By?"

"I do."

Fitz had earned his stripes in the Mekong: He was roughly five feet tall and approximately five feet wide. His heart was slightly bigger than those dimensions: He'd earned himself his Congressional Medal of Honor for single-handedly taking out a heavily entrenched mortar nest and saving his platoon. He'd carried two wounded to safety under heavy VC fire. He'd been missing a good portion of his stomach at the time.

In that other lifetime, Stoke had been Fitz's squad leader, SEAL Team 3. Also in that legendary squad, Charlie Rainwater, now wearing his trademark shoulder-length ponytail, buckskins, and a faded navy and gold SEAL T-shirt. Chief, as he was known, had been the squad's UDT demolitions expert. Chief, and the man sitting next to him, a tough little nut called the Frogman, were the best in the business. They were going to need both men tonight.

Stokely Jones, having now seen Fort Mahoud up close and personal, was glad as hell Hawke had had the wisdom and foresight to fly all of Stoke's old badass buddies from Martinique in for the party.

"Okay, here goes," Stoke said. "Me and Alex in the submersible SDV. We splash in the cove off Point Arras at 0200 hours. Descend to fifteen feet and maintain that depth. We proceed north around the point and then southwest to the powder magazine entrance. Arriving at approximately 0215, we reverse direction and enter the magazine tunnel stern-first. We make our way, backing full slow inside the tunnel to Point R-2 on the diagram. We disembark and remove the five RIBS stowed aboard. We inflate the boats, securing them in a daisy-chain aft of the SDV. We secure the vehicle. We rig satchel charges with detonators and fuse igniters on both doors leading to the tunnel and use the right-hand door to enter the magazine itself. Time: 0230 hours."

There was a smattering of ironic applause at this recitation and Stoke held his hand up for it to stop. They were all punchy as hell.

"Well done," Fitz said. He then turned to Chief Charlie Rainwater, who was rolling condoms over fuse igniters and tying off both ends so as to make them waterproof, another old trick he'd learned in the Delta.

"How about you, Chief Rainwater? You got enough rubbers there for a division. You going fucking or fighting tonight?"

Rainwater's teeth showed white in his dark face.

"Rule One," Rainwater said. "Fight first, fuck later."

McCoy smiled. "You know what to do?"

" 'Arrow,' my squad, disembarks and gains entrance to the fort. We do it the easy way or the hard way. We dock at 0215 hours and offload the equipment. After rigging charges at the base of the two towers, we enter the fort. At 0230, we rendezvous with 'Bow' squad, Stoke and Hawke, in the powder magazine. Designated Point Q. We ascend the stairs leading to this level where Ahmed believes the hostages to be held. At that point, all hell breaks loose and Bow and Arrow kill all the tangos and save all the women and children."

Fitz tried not to laugh and saw that it was impossible to continue. They all had to get some sleep. Even Rainwater, who habitually chewed some kind of plant root to stay awake, looked done in. The flight from Martinique to Oman in their old C-130 had not been relaxing. Their brains were weary from planning the operation. Sleep was imperative. They'd reconvene at noon for a final run-through. They were useless now. He had twelve hours left to get them ready.

Rainwater told Froggy to get some sleep. The Frogman sat there staring silently at him with eyes wide open. He was already asleep. That's how exhausted they were.

Until it all went to hell, it was going pretty good. The cranky diesels worked, at least well enough to get *Obaidallah* out to her designated location, an anchorage one mile northwest of the target island. They doused the lights and the ship was plunged into darkness. Ali put his first mate, Abu, on the radio, informing the French supply officer on Masara that he was very sorry, sir, that they were late, but they were having engine trouble. They'd lost power and had heaved an anchor until they could determine the problem.

Abu informed the sleepy Frenchman that repairs were well under way and he expected *Obaidallah* to arrive at the dock sometime just after midnight. The Frenchman accepted this at face value. And why not? The supply ship broke down all the time. He promised to have two dockhands waiting for their arrival.

Point Arras loomed up Sphinx-like against the dark sky. Standing on the foredeck of the darkened vessel with Hawke and Stokely Jones, Captain Ali raised his glasses and watched the lights of the patrol boat disappear around Point Arras. The first mate had clocked two or three circumnavigations now, and reported that a round-trip was averaging one hour and twenty minutes. When the patrol boat was gone, Ali gave Hawke the thumbs-up.

"All right, Stoke, let's go hunting," Hawke said. He checked his watch. They were already three minutes behind the atomic clock in his head. The three men walked swiftly aft to where the SDV hung in its sling off the stern. As they passed the wheelhouse, Hawke could hear the murmurs of the men inside, suiting up, checking weapons in the dark. Many of them were donning loose-fitting white garments over their tigerstripes and camo war paint. And substituting turbans for the white kepis the Legionnaires traditionally wore.

At the Masara dock, only a skeleton crew would be on duty at this hour. Maybe, if they were lucky, only a few sleepy Omanis who helped with the lines, pumped gas, and helped unload supplies. It was hoped the guards posted at the front gate wouldn't look too closely at the men unloading supplies. And that the machine gunners looking down from the twin towers wouldn't notice anything un-usual when *Obaidallah* arrived at the dock.

Fitz believed that with Abu or Ahmed doing all the talking as they stepped ashore, and some good body language on the part of his disguised troops as they off-loaded equipment, he could get all of his men and materiel inside the front door without firing a shot. That was the plan anyway.

Hawke paused by one of the opened portholes. Fitz was in there now, moving among his men, encouraging them, issuing last-minute instructions, making sure his team was mentally and physically ready to peak. Something was bothering Fitz, Hawke had seen it in his eyes. There just hadn't been enough time for adequate preparation. But was there ever?

They'd all been cooped up at sea aboard an old rust bucket for two days, with no place to run or stretch or hide. Because of the lack of quarters aboard, they'd been forced to "hot rack" or use the same bed in shifts. These men were jungle and desert warriors, not sea pi-rates like Stoke and Hawke. Fitz had asked Hawke for another day. Hawke had said no. And, to McCoy's great chagrin, he didn't say why.

He couldn't. Kelly had ordered him not to reveal the truth, be-lieving, correctly, in Hawke's view, that it would be bad for morale to ask men to put their lives at risk for a hostage who might well be dead already.

"Hoo-ah," Stoke said, staring at Hawke as he approached, looking like an interplanetary traveler in his undersea warfare gear. Stoke, who'd be driving the boat for a good portion of this mission, had a red-lensed pencil flash, studying their route one last time. On the stern, a crewman was lowering the torpedo-bodied SDV slowly to the surface.

"Let's go get this bloody thing over with," Hawke said, putting on his half-helmet and adjusting his lipmike.

Stoke's gut was talking now, saying it was going to be bad.

It just didn't say how bad.

Chapter Forty-nine

Southampton, New York

"FINE DAY FOR IT, CHIEF INSPECTOR," THE HEAD DOORMAN, Michael O'Connell, said, tipping his cap as Ambrose pushed through the hotel doors onto Seventy-sixth Street. He was a cheery rosy-cheeked fellow who'd been on the door at the Carlyle for years. He had Ambrose's rather tired-looking leather grip in one hand and held a silver whistle to his lips with the other, scanning the solid phalanx of traffic headed north on Madison for a taxi. The sun was out with a vengeance now and steam was rising from the glistening streets.

Something in the air: You could sense the green acres of Central Park baking dry after a good soaking.

"British Airways, sir?"

"No, no taxi to JFK this morning, Michael," Ambrose said. "Someone's picking me up."

"Enjoy your stay, sir?"

"Most enjoyable, Michael. Always feel at home here."

"Where to now, sir?"

"Out to Long Island for a country weekend. Friends of friends out at Southampton. Some kind of house party, I believe. Chap named Jock Barker. Ever hear of him?"

"Oh, yes. Quite famous, sir. Jack 'Call me Jock' Barker. You're sure to have a good time at Stonefield."

"Stonefield?"

"The old Barker place. One of the loveliest homes out on the island, sir. Mr. Barker throws this party every summer. Legendary. I believe that's his car coming around now."

The car, a Rolls, was one of the new Phantoms. As it swung mightily around the turn into Seventy-sixth Street, it looked as if it had been carved singly from a massive block of black steel. It had a haughty, imperious aspect that Rollers had lacked for the last decade or two. The car seemed to say, "I'm back. Move over."

The chauffeur, dressed in robin's-egg-blue livery and wearing matching gloves, leaped out and opened the boot. He was a strapping, freckle-faced boy of about twenty and had the earnest look of a chap who loved his work. Ambrose slipped Michael a twenty and thanked him. The opaque rear window nearest the curb began to slide down. Ambrose's eyes went to a beautifully rendered monogram, in the same light blue, on the door. Below a prancing horse, the words *Spe Labor Levis*. Hope lightens work. A worthy sentiment.

A face appeared, pale and lovely, china-blue eyes framed by soft auburn curls, the small red bow of a mouth done up in a smile. Ambrose staggered a step, but recovered quickly by pretending to lean over and place a hand semicasually on the roof above the rear window. The prettiest girl in the world said, "Oh, hullo, stranger. Need a lift?"

Ambrose climbed inside the sumptuous coach and sank into the soft leather beside Lady Diana Mars. She gave him a chaste peck on the cheek and took his hand. Her hand felt small and cool and fragile inside his own. She regarded Ambrose for a moment, her eyes softening, then leaned forward on the seat and said to the driver, "Gin Lane, Buster, and step on it."

Ambrose was astonished, but the chauffeur was apparently accustomed to this sort of behavior. He looked over his shoulder and smiled. "Yes, ma'am. We should be out there in less than two hours if we get lucky leaving the city. A bit more if Route 27 is backed up."

"Let her rip," Diana said and then whispered into Ambrose's ear, "I'm not being cheeky. He's Jock's bodyguard. His name really is 'Buster.' "

Buster steered the stately battle cruiser up the Northern State Parkway east to avoid any traffic that might dare cross his path, and then picked up the notorious Long Island Expressway. The LIE, all eight lanes of it, ran due east the length of the island, stopping just shy of Montauk Point. The traffic was bumper-to-bumper all the way to Manorville. The passengers, at least, had the luxury of ignoring it, happily bringing each other up to speed on events on either side of the Atlantic. Diana's brush with an intruder seemed the furthest thing from her mind as she pressed Ambrose for all the lurid details of his Coney Island escapade.

"How perfectly dreadful, Ambrose. But you got your confession. Now what?"

"I've merely provided the CIA, FBI, and Interpol with ammunition. It's up to them when and if they choose to use it."

"Murdering your own father. The man *should* be shot."

"Don't worry. I've a feeling he will be."

After the Pine Barrens and Manorville, the scenery grew much more agreeable, an expanse of rolling green hills criss-crossed with white picket fences and brown potato fields stretching into the distance. Once they reached Route 27, Buster was able to open the mammoth Roller up a bit, give the Phantom her head. They were probably doing well over a hundred but it felt like fifty. Ambrose and Diana lapsed into silence, each content to watch the sunlit summer day slide peacefully by the windows.

"Mr. Congreve?" Buster said, his eyes in the rearview mirror. "Sorry to disturb you."

"Yes?"

"I believe we've picked up a tail, sir."

"Really? When did you notice it, Buster?"

"On the Triboro Bridge, sir. It's a white van."

"Lots of white vans," Ambrose said.

"This one's got a cracked windshield, sir. Sun catches it."

"Does he know you've made him?" Ambrose craned his head around and peered out the small rear window.

"I don't think so. Four or five cars back, sir. Behind the red Porsche."

"Is there a back way into Southampton?"

"Yes, sir. Through Hampton Bays. The turning's coming up in about two miles."

"What's the top end on this machine?"

"She'll do one-fifty if you push it."

"Push it. After you make the turn, pull over. We'll see what happens."

"Someone's following us?" Diana said. The acceleration was noticeable but not uncomfortable, pressing her firmly back into the deep leather cushions.

"Perhaps. We'll know soon enough . . . hold on, we're going to take this turn very, very quickly. Well done, Buster. Let's just nip into this car park and see what transpires."

Buster swung into the lot and turned the big car around so that they were out of sight but had a clear view of the highway they'd just left. After a minute or two, Buster said, "No sign of him, sir."

"Did he speed up when you did?"

"I don't think so. He'd have passed us by now, sir. May have turned off."

"There you have it, then. Nothing to worry about."

"Sorry to alarm you, sir. I just thought that—"

"No apologies necessary. Caution is always rewarded. Let's get going, shall we?"

Soon enough, they came to a traffic light and were moving at a snail's pace through the lively town. Southampton looked to Ambrose as if it had once been a sleepy village and quaint. Main Street was lined with trees and the sidewalks were still of brick. What had once plainly been a residential street in a small town was now lined with an assortment of shops, restaurants, and even an old-fashioned hardware store standing cheek-by-jowl with an emporium selling surfboards and sunglasses.

Town was certainly busy on this Saturday afternoon in high summer; the sidewalks were crowded with strollers, shoppers, women in tennis whites pushing baby prams, men in colorful Lacoste polo shirts with the collars turned up. Main Street proper was clogged with vintage convertibles and big black Range Rovers with blacked-out windows. The summer people crossing in front of the Rolls at each corner stop looked tan and fit and desperately happy to be here. And, for the most part, they looked quite rich.

"What sort of house party is it going to be?" Ambrose asked Diana as they rolled to a stop at a dead end. Main Street ended abruptly at a leafy, shady cross street with the charming name of Gin Lane. They turned right and he caught glimpses of the blue Atlantic sparkling in the sun on his left. He was most curious to see the great ocean palaces, but they were all well hidden behind severely manicured hedgerows twenty feet high. "I've never ventured out here before and I've no idea what to expect."

Diana squeezed his hand. "You'll see, dear. Jock's parties are legendary. Look, we're pulling into the drive now!"

The Rolls cruised through a tall pair of very ornate gates, wrought-iron vines forming the letter B when they were shut. The gravel drive that curved toward the ocean was lined with stately elms boasting great bursts of leaves that formed a solid green canopy over the road. Ambrose lowered his window and was rewarded with the sharp tang of ocean air mingled with the delicious scent of freshly mown grass.

Presently, the drive widened and they came upon Stonefield standing on a gentle knoll amid a profusion of blazing rhododendron. The house itself resembled a hotel in France where Ambrose had once spent a week recovering from a gunshot wound to the posterior. The Hotel de Ville in Normandy. There was a tower to one side, old brick under a thin beard of dark green ivy. Sprinklers were flashing on the lawn in front, their arching spray reaching the sundials and brick walks and flame-red gardens.

The front of the stone house was broken by a line of French doors, all of them aglow with mirrored gold, and all flung open so the great house might inhale the delicious scents of summertime. There was a man standing with his legs apart at the front door. He was wearing riding clothes and Ambrose guessed he was the host, Jock Barker. When the Rolls glided to a stop, he rushed down the steps and whipped Diana's door open before Buster had even switched off the ignition.

"Diana, my darling, it's so good of you to come," the tall and well-made fellow said. He was perspiring mightily, and Ambrose assumed he'd just returned from his stables. He spoke in a husky tenor and he had a good smile full of white teeth, startling against his tan.

"You look lovely, girl," Jock said as she climbed out.

"So good of you to have me," Diana replied, putting her arms round his neck and kissing his cheek. "Come say hello to my good chum Ambrose Congreve."

Ambrose climbed out of the back of the Rolls and shook the man's hand.

"I'm Jack, call me Jock, Barker," the big chap said with a smile. "Welcome to Stonefield."

"Ambrose Congreve. Pleasure to be here. What a splendid car you have there, Jock."

"Why, thanks. It's brand-new. My wife, Susan, hates it."

"Really? Why?"

"She says a car like this makes me look like I want people to think I'm rich."

"What does she want you to drive?"

"According to Susan, the truly rich all drive beat-up Volvo station wagons."

"But then you'd look truly rich."

Barker laughed and turned to Diana. "I think Ambrose and I are going to get along just fine. Come on inside and say hello to everyone. We're just having lunch served down by the beach. Then we're going for a swim."

"Swim?" Ambrose said, a tremor in his voice. "In the sea?"

"Or not," Diana said.

"What's that?" Jock asked.

"Oh, nothing," Diana said. "Ambrose doesn't care for swimming. He's allergic to water."

Later, from the beach, where the sand was still warm even though the sun was long gone, the house looked as if it was afire. It stood bathed in a blaze of lights, white floodlights picking out the seaward windows and many-gabled rooftops, colored lights dancing above the pool complex, and millions of tiny white lights winking gaily in all the trees that marched down to the water.

Four massive commercial searchlights, positioned straight up at the four corners of the lawn, created columns of pure white light and a space for the chorus of voices that rose up from the lawn, bits and snippets that existed and then twinkled out like stars looking down from above. This heady cocktail buzz, the familiar Hamptons' comic opera of summer small talk and instantly forgotten introductions, was fueled by champagne. The Bob Hardwick orchestra flown in for the occasion accompanied it.

The only competition for all this grandeur was the moon, rosy-gold with a haze around.

"I see him," the waiter said, pushing his black glasses up on the bridge of his nose. "She's gone inside."

The tall, white-jacketed waiter, who'd dyed his curly blond hair

jet black for the party, stood in the lee of a sand dune smoking a cigarette. The thin line of a smile appeared. He'd been waiting a long
time for this night. A very long time indeed.

"Anyway, I think they're coming," he told the woman standing beside him in the shadows.

"Why?"

"Why? Why, because I fucking said so, didn't I? That's *why*. I
heard *him* tell *her* to get her wrap. That they were going for a little
stroll on the beach. I made it my job to keep track of them, didn't I?
Without being recognized, I might add."

"I can't stand out here all fucking night," the woman said. She was
wearing a thin black raincoat. Her jaws were clenched to keep her
teeth from chattering. Even in summer, the rolling ocean cooled the
night breezes blowing onshore.

"You want some of this?" the waiter hissed, raising the back of his
hand and giving her face a near miss.

"No. I'm done with all that."

"Don't lie to me. Look. Here they come," the waiter said. He
threw down his cigarette butt and crushed it into the sand with his
heel.

"That's them?"

"That's them all right. Good hunting."

The waiter made his loping way across the dunes and back to the
party, careful to avoid the happy couple strolling hand-in-hand
through the sand toward the low-hanging moon.

Chapter Fifty

Masara Island, Oman

HEAVEN, AT LEAST FOR THE TIME BEING, WAS ON HAWKE'S side. The inverted bowl of sky above was an ideal shade for his purpose: black. There was no moon to speak of and only a silver sprinkling of stars across the northern sky. Since the winds were calm, so were the seas. Not that you would dare say it aloud: perfect spec-ops conditions. Fifteen feet below the surface, Hawke's thirty-foot-long vehicle, dubbed *Bruce*, was sliding silently forward. Given the conditions, the sub was, Hawke hoped, invisible to the tower guards manning the heavy machine guns.

"All stop," Hawke said, looking over at his navigator.

"All stop," Stoke said.

The two men were adjacent to each other, each tucked into a separate flooded compartment in the nose of the SDV. Both were hooked into the vessel's internal communication and auxiliary life support systems. They could speak and breathe easily. Easing the throttles back in sync to the neutral position, they felt the sub slow and stop. There was no sound.

Buoyancy systems kept them hovering at the desired depth in the black water. Visibility was near zero. Only a hooded four-color GPS screen in front of Hawke allowed him to see precisely where he was in relation to the island dead ahead. They'd made good time from the mother ship, arriving off Point Arras right on schedule.

The minisub's all-electric propulsion system was powered by rechargeable silver-zinc batteries and designed for silent running. Only the most sophisticated underwater auditory monitors could pick it up. At idle, and three hundred yards offshore, Hawke felt the chance of audible detection was very slight indeed.

"You have the helm," he said, removing his hand from the control stick.

"I have the helm," Stokely replied, taking it.

Hawke completed his preparations to disembark from the portside pilot station. It had been previously agreed that he would now leave the vehicle, alone, and swim the three hundred yards remaining to the entrance to the docks. He disengaged from the onboard underwater breathing apparatus, called a "hookah" because of its uncanny resemblance to a water pipe. He now switched over to his Draeger LAR-V underwater breathing apparatus.

Opening the small hatch cover, he levered himself out of the cockpit and kicked away from the vehicle. Moving his fins with slow, scissorlike movements, he remained in Stokely's view just long enough to make a circle with his thumb and forefinger. Stokely gave the return thumbs-up and Hawke swam away. Hawke would make sure there were no unpleasant surprises at the dock before Stoke brought the sub in close.

Once he had the all-clear signal, Stoke would pilot the SDV directly to the tunnel entrance. On the panel before him was an array of sophisticated instruments including Doppler navigation sonar displaying speed, distance, heading, and other piloting functions. A ballast and trim system controlled his buoyancy and pitch attitude. A manual control stick was linked to *Bruce*'s rudder, elevator, and bow planes. Pure functionality, no frills, just the way Stoke liked his war machines.

But the beast also had sharp teeth. A shark's toothsome grin was depicted on the nose, hand-painted on the bow by some boys at the Naval Amphibious Base at Little Creek, Virginia. Boys, Stoke said, who clearly had too much free time on their hands. Still, he had to admit the grinning shark's teeth did give *Bruce* a very intimidating appearance.

It sort of screamed *Don't mess with me. I bite.*

Hawke covered the remaining three hundred yards swiftly and without incident. He surfaced under the dock, swinging the Beretta nine in his right hand through a tight arc. There was a round prejacked into the chamber.

All quiet. No beeping, screeching alarms, no whispered shouts and frantic running feet on the network of steel docks above his head. Only the soft lapping of the water against the pilings. He flipped down the NVG goggles atop his helmet and quickly located the three marks he'd slashed into the barnacle crust on one of the pilings.

He studied the water's swift flow against the piling. The tide was running, well into the ebb. If they could manage to stick to their mission schedule, the entrance would be fully exposed when they exfiltrated at high speed.

They would have the newly freed hostages in tow behind the speeding sub, an idea Hawke had gotten on that first day, watching a blue fishing boat towing a string of white dinghies. The sight recalled a favorite children's book, one his mother had brought him as a present from America. *Make Way for Ducklings*, it was called. There was a problem with the idea, however. When you have your ducks in a row, they make for a very easy target.

If all went well, though, the machine guns would be silent, the twin towers by then a heap of rubble, brought down by massive charges at the base rigged by Chief Charlie Rainwater. Egress from the fortress via the main gate would be blocked. The tunnel the only way out. It might work.

And the dock he was swimming beneath would no longer exist. He reached up and attached an MK-V Limpet assembly module to the underside of the dock. The module contained more than one hundred pounds of high explosives. He set it to detonate in the standoff mode at 0330 hours. By that time, it was expected, the infiltrators would be gone.

That, at least, was the plan.

Hawke submerged once more and located the pinpoint violet beam they had affixed to *Bruce*'s nose. Two seconds on, two seconds off, invisible from above. Hawke had a portable version, a pencil light sheathed in rubber. He signaled three times rapidly, flashing the all-clear, and saw three short flashes in return from the SDV. Stoke had acknowledged and was proceeding directly toward Hawke.

The tricky part now would be maneuvering the cumbersome vehicle in reverse at one knot. Once they'd gotten the thing inside the tunnel, they'd be backing down until they reached the powder magazine. It had been agreed that Stoke, who had trained in undersea warfare at Little Creek with both an early version of the vehicle, the

Mark VII, and newer, larger versions, would now pilot *Bruce* from the navigator's helm on the port side.

They would run dead slow. Swimming, Hawke would position himself at the new "bow," grasping the handhold and kicking off from sides of the tunnel to keep them on course as they moved deeper within. The screeching sound of metal on stone was to be avoided at all costs. So was damaging the props and disabling the vehicle, which would be disastrous.

"Anything exciting up in the real world?" he heard Stoke say in his headset. *Bruce* was now hovering just ten feet from the surface and five yards outside the underwater entrance. Hawke swam over and grabbed a rail running the length of the vessel.

"Negative. Let's turn this brute around."

"Jaws of death, man. Come to call." Stoke was psyched; Hawke could hear it in his voice.

Stoke reversed the port motor and shoved the starboard throttle half ahead. The painted nose began to swing slowly to the left and Hawke, using his flippers, started kicking, helping to push the nose around. After five minutes of heavy exertion, they had the thing correctly positioned, stern-to, just outside the entrance. Time for *Bruce* and his unexpected guests to go calling.

Hawke checked his watch. He and Stoke were due to meet up with the rest of the force in less than twenty minutes.

On the surface, things were going pretty much according to the plan Hawke and McCoy had agreed upon. Everybody was awake and sober, nobody had fallen overboard, and nobody was shooting at them as of this moment. This, based on FitzHugh McCoy's vast experience of the counterterrorist trade, was an exceedingly dangerous state of affairs. Something was bound to happen in the next thirty minutes or so that would blow all his plans out the window and everything else to hell and gone.

He imagined Hawke and Stokely had the sub just inside the tunnel now. In twenty-two minutes, they would all regroup inside the large ammunition storehouse just inside the entrance to the fort on the left. A stone staircase led down from that storeroom to the old powder magazine and the tunnel. If there were to be trouble for

Hawke, it would most likely be on those steps leading up from where he moored the sub. If an alarm sounded, if the garrison realized they'd been breached, that's the first place armed guards would go. It was a weak point in the plan but it couldn't be helped.

Fitz was standing on the bow of the good ship *Obaidallah* in his Arab regalia. His hands were on his hips, his eyes were everywhere as the battered supply boat slowly approached the docks just below Fort Mahoud. He could feel many pairs of eyes on him, imaginary death beams coming from the gunners manning the tops of the twin towers.

The old boat was running dead slow, black smoke leaking aft from her stack. She had only her running and navigation lights on. A reddish glow illuminated the first mate, Abu, standing at the wheel. His would be the familiar face to anyone on the docks. Fitz had told him to angle the overhead light so that his face was clearly visible from the dock. To a casual eye, Fitz believed, all was precisely as it should be aboard the weekly supply ship.

Two men, dockhands, were lounging on the dock silently watching their approach. One of them leaned casually against a bollard, smoking a cigarette. He looked just like he should look, Fitz observed, sullen and lazy. Both men had lines loosely at the ready. There was nothing at all about their body language or facial expressions to cause Fitz any concern.

It was two-thirty in the morning.

Except for the soft yellow lights at either end of the dock, it was pitch dark in the little marina. The docks, as anticipated, were empty. The French patrol boat had left the dock on schedule, fifteen minutes earlier. Fitz checked his watch again. Forty-five minutes, roughly, until the cutter returned. Enough time to do this thing, maybe.

Fitz had his eyes peeled, taking it all in. These rascals with the dock lines had probably been roused again from their bunks to greet the delayed supply ship. They'd be cranky and sleepy, nothing more. He hoped.

Brock's man, Ahmed, who was standing on the stern, lifted his right hand in a vague greeting as the boat neared the dock. He muttered something in Arabic to one of the dockhands as the vessel bumped up against the pilings. The hand tossed him a line, and Ahmed made it fast to a stern cleat. The other line came aboard amidships and Abu stepped outside and handled that one. The old diesel was still throbbing, and Captain Ali shut it down.

Ahmed stepped easily onto the dock and after a brief exchange sent one of the two hands scurrying for the hand carts. He remained with the other, amiably chatting him up. Ahmed was their point man in dealing with any Arabs they encountered. Without him, Fitz had told Hawke, this mission would have been virtually impossible.

Fitz remained on the bow, checked his watch, and did a surreptitious weapons check beneath his loose-fitting white garments. He had two weapons at the ready. A Heckler & Koch MP 5 machine gun. And a Fairbairn-Sykes fighting knife in a leather sheath.

The knife was the pride of the McCoy armory back home at Fort Whupass in Martinique. Designed by two British officers based on their close-quarters combat experience with the Shanghai police, it was designed specifically for striking accurately at the target's vital organs. It had been a standard weapon for commandos during World War II. Fitz touched the hilt, reassured by the well-worn smoothness of the leather wrapping.

He looked aft. Abu and Brock had gotten the heavy iron after hatch open and the first of the supplies were being passed up from the men below. The words SUGAR and RICE were stenciled on burlap sacks. Some actually contained sugar; many others contained satchel charges, Semtex explosives, and nine-millimeter cartridge belts. The dockhands had returned with dollies and were loading up the carts under the supervision of Ahmed.

Rainwater stepped suddenly out of the shadow of the wheelhouse and joined Fitz standing on the bow. With his dark skin and flashing black eyes, Charlie Rainwater looked like some children's book illustrator's vision of a terrifying Barbary pirate. All he needed were brass hoops in his ears and a flashing scimitar.

"Looks good," Rainwater murmured under his breath.

"Doesn't it just?" McCoy said, also keeping his voice low.

"You see the guys up in the towers?"

"See 'em? I can feel their fooking breath down my neck. Don't look up there. They appear to have lost interest in us."

"Here's some good news. That metal surveillance platform that runs around the top of the tower? They can't see me rigging charges down at the base unless they happen to lean way out over the rail and look down."

"I noticed that. I thought you'd be happy. You like your privacy when you work."

"I'm ready to do this, Fitz. Now. I like the timing. I'll throw a sack of 'Semtex sugar' over my shoulder and take a casual stroll down the dock. Have the charges rigged at both towers in five minutes or less."

"I agree wholeheartedly, Chief. Do it. Go."

An ad hoc change of plans was not unusual in McCoy's world. Thunder and Lightning as a counterterrorist group was still alive and kicking butt the world over precisely because they weren't afraid to toss the best-laid plans right out the window. Rainwater disappeared aft, careful to maintain a lethargic pace as he made his way past the wheelhouse. Although blowing the towers wasn't scheduled to occur until just before egress, it made sense to set the charges now while everybody was so relaxed.

Fitz made his way aft to check on the Frogman. Froggy and his men were doing the unloading. The wooden crates containing the automatic weapons were coming up now. The Frogman, a squat, tough ex–French Foreign Legionnaire, had been with Fitz since the very beginning. He was a founding partner of Thunder and Lightning. He and his sidekick, the Great Bandini, with the help of Abu and Captain Ali, were all stacking crates on the dock and sending them off as fast as they were handed up.

"Froggy?" Fitz said quietly.

"That's the last of it, Skipper. Shall I bring the boys topside?"

"Not yet."

Fitz cast his eyes quickly up at the twin towers and around at the docks one last time. The eight commandos, all dressed in Arab kaffiyehs, were more than ready to emerge from the stifling hold. Each man had given a brief, imperceptible nod to Fitz, who'd looked each in the eye one last time before going up on deck. They were bloody ready. But something didn't look right. One of them was missing.

"Where the hell's Ahmed? He was here on the dock not two minutes ago!"

Froggy said, "He and Brock went with one of the dockhands to open up the gates and the storehouse."

"Damn him," Fitz said, more in shock than anger, "He's supposed to remain here. Brock, too. Oversee this lot. Deal with contingencies."

"There was a lot of Arabic going back and forth with Ahmed and Brock and the dock guys," Froggy said. "Maybe there was a problem."

"Brock doesn't speak Arabic."

"He does now."

"Arrow?" Fitz said into his lipmike. "Where the hell are you, Chief?"

"Base of the north tower. Charges set, both towers. Front door is wide open. No tangos visible. I'm headed back to the boat to collect Froggy and company," Rainwater said.

"Belay that. Stay where you are. We're coming to you. Is Ahmed with you?"

"Negative. He's inside. Said he and Brock were headed for the storehouse for the rendezvous with Hawke."

"For fuck's sake. All right. One minute, mate. Keep your bloody eyes open. I don't like this."

"Affirmative. Hold on, Skipper, I think something—"

That's when the staccato sound of automatic weapons came from inside the fort. The moment when all the lights went on and all the alarms started screaming like Irish banshees announcing that everyone within spitting distance was going to die.

That's when the real goat-fuck got started; when anything and everything turned to pure, unadulterated shit.

And FitzHugh McCoy realized too late he'd had a man named Judas aboard his boat. I've just got no fooking clue which man was the traitor, he thought.

But if he was a betting man, right now he'd be betting heavily on Harry Brock. Hawke said he'd been in a Chinese prison for three months. A lot can happen to a man's brain in one of those bloody hellholes. They rewire the damn things!

Chapter Fifty-one

Southampton, New York

"WELL! THAT WAS CERTAINLY CHEEKY," DIANA SAID, TAKING his hand while sipping from a fresh flute of champagne. Not that he was counting, but it was her third. Or fourth. He'd lost track. It was that kind of party. No half-empty glasses. Frantic, but intimate in that odd way truly large parties can be. Since he knew absolutely no one, he could be alone with Diana, two blithe spirits, apart in the midst of the social whirlaway, in an imaginary space of their own making.

"What was certainly cheeky?" Ambrose asked, leading her toward the sand dunes. "Mind your step. There's a broken board here and there."

They'd left the raised wooden walkway that stretched out from the lawn and were on the steps leading down to the beach proper now, threading their way through clumps of wild sea oats that dotted the sand dunes. Beyond, the surf was pounding gently, its low rumble a blessed relief from the all-too-familiar strains of "Jeremiah Was a Bullfrog" and "Bad, Bad, Leroy Brown."

"That man passing the champagne was cheeky," Diana said. "One of the wait staff. You must have seen him. The one who looked like that wonderful English actor, what's his name."

"What *is* his name?" he said, his eyes bright with happiness. She did look so pale and lovely in the moonlight. She wore an emerald-green dress, satin, with a deep neckline that was positively awe-inspiring, and a simple necklace of diamonds.

"Don't make fun, Ambrose. You know exactly who I'm talking about. Michael Caine! That's the one I mean."

"Ah. Alfie."

"You did see him then? The waiter? The one with the thick black glasses?"

"No."

"Well, he winked at me. You must have been looking the other way at some other woman. Winked at me and said something rude. Like 'bang' or something like that. I think that's rather cheeky, don't you?"

"*Bang?*"

"I don't know. I couldn't hear him in the middle of that riot. Bang-bang, maybe."

"It's damned rude, Diana. Also, given the circumstances, a bit un-nerving. Which one is he? I'll go have a word with him."

"Oh, don't go back there. I don't want to make a fuss. I want to walk along the beach and look at the stars. The moon. It's a wonder-ful night. Magic. Let's forget about it."

"Very well, Diana. Just point him out when we get back. I'll say something to Jock. I don't think he'd find it amusing. At all."

"Don't be stuffy. Come on! I'll race you down to the water! There's something I want to show you down there. Come along, now . . ."

"Diana, don't—"

But she'd flung her shoes off, hiked up her skirts, raced ahead, and disappeared over the dunes. Ambrose was not fond of walking in sand, much less running in the stuff. Still, he sat himself down and began unlacing his shoes and rolling up his trouser cuffs.

"Come on!" she cried, "You must come and see this moon!"

"I'm coming as fast as I can," he said, getting to his feet and trying to brush the sand from the seat of his trousers. What was the attrac-tion? People seemed to flock to beaches in droves and—

"Ambrose! What *are* you doing?"

When he caught up with her, Diana was strolling barefoot through the surf, her face turned to the moon, her hair falling in lus-trous ribbons on her pale shoulders. He reached out and put a hand on her—

"Oh! You frightened me. I didn't hear you coming."

"The strong, silent type."

"Ambrose, isn't it beautiful? The waves. The moon on the water. I'm so glad you could come."

"So am I."

"Will you hold me for a second? I haven't been held in the moon-light in a very long time."

"Well, I—"

"Are you shy, dear?"

"No, no. It's just that I—well, to be brutally honest, I haven't held anyone in a very long time myself."

"One step at a time, then. Put your arms around me."

"Like this?"

"Perfect. Maybe just a wee bit closer."

"You said you wanted to show me something . . ."

"Shh. Now. I lift my chin to a certain angle."

"I must tell you, Diana, you are the most beautiful woman I've ever known. I simply—"

"I said 'shh.' That means be quiet in English."

"Sorry."

"Ambrose?"

"Yes?"

"It's time."

"Ah."

"Go for it."

"Yes."

"Do it."

He did it. He kissed her. He'd meant it to be brief, that kiss, but it seemed to take on a life of its own. It grew warmer, and longer, until there was simply nothing else on earth he knew about or cared about, nothing at all in his world except Diana's warm lips. His hand moved down her back and he felt the curve of her hip. He pulled her to him and kissed her harder, fearful he was hurting her, but she was crushing her lips against his and he felt her tongue darting about and he parted his lips.

Later, he would not remember how long that first kiss lasted. Only that it was seared in his memory and that it was filled with promise. And that it came within a hair's breadth of being the very last kiss of his life.

"Golly."

"My sentiments exactly."

"I had no idea."

"So that's what all the fuss is about."

"We really must do that again sometime."

He wouldn't remember who said what to whom in those few moments afterward, only that they clung to each other for a brief while, just whispering silly things, feeling each other close, and then somehow started walking along the wet sand, seeing the silver reflection of the moon in the waves that rushed up over the beach in a froth and then slipped away.

"What was that?" Diana said, suddenly squeezing his hand.

"What?"

"I saw someone. Over there. They ducked behind that clump of grass on the dune."

Ambrose turned and looked in the direction she was pointing. He saw a solitary figure, a woman wearing a black coat, appear at the top of the dune and make her way toward them. She was walking rapidly and was strangely silent.

"Hello!" he said, but she made no reply.

Then he saw her arm come up and knew in that moment what he should have known a moment sooner. The woman had a gun. And she clearly meant to kill them. Here, in the beautiful moonlight, they were both going to die.

She fired at Diana first. He heard her cry out and saw her collapse on the sand. He thought the woman would turn the gun on him, but, no, she moved rapidly toward Diana, her heels kicking up sand, the small gun held out at the end of her extended arm. She was going to fire at Diana again! Shoot her where she lay. Helpless on the ground!

Ambrose dove.

In the act of diving, he had an impossible choice. To go for the gun or use his body to shield Diana.

In that horrible instant he saw himself reaching for the gun and missing his one chance to save the woman he loved. And so he flung himself headlong toward Diana, face-down, and landed hard atop her body, covering her. He tensed, waited for the burn of the rounds, the hard slam of lead into his back or shoulder or leg. He'd been shot at before. He knew how it would feel.

The first round burned into his shoulder, struck bone, and careened off inside his chest, tearing something. She must have stumbled in the sand, because the next shot was wide of the mark. He heard it whistle past his ear and burrow into the sand. The next one would be to the head. She was close enough now to dispatch both of them with one bullet. She was close enough to—

He just kicked. He had no hope of hitting anything, but neither had he any hope of surviving the next bullet. His foot connected with the woman's knee, forcing the joint backward with a satisfying snap. She cried out. He felt her go down.

He remembered rolling off Diana at that point, going for the gun. The woman was struggling to get to her feet. The gun was in her right hand, half-buried in the sand. Ambrose, who was feeling a black redness crowding round the edges of his mind, managed to wrench the gun away. She snarled as he tore it from her fingers and he saw her face. He recognized the face. He'd seen it that day in the pictures at Henry's flat. It was Bianca Moon, of course, the China Doll.

"Don't move," Ambrose croaked, pointing the gun unsteadily at the woman.

"You're going to shoot an unarmed woman, Inspector Congreve? I think not."

She got to her feet, clutching the wounded knee with her right hand. Ambrose could see her calculating her next move, whether he had the strength to hold on to the gun. He heard Diana moan. He would hold on to that gun if it killed him.

At that moment, all the sky exploded in sound and light.

Red rockets screamed suddenly overhead, arcing hundreds of feet into the air, expiring in a concussion of sound. Massive blue-and-gold fireballs bloomed over the sea; a falling shower of radiant silver sizzled and fried in the sky and then blinked out. He saw the silhouettes of Jock and Susan Barker appear on the dune followed by hundreds of guests come to ooh and ahh. When he looked for the woman, she was gone. Bianca.

"Help!" he cried weakly, "Over here!"

He couldn't sit up any longer. He collapsed beside Diana and cradled her head in his arms. They were both looking up at the sky. Jock was first to reach them, having seen a starburst illuminate two dark figures sprawled in the sand and one running away. He took one look at Ambrose and Diana and started barking orders at the closest bystanders.

"Look how lovely, darling," Ambrose said to her, "Chinese fireworks."

Then he was gone.

Chapter Fifty-two

Masara Island, Oman

FITZ BEGAN TAKING HEAVY FIRE ABOARD THE *OBAIDALLAH* just as the first of his men started clambering up out of the hold and onto the deck. Two .50-caliber machine guns on the south tower were raining death from above. One man who managed to survive and make it to the shelter of the wheelhouse was the Italian stalwart Bandini. But the next man up, a tough little Gurhka named Sim, took a round in the head and collapsed back inside the hold. That, and Fitz's screaming at his men to stay put, was enough to convince everyone remaining to stay below for the time being.

Fitz whirled around, anger glittering in his eyes. Why the hell hadn't Rainwater blown both towers as soon as the shooting started? Clearly, any hope of surprise had been lost. "Arrow! You copy? What the hell, man? Blow the tower!"

No response.

Fitz, trapped on the stern, peered around the iron hatch cover he was using to stay alive. It was clear at this point that Thunder and Lightning was smack dab in the middle of a major goat-fuck. Rounds were ricocheting off the hatch cover, making an unpleasant hollow, ringing sound. There had to be at least two .50 cals up there, maybe three. Fire was coming only from the top of the near tower. The north tower, thank merciful God, didn't have clear line of sight at the supply ship's deck.

But there were three heavy spotlights mounted halfway up the south tower and they were making life hell for the men from Martinique.

"Froggy," Fitz barked into his lipmike, "where are you?"

"Wheelhouse, Skipper. I've got Bandini back here with me. Thought we'd wait this little storm out."

"Listen up, Froggy. One. I can't raise Arrow. No response. Something's wrong or he would have blown the towers. He may be down. Two, the troops are pinned down back here. Getting hammered. Can you take out those fucking spotlights? It's like daylight back here."

"Mais oui . . . I can, if I can get forward."

"So get forward. Now. Use the foc'sle for cover. Come on, Froggy, we can't take much more of this!"

"I'm moving—"

"I see you. Now, Bandini, you get up on the roof of the wheelhouse with the RPG. You copy that? Take out those fucking machine guns as soon as Froggy kills the lights and you've got a shot. Copy?"

"Va bene, va bene," Bandini said.

"Consider it done, *mon capitain!"* said Froggy.

Froggy didn't waste any time. He'd shed his Arab costume, which clearly had outlived its usefulness, and scrambled forward, drawing fire. Rigging was collapsing on the deck around him, brought down by withering hail of lead from above. Meanwhile, Bandini was crouched in the shadows aft of the wheel, assembling his RPG tube. Good.

Fitz stepped out from behind the hatch cover and delivered a sustained burst of automatic fire into the top of the tower. His aim was true. It was enough to distract them long enough for Froggy to get on his feet, take careful aim, and extinguish the powerful spotlights lighting up the decks of the *Obaidallah.*

POP! POP! POP!

The three spotlights exploded one after the other, extinguished by one of the world's preeminent sharpshooters. Now it was Bandini's turn. The Great Bandini had a very simple solution for all of the world's ills, from cold eggs to unruly governments or bad-mannered insurgents: Nuke 'em.

"Bandini!" Fitz said, stepping out from behind the hatch cover, his weapon on full auto. "It's all yours!"

Bandini scrambled atop the stacked crates and onto the roof of the wheelhouse. He had the tube on his shoulder and his legs braced. He was an easy mark, but Froggy on the bow and Fitz on the stern were doing a good job of fire suppression, tracer rounds screaming toward the top of the tower. The sudden loss of the spotlights and the heavy incoming fire had momentarily disoriented the gunners.

There was a whoosh from the wheelhouse roof and a tongue of fire licked out the back end of the tube. A trail of whitish smoke streaked upward toward the top of the south tower. The gunners must have seen it coming because there was time for several loud screams before the top of the tower erupted into a brilliant fireball. A second later, the ammunition went up, sending great gouts of flame skyward. It resembled nothing so much as a giant Roman candle standing at the edge of the sea.

"Go! Go! Go!" Fitz screamed at his men now flying up out of the hold and exploding up onto the deck. They'd all shed their disguises when the shooting started. In their Kevlar body armor and helmets, bristling with weaponry, they now looked like exactly what they were, the deadliest hostage rescue team on the planet.

It was clearly time to hop and pop.

Moments earlier, Hawke and Stoke had still been inside the tunnel.

"How you say 'Oh, shit' in Arabic?" Stoke said to Hawke from the top of the steps. *Bruce* was floating on the surface, his grinning face pointed in the right direction, having sustained minimal damage on the way inside. Hawke pulled the tabs that inflated the daisy chain of five IBS boats they'd strung behind the sub. Each inflatable could carry only seven adults. Somehow, he'd have to get the women and children safely down here and into these boats, and just pray he had enough space for everyone.

Once they'd boarded the hostages, he and Stoke would swim aboard *Bruce* and they'd make a full-bore run, back through the tunnel and out into the open sea and—

Stoke had run up the stone steps to do a quick recon of the storehouse. Now he was back and he didn't look happy.

"*Jara*," Hawke said, moving the selection lever on his HK 9mm automatic weapon from semiautomatic to fully automatic.

"What's that?"

"*Jara*? That's how you say 'Oh, shit' in Arabic. What did you see up there, Stoke?"

"Tangos. Chinese mercenaries, looked like. And there's a man down on the floor. Couldn't tell who it was."

"How many tangos?"

"Four."

"Did they see you?"

"What do you think?"

"Let's go get the sultan and his harem and get the hell out of here."

Stoke and Hawke went through the door at the top of the steps high and low. The flash-bang Stoke tossed into the room took the Chinese mercs by surprise. Stoke dispatched them quickly with his Sig Sauer nine. The gun had a hush puppy attached to the muzzle. *Pfft-pfft.* Four whispers, head shots, and the four men crumpled. Hawke raced to the body Stoke had seen lying near the door, muttering a silent oath as he saw the man's face.

It was Charlie Rainwater.

"Aw, shit," Stoke said. "Is he dead?"

He wasn't dead, but that was the only good news. He'd been stabbed repeatedly, and there was a particularly severe wound under his left earlobe. His chest was rising rapidly, thin, shallow breaths. Hawke got his hands under the big man, dropping to one knee for leverage, and squat-lifted him up, getting him onto his shoulder.

"Do a quick recon," he told Stoke. "Then rendezvous with Fitz. I've got to get the Chief here back to the boat. Maybe Ali can stitch him up. Pump some morphine and ease his exit, if that's how it goes."

With the big man levered onto his shoulders, the last thing Hawke needed was somebody shooting at him. But that's what happened as soon as he emerged from the main gate and turned left for the docks. Twin .50 cals from the sound of them, up on the south tower. Their fire was concentrated on the *Obaidallah*. Nobody on the old boat was shooting back, which was bad. It meant he was taking Rainwater out of the frying pan and directly into the fire. It was the damn spotlights up on the tower. If somebody could just—

Somebody did. He heard a succession of three loud pops and the docks were plunged again into darkness. He saw the silhouette of a man standing on the wheelhouse roof with an RPG tube and the trail of white smoke streaking toward the tower. The chattering .50s fell silent a beat before they disintegrated. The remaining north tower wasn't a problem for now: still no clear line of fire at the docks.

But it would certainly be a problem later when *Bruce* came racing out of the tunnel on the surface towing a train of helpless women and children. In open water, with no cover, the big fifties on the tower would chew them up alive. Hawke saw that Rainwater had set his charges at the north tower base and jammed an iron rod into the door, sealing it. The men manning the tower were trapped inside.

Hawke bent down, balancing Rainwater on his shoulders, and found one of Charlie's condom-covered igniters.

He was almost to the boat when the second tower blew. The explosion lit up the sky and helped him see where he was going. He ran into Fitz and his men who had scrambled off the boat and were headed to the rendezvous.

"Holy Jesus," Fitz said, seeing Rainwater's condition. Two of his men took the injured man from Hawke, got him into a makeshift fireman's sling, and headed back to the boat. Captain Ali had already rigged an emergency sickbay on the table down in the saloon. He had iodine, gauze, needles, and morphine. As captain of an offshore trawler, he knew how to sew well enough, long as you weren't too particular about scars.

"Somebody got him with a knife from behind, Fitz," Hawke said. Fitz McCoy watched his old friend and partner get carried inside the wheelhouse. His face was clouded with sorrow and anger in the light of the flames from the tower.

"Which means it was someone Chief knew. Rainwater would never let anybody else get that close. Where'd you find him?"

"Inside the storehouse. Four dead tangos, too, but they didn't do it. No knives on them."

"Did you see Ahmed? Brock?"

"Negative."

"It's one of them did this," Fitz said, "Maybe both."

"Let's go find out."

The interior courtyard was strangely silent, considering the recent havoc that had taken place here. Fitz signaled a halt just inside the main gate. To the right, a large mosquelike structure with darkened windows. To the left, the old storehouse where Hawke had found Rainwater and left Stokely. Straight ahead, about five hundred yards away, was the fort's central structure. Rommel's former headquarters was a massive stone blockhouse, a squat four stories high, and looked to have been built in the nineteenth century. There were period battlements on the roof, a defensive parapet with indentations on all four sides. It looked completely impregnable.

"Holy Jesus," Froggy said, looking at the thing, "When I packed my bombs I forgot to bring my bunker-busters."

Fitz whispered, "You'd need a fooking nuke to take that big bastard out."

"Sorry. Forgot my nukes, too," Froggy said.

There was a cricket-rattle of safeties being flicked off and the clacking of Kevlar armor in the dark. A giant black apparition was sprinting toward them through the shadows, hugging the wall, coming from the direction of the mosque. Hawke had asked the man to do a quick recon.

"Easy," Hawke said, "it's Stokely."

"Rainwater?" Stoke asked. "How's he doing?"

"Not good," Hawke said. "Ali's doing all he can for him in sickbay. How's it look out there, Stoke?"

"They want us to waltz right inside, looks like to me," Stoke said. "Side door to that building is wide open. No guards inside. Nobody standing guard behind that bulwark either, that I could see. You can't see 'em now, but there are snipers up on that roof."

"What's inside the mosque?" Hawke asked.

"It looks like a mosque, but it ain't anymore. Some kind of dormitory. I heard lots of women. Crying and wailing and shit. Kids crying in there, too, boss, a whole lot more of them than we got room for in the inflatables."

"We'll think of something. No guards?"

"Not outside that I could see. All inside with the women and children."

"So first we take down the main building," Fitz said. "That's where we'll find the sultan."

"Right. Let's split up," Hawke said. "I'll take Froggy and his squad to the right. You and Stoke take the remaining men around the left side. We'll rendezvous at the bulwark, up the front steps, and go in shooting. Move!"

"Shuck and jive, *mon ami*!" Froggy said, happy the thing was finally going down.

The two teams took off, hugging the walls at the opposite edges of the courtyard, moving at a half run through moonlight and shadow. When they rejoined under the overhang of the bulwark that stood before the wide stone stairs, weapons were flicked to full auto. Just as they prepared to mount the steps, Hawke suddenly showed the raised flat of his hand.

He whispered, "Nobody move."

The heavy wooden doors had cracked open a few feet. Light spilled out from inside, silhouetting a lone man. He stepped outside and paused at the top of the steps. He was a tall, elegant fellow, wearing a white linen suit and smoking a cigarette in a slim ebony holder. At his neck, a navy bow-tie. He was Chinese, with a distinctly military bearing, but he dressed in the English fashion. The fact that ten automatic weapons were suddenly aimed at his heart seemed not to bother him in the slightest.

When he spoke, his English was flawless. "Good evening, gentlemen. I've been expecting you. Is Alex Hawke there among you? Sorry, everyone looks the same in body armor."

"Who the bloody hell are you, man?" Hawke barked.

"Quite right. I haven't introduced myself. I am Major Tony Tang of the Chinese People's Liberation Army. I am currently here as an advisor to the French commander of this garrison."

"Advisor, my royal butt," Alex said, taking a step forward and removing his helmet and balaclava. "I'm Alex Hawke."

"Lord Hawke," the major said with a slight bow, "The pirate himself. I'm so glad you made it. I was hoping we'd have a chance to chat before you were killed. Won't you come inside? I've alerted the sultan that you're here."

"He's still alive?"

Hawke instantly regretted this show of hope that the hostage had not already been shot or otherwise murdered. This was no time to display weakness or anxiety.

"I'm sure he would appreciate your concern. He's—not well."

Hawke bent and whispered to Fitz, "I'm going in there. Alone. Give me twenty minutes or until you hear something spectacular. Then go in that side door Stoke found. And when you come, come shooting."

"What?" Fitz whispered back, "Are you insane, man? You can't go in there by yourself, for all love! Why—"

"Quiet, Fitz. Let's hear what he has to say."

"As you can see," the major said, "I've closed the main gate behind you. It's the only way out. There are men with weapons on the roof and many more inside."

"I'm going inside," Hawke said.

"No you ain't," Stoke said, "I agree with Froggy. You can't go in there alone, boss. I'm dead serious."

Hawke looked at him. He and Stoke had been in spots like this many times before. Stoke had an uncanny ability to talk his way out of tight situations. But it was the things they could leave unsaid between them that would offer them a slight advantage. Stoke would go in with him. Together, they mounted the steps to meet Tang.

"This is Captain Jones, Major. He comes with me. The rest of these men will remain here, unharmed, under the command of FitzHugh McCoy. I should warn you that there is a squadron of U.S. Navy F/A18 Super Hornets circling overhead at ten thousand feet. If any one of these men is harmed, this fort will be reduced to rubble in less than five minutes. Do we understand each other?"

"We do. Delighted to meet you, Captain Jones," Major Tang said, "Won't you both leave your weapons here and follow me?"

And they did.

"*Captain?*" Stoke whispered, "Why'd you make me a captain?"

"What the hell do you want to be?"

"An admiral at least. I didn't know we had Super Hornets upstairs."

"We don't."

Chapter Fifty-three

Southampton, New York

THE OLD TOPPING ESTATE, NOW SOUTHAMPTON HOSPITAL, had sprouted wings over the years. New, modern additions had been built in the last century to better serve the current local population of four thousand souls. That number tripled in the summertime when New Yorkers fled the city for the beaches of the South Fork and the Hamptons. July, especially, put more stress on everyone at the hospital, from the emergency room to the very expensive florist in the main wing.

Ambrose Congreve was lucky on two counts. Despite multiple gunshot wounds, he was still alive when the EMS personnel rolled him into the ER. And, having survived that ordeal, he was soon removed from Intensive Care to a private room on a private floor. The room became available after its occupant, a society matron with a liver condition, expired. And after Jock Barker, a member of the hospital's board, had let it be known that he was to be notified immediately should such a room become available.

The English detective was ensconced, still in critical condition, on the top floor of the old original building. His view, though he could not see it, was a good one. His two windows had eastern exposure, overlooking potato fields blooming with snow-white mansions and aqua swimming pools. Beyond lay the blue Atlantic, sparkling in the midday sun.

Ambrose lay propped up in his bed, his face pale, asleep under the blissful wand of sedation. A woman sat in a comfortable chair by his bed, reading. She had suffered a gunshot wound as well. However, hers was not severe. The flesh wound to her shoulder had been dressed and she had been discharged just two hours after she and Ambrose had arrived some time after eight the previous evening.

Lady Diana Mars was reading poetry to Ambrose, even though she was well aware that he was drifting in and out of consciousness. His breathing sounded more regular when she read aloud to him, and the nurses all agreed that the poetry was beneficial. At the moment, she was reading a favorite poem in a loud, clear voice:

> *"I know that I shall meet my fate*
> *Somewhere among the clouds above;*
> *Those that I fight I do not hate,*
> *Those that I guard I do not love;*
> *My country is Kiltartan Cross,*
> *My countrymen Kiltartan's poor,*
> *No likely end could bring them loss*
> *Or leave them happier than before.*
> *Nor law, nor duty—"*

"That's lovely," the man entering the sunny room said. He took off his grey fedora. "Please, don't let me stop you."

She put the slim volume down across her knees and slowly looked up. The man was not tall, but ruggedly handsome, dark hair, silver at the temples and built like a footballer. "I'm sorry. Who are you?"

"I'm Detective Captain John Mariucci," he said, offering his hand. "New York Police Department."

"Diana Mars," she said, shaking it. "Won't you sit down? Now I know who you are. I'm sure Ambrose would appreciate your coming."

"Yeah, well, we're buddies, you know. Pretty tight. He's asleep, huh?"

"Hmm."

"Hey, you know what I'd really like?"

"Please tell me."

"If you'd finish that poem."

"I'd be happy to, Captain. Ambrose keeps asking for it when he's awake. Sit."

He pulled up the second chair and sat. "That would be nice, hear how it turns out."

She continued,

> "Nor law nor duty bade me fight,
> Nor public men, nor cheering crowds,
> A lonely impulse of delight
> Drove to this tumult in the clouds;
> I balanced all, brought all to mind,
> The years to come seemed waste of breath,
> A waste of breath the years behind
> In balance with this life, this death."

Diana Mars closed the book and smiled at the policeman.

"I'll tell you something," Mariucci said, wiping some speck from the corner of his eye, "I don't know anything about poetry, but that's a hell of a poem. Who wrote that?"

"William Butler Yeats. An Irishman."

"Figures he'd be Irish, right? Fucking micks can write like angels—I'm sorry—excuse the language. I'm just a little emotional right now, you know what I'm saying?"

"Don't worry about it, Captain. I've heard worse."

"What's it called, that poem?"

" 'An Irish Airman Foresees His Death.' "

"He knows he's going to die but he's okay with it. Man oh man."

"Yes."

"Doctor says it looks pretty good. The prognosis."

"Pretty good."

"He'll probably pull through, I mean. If they can keep him stable long enough to operate. They're moving him to New York Hospital. He'll undergo surgery there. Remove the bullet from his spine."

"That's what they said this morning."

"Awful. Just goddamn awful."

"He's alive. He saved my life."

"Yes, he did. I read your statement, Lady Mars. You got a good look at the assailant. She was actually known to you, is that correct?"

"Yes. Bianca Moon is her name. She's apparently been in league with my former butler, a murderer named Simon Oakshott, for some time now. According to Ambrose, probably on her payroll. He killed a man named Henry Bulling, Ambrose's cousin. I think he was there last night, too, at the Barkers' party. He'd cut off all his hair. Changed the color. He was wearing heavy black glasses. Disguised himself as a waiter. Unfortunately, I'd had more than a bit of champagne. Wasn't really paying too much attention to anything and I—didn't recognize him in time to—to prevent—to stop . . ."

"No need to go through all that now, ma'am. The Southampton detective got it all in your statement last night. I, uh, I just came here to see Ambrose. I brought him this. Maybe you could give it to him when he wakes up?"

"What is it?"

"It's a get-well card. My granddaughter made it for him."

"Very kind, Captain. I'm sure he'll appreciate it."

"Hey! What are you going to do, right?" He laughed, but he had something in his eye again. He got up and went to the window.

"Do you think you'll catch her?"

"Absolutely. I got two men sitting not twenty feet away from her right now. Interpol."

"Seriously?"

"She's on a British Airways flight to Hong Kong. Took off two hours ago from JFK. We found Oakshott washed up on the beach with a bullet in his brain. Disposable. We're going to watch her for a few days. See where she goes, who she meets."

"This woman, Moon. She's somehow connected to the case you and Ambrose were investigating. That awful business out at Coney Island."

"Very definitely connected, Lady Mars."

"Call me Diana. Please."

Mariucci sat back down. He leaned forward, placing his hands on his knees, and said, "She's Chinese secret police, Diana. She was in this country to kill the two remaining witnesses in this old homicide Ambrose was working on. Ambrose screwed up her plans. She was looking for revenge, maybe."

"He told me about the confession. At the Ferris wheel."

"Yeah. Weird case. We're about to charge the president of France with murder."

"A delicate political situation."

"Yeah. With an indelicate solution."

"What do you mean, Captain?"

"Well. The Chinese put this guy Bonaparte in power. They'd like him to stay there. He's promised them a million barrels a day of oil from Oman. And that's just for starters. We've got other plans for him. I want to introduce him to Old Sparky."

"Sorry?"

"That's the electric chair, as we call it."

"Ah," she said.

"You didn't see the news this morning?"

"No."

"French troops are preparing to come ashore in Oman. They claim the sultan of Oman invited them. Put down some kind of insurrection. It's total bullshit. But the Chinese are backing them up."

"What's going to happen?"

"That's the big one. The United States and Britain are giving the French forty-eight hours to withdraw their troops. The French refuse."

"Now what?"

"China needs the oil. She's ready to go to war over this."

"Good heavens."

"Hullo?"

Ambrose's voice was so weak he barely made himself heard. His eyelids were fluttering and he was trying in vain to lift his head from the pillow.

"Darling," Diana said, taking his hand, "Look who's come to see you."

"Alex? Alex Hawke?" Congreve said, struggling to sit up.

"Lay back, dear. It's all right. It's not Alex. It's Captain Mariucci come to see you! Isn't that nice?"

Ambrose's voice was ragged. "I had—had a dream. An awful dream. Something . . . bad happened. Something terrible happened to Alex. The most horrible thing! I—I must help—help him . . ."

Diana rang for the nurse.

"I'll give him your granddaughter's card, Captain. Thanks so much for coming."

Mariucci put on his hat and went to the door.

"Take good care of him, Diana."

"Perhaps that's exactly why I met him, Captain."

Chapter Fifty-four

Masara Island, Oman

THE DUNGEON WAS A FOUL, EVIL-SMELLING PLACE. THE nether regions of Fort Mahoud appeared to have escaped any attempt at modernization. No electricity, certainly. The minimal light was provided by large guttering candles in wrought-iron brackets every few feet. Below in the darkness, a beating of tiny wings: bats. Small gutters on either side of the stone stairway ran with what could only be raw sewage.

Hawke and Stokely descended the worn steps side by side behind the major. Six heavily armed French mercenaries wearing kepis clumped heavily down the steps behind the three men.

"Sorry about the stinking mess down here," the major said. "We left this part pretty much as we found it." He spoke with a kindly solicitude that was both pleasant and infuriating.

"Captain Jones and I were just admiring it," Hawke said, unable to stop himself. "The Chinese enjoy a well-deserved reputation for their unique ways with hygiene."

Ignoring the sarcasm, Major Tang said, "Fate has finally brought you and me together, Lord Hawke. Your timing is quite good. The sultan is preparing to address the Omani people. It occurs to me that you and Captain Jones should also address the citizens of your respective countries. Seeing one's countryman on his knees begging for his life has enormous propaganda value, as I'm sure you know. The sultan's temporary quarters are just at the end of this passageway. Mind your step."

"Can we step on the rats?" Stoke said.

The Chinese major stopped in midstride and whipped around to confront his two prisoners, one hand on his holstered sidearm.

"It is I who shall make the waves, gentlemen. We'll see soon enough if you can walk on them," he said.

"Full of piss and vinegar, ain't he?" Stoke said to Hawke. "Mostly piss."

Two well-armed Chinese People's Liberation Army officers stood on either side of the heavy oak door. They stiffened in salute as soon as Tang was visible in the guttering light. The major checked and returned the salute. One of the guards unbolted the door and pulled it wide. Hawke was surprised at the sudden gust of cool sea air that greeted him as they stepped inside. It wasn't a cell at all, but a large hangarlike space hollowed out of rock and open to the sea.

Major Tang was having a quiet word with one of the uniformed French Foreign Legion officers and a group of casually dressed civilians standing just inside the door. They were all speaking French in low tones, arguing about something. Hawke edged nearer the wide arched opening to the sky. He could see a glint of moonlight on the water far below. He estimated they were perhaps a hundred feet above the sea.

The sky was dark with no hint of dawn. The cave's interior glistened in the light of torches, the iron sconces and a heavy chandelier providing the illumination. The barrel of the ceiling disappeared into darkness above and the candles cast long, medieval shadows on the stone walls and floor.

A long, narrow-gauge rail track led from where Hawke stood all the way to the lip of the cave mouth. Hawke could see it now, could imagine what this odd space had been. A large gun, massive, had once been in place here, standing guard over the southern approach to the Strait of Hormuz. Judging from the size of the heavy iron tracks, this space could well have been the emplacement originally built to accommodate the Nazi V-3 Supergun.

Hawke had seen plans for just such a mammoth gun in the British Imperial War Museum. A British agent in a bombed-out munitions factory had discovered the plans in late 1945 and turned them over to MI5. The V stood for "Vengeance." The barrel was reported to have been over three feet wide and more than one hundred yards long. Such a weapon, updated, could easily fire a nuclear-tipped projectile many hundreds of miles. Rumor had it that Saddam had been trying to replicate the V-3 just before the first Gulf War, building a massive gun called "Baby Babylon."

The 512-foot-long gun had been installed at Jabal Hamrayn, a mountain ninety miles north of Baghdad. It was capable of firing a six-hundred-kilogram projectile to a range of one thousand kilometers. The allied forces conquering Iraq had never found it.

Hawke had a sudden flash. The massive O-rings that the *Star of Shanghai* had been loading that night at Cannes. He remembered glancing inside one, thinking nothing of it. But the thing had been *rifled*. Each ring was to be a section of the five-hundred-foot-long barrel. The *Star* would have been stopping at Oman on her trip to Shanghai. To deliver the missing Babylon Supergun for the Chinese to install here on Masara Island. With that gun emplaced in this location, they could do what military men had longed to do for centuries: exert total control over the Strait of Hormuz.

It made sense. Perhaps the Chinese garrisoned here at Fort Mahoud were planning on taking up where Hitler and Saddam had left off.

There were further surprises.

To Hawke's left, a man was seated at a plain wooden desk. His head and shoulders were completely hidden under a canvas hood spotted with ominous dark stains. The sultan, Hawke thought, surely. On the stone floor in front of the desk, kneeling, hands bound behind his back, another hooded man. Sitting casually on the edge of the desk and smoking a cigarette was the one familiar face in the room. The handsome mustachioed face grinned up at Hawke from out of the black cowl that covered his head.

It was Harry Brock's old chum from Muscat, Ahmed Badur, favored architect of sultans and beloved friend of princes, the great provider himself.

"Your sense of loyalty is remarkable, Ahmed," Hawke said. "Frankly, I'm relieved."

Ahmed smiled. "You thought the traitor might be Brock?"

"I did."

"You should have known better, m'lord. Oh, we tried to buy him, believe me. But old Harry is just what he appears to be. A good soldier. And so brave. Look at him now. Awaiting his fate without so much as a whimper."

Ahmed kicked the kneeling Harry viciously in the ribs. The strength of the blow was sufficient to lift the man from the floor. Stokely made a move toward the desk, saw Hawke's look, and stopped in midstride.

"You do that to my friend again and you're dead," Hawke said to Ahmed, his eyes as cold as his voice.

Ahmed laughed, showing his white teeth. "What do you care? He's already dead. So are you, my esteemed friend."

"Ah, Ahmed!" Major Tang said, striding across the room, "I see you've renewed your acquaintance with your former shipmates. Lord Hawke, I'm sure Mr. Badur would appreciate being treated in accordance with his new rank of general. General Badur is a newly minted officer in the Omani Liberation Army. In his forthcoming television address, the sultan will name him interim president of the new government. Now, I think the camera crew is ready, if you are, gentlemen?"

"Camera crew?" Stoke said, as the French civilians in jeans and T-shirts approached, equipment in hand. "What the hell you people doing here?"

A grinning Ahmed hopped off the desk and withdrew a long, curved sword from the folds of his hooded black djellaba cloak. He said, "A new reality show."

"Riveting," Hawke said, edging closer to the sultan.

"Isn't it? It's called 'Invitation to a Beheading,'" Ahmed said, flashing the sword before Hawke's eyes, taunting him, disappointed when he got no reaction from the cold eyes at all. He spun and whipped the hood off the man on the floor. It was indeed Harry Brock. Ahmed placed the blade of the sword gently across Harry's bare neck. A thin line of blood appeared.

"Just do it," Harry Brock said, his voice devoid of any discernible emotion. Ahmed raised the blade.

"This ain't happening, Ahmed," Stoke said, lunging for the traitor and stopping his arm as it came down. The sword clattered on the stone floor. Instantly, four heavyset Arab guards grabbed Stoke from behind and wrestled him facedown to the ground. Stoke managed to fling two away, but one of them pinned his legs and the other had his left forearm jammed up between his shoulder blades. The guy seemed to think he had Stoke in a tough spot.

Stoke craned his head around and smiled at the snarling gorilla on his back.

"Rock me, baby, rock me like my back ain't got no bone," Stokely said.

Then, with his right hand, Stoke casually got the man by the throat and dug his fingers into the larynx. The guard's face was turning blue. Ahmed stuck the tip of his scimitar an inch into Stokely's shoulder joint.

"You cut my arm off," Stoke said softly, "I swear I'll beat you to death with it."

"Stoke," Hawke said. "Relax. Let him go. Let's be gentlemen about this."

"I'll let him go soon as they let Brock go . . ."

Ahmed lifted Harry Brock to his feet and said, "All right, then. You gentlemen are all going straight to Paradise as soon as we have completed filming your heartfelt pleas for mercy. A casual observer will think you ran into some very nasty terrorists on your way to rescue the sultan."

Stoke got to his feet, glaring at the traitor. "Hey, Ahmed. You familiar with that old American expression, 'Go fuck yourself'?"

The mercenaries and Chinese guards had the guns leveled on them now. Stoke knew there was little he could do now but wait. Wait and pray Hawke knew what the hell he was doing. He saw Alex look down at his watch and relaxed a little. Hawke was playing for time, all right, and it might just work.

The French camera crew positioned the digital video camera on a tripod a foot away from the desk. Two floodlights also on tripods were similarly positioned and turned on. In the stark white light, the figure behind the desk, a pale shadow of the man who had appeared before the cameras in Paris just three short weeks earlier, was trembling visibly. On the desk in front of him, some kind of documents. A formal agreement, it looked like. Ahmed stepped behind the man and pulled the cloak from his head.

"State your name," Major Tang said from behind the camera. The man at the desk was red-eyed with fear and exhaustion. On either side of him, out of camera range, stood two men with ugly black automatic pistols aimed at his head.

"I am Sultan Aji Abbas."

"Your Highness," Tang said, "our first order of business. If you'll please sign the agreement?"

The sultan picked up the gold pen with palsied fingers and dipped it into the inkwell. With great difficulty, he inscribed his name in the place indicated.

"What's he signing, Harry?" Hawke said. Tang smiled and made a sweeping gesture to Brock. Go right ahead, why not?

"That's the Muscat Agreement," Brock said, shaking his head to clear out the cobwebs. "Big bad secret. The French government agrees to supply five hundred thousand tons of tanker shipping toward the establishment of the Omani Maritime Company. OMCO will be exempted from Omani taxes. Ships will fly the Omani flag and the officers will be drawn from an Omani maritime college established and funded by Bonaparte himself. OMCO gets priority rights on all oil shipped to China. Bonaparte gets an initial guaranteed 10 percent of the country's annual output."

"Good idea," Hawke said.

"Yeah. Gives France the monopoly on about fifty million tons of Omani oil shipped to China. But Bonaparte knew it couldn't be implemented without a royal decree. He couldn't make this fly legally without the sovereign's signature."

"So, now, everybody's happy," Hawke said.

"Yeah. And if this little beauty works, China takes this show on the road. Replicate this scenario in other Gulf States. That's the plan, anyway."

"That's the plan," Major Tang said, smiling at Hawke. "Now, if you'd please be so kind, Sultan Abbas, we'll begin taping your broadcast."

The sultan gathered himself and, his voice strong and unwavering, spoke directly into the camera.

"Tonight, I wish to address the brave people of Oman. As you know, a grave crisis looms over our small nation. Insurgents and insurrectionists are at our back door. In this dire time of our peril and need, I turned to my good friend, President Bonaparte of France. A man whose love for our country knows no bounds. Even now, French troop ships are steaming toward our shores. They will help us repel the barbarians and save us from—"

The heavy doors were blown off the hinges by the force of the explosion outside. The sound of shouting and automatic weapons fire could be heard just outside the entrance. Stun grenades, both flash-bangs and smoke, were lobbed into the room and immediately exploded, creating deafening, mind-numbing noise and a roiling white fog that obscured everything.

A momentary smile crossed Hawke's face as he saw Thunder and Lightning come through the door.

"Fitz!" Hawke cried, "Over here! I've got the sultan!"

Hawke was trying to pull the old man to the floor and out of harm's way. Rounds were sizzling overhead, fired randomly in every direction. He'd seen the yellow twinkle of muzzle flames in the smoke not six feet away. It was Major Tang, firing his pistol blindly in their direction, hoping to take out the sultan with a lucky shot. Ahmed, who was barely three feet away, instantly saw what was happening.

"Death to tyrants! Death to America!" Ahmed cried, slashing downward with the curved blade as he fell, wounded, to the floor. Hawke felt a gush of the sultan's hot blood splash against his face and the old Arab crumpled in his arms. The sultan was breathing, but his right leg was hemorrhaging horribly. Ahmed had left his blade buried in the man's thigh. The femoral artery lies deep within the thigh, but if a blade can find it, the chances of stopping mortal blood flow are almost nil.

"Froggy! Get over here!" Hawke cried aloud. He pressed his balaclava into the sultan's wound. "Here, Your Highness, press this into the wound as hard as you can. I'll get help!"

First he needed a weapon. He saw a boot a foot away and grabbed it, pulling the man wearing it down. The Kalashnikov in his hands clattered to the floor and Hawke grabbed it. He used the butt end of the gun to put the former owner out of his misery, and then came up on his knees. He saw Ahmed, crabbing across the stone on hands and knees. He seemed to be headed for the mouth of the cave. A hundred-foot drop? He wasn't going anywhere. The firefight was intense now.

Where was Stoke? Was he down?

Hawke got to his feet. He had to find Froggy somewhere in this interior cloudbank. The little French sharpshooter and medic was the only one with a prayer of stanching the sultan's bleeding artery.

Hawke had only one thought now: getting the leader of Oman on tape telling the truth. The swirling smoke made identification of anyone in this fight damn near impossible. If he couldn't get to Froggy, Froggy would have to get to him.

He aimed the AK-47 straight up, flipped the lever to full auto, and fired a sustained burst at the ceiling.

"Froggy, I'm going to fire a second burst into the overhead. Make your way to me!" He pulled the trigger and emptied the magazine into the vault of stone.

Someone was tapping on his knee. Hawke looked down and saw the smiling face looking up at him. *"Mon ami,"* Froggy said, "how may I be of service?"

Ten minutes later, it was almost over. Thunder and Lightning had taken casualties. Stokely was missing. Bandini had been the first to go down, instantly killed with a clean head shot coming through the door. Two of the Gurhkas had suffered gunshot wounds to the neck and chest but Froggy was tending to them. If they had any chance at all, he'd make sure they got it. Major Tony Tang and most of his men were dead. Tang, Hawke was less than shocked to notice, had been nearly beheaded. Harry Brock was standing over the corpse with Ahmed's bloody scimitar in his hand.

The few mercenaries and French regular troops who weren't dead were either down with injuries or being cuffed by Fitz's men. Thunder and Lightning, wounded, had struck back with a vengeance. Hawke was sure the searing memory of the grievously injured Chief Rainwater had been in their hearts and minds when they entered the room.

Fitz had posted four of his commandos outside the door to deal with any curiosity seekers who came to see what all the noise had been about. He and Harry Brock were now helping Hawke with the sultan. They'd gotten the mortally wounded man back into his chair and were tightening the tourniquet Froggy had applied. The Omani sovereign's breathing was shallow and his pulse was faint.

"Fitz," Hawke said, putting a canteen of water to the sultan's trembling lips, "get the camera set up. See if the lights are still working. We haven't got much time."

"I am worried about Stokely," Froggy said, erecting the camera in its old position. "We cannot find him."

"We don't have time to worry about anybody but the sultan right now. We need to get this man on record. Damn it, he's got blood in his eyes. Bring me some water and a cloth, will you?"

"I've no idea who you are," the sultan croaked, his voice barely audible as he gazed up at Hawke, "but what you've done here today is save people."

"Bien sûr," Froggy said, "The camera is recording."

Hawke saw the flashing red light under the lens and carefully lifted the dying man more upright in the chair. The sultan seemed to sense what was happening. He placed his hands on the desk, squared his shoulders, and stared into the camera. A steely light came into his eyes and Hawke knew it would be all right.

"Your Highness," Hawke said, "I'd like you to finish your address. It's very important that your people hear your words. The world needs to hear the truth about what is happening this day in your country."

"Yes," Aji Abbas said, "I will do it now."

With his dying words, the sultan of Oman did just that.

He told his countrymen about the treachery and lies of the new French government. Of President Bonaparte, who had betrayed them. He spoke of the suffering his family had endured at the hands of the many Chinese "advisors" and French soldiers who were in Oman illegally. He asked that world leaders, especially England and America, ensure that Oman's borders were respected and that no foreign troops were ever again allowed on her soil. Oman was a peaceful, law-abiding nation, he said in closing, and, with the help of Allah, the true and just God, it would ever be so.

The sultan sat back in the chair and closed his eyes.

"Thank you, Your Highness," Hawke said, smiling at him. The old man's bravery in the waning moments of his life was undeniable.

"Hey, boss," Hawke heard Stoke say. "Come take a look at this." The big man had suddenly appeared and was standing at the edge of the cave mouth. The sky behind him was dusky pink.

"What is it?" Hawke said, not wanting to leave the sultan's side. The man had only a few more moments to live.

"Fishing boats," Stoke said, smiling. "All kinds of damn boats.

Trawlers, schooners, little baby scows. Hundred or more of them leaving the mainland and headed this way. Looks like everybody in Oman with a boat and a paddle is coming out to show the flag. Must have heard all the explosions, seen the fires burning. Coming to rescue the sultan's family and kick the damn Frenchies off this island."

Hawke and Brock crossed and stood beside Stoke, neither man believing his eyes. It was, as Stoke had said, a magnificent sight. Perhaps a hundred vessels of every size and description, all lit by the first red-gold streaks of sun, and every one of them headed due east, bound for Masara Island.

"Where's Ahmed?" Hawke asked.

"Down there on the rocks where I left him," Stoke said. "We had a little disagreement about the future of the world. He lost."

"Fitz," Hawke said quietly, "Could you and Froggy carry His Highness's chair over here? I think he ought to see this."

"Aye, we're bringing him," Fitz said. They gently lowered the sultan's chair to the ground. "What is it?"

"It's quite something, Your Highness," Hawke said. "Just have a look."

"Yes," Aji Abbas said softly, his cloudy eyes taking in the vast armada come to his family's rescue. "A miracle. Like Dunkirk, isn't it?" he whispered.

Then his eyes slowly closed and he slipped away.

The little boats began to arrive an hour later. It seemed every fisherman and fisherman's son in Oman had steered his boat across the dangerous stretch of water that lay between the mainland and the island of Masara. Two or three of the tiny vessels had been sunk by the patrol boat before Fitz realized what was happening and got on the radio to tell the French captain and crew it was over. The Fort Mahoud garrison, composed of Chinese and French mercenary forces, had surrendered.

The patrol boat captain, delighted at any excuse to leave the godforsaken place, had surrendered over the radio. Half an hour later he was steaming into the dock, all of his crew's small arms in a pile on the afterdeck.

Down at the docks, Hawke was standing with Stokely and Harry

Brock. They saw *Obaidallah*'s captain, Ali, and the patrol boat crew helping all the hostages, women and children mostly, into the waiting fishing boats. After a few minutes, they went back aboard their boat to check on Rainwater. They ran into Froggy coming out of the captain's cabin. He had been in with him for the last hour, doing what he could.

"How's he doing, Froggy?" Stoke asked, unable to read the little Frenchman's expression.

"The lord, he is still making up his mind," Froggy said, with a shrug of his broad shoulders, "but I think he's going to decide in the Chief's favor."

Chapter Fifty-five

The White House

"MR. PRESIDENT?"

Jack McAtee looked up from his desk in the Oval Office to see his longtime secretary, Betsey Hall, standing in the doorway. She had the *look*. Something was up. It was nearly ten o'clock at night and he was only now getting around to reading his goddamn PDB. The president's daily brief was so sensitive only a dozen people shared it. He was bone-tired. Dr. Ken Beer, his newly appointed White House physician, had told him just this morning that he needed to get more sleep and more exercise. And cut down on the cigars. The bourbon and branch water. And that golf didn't count as exercise and—

"Mr. President?"

"Yes?"

"I'm sorry, sir. It's apparently urgent."

"Who?"

"Mr. Gooch and General Moore to see you, sir. Assistant Secretary Baker from the State Department is in the Roosevelt Room, if you need him."

"Please show them in, Betsey," McAtee said.

His national security advisor, John Gooch, and the chairman of the Joint Chiefs, General Charlie Moore, walked in. He closed his PDB file and pushed it aside. Maybe he'd get to it before tomorrow's report arrived on his desk at 6:45. He got to his feet and moved over to the sofa near the fireplace. Might as well be comfortable. The two men filed in and took the two chairs opposite him.

"Let me guess," McAtee said, smiling at each of them in turn, "Something troubling is afoot."

Gooch, a tall, thin Boston Brahmin, St. Paul's and Harvard, spoke first. This was not at all unusual. The NSA talked and the JCS chairman listened. Moore would hold his fire until he heard something he and the president would construe as actionable. Sometimes this happened and sometimes it did not.

"Mr. President," Gooch said, riffling through a sheaf of reports, "I don't like what I'm seeing here. There are patterns here that—"

"Tea-leaf reading again, John?" McAtee said, firing up his Partagas Black Label despite doctor's orders.

"I'm afraid it's a bit more than that. We've got French naval assets—here, have a look at the overheads. Time-sequenced satellite imagery shows French assets moving rapidly out of the Indian Ocean into the Gulf of Oman . . . go ahead, sir, take a look."

"What am I looking at?"

"That's the nuclear carrier *Charles de Gaulle*, sir, their flag vessel, and—"

"Just last month you—or someone—told me the *de Gaulle* was laid up in dry dock for repairs," McAtee said. "Her reactors were throwing off too much radiation. The crews were getting sick and suing the goddamn French government."

"They've apparently repaired her, sir. At least temporarily. Here you've got tankers, destroyers, frigates, subs . . ."

"Goddamn it, this is an offensive configuration—or am I wrong?" McAtee said, holding up a photo for closer inspection. "These smaller boats here and here are amphibious landing craft, right?"

"Indeed they are, sir."

"So they're going ahead with this damn thing, John, this invasion."

"Yes, sir."

"Goddamn it! Are they fucking nuts?"

"Not all of them. You can point the finger directly at this man Bonaparte, sir. He's going to have to be dealt with, sooner rather than later. We're building the Interpol file now. It's only a matter of days before we go public with the patricide story."

"Guy murdered his own father to get ahead in the Union Corse. At sixteen. You believe that, Charlie?"

"From what I've heard about him, yes, it's believable."

"He's guilty of homicide and we can prove it, sir. We've got an eyewitness to that crime. I just got a call from Captain John Mariucci, NYPD. He and a Scotland Yard man named Ambrose Congreve located a witness in New York."

"I know Congreve. Through Alex Hawke. Any news from him, John? Hawke, I mean."

"As you know, Hawke is involved in an arm's-length operation to get the sultan out of Oman alive, Mr. President."

"Right. Put him in front of a camera. Have him tell the truth about Oman asking France to invade. France has pulled the wool over the world's eyes for long enough. Suppress an insurrection, my ass. They're going in for oil to sell to China."

"Our team is inside the fortress on Masara Island now, Mr. President. They went in to pull the sultan out at 1140 hours EST. About twenty minutes ago. We are monitoring real-time."

"Hawke and I go back a long way. Not the kind of man who'll let us down. But the sooner we get Sultan Abbas out of that hellhole, the better. Do what you have to do, John."

"We're on it, sir."

"All right, Charlie. What do you make of this French navy in the Arabian Sea bullshit? All this faux muscle-flexing?"

"It may be just that, Mr. President," General Moore said. "The CNO has been on the horn with Frank Blair, who commands the Sixth Fleet now . . . they're trying to get a read on it, sir."

"Is the fleet moving?"

"Yes, sir. The Pentagon confirmed that Admiral Starke's lead units entered the canal at 1700 hours. They're positioning for a holding action. Assume we control the canal at this point—no one in, or out, unless we give the word."

"Good! Now that's thinking ahead."

"That is good," Gooch said, "but we haven't heard from the Egyptians, or the Chinese, or the rest of the 'striped-pants' crowd yet."

General Moore leaned forward in his chair. "Frankly, Mr. President, the French are overextended and they know it. Probably a little tension in the dialogue back in Paris. They know we could take them down in about four hours."

"I know we could. We could, but we won't. Because France, as we all know, is just a goddamn shill for the Chinese, a prophylactic in this whole thing. Hell, if China wasn't involved—let's talk seriously about this China gambit. Where are we with them? John?"

"Certainly, sir," Gooch said. "Here's where we are now. There are—"

"Don't tell me. Two schools of thought," the president said with a wry smile. He'd been down this well-traveled road before.

"Exactly," Gooch said. "That much hasn't changed. On the one hand, the State Department's position. State says don't rock the boat. We can go along to get along. Because we *have* to."

"On the other hand," General Moore said, "there's my position. Send a signal to the French and the Chinese that we won't tolerate interference with our oil supply in the Gulf. The kick-ass-and-take-names position."

The president smiled and waited for Gooch's reaction.

"Mr. President," Gooch said, "we probably ought to round-table this in the morning. Get a fresh look at it from State, the Pentagon, and the Agency—especially if you are considering a policy change. I have to tell you I firmly believe we can get along with China once we move past this situation in Oman. We *have* to, sir. In all honesty, we're in a very tight spot with Beijing."

"You mean we find a way to get along with them or we'll tank our own economy."

"Exactly my feeling, Mr. President."

"John, the bullet points. Just briefly."

"There are two pressure points with China, sir. Our economy and Taiwan. The one that concerns me most right now is the former."

"Because?"

"Because if we lean on China about the OOTB in Taiwan or their little misadventure in Oman, we run the risk of an economic—"

"OOTB? What the hell is that? Why does everybody who comes in this office have to sound like a walking Tom Clancy novel?"

"Mr. President," General Moore said, "It's an acronym for 'out-of-the-blue.' It's a top-secret plan on the Chinese books to use wargames in the Formosa Strait as a cover for a general invasion of Taiwan. It looks like typical peacetime maneuvers . . . until the troops involved suddenly move. China's got over six hundred ballistic missiles and several hundred warplanes stationed within range of Taiwan. Launch in the predawn hours and, well, it could be nasty. You'd catch most of the Taiwanese troops in their barracks and their ships, tanks, and warplanes lined up like ducks. We don't necessarily believe that—"

"Wait a minute!" McAtee said, stubbing out his cigar. "Hold the phone. Didn't Brick Kelly say in our morning briefing three days ago that they are in the goddamn Taiwan Straits? The Chinese fleet?"

"Yes, Mr. President," Gooch said. "They are."

"Holding joint exercises with France, if I'm not mistaken. A shakedown cruise for that new Russian carrier they bought."

"That's correct, sir. Although France has now shifted the bulk of her assets to the Arabian Sea."

"And you two are concerned with the economy?"

"He is. I'm not, sir," General Moore said.

"No grandstanding in here, Charlie," the president said.

"Okay, John and I are concerned about the economy in varying degrees."

"Much better."

"Damn right I'm concerned about it," Gooch said. "Mr. President, if what Assistant Secretary Baker says is correct—"

"Who?"

"Anthony Baker. NSC staff member, sir. East Asian Affairs. He's across the hall in the Roosevelt Room if we need him."

"Go ahead."

Gooch cleared his throat and adjusted his pale-blue Hermès tie. "We push France, in effect, China, on this Oman thing and China pushes back, big time, economically. As you are only too aware, sir, they are the largest holders of U.S. Treasury bonds in the world. Which keeps our interest rates low. China gets pissed off, sir, and stops buying U.S. bonds—well, I don't need to tell you what happens."

"Tell me anyway."

"What happens is, to get new buyers, Treasury has to increase interest rates they pay on bonds. Ripple effect—everyone's interest payments go up. Next, China stops selling cheap goods. The average American's cost of living shoots up, China's unemployment spikes, their export sector shuts down. U.S. inflation goes through the roof and so does everybody's mortgage and credit card charges."

"A lose-lose situation for both of us. Charlie?"

"I'm far more concerned about Taiwan, sir. What John says about the economic implications of any showdown with China is indisputable. Currency is the most decisive factor in foreign affairs. And they can sink our currency. But, here's the thing. And, this point is nonnegotiable. China *must* have oil. It is absolutely essential. Everything else is bullshit. Push them and they will, Mr. President, I repeat, they *will* play the Taiwan card."

"They're doing just fine without Taiwan. Double-digit growth. Why are they so goddamn obsessive about it?"

"Because they're not too keen on having a model of democracy just off their coast and they don't particularly like us using Taiwan as our personal naval air station."

"General Moore, put this whole goddamn thing in English for me."

"If we order France out of Oman, China will push back using Taiwan. And I'm not talking about rampant U.S. inflation or goddamn spiking credit card charges. I'm talking about a nuclear confrontation that could change the quality of American life, sir. They will put Taiwan on the table because *they have no choice.* They will make that move."

"That's it?"

"That's it for me, Mr. President," Moore said.

"John?"

"I've been saying this for four years, Mr. President. We're vulnerable where China is concerned. But it's a perfectly balanced symbiotic relationship, sir. They need us every bit as much as we need them. Economically. They won't touch Taiwan. It would destroy everything they've worked to build. Wipe it out. They won't do that."

"Thanks for stopping by, gentlemen. Charlie, could you stick around for a couple of minutes? I've got something else."

As the president got to his feet, the two men were already up. As they turned to leave, the president put his hand on General Moore's shoulder. Gooch kept moving. As he left, the president took the chairman of the Joint Chiefs of Staff by the arm and guided him over to the bourbon decanter. He poured each of them a healthy one.

"If you think they'll move on Taiwan, Charlie, that's good enough for me."

"Yes, sir. Thank you, sir."

"So, we damn well better be ready for them. Operation Wild Card."

Moore looked at the president. Those were the three words he'd been dreading.

"We will be ready, Mr. President," Moore said.

"Harry Brock's working directly for you on this, right? Not CIA?"

"I sent him to China. I sent him to Oman, sir."

"You getting any direct word from Brock or Alex Hawke? This whole Gulf thing gets a lot less nerve-wracking if we can point the finger directly at France. At this fucking Bonaparte."

"Not a word since they went in. We should know within the hour, sir."

"You'll let me know as soon as you've got something?"

"Aye, aye, sir."

"Cheers."

"Cheers."

"Mr. President?" Betsey Hall had reappeared in the doorway.

"Yes?"

"Sorry, sir. Mr. Gooch would like to—"

Gooch brushed past her and came into the room, his face drawn.

"I've just received word, sir. French troops and armored vehicles are landing on the Omani coast. They've opened up a naval bombardment of the capital of Muscat and certain important coastal cities. Paratroops are on the ground at the airport."

"Jesus," McAtee said. "Any word from Hawke?"

"Just now, sir. He's safely out."

"Did he bring Sultan Abbas out with him?"

"No, sir. The sultan is dead. He was killed during the rescue attempt."

"Goddamn it."

"There is some good news. Hawke's got it, sir. He's got the sultan on tape pointing the finger straight at France. Denouncing Bonaparte. Denying that he invited France in."

"Thank you, John. Call the networks and get that tape on the air immediately. CNN, FOX, Al Jazeera."

"Done."

"And get Mr. Bonaparte on the phone. It's time I had a little tête-à-tête with this asshole."

Chapter Fifty-six

Hong Kong

OF ALL THE WATERFRONT DIVES IN MACAO, STOKE THOUGHT, she had to pick this one.

He'd called Jet as soon as he'd arrived that morning. Twelve hours after saying good-bye to Hawke at Muscat airport, he was checking into his hotel in Hong Kong. Hawke wanted him to follow the threads he'd picked up in Berlin. To find out what the hell this General Moon was up to and fast. He stretched out on his bed overlooking the beautiful harbor. Thinking about what he'd say, he called the number on the card she'd handed to him in Berlin. On the phone, she'd sounded good. Upbeat. Staying out of sight at some girlfriend's house in Macao.

Before he could even get to the purpose of his visit, she asked about Alex, which Stoke found pretty interesting. Wanted to know how he was, what he was up to. Yeah, he'd been right all along. The girl was a torch-bearer for Alex Hawke, all right. Get in line. Well, if it was true, good luck. Hawke had only loved two women in his whole damn life besides his mother. Consuelo de los Reyes, who wasn't talking to him right now. And Victoria Sweet, who was dead.

Stoke told her that a good friend of Alex's, a wonderful guy named Ambrose Congreve, had been shot at some fancy party out on Long Island and had been rushed to a hospital. All they knew, so far. Alex was en route to New York now to be by his friend's side. Stoke was headed there, too, soon as he'd done what needed doing here in Hong Kong.

Said she was sorry about the friend; that she wanted to help Alex in any way she could. Help *them*. Alex needed her help more than he knew, she said. Stoke was still thinking about that one when she added, "Whatever you've figured out about von Draxis and

Leviathan, I'm guessing it isn't the whole story. As I told you, I don't know the whole story myself. But I know one thing, Stokely. You don't have China. You don't have my father."

"You can't tell me."

"I can't tell you because I don't know. And I don't want to know. My relationship with him is complicated enough."

Stoke told her some stuff he and Alex had discussed with Brick Kelly at CIA and she said, yeah, that was the right direction. It was definitely a French, German, Chinese connection. It was all about oil. But there were a whole lot more pieces to this puzzle. Bad pieces.

They should meet, she said. Tonight.

Stoke had learned a few things as an NYPD detective. One of them was that prearranged meetings with people you didn't completely trust were always interesting. A lot of things could be prearranged. Stoke knew this was the final act with Jet. It would go one of two ways. Either she was going to hand him the keys that would lead to the kingdom. Or, another possibility, she was leading him smack into a very dangerous situation.

He had a vision of himself drugged and shanghaied. Bound for nowhere on a tramp steamer or sent to some farm for reeducation. Maybe even something more deadly.

Nothing to do but find out. Her idea was they'd hook up tonight at a place called, believe it or not, the Krazy Kat Klub. It was long on atmosphere, you had to say that. A cross between a hooch house and an opium den. The smoke-filled joint was full of wharf rats and zombies who looked like they had serious opium or smack issues. Jet said be there no later than eight. It was now almost nine. He was still sitting at the bar nursing a warm Coke with his eye on the door, waiting to see her waltz in.

She had told him they'd need some kind of boat. Nothing fancy, but something fast. Something that could get them over to Hong Kong Harbor, even if the weather was bad. The weather was bad. There was a typhoon brewing out in the China Sea. The leading edge had rolled into Macao about two hours earlier. It was blowing like stink outside. No rain yet, but that was coming.

He'd done the best he could with the boat. But it hadn't been all that easy. You don't just walk into Hertz Rent-a-Boat in Macao and get the keys to a Chris-Craft.

He'd finally paid cash to a guy he'd met down on the docks that afternoon. His name, believe it or not, was He Long. Bought a little stinkpot from him, mainly because he was the only guy Stoke could find who spoke a little English. *Foo Fighter* was only twenty-four feet or so but she had an enclosed flat-roofed wheelhouse to keep Jet dry and a big Chevy 327 gas engine that looked pretty clean, points and plugs looked after, well-maintained. Owner said she'd do thirty knots and Stoke believed him. Had a fresh paint job, too. Bright red.

"I like your name," Stoke told the owner before he left the dock. "Guy could get a lot of mileage out of a name like that. Hormone replacement business, Viagra shops, something like that."

He Long was still bent over on the dock and laughing his ass off when Stoke rumbled away. Stoke was pretty sure He Long didn't have a clue what was so funny but everybody was pretty polite here in Macao. Maybe He Long was just giggling because Stoke had just paid him twice what his boat was worth.

Stoke was just about to check his watch for the umpteenth time when Jet Moon walked in. She looked spectacular, her black hair held up with a pearl comb, all dressed up in a tight white dress. Guy next to him never even noticed. Gay bar? No. Just the last guy on the last stool in the very last bar at the end of the road. Stoke looked at the guy's eyes for a second, then looked away. The Chinese Thought Police would have a field day in here. Some crazy shit going on behind those eyes.

Jet headed straight for him. Guess he wasn't too hard to spot in a crowd of pint-sized Oriental drug addicts.

"Sorry I'm late," she said. He could tell she meant it, so he smiled and slid off the stool.

"Hey. Have a seat. Want a drink?"

"A glass of white wine?"

"Really? Here?"

"That was a joke, Stokely. I'll take a brandy. Neat."

Stoke ordered from the little guy with the Fu Manchu goatee and got another Coke. Unlike American bars on a Saturday night, this one was pretty quiet. Everybody zoned out on China White maybe. At least you could have a private conversation without screaming.

Jet said, "So, you got the boat?"

"Yeah. It's that bright red one tied up outside."

"That will do. Good work."

"Can I ask where we're going?"

"A restaurant over in Hong Kong Harbor. The Golden Dragon."

"Really good food, must be, go all the way over there. With this weather and all."

"We're having dinner with my father. It's his restaurant."

"Yeah? Wants to meet your personal trainer, huh?"

"You're my fiancé now. I just told him an hour ago."

"Hey, I'm moving up in the world. Even if you're just using me to get to Alex Hawke, I'll take it."

"That's not funny, Stoke."

"Yeah, it is. You were supposed to kill him but your heart wouldn't let you. Right? Tell me I'm wrong."

She waved his smile away. "Look, Stoke. I'm doing you a huge favor here. My father's a very important man in China. There are worlds within worlds in Hong Kong. I'm saving you a lot of time sorting them all out."

"Tell me what I'm looking for here, Jet."

"My father, I learned last night, is privately selling nuclear materials. Off the books."

"Materials. You mean weapons?"

"I don't know."

"Off the books. You mean Beijing doesn't know about it?"

"I have no idea. I told you, I'm just a cop."

"Selling to who? France?"

"To Germany."

"And what are the Germans doing with these weapons?"

"That's why you're here, Stoke. My father's house has many rooms. I'm sure there's something horrible in every one of them. But I've just told you all I know."

"I know what kind of man your father is, Jet. Just like I know who you are. But I got to say, I'm kind of surprised at the way you're handling this part."

"You don't trust me? After all I did in Berlin?"

"I trust you, Jet. Yeah. I do. Pretty much."

"Thank you. Really."

"Jet, let me tell you something. I appreciate all you're doing. You know I do. But I don't see how you survive this, girl. Going against a man like your father. Maybe we'll get out alive tonight. But they'll find you, Jet. He'll find you. He won't let you go after this."

"That's my problem, isn't it? You ready?"

"Let's go."

"Sorry about the choppy ride," Stoke said, the two of them side by side at the wheel of *Foo Fighter*. The storm was kicking up now and they were getting bounced all over the tiny wheelhouse. Rain was beating against the windshield but the wipers worked pretty well. And it was warm and dry inside. "Want me to slow down?"

"Actually, I'm amazed at how you keep missing all these sampans. You see that thing all lit up on the horizon? That's the Golden Dragon. We'll tie up on the other side."

"Got it."

Jet looked at him. "How much do you know now, Stoke? From what you took out of Schatzi's office?"

"Not enough, Jet, or I wouldn't be here. I work for Alex Hawke. And Alex, at least for right now, is working for the U.S. government. I'm here in Hong Kong because Alex Hawke told me to be here. Just so we're clear. Who's doing what for who, I mean."

"I'm clear, Stoke. I want you to be. I'm on your side."

"Good. Anyway, Washington is still busy examining everything I stole from Schatzi's office. We know the Germans are building a supertanker fleet for the French. Ultralarge crude carriers in the half-million-ton range. We know the French government-owned company, Elf, is setting up a massive operation of ship terminals, refineries, and tankers to transport oil from the Gulf to China."

"What else have you got?"

"China gets oil. France gets money. End of story."

"And *Leviathan*?"

"Same story. She was built in Germany for the French by your pal, Schatzi. Just like the tankers. Good business idea, if you ask me."

"My father's got a lot of ideas, Stoke. Some good, some no doubt very, very bad. That's why we're having dinner with him on the Golden Dragon."

"Just the three of us, huh? Nice and cozy."

"There'll be four. I don't know who the mystery guest is. Probably his righthand man, Major Tang."

"Tony Tang? Charming guy."

"You know him?"

"We just met. He's dead."

"You might not want to mention that to my father. Major Tang was his best friend."

"Lips are sealed."

She looked at him a second, then said, "Okay. Slow down. We tie up over there at the restaurant dock. Where all the water taxis wait. We're going to his private dining room up on the top deck. About halfway through the meal, I'll figure out some kind of diversion. At that point, you're going to excuse yourself. Say you're going to the loo. But you're really going to the kitchen that prepares meals for my father and his staff. Don't worry. The kitchen staff is too crazed to pay any attention to you. Just act like you're lost."

"That will be easy."

"There's a young sous chef down there who works for me. He's expecting you. His name is Wan Li. He'll ask if he can help you. You tell him you're looking for the lavatory."

"Then what?"

"I've drawn a diagram of the Dragon's upper deck. My father's private offices are here. Here's the small dining room where we'll be having dinner. The kitchen is here. Wan Li will take you where you need to go."

"Where's that?"

"You'll see. From what I know now, the answers to all your questions is down in the bowels of the Golden Dragon. Wan Li will show you."

"And after that?"

"I'll give you twenty minutes. That should be enough time. Then I'm storming out of the dining room and returning to the boat. Leave the keys in it. I'll bring it around and pick you up at this cargo door on the stern. Wan Li will show you. It's a gangway where the produce barges unload for the kitchen."

"You have a weapon?"

"In my handbag. I hope I don't need it."

"You might."

"He's my father, Stoke."

"I know."

Chapter Fifty-seven

The Golden Dragon

"GUESS WHO'S COMING TO DINNER?"

"What did you say?" Jet asked him, plainly irritated. This cozy dinner wasn't going all that well. He could tell the general wasn't too jazzed with Jet's choice of a fiancé, either.

"That's the title of the movie," Stoke said.

"The title of what movie, Stokely?" she said, firing daggers at him across the table. She looked like she wanted to kill him, but the one she really wanted to kill was sitting right next to her. Dressed in an emerald-green silk number that looked sensational was the mystery guest. That would be her sister, Bianca, who was the surprise at this cozy little dinner party.

Bianca looked *exactly* like Jet. A duplicate twin, Stoke thought they called it. Same beautiful black hair, green eyes, identical. But the sisters were not close. In fact, the mood in the general's private dining room was a little tense. Stoke was trying to lighten things up, striving heroically to keep the old conversational ball rolling. He was playing for time until Jet gave him the signal it was time to split.

The two sisters gave the impression that only one of them was going to get out of this room alive. When they first sat down, they'd been speaking Chinese to their father and you could tell the general was trying to calm them down about something. Stoke figured he should just stay out of it. Family business. But light and airy it was not.

Jet was supposed to create some kind of diversion. He couldn't wait. He was all out of conversation and the general's fuse was burning up pretty fast. Jet was looking at him funny now and he remembered she'd asked him a question. What was it? Oh, yeah. That Poitier flick he was talking about. Since Jet was an actress, he figured movies would be a safe topic.

"That's the name of that movie I was trying to think of. The one with Sidney Poitier. Remember? The one where he goes to dinner at Spencer Tracy and Katherine Hepburn's house in San Francisco. Asks them can he marry their daughter. You remember that one, General?"

"No."

"Pretty good movie," Stoke said, getting into it now. "About this black dude, right? Who shows up at this white girl's house to have dinner with her parents? It's kind of awkward and nobody knows what to say, see? So, Sidney, he's the black guy, he starts talking about—"

"Jesus," Jet said to him, and went back to her lobster soup with the claw sticking out of it.

Jet's father, General Moon, wasn't much of a conversationalist. Or movie lover. He was just staring at Stoke. If you had to guess what he was thinking, it would be how to commit a murder that took a really, really long time and hurt really, really bad before the victim expired.

"You like football, General?" Stoke said. "I used to play for the Jets."

That was all Jet needed to decide it was time to create her diversion.

"You lying little bitch," Jet hissed at her sister.

"Don't call me a liar, slut," Bianca said. "You're the one who—"

Jet picked up her soup bowl and threw it across the table. The lobster claw sort of bounced off Bianca's shoulder but the soup ran down her face and into her cleavage. That was enough to bring the whole evening to a boil. When Bianca swept all the china off the table and picked up a knife, Stoke stood up and put his napkin on the table.

"If you folks will excuse me, I need to use the restroom."

He smiled at the two hefty guys in dark suits standing outside the door and kept on walking. At the end of the corridor he hung a right and headed for the kitchen. It was down on the next deck, just like Jet had drawn it on her little map.

It was hot in there, really hot, and full of steam. Stoke wandered in and was immediately approached by a young guy who said, "May I help you, sir?"

"Looking for the men's room," Stoke said, bending down to talk because he felt like his head was in the clouds.

"Ah-so." Wan Li smiled, just like in the movies. He motioned for Stoke to follow him through the madhouse that served as a kitchen.

They went through a metal door and stepped onto a catwalk that crossed over what looked like a large holding tank. Stoke saw some dorsal fins slicing through the water. It had to be the only floating restaurant in the world with shark-infested waters on the *inside*. No wonder that shark soup had tasted so fresh.

"You find what you look for just in there," Wan Li said, indicating an anonymous blue-painted metal door at the bottom of a short ramp off the catwalk. "Door open. All empty. Nobody home this hour of night."

"Hey, thanks a lot," Stoke said. Wan Li hurried back to his kitchen. Stoke turned the knob and went inside. It was a long, narrow room with a low ceiling. It was dark except for the harbor lights coming in through the row of windows to his left. Stoke, who had spent some time at Newport News helping navy draftsmen design a faster river patrol boat, knew instantly why Jet had brought him here.

This was where the giant cruise ship *Leviathan* and the German-built supertankers had been designed.

He looked at his watch. Jet had given him twenty minutes. He had sixteen left. Not a lot.

He pulled the small, flat flashlight from his pocket, switched it on, and made his way past rows of old-fashioned drafting benches and banks of oversized computer monitors. There were half-hull forms mounted along the wall to his right. Tankers, he saw, mostly hundred-thousand-ton displacement by the looks of them. Ships that drew about ninety feet of water. Ships that required deepwater ports.

There was a wall of glass at the end of the room. A glass door opened into a smaller drawing office on the other side. He went in. More models on the wall, this time VLCC and ULCCs. Very large and ultralarge crude carriers of more than four hundred thousand tons. With global oil consumption up about 8 percent a year, he could see why the French and the Chinese were getting in the business. A ULCC could make a profit of four million dollars on a single run from Kuwait to Europe. He wouldn't even hazard a guess as to what a run from the Gulf to Shanghai might net.

Stoke looked at the blank monitor. It was no secret that China desperately needed oil and would do anything to get it. So what deep dark secrets was the Golden Dragon hiding?

He sat down at the computer CAD workstation and started scrolling and searching. He was looking at the shipwright's plans for a huge tanker named the *Happy Dragon*. He scanned her prefabricated units—cross-sections, diagonals, buttocks, and waterlines—looking for something unusual. Nothing. Then he moved on to the completed hull form and its vast tanks and watertight bulkheads. Finding nothing interesting there either, he moved quickly to the propulsion files.

It took ten seconds to discover her first secret. She was nuclear-powered. So that's where General Moon and the Chinese came in. They provided the reactors and fuel for the German-built vessels. Next stop, her reactor room, he said to himself, scrolling as fast as he could.

She had fourth-generation naval reactors similar to the KN-3 reactors used aboard a vessel he was very familiar with, the Russian Arktika-class nuclear icebreakers. He'd been a stowaway on one for a month. He looked at her twin reactors and uranium core fuel plans for no more than a minute when something made him move on. He flashed on that night aboard *Valkyrie*. The gadget he'd found in the guard's pocket and the missing keel. The dosimeter. Both had been tickling his subconscious ever since. Yeah, and those iodine pills for radiation sickness. So? Keels were lead. Lead was the ideal shield against radiation. So where the hell did that lead?

He'd just opened a new file when the thing caught his eye. There it was, in a small cross-section of the *Happy Dragon*'s keel in the lower righthand corner of the screen. Something definitely didn't look right.

Keels were built of solid lead. That was the whole point. This one wasn't solid at all.

This one had something buried deep within it.

Holy shit.

All the pieces clicked into place in an instant. There was the barrel, surrounded by the tamper, with all the plutonium pieces arranged in a perfect pie shape around the beryllium/polonium core. Oh, yeah. It was an implosion-triggered fission bomb. Buried deep inside the lead keel of a fifteen-hundred-foot-long supertanker. A ship built to sail the endless seas without restriction. Built to traverse the world's most vital waterways—

Wait a minute. The lead, that was the key. It wasn't only good for keeping radiation *out*. Like a lead shield. It would also work to keep radiation *in*. The dormant bomb inside the tanker's keel could remain shielded in place for decades. And without any possibility of detection until the instant it was detonated! Jesus. A keel was the *perfect* place to hide a nuclear weapon. Underwater and out of sight, completely encased in a solid lead shield that would prevent even a trace of radiation from being detected.

But how many of these damn things had they built?

Check it out—right there—he had clicked through to a page showing von Draxis hull design comparisons: looked like four hulls completed in the last four years. All ULCCs. Three of them with the nuclear option package in the keel, one without. Three out of four ain't bad!

He could see it. You blow, or even threaten to blow, one of these things in a major shipping chokepoint, and you've got the whole world by the short and curlies. Strait of Hormuz, Panama Canal . . . you shut down the U.S.A. in a heartbeat. And they already had three of these things out there somewhere. At least one more on the way!

He grabbed a pencil and scribbled down the names of the ones that had the weapons as fast as he could. All Dragons. The *Happy Dragon*, the *Super Dragon*—and the *Jade Dragon*. Dragons roamed the earth. Right now. He ripped the page off the pad and stuffed it inside his pocket.

Thanks to Jet, he thought he had all the pieces now. She'd given him all she could. All she knew. And it was far worse than she knew. Anyway, he had the big picture now. German shipyards owned by von Draxis build the tankers. France buys the tankers to transport oil to China. China sells the nuclear reactors and enriched uranium fuel to keep those tankers smoking. Everybody's a winner.

And in the belly of each beast that circles the globe, an invisible bomb that gave the Chinese and the French a huge sword to dangle over the world's head.

He kept scrolling, looking at his watch. He was already way late for Jet's pickup on the stern. He didn't care. Somehow, he needed to find the goddamn detonating mechanism. He scrolled through end-less pages, looking for a timer or a radio receiver. Knowing where the fission bomb was was useless unless you knew how it was detonated. That was the only way you could stop it.

After a few minutes, he had to give up. Either there was no inter-nal timer or they'd designed the bomb to be detonated at a distance by radio or satellite signal. He had to get the hell out of here before General Moon's bullyboys came looking for him. But first he had to do just one more very important thing.

He moved the cursor to the "search all" function and typed in a single word: LEVIATHAN.

If the goddamn tankers had bombs in their keels, then why not—shit. No files came up with that name. He banged his fist on the desk and tried again.

Nada.

He raced out of the marine drafting studio, across the shark-bait cat-walk, then slowed to a mild run through the crowded kitchen. Wan Li caught his eye, giving him a worried look, and pointed to an exit leading to the stem. He'd been gone way too long. He might have missed his ride. Or maybe there was some other complication. He'd deal with that. Right now, all he could think about was *Leviathan*. You really had to wonder whether there was a bomb in her keel, too. Cruise ships, like ocean tankers, go everywhere.

Question was, where the hell was that cruise ship located now? There was only one way to find out.

Foo Fighter was just pulling away from the barge when he got to the cargo door at the stern. There was maybe six feet of open water between the hull and *Foo Fighter*. The doorsill he was standing in was about twenty feet above the water. No way she could hear him now, even if he shouted loud as he could. If he jumped, he just might make it to the flat roof of the wheelhouse. It was pitching pretty badly. Still, it beat the hell out of swimming ashore in Hong Kong Harbor at night.

He jumped, clawing at the air, because Jet decided to hit the throttles while he was in midflight.

He made it, barely.

Fear lent him wings, as the saying goes.

When he clambered down to the afterdeck and ducked inside the wheelhouse, Jet was frozen at the helm. She was staring straight ahead, hands locked on the wheel at ten and two. Her pretty white dress was torn and bloodstained. She was barefoot. Her hair was messed up and matted with dark blood. He put a hand on her shoulder and she turned to look at him. There were black streaks down her cheeks under both eyes.

Already knowing the answer, Stoke said, "Hey. You okay?"

She looked away without answering.

"Hey. You have to talk to me."

"I hope you found what you were looking for," she said. Her voice, like her eyes, was dead.

"Yeah. I did. But I need to know something. Right now. I need—"

"He'll be coming after us. You. Me. Most especially me."

"What happened?"

"My father and my sister. When you didn't come back, they figured it out. He was holding me down. The guards came in and he told them to go away. Locked the door. It was a family matter. He gave Bianca the knife. Told her to cut the traitor's throat. Mine. And she would have, too. You should have seen her smile. So I hope you got the information you needed."

"Jet, I'm sorry. If it's any consolation, you did the right thing."

"The right thing? I killed my own sister. I almost killed my father."

"That was self-defense, Jet. Cut yourself some slack."

"Slack? My own father wants me dead. When General Moon wants you dead, there's nowhere to run. It's over, Stoke. We're not getting out of China alive."

"How did you leave him?"

"Unconcious. I shot him up with ketamine. A liquid anesthetic. He should be out for a couple of hours if I hit the right vein. After that—"

"Listen, Jet. I knew I'd have to leave in a hurry. Didn't know for sure if you did. Now I do. There's a seaplane."

"Where?"

"On a temporary mooring in Kowloon Harbor. Six minutes from

here. I'm taking it to Taiwan. There's a State Department jet on the ground at Chiang Kai-shek Airport with its engines warming up. I'm taking you out of China. Okay?"

There was an imperceptible nod of her head.

"That's a good decision," Stoke said. "Thank you for what you did back there. One question I have to ask you. Where are the tankers? Where are all these big surprise packages, Jet? Now?"

"I don't know."

"Of course you do. Tell me."

"I don't *know* where the tankers are, Stoke! How would I? I know *Leviathan* sailed from Le Havre five days ago. She's probably at the dock by now."

"Which dock is that? Schatzi happen to say?"

"Pier 93, I think. New York City."

"Jesus, Jet. Is there a plutonium bomb on that cruise ship?"

"What?"

"I think there is a bomb aboard that ship. Remember that weird-looking keel on that *Leviathan* model in Germany? Big damn bulge at the bottom of it. A bulb keel you called it. There's a bomb inside that bulb, Jet."

"He wouldn't do that, Stoke. My father's not that evil. He's no mass murderer. I don't think he—oh, god, I hope to hell you're wrong."

"I think a bomb that big will take out the whole West Side of New York. And, what's left of the city after the explosion will be flooded with dirty water. Radiation levels so bad no one can live there for at least ten years."

She looked up at him. Tears were running down her cheeks.

"I can't believe he'd do that, Stoke. Blow up the whole goddamn world. Even for my father, that's complete, utter fucking insanity."

"Okay, Jet, tell me this. Do the French know about these bombs? Are they in on this?"

"I don't think so. This isn't about France. France is fucking clueless. This is all about who rules the world, Stoke. It's about China and America, dividing the spoils, upping the ante. In case you haven't heard, the next world war is going to be over oil. We're running out."

"Listen. You see that berth down there? Why don't you go lie down for a few minutes? I'll take the helm, okay? I'll call you if I need you."

"Need me?"

"We got company, Jet. Back there. Couple of blue-light specials. This is a pretty crowded neighborhood and maybe I can lose 'em. I stowed some weapons under that berth. Two HK machine guns and a grenade launcher."

Stoke took the wheel and put the boat hard over to avoid a suddenly oncoming ferry. Jet ducked down into the little cabin and lifted up the cushion, moving very slowly and deliberately. She handed up one of the HKs, but she was clearly in shock. If he did need her, she wasn't going to be much help.

A rapidly blinking blue light had flickered across Stoke's peripheral vision. Then it disappeared into the great floating city of barges, scows, and sampans. He thought he'd lost it. A minute later, they were everywhere. Two or three fast patrol boats, maybe more. He saw their flashing blue lights bearing down on *Foo Fighter* from astern and abeam, weaving through traffic at ridiculous speeds.

He was smaller, though, and, he hoped, faster.

He was sure more would be on the way any second now. Shit, General Moon would have the whole Chinese navy out here as soon as he came to his senses. Stoke leaned on the throttles, firewalling them. The answering roar and the little hull's great leap forward was reassuring. The good news here was *Foo Fighter* was a screamer. He'd seen the chrome-plated heads and that big Holley hot-rod four-barrel carburetor sitting on top. He knew that big block Chevy V-8 might come in handy.

He was running flat-out in open water now, a blurred neon skyline out his window, ahead the dark silhouettes of sampans moving on the water, merging into the darker mass. He was doing nearly fifty miles an hour, headed straight toward that big black wall. The almost solid city of sampans and ferries between him and Kowloon Harbor would be tough to navigate with the throttle wide open. But slowing down was definitely not an option. He leaned forward over the wheel, ignoring the rapidly gaining patrol boats, his concentration total.

The window about six inches in front of his face exploded a second before he heard a sizzling round just below his left ear. Now he heard and felt the heavy thunk of rounds slamming into the transom and the deck behind him. They'd found his range all right.

Oh, shit. He cranked the wheel hard to starboard and missed a big sampan by inches. He saw a hole in the black wall that loomed up in front of him. The alley created by two hulking barges was about six inches wider than his beam. A bullet in the back or collision at sea can ruin your day. But he didn't slow down. He didn't really have time for a shootout with Chinese gunboats right now. He had a plane to catch. And a phone call to make.

Alex Hawke was in New York City. He was probably at New York Hospital this very minute, sitting in a room somewhere with Ambrose Congreve. He kept his left hand on the wheel and took out his sat phone. He and Hawke needed to have a very serious conversation.

Right now.

He put the wheel hard to port and *Foo Fighter* ducked down another blind alley at full bore.

Chapter Fifty-eight

New York City

"OH, HULLO," AMBROSE CONGREVE SAID, HIS EYELIDS FLUT-tering. A wavering shape had mysteriously appeared at his bedside. Yesterday, he'd come into New York City from Southampton by ambulance. The surgery to remove the bullet from his spine took place at New York Hospital. That was six hours ago. Congreve's voice was very weak, his face a kindred shade to the grey-white pillow beneath his head.

"Is that you there, Alex?"

"Indeed, it is."

"You're in New York City."

"Yes. I came just to see you."

"Oh. How am I?"

"That's what I came to find out. How are you?"

"In hospital, I'm afraid. I, uh, had a bit of surgery."

"So I understand. It went very well, according to your doctor. How do you feel?"

"All right, I suppose. My eyes are a bit wonky. Sleepy."

"Well, you're still in the arms of morphine. You'll be swell in the morning. The doctor assures me that with a little bed rest, you'll make a full recovery. Back to fighting strength in no time, old scout."

"What pretty flowers. Dahlias. Who are they from?"

"I believe they're from Mrs. Purvis. The roses are from Ross Sutherland."

"Ah. Who's that? In the chair?"

"That's Detective Mariucci. He and I have been getting acquainted while we waited for you to wake up."

"Whom is he talking to? I can't hear what he's saying. I don't see anybody in the other chair."

"He's on his mobile to someone in Washington. The game is afoot, as your idol Mr. Holmes would say."

"Watson. The game?"

"I'll explain later."

"Is Diana here?"

"She was. She's been in that chair for the duration. I told her to go out and get some air. She should be back any minute."

"You met her?"

"I did. She's everything you said and more. Lovely woman. I'm very happy for you."

"She's too good for me, Alex."

"That's true, obviously, but I think given enough time she'll bring you up to speed quite nicely."

Ambrose closed his eyes and whispered so softly that Alex had to bend down to hear, "What, when drunk, one sees in other women, I see in Diana, sober." After that he made no sound. He'd drifted away again.

"Alex?" Detective Mariucci whispered, "I need you over here a second."

"Yes?"

"That was ATAC Command in D.C. The friggin' French have invaded Oman. Bonaparte's sticking with his story."

"What about the sultan's tape?"

"Claims the Oman tape was made under coercion by the West. By you, specifically. French TV is showing the beginning of the tape where you're wiping blood off the guy's face before he speaks. Jesus Christ. Here, take this phone. Somebody's patching an urgent call through. Stokely Jones calling you from Hong Kong. Ten seconds."

Hawke put the phone to his ear, his eyes cold as stone. He spoke to Stokely for two minutes, max, disconnected, said good-bye, and punched in another number.

"I'm putting this call on speaker," Hawke told Mariucci and collapsed exhausted into the chair next to him. He placed the phone on the small table between the two of them and tilted back the rest of his cold coffee. He *had* wiped blood off the sultan's face. And the sultan had thanked him for—wait. Bonaparte was running that part of the tape *without sound*.

"Jack McAtee," they heard the gravelly voice of the president say a second or two later.

"Mr. President, sorry to disturb you at this late hour. Alex Hawke calling."

"Alex! Good to hear your voice, partner. Good work over there. I'm in the Situation Room with Kelly, Gooch, and Charlie Moore. We've already got your videotape on the air. Al Jazeera's running it every ten minutes and France is already taking serious heat from the Arab world."

"Glad I could help, Mr. President. About the tape. The French media are running the first part without sound. Under government orders. We need to get the whole thing on the air, sir, the entire thirty seconds preceding the sultan's speech."

"Done. Tell me what you need, Alex."

"Mr. President, I'm on speakerphone in New York with Captain John Mariucci of the NYPD Anti-Terrorist Task Force, sir. I'm afraid I've got some bad news."

"Just got the news, Alex. I was on the phone with Bonaparte not three hours ago. I told the crazy sonafabitch that unless he wanted to be on the wrong end of another invasion at Normandy he should keep his ass out of Oman. He assured me he had no intention of invading. Now I learn the French have gone into Oman anyway."

"I just heard that, too, sir."

"Will we never learn?"

"Sir, I have news of a different nature."

"Talk to me, Alex."

"Mr. President, fifteen seconds ago I got a call from Hong Kong. As Director Kelly knows, I sent a man out there early this morning to finish sorting out General Sun-yat Moon's activities."

"Right."

"I believe we have a complete understanding of that operation now. It's not good, Mr. President. In the last four years, four supertankers were launched at various von Draxis shipyards in Germany. All were purchased by the French oil company Elf. Three of the four have extremely powerful nuclear devices secreted inside their lead keels. The keels were hung at Shanghai Shipyard at the same time that Chinese reactors and enriched fuel cores were installed."

"Alex, what kind of devices are we talking about?"

"Implosion-triggered fission bombs, Mr. President. Heavy duty."

"Christ. Hold on a second, Alex. I've got you on speaker. Brick Kelly wants to know if these devices are plutonium or weapons-grade uranium?"

"Stokely definitely said plutonium, sir."

After a few moments of muffled conversation, the president continued, "Go ahead, Alex. As of this moment, I have to inform you that this is a completely compartmentalized operation. It now has its own ticket. Codename: Wild Card. Langley's putting the steel in it right now. Nobody gets in without that ticket."

"Acknowledged, sir. The devices are shielded inside the ship's solid lead keel. Brilliant concept. Detection is virtually impossible by harbor security. No leaks. Impervious to X-ray inspection. No port security team in the world could screen them out."

"Location of these tankers now?"

"Locations unknown at this point, sir."

"Names?"

"*Happy Dragon*, *Super Dragon*, and *Jade Dragon*, sir. All sailing under French flags, sir."

They could hear the president barking orders at various staffers inside the Situation Room. Then he was back on the speaker.

"Alex, we're already all over the tankers. We'll find them. I get the feeling there's more to this story."

"Sir, such a device was also designed into the keel of the cruise ship *Leviathan*."

At that moment, Mariucci grabbed Hawke's arm.

"Holy mother of god!" Mariucci cried, jumping to his feet. "She's here! *Leviathan*? She arrived this past Tuesday! I was on one of the Moran tugs that—"

"Alex," the president said, his voice steady, "you are talking about that huge ocean liner that arrived in New York earlier this week?"

"Yes, sir. The new French ship. *Leviathan*."

"And you say her keel contains a large fission bomb?"

"Yes, sir. That's what I'm saying. I want to confirm that fact. But I believe it."

"You believe it's a Chinese device? Put there by the Chinese? She's a French-flag vessel, Alex. Built in Germany."

"Mr. President, her reactors were installed at Shanghai Shipyard. The keel was hung there, too."

"All right, Alex, listen carefully," the president said, "Nobody says boo about this until I say so. Captain Mariucci, do you hear that?"

"Yes, Mr. President, I do."

"Nothing, I mean not a single word, gets said about this *Leviathan* situation until you two get over to that vessel, alone, and confirm the bomb's existence. That includes you, too, Captain Mariucci. You're the only one with a ticket. I don't want any helicopters in the sky, harbor police boats, none of that crap. Nobody even breathes until we know exactly what we're dealing with here. Understand what I'm saying?"

"We do, sir," Mariucci said. "The danger of panic far outweighs the chance of immediate detonation. If we find there really is a bomb hidden aboard that monster."

"Right. Okay. Get going. Alex, you've got my secure number. It's what, ten-fifteen? Call me one-half hour from now no matter what. We're nose-to-nose with the Chinese over this goddamned Oman incursion. Until I have a definitive answer from you on this thing, I'm paralyzed in these negotiations."

"Sir—"

"Unless we get that bomb out of New York, there's a very good chance we're going to war with China."

The president was gone.

Chapter Fifty-nine

New York City

NEITHER HAWKE NOR THE CAPTAIN SAID A WORD DURING the elevator ride to the ground floor. Nor did they speak crossing the lobby. Instead of taking the cruiser idling out front of the hospital entrance, they jumped into a cab at the corner of York and Seventieth Street and headed across town. It was Sunday night and the traffic was light going through the park. They pulled up at the passenger ship terminal, Pier 93, just after nine-thirty.

"Got any ideas?" Mariucci said to Hawke as they climbed out of the cab.

"Nothing yet," Hawke said, "I was hoping you'd have one by now."

Hawke handed the driver a twenty and joined the captain on the sidewalk. The upper decks of the enormous ship, illuminated, blocked out the sky above the terminal. She was, Hawke knew, two times longer than the Eiffel Tower was high, and four times the size of the *Titanic*. Hawke saw the word *Leviathan* stenciled in gold on her beautiful black bow. No doubt about it, she was monumentally impressive.

"Let's go find the captain," Hawke said.

They raced through the terminal and arrived at the deserted check-in area. The floor was still littered with streamers and confetti. The French Line had decorated the entire area with paintings, ribbons, and pictures of the great liners of the past, the *Île de France* and the *Normandie*. A massive oil painting dominated the scene. In the foreground of the painting, the largest ship ever built, *Leviathan*. In the background, almost hidden by the arcs of water jetting from the fireboats, the Statue of Liberty.

There were two desultory guards at the boarding door who barely looked up from their newspapers as Mariucci flashed his shield and barreled through. When they got outside on the dock, they couldn't even see the ship. It was too close to the building. It looked like a black wall.

There was a gangway leading up the side of the black wall, its rails festooned with wilted red, white, and blue streamers. Hawke raced up, followed closely by Mariucci. There was an officer in white at the top with a clipboard. At the sight of two men running toward him, he put on a welcoming smile to hide his confusion. The passengers were all long gone and these two men didn't look like crew.

"Good evening, gentlemen," the officer said.

"Yeah, how are you doing tonight? Listen, I'm Captain John Mariucci, NYPD, and this is my colleague Alex Hawke. Royal Navy. Mind if we take a look around?"

"I am so sorry, sir, but you see we do not allow tours or uninvited visitors. The ship is—"

"I'm sorry, I didn't get your name," Mariucci said, moving right up into his face. "You are?"

"I am the ship's chief purser, monsieur. And, I will have to ask you to—"

"Look, Alain, that's what it says on your security tag thing there, you're new, so let me explain how this all works. This is New York City, see. We have our own unique style. Like, I'm a cop here. I don't have to be invited."

"We'd like a brief word with your captain," Hawke said. "Would you be so kind as to take us to the bridge?"

"Well, I—"

"After you, Alain. Lead the way."

"As you wish."

As it happened, the ship's captain, Francois Dechevereux, was not on the bridge at all. He was standing alone on the open observation deck, high above the graceful curve of the bows, looking at the pristine New York skyline. He was a tall man, angular, and his white uniform hung on him the way a tent hangs on poles. Hawke noticed his yellow fingertips and the unfiltered cigarette that seemed a permanent fixture in the corner of his mouth.

"Beautiful ship, Captain," Hawke said after they'd been introduced by the purser. "Magnificent lines."

"Yeah, nice," Mariucci said. "Big. But nice."

Captain Dechevereux whispered something in the purser's ear and sent him scurrying away. Then he turned to Hawke, removing his cigarette only to speak. He didn't look happy to see them.

"*Leviathan* is a wonder, Monsieur Hawke, a symbol of the new French Renaissance. Our great leader, President Bonaparte, has given her to France as proof of her restored glory. *La Gloire*. I am glad you appreciate her. I don't mean to be rude. But, may I ask why you gentlemen wished to see me? Is there some problem? Some irregularity with our paperwork?"

"There certainly is a problem, Captain," Mariucci said, "But I'm here to make it go away."

"How can I help you?"

"It's the mayor, Captain. Of New York. He's a greenie, see? One of those tree-hugging environmental wackos, right? Hizzoner has never much liked the idea of a nuclear-powered vessel with a foreign flag zipping in and out of New York Harbor and—"

"He is anti-French," Captain Dechevereux said with disdain, flicking his cigarette over the rail and immediately lighting another. "I have read this about him."

"No, no. The mayor of New York loves France. It's not that. He—"

Hawke cast a sidelong glance at Mariucci. "Captain," he said, "I've heard you can do well over thirty knots. Staggering. Please tell me about your propulsion system."

"Ah. The most advanced in the world, monsieur. Two pods, submerged under the stern, that can rotate 360 degrees. Driven by 4.2-megawatt thrusters controlled by a joystick."

"Amazing. How many reactors? Four?" Hawke asked.

"*Mais certainement*. Four nuclear reactors each generating one-hundred-thousand-shaft horsepower. We keep her speed confidential. In brochures we say 'It's sufficient.' "

"That's great," Mariucci said. "But look around you here. Pretty densely populated area here in Manhattan. People get nervous when they even hear the word 'nuclear.' You understand that."

Hawke said, "Captain, I saw a poster depicting Alaska at the dockside check-in. I take it you intend to sail in waters where there are strict environmental controls?"

"*Mais oui*. But we are very conscious of the environment issues. President Bonaparte, who, perhaps, found it expedient to become a great conservationist, insisted she exceed every requirement. The ship is designed to operate—"

"Precisely why we're here, Captain," Hawke said, leaping through the opening. "Environmental issue. We're going to need to do a thorough inspection of your reactor rooms. Immediately. I understand you're sailing back to Le Havre tomorrow evening?"

"No."

"No? That's the announced schedule. A six o'clock sailing."

"There will be an unfortunate delay. A mechanical problem—one of the propulsion monitors has shut down our reactors. The ship is to remain here indefinitely. It is not my decision."

"Really? You being the captain and all, I'd think—whose decision is it?"

"The builder. He was a passenger on our maiden voyage. All over my ship, with his little notebook, writing and writing. Now, he says we cannot leave. He is flying in some more Chinese technicians to make the repairs, and who knows how long that will take? I've just learned all of this myself, Captain. The man was standing here not ten minutes ago. To tell you the truth, I am furious with this decision. It is an embarrassment."

"The builder is onboard?" Mariucci asked, looking around.

"*Mais oui!* You know what he said to me? That we have too many screws in the coat racks on the stateroom doors! Eh? Too many screws?" The captain was getting a little hot under the collar. Whatever was going on aboard this behemoth, the captain obviously wasn't in on it. And he was pissed.

"Bonaparte had Baron von Draxis build this ship in Germany," Dechevereux said. "The new *Queen Mary*, she was built in France. Many jobs for Frenchmen. But Germans built this great ship for our beloved President Bonaparte. Germans! Make sense to you? No. Go. Find him. He went to the Normandie Bar for a nightcap before turning in."

"One more question before we go, Captain," Hawke said. "Tell me about your keel design. Anything unusual about it?"

"No. It's lead."

"Nothing inside? No electronics? Side thrusters?"

"It's a *keel*, monsieur. A dead weight. Please. Leave me alone. I am very upset at the moment."

"Thanks for your time, Captain," Mariucci said. "We'll find our way to the bar."

Under his breath, Mariucci said, "Von Draxis is faking some mechanical problem so his ship can remain in New York indefinitely. Like a permanent Trojan Horse."

"Right. But I've an idea," Hawke said as they walked quickly aft to find the builder.

"Don't be shy," Mariucci said as they entered the vast Art Deco lounge.

"We tell this von Draxis we're here to save him, and France, a lot of embarrassment. Tell him Port Security was doing random samples and picked up a radiation leak."

"I like that—look. That's got to be him, headed this way. Looks like a friggin' bull."

"In a bloody China shop," Hawke said, lowering his voice. "Remember, no inspection, his ship has to leave immediately. Got it?"

"Got it."

"Gentlemen, good evening! Zo, I understand there is some kind of problem. I am the proud builder, Augustus von Draxis. Perhaps I may be of service?"

The captain flashed his creds. "Mariucci, NYPD Anti-Terrorist Task Force. This is my driver, George."

"Evening," Hawke said, smiling.

The baron eyed Hawke suspiciously and said, "What seems to be the problem?"

"Pollution," Mariucci said.

"Pollution? Ha! This is the cleanest ship afloat, Captain. A zero-waste ship."

"Radioactive leak, Mr. von Draxis. One of my Port Security boats in the East River picked it up in a random sample. Just this afternoon. We'll need to do an immediate inspection."

"Inspection? Impossible. If there is a leak, which I doubt, we'll find it and fix it ourselves."

"I knew you'd say that. But, frankly, I can't take your word for it.

Two choices, sir. Allow my divers and inspectors and their mobile X-ray scanners aboard, or get out of Dodge. Your call."

"This is ridiculous. In any event, we are scheduled to depart for Le Havre tomorrow."

"But you're not, right? You're waiting for a powwow with some Chinese technicians?"

"Who told you that?"

"That would be your captain. Dechevereux is his name? Am I right, George? Dechevereux?"

Hawke nodded.

"This is insanity," von Draxis said, the color rising in his cheeks. "My family has been building the finest ships afloat for four generations. And I am telling you there is no leak. I know her every bolt, every screw on this vessel! You know how some people talk to horses? I talk to boats! She is not leaking radiation. I will not tolerate this!"

"What a world, huh?" Mariucci said. "Hey, listen, Mr. von Draxis. I know it's a royal pain in the ass. But save yourself a lot of bad PR, all right? We'll be in and out of here in two hours, max. You don't want to see your pride and joy on the news tomorrow with police barricades up all around it, do you? What do you say?"

The baron looked like he was about to detonate. "What exactly is it you people wish to see?"

"What we the people would like to see is your fat ass headed due east out of our fucking harbor. But what we will settle for is a complete inspection of your reactor rooms, your hull, your keel, and any other part of this fucking ship I want to look at. Got all that?"

The German, Hawke noticed, was balling his fists and rising up onto the tips of his toes. His thickly corded neck was bulging and his shoulder blades looked like tectonic plates shifting under his dinner jacket. But somehow he managed to control all this and not to take a swing at Captain Mariucci.

"The governor of New York will hear about this outrage. He is a close personal friend of German chancellor Gerhardt's. I will squash you like a bug."

"Fine, we'll do it the hard way, pal. Come on, George. We're out of here."

Chapter Sixty

Washington, D.C.

"HERE'S HOW I LIKE MY BAD NEWS," PRESIDENT MCATEE said, striding into the Sit Room.

"Like a frozen rope, for you golfers: straight and to the point. For you baseball fans, I like a hard fastball over the heart of the plate. Let me have it, boys. Batter up."

Wild Card, the top-secret, highly compartmentalized White House team devoted to the Chinese crisis, had gathered in the Situation Room. The team was now composed of a dozen men and women, including members of the JCS, CIA, National Security Council, and National Security Agency officers. You could read the faces; it wasn't good news.

The long, narrow office had the air of a stale boardroom after a marathon meeting. One where all the details had obviously been sweated. The long burl table, with seats for about eighteen, was full. So were the few chairs along the walls. The far wall, which converted to a giant screen with real-time media capability, now displayed a brilliant four-color map of China and its troublesome neighbor, Taiwan. The mood was tense, but still informal.

As the president took his chair, the national security advisor, John Gooch, was the first one on his feet.

"Mr. President. We are now looking at three distinct threat scenarios," Gooch said, nodding to the Marine who was manning the computer. "Number one—"

"Only three?" the president said with a smile. "That's not too bad. Hell, that's hardly enough for a full-blown global crisis."

"Mr. President," John Gooch said when the nervous laughter had died down, "I'm afraid the situation has sharply deteriorated since your last briefing."

"Sorry. Go ahead, John. Can I get a Diet Coke?"

"One, the nuclear device in New York City has been confirmed. The—"

"Excuse me," the president said. "Confirmed?"

"Yes, sir. We dropped a black ops team onto the roof of the Golden Dragon in Hong Kong Harbor. Surprise visit. We overpowered the resistance, took a few casualties. No sign of General Moon. Our boys hacked into the naval design computers."

"And?"

"There is a device in *Leviathan's* keel, sir. Twice the destructive power of those in the tankers."

The president's face went suddenly cold. All traces of humor disappeared from his eyes. All who knew him well saw the omnivorous intellect and distilled, probing presence that had propelled him to the very top of his party and the presidency.

"How bad is it?" McAtee asked, rubbing his chin.

"A fission bomb of sufficient size to take out half of Manhattan, sir. And flood what's left of the city with dirty water. Seven years' contamination, minimum."

"I want Hawke and Mariucci to have whatever federal, state, and city resources they need. I'm giving them one hour to get that floating French flophouse out of New York Harbor. Okay? And do it without causing alarm. All right? That's one threat. Give me another one."

"Two, Mr. President. Beijing's recent behavior is appalling. The relationship we thought we had has gone downhill in a hurry. As you well know, they passed a law authorizing the use of force against Taiwan. They encouraged anti-Japan riots in China. They're using the Rape of Nanking to whip up the population. Now, they threaten to sink our currency if we don't back off the French in Oman. Will they do it? I honestly don't know."

"That's it?"

"The Cheshire Cat is showing us a new and totally unexpected face, Mr. President. That's all I've got at the moment."

"That's enough. Charlie?" the president said, swiveling his head to regard the chairman of the Joint Chiefs.

"To hell with our currency. Right now they're threatening to sink our ships. And invade Taiwan."

"I was just coming to that, Mr. President. Number three, the presence of significant Chinese naval and air forces in the Taiwan Strait. By significant, I mean a battle fleet centered on their new carrier, *Varyag*, purchased from the Ukraine and carrying forty of the new Sukoi SU-30 fighter jets recently purchased from Russia. Questions?"

A hand went up. "Subs?"

"Right. China is fielding two Han-class and one of her Xia-class nuclear missile submarines recently launched at their shipyard near the Gulf of Bohai. Both carry twelve solid-fuel 'Giant Wave' model-1 missiles with a range of twenty-four hundred kilometers."

"And that area includes?" the president asked.

"That includes Japan, Taiwan, Korea, and Alaska. In addition, a Song-class diesel sub is off Kaochung at the mouth of the Straits. She's equipped with a new sonar facility that can simultaneously and automatically monitor and operate five combat targets."

"No model-2 missiles?"

"We don't know. That's one reason I'm sweating right now. The model-2, as some of you know, has a range of eight-thousand kilometers. Any Chinese sub now operating in the West Pacific or Philippines with model-2 missiles on board can aim at and reach any target within Russian and U.S. territories."

"Who gives a flying fuck about Russia at this point?" General Moore said.

"I do," Gooch said. "We're at the stage in the game where everybody damn well better give a damn about everybody else. We're all on this goddamn planet together. The president just got off the phone with Putin. He called to say he had two Russian Victor III submarines in the theater and headed into the Straits. As I say, everybody needs to know everything. Or *almost* everything."

"So what happens next? Charlie?" the president said.

"As you know, the CNO put the fleet on Level Three—canceled shore leave and ordered all units in San Diego and Norfolk to sea four days ago. CINCPAC has informed me through the CNO that the *Theodore Roosevelt* and her battle group have reached the Straits and await orders; *Kennedy* and *Nimitz* with their groups are a day out, moving at flank speed through forty-foot seas. Lead units from both are within three hours of the Straits."

"Good news," the president said, staring down at something he'd written on his legal pad.

"Yes, sir. The bad news is the tankers are having a tough time keeping up and we may have a fuel problem if things get really spicy."

"Well, we'll just have to handle that," the president said. "How about the psyops? Director Kelly?"

The lanky CIA man put down the slice of cold pizza he'd been about to eat and got to his feet. His suit was rumpled and his eyes were red and swollen with strain. Like many of his colleagues, he'd gone a day and a half without sleep. He straightened his tie and addressed the president directly.

"Uh, right, on the psychological operations front, Mr. President, we have at your order, activated—sorry—may I just confirm, sir, that everyone in this room has a ticket for Wild Card? Please confirm by raising your hand and stating your name and agency . . . sorry, folks, this is just for my records . . . okay. Thanks. Sorry. Regarding Wild Card, sir. That went operational at 0800 hours this evening, EST."

"Good. Tell them what it is, Brick."

"How much can I say?"

"Just enough."

"All right. Operation Wild Card is a 'deep sleeper.' It's, uh, a contingency asset already in place inside Mainland China. A linked chain of our most powerful nuclear weapons. Deep inside one of their major cities. They know about it. They even know its name. They just don't know where it is. What city, what time. That's it."

"Jesus Christ," John Gooch said. "What are you going to do? Blow up Shanghai? Take out Beijing? Brick, you are talking about killing a couple of million people, for god's sake."

"It won't come to that," Brick Kelly said.

"I hope to hell you're right," Gooch said.

Kelly continued, "We put Wild Card on the table tonight through a deliberately careless radio operator in a transmission from Hickham Air Force Base in Hawaii. He used a code we know they've broken. The operator's message was, 'Wild Card is in play.' We're reading their traffic. They've intercepted our transmission. Right now, I would say there is something approaching tense discussion within the halls of the Politburo."

"So Wild Card is working, Brick?" the president said. There was hope in his question. He'd originally been against the concept of the grievous, last-resort contingency asset. Then came his first post-inaugural briefing. The asset, deep inside Mainland China, would be impossible to remove without destroying the thin line of civility that had existed for some time between Washington and Beijing.

"Let's just say we have reason to believe the Mandarins in the Forbidden City are rapidly losing their cool. In a severe crisis, their pyramid structure at the very top is hardly conducive to well-reasoned consensus management. You get the top five alone in a room, throw in Wild Card, and, hell, they're bouncing off the walls."

"Somehow, I don't find that image very reassuring," the secretary of state, Consuelo de los Reyes, said.

"Madame Secretary," Kelly said to the secretary of state, "I understand your feelings. But Wild Card is the very best chance we have of preventing an all-out nuclear war."

Consuelo de los Reyes, Cuban-born and Harvard-educated, was the person Jack McAtee was closest to in his administration. He smiled at her and said, "Conch, could you give us an update on what State is doing, please."

"Yes, Mr. President. Two hours ago, Barron Collier, the U.S. ambassador in Beijing, demanded to see the Chinese foreign minister. Ambassador Collier just came out of that office twenty minutes ago. While there he presented a demarche to the Chinese government. Three demands: one, get the bomb out of New York Harbor. Two, get all French and Chinese forces out of Oman. Three, stop this bullying harassment of Taiwan."

"And what, pray tell, was their initial response?" the president said.

"Knowing Collier as I do," Charlie Moore said, "He probably found grounds for productive discussion."

"Unfortunately he did not, General," the secretary said, glaring at the former Marine. "The Chinese are playing us—which, to my mind, means they have a lot of equity in this and they've thought it through. Or, at least they think they have."

"The bomb," the president said as he looked up from his pad. "What did they say about the damn bomb, Conch?"

"China's opening position is a remarkable display of plausible deniability. They said, 'What bomb?'"

"Right. The bomb they put in *Leviathan*'s keel, goddamn it!" General Moore said.

"What about the Gulf?" the president asked.

"They say they aren't in the Gulf. France is. Suggested we speak with Monsieur le President Bonaparte about Oman. He's the one who ordered the French troops to invade."

"And Taiwan?"

"Taiwan is their property. That's the view. They actually quoted the Taiwan Relations Act. In an odd way, they seemed to be advising prudence on our part."

"Prudence?"

"Just a feeling. That we should tread lightly."

"Ah. And this veiled warning took place prior to the Chinese foreign minister knowing Wild Card was on the table, correct?"

"Correct, sir."

"I just had a thought, Mr. President," Gooch said.

"Go ahead," McAtee said.

"This *Leviathan*. It's been their plan all along. That ship is the Chinese attempt to check Wild Card."

The room went silent.

"What does that mean, John?" the president said.

"Check. Checkmate."

"How so?"

"Trigger one, trigger all. We initiate our detonation sequence, they initiate theirs."

"I think John's absolutely right. Only we know where their bomb is," CIA Director Kelly said.

"That's correct, Brick," the president said. "We do know where it is. I just pray to God we get that damn thing out of New York before they pull the trigger."

"Until we do, we're in an undeclared state of war with Red China, Mr. President," John Gooch said.

Chapter Sixty-one

New York City

2:01 A.M., EST

NEW YORKERS ARE HARD TO SPOOK. THAT'S WHAT MASTER Chief Petty Officer Ken Tynan was thinking, anyway. People in Manhattan, they've seen just about everything in the last four or five years. So, when drivers on the West Side Highway see a line of NYPD cruisers an entire city block long, bumper-to-bumper out front of the Passenger Ship Terminal, you know what, they don't pay a whole lot of attention to it. All those cop cars in a row, lights flashing; it was cool-looking. Good scene. Like some Bruce Willis or Arnold movie on one level. Reassuring on another.

Nor did New Yorkers think much of the six Moran tugs that were currently steaming up the East River toward Pier 93. Any insomniac looking out the window in Midtown, or over in Jersey, wouldn't think twice about a few tugboats, even though it was just after two o'clock in the morning.

Except for all the uniforms swarming around, the French Line check-in area at Pier 93 was deserted. Outside on the dock, at the foot of the gangway where Tynan was located, guys from the NYPD Marine Units were standing by. Everybody was shooting the shit, occasionally looking up at the draught markings rising up the side of the big black wall and wondering what the hell was going on.

All anybody knew was that Captain John Mariucci and his Anti-Terrorist guys had some kind of operation going. There was a rumor fragment just circulating that the giant cruise ship had sprung a radiation leak. Divers were down, examining the hull and the bulbous keel. You could see their work lights bobbing around down there, fuzzy white orbs in a halo of green.

Some scientist wonks had set up shop on the counters inside the check-in area, crunching numbers on their laptops. With all the streamers, it looked like the back room at a political rally. They'd evacuated the whole crew of the boat an hour ago. Tynan, who was a gas turbine tech himself, was amazed at the number of Chinese technicians streaming off that boat. They all had that nerdy "nuclear" look. Now, only the ship's captain and a couple of other guys remained on board, far as he knew.

Pretty exciting stuff for a Sunday night in June. You never know, right?

All Chief Tynan was sure of, he wasn't supposed to let anybody get on or off this ship, period, and that's just what he was doing. So far, it had been pretty easy. People didn't generally mess with him. Before he'd trimmed down to meet the Coast Guard regs, he weighed two-fifty, two-sixty; this was when he'd been on the U.S. wrestling team that had gone to Athens. One match, he'd dislocated his wrist seven times. He'd won anyway. "You go for my wrist again, I'm going to go for your head," he'd told King Kong, Russia's thirteen-year undefeated legend, Alexander Karelin.

"Tynan!" he heard somebody shout at him. He turned around and saw his boss Mariucci and another guy heading toward him. Ken saluted and said, "Yes, Captain?"

"We're going aboard," Mariucci said. "Everybody get off?"

"All the crew was evacuated, sir. About an hour ago."

"Anybody try to leave or get on this thing since then?"

"No, sir," Tynan said. "Nobody."

"Good. If they do, arrest 'em. If they resist arrest, shoot 'em."

"Yes, sir."

"I'm putting the Coast Guard, namely you, in charge of this NYPD Marine Unit, Tynan. Here's a packet of sealed instructions to be opened on my verbal order. Stay tuned, you'll hear from me on your headset. I'm wearing a mike."

"Yes, sir."

"You hear me say the word 'Moran,' you and the Marine Unit captain open the envelope together. Got it, Tynan?"

"Aye-aye, sir."

"Where's the captain of this vessel now?"

"In the owner's private stateroom, sir, talking to the builder. Big two-story penthouse flanking the bridge on the right side. I've got two of my men outside the door and one more by his private elevator. They're not going anywhere, sir."

2:06 A.M., EST

Hawke and Mariucci found Captain Dechevereux and von Draxis sitting in the baron's movie set Art Deco living room. Everything was done in black and white. A wall of windows rose two stories high and gave a breathtaking view of Manhattan. They were sitting on a sofa beneath a scale model of *Leviathan*, the model itself more than fifteen feet long. A third man, huge, with a shaved skull, sat in a chair opposite. He wore white duck trousers and a black T-shirt that said VDI Security. On the floor near his feet was a dog, size large, a Doberman pinscher.

"Nice view from up here," Mariucci said. "Too bad you got to leave."

Von Draxis got to his feet.

"Ah, Captain Mariucci," he said, "won't you join us? You, too, uh . . . George. Please, sit. Have a drink. I was just telling the captain here about the time my hero Onassis was ordered to change the Olympic logo on all his airliners. You've heard this one?"

"No," Mariucci said, looking at Hawke.

"Olympic Airways had the same logo as the Olympics, five interlocking rings, you know? The Olympic Committee, the IOC, said legally he couldn't use that five-ring logo on his planes. Cost him a fortune to change them. You know what he did, that wily Greek bastard?"

"He added a sixth ring," Hawke said.

"What? That's exactly right! Good for you, George."

"*Danke vielmaus,*" Hawke said with a slight bow. The baron looked at him again, shaking his head.

"Here's the deal, Mr. von Draxis," Mariucci said. "You are hereby—"

"*Baron* von Draxis. Please."

"Fine. Here's the deal, Baron. With the authority invested in me by the United States government, I am hereby rescinding your landing rights. If you do not remove your vessel immediately, you will be in violation of U.S. federal laws and subject to seizure."

"Seize away, Captain! We're not moving. I told you. The ship's propulsion monitors have malfunctioned. Besides, we have shut down the reactors."

"Is he telling the truth, Captain?" Mariucci asked Dechevereux.

"The reactors are down. It would take hours to restart them."

"Zo. You see? I am, quite literally, powerless. Now. If you'd be so good as to leave my ship, Captain Dechevereux and I can continue our conversation."

"You want us to leave?"

"*Ja*, I do. Arnold? Be so kind as to escort these gentlemen off my ship."

The bald giant smiled and got to his feet. So did his dog. He had a strange weapon in his hand. It looked like a German machine gun from World War II.

"Lovely weapon," Hawke said to the big man, "A Schmeisser machine pistol, if I'm not mistaken."

Hawke had heard all about the gun when Stokely debriefed him upon arrival in Oman. The gun, the twin Arnolds, and von Draxis's pet Doberman.

"This is your driver?" the baron said, incredulous. Mariucci smiled and nodded.

"Baron, come over here a second," Mariucci said.

"What?"

"Just come over here to the window. I want you to see something. Beautiful sight."

"If you insist," von Draxis said, moving slowly toward where Mariucci stood at the window.

"What is it?" the baron sighed.

"Look down there on the street. Tell me what you see."

The baron stepped closer to the window and looked down. The line of flashing NYPD cars now stretched the length of the block and around the corner all the way to Eleventh Avenue. Von Draxis shook his head sadly and made a clicking sound with his tongue at the top of his mouth.

"Polizei," he said.

"Yeah. You want to save yourself a whole lot of trouble? Show me what's in your keel. Tell me how to get at it."

The German froze in place. His small eyes took on a ball-bearing hardness.

"Arnold," von Draxis said quietly, *"Bitte,* please ask George if he's carrying a weapon. If he is, relieve him of it. If he refuses to cooperate, kill him."

"Little late for this kind of drama, Baron," Hawke said.

"Do it, Arnold!"

Hawke pulled the Walther out of the holster in the small of his back, reversed the muzzle, and handed it to the German thug.

"Are you armed, Captain Mariucci?" von Draxis asked.

"Nope. Clean."

"Sehr gut. I want you both to go over there and sit down. You and your charming driver. Sit side by side on that sofa where Arnold can keep an eye on you. All right? Please?"

"Whatever you say," Mariucci said, looking at Hawke. "Hey, Moran? Pick a seat."

"Moran?"

"His last name, Baron. His first name is George."

"Ah." There was an ornate French desk by the window, bare except for an Apple G5 laptop and two telephones, one white and one black. Von Draxis sat in the gilded desk chair and lit up his computer. He punched in a series of commands, staring at the screen. Hawke leaned forward, attempting to see the display. There was a low growl from the Doberman, staring at him with big black eyes.

"Nice dog, Baron," Hawke said, reaching out to it. "Come here, Blondi, *kommen Sie hier."*

Von Draxis swiveled on his chair, staring at Hawke in utter disbelief. "Blondi, did he say?"

"That's what he said." Mariucci smiled.

"But this is the dog's actual name!" von Draxis said, a look of incredulity on his face. "How does George—"

"He's a dog psychic," Mariucci said. "What can I tell you?" Mariucci got up and walked back over to the windows. Chief Tynan had heard the magic word, all right. The six Moran tugs were moving into position just off the pier. His own guys, Marine Unit officers, were running fore and aft readying the lines that would secure *Leviathan* to the tugboats.

The white phone rang.

Von Draxis picked it up.

"General Moon, thank you for responding so promptly to my e-mail. I'm here in New York aboard the vessel with a Captain Mariucci from the New York Police Department. Yes, yes. Here at the dock. Everything is fine. Don't worry. Your ship is not going anywhere. You may initiate the sequence whenever you wish. Good-bye, General, and may I say what an honor it's—I'm sorry, sir? Yes, you may. Please hold the line."

"Initiate the sequence?" Mariucci said. "What the hell does that mean?"

Von Draxis looked at Mariucci. "He wants to talk to you, Captain."

Mariucci stood up and took the phone from von Draxis.

"This is Captain Mariucci," he said. "Who is this?"

He listened intently for roughly sixty seconds, all the color draining from his face.

"Wait a second, General," he said, picking up a pen, "I think I better write that last part down."

Mariucci scribbled a line on the pad. "Okay, repeat that for me one more time, please? Yeah. Okay. I've got it. Good-bye, General. I'll convey your message." He tore the top page from the pad and stared at it for a second.

There was a noticeable tremor in his hand as he replaced the receiver. He drew himself up and turned to Alex Hawke.

"That was General Sun-yat Moon of the People's Republic of China," Mariucci said, his voice devoid of emotion. "He wants us to call the president and deliver a message for him."

"A message."

"Yeah. I think you should do it, Alex. He knows you."

"Mind if I use your phone, Baron?" Hawke said, getting to his feet.

"Please," the Baron said, a look of smug satisfaction on his face.

"What's the message?" Hawke asked, punching in the president's direct line.

"Here. I wrote it down."

Hawke heard the president say, "Jack McAtee."

"Mr. President. Alex Hawke."

"Alex. Where are you now?"

"Aboard *Leviathan* at Pier 93 in New York, sir. I have an urgent message for you, sir. Just received directly from General Sun-yat Moon in Hong Kong. You may wish to have others hear this, sir."

"I'm putting you on the Sit Room speaker. Go ahead, Alex."

"Mr. President, the general has issued the following demand—I am quoting him now, sir. 'The United States must rescind her order to initiate Operation Wild Card immediately. Failure to do so will have disastrous consequences.' "

"All right. We've got that. Did he give you a time frame?"

"Yes, sir, he did. He just initiated the sequence. The device will detonate at 4:00 A.M., Eastern Standard Time. Once initiated, the detonation sequence is immutable and irreversible without his code. Can't change it. Can't stop it."

"What time is it now? Damn it. Two-oh-nine."

"Yes, sir. We have less than two hours."

"Christ. We're already working on something here. You need to get that boat into deep water in a hurry. Can you manage that, Alex?"

"I think we have to, Mr. President."

"Anything else?"

"Yes, sir. He said unless he receives certifiable confirmation that Wild Card has been neutralized, you can kiss New York City good-bye."

Chapter Sixty-two

New York Harbor

2:16 A.M., EST

HAWKE, STANDING AT THE STERN RAIL ON THE LINER'S uppermost deck, watched the tugboat operation with mounting dread. If ever he'd had a time-critical mission, this one was it. The tug *Karen Moran*, one of six tugs assigned by the U.S. Coast Guard, had moved into position off the great liner's stern. The hawser, a thick towing cable, looped down from a bollard on *Leviathan*'s stern out to the tug's bow. Suddenly, the slack snapped out; the tug began to pull mightily. Against her will, *Leviathan* was about to back out of the berth. It was a painfully slow process.

Every passing minute darkened his thoughts.

Still, New York City slept, ten million dreamers blissfully unaware of the deadly drama unfolding in her harbor. Imagining the lives behind every dark window along the river, Hawke had a sudden, stinging thought. Ambrose Congreve across town in his hospital bed. Perhaps the bedside lamp was lit. And Diana Mars was sitting quietly by his bedside reading Yeats to him.

As for himself? He'd always felt he'd been born with one foot in the grave. He'd lost his wife to a sniper's bullet. The bullet that found her heart had been meant for him. Living on borrowed time has a numbing effect; any thoughts of death Hawke had now were centered on others. Ambrose and Diana, at this late date, had finally found love. Mariucci was a true New York hero. That Coast Guard kid, Tynan, who'd won a gold medal for America in Athens. None of these people deserved this. To vanish like—

He looked at the radio in his hand.

He had an open line to the president. But calling him again so quickly with such sketchy information would serve no good purpose. There were a lot of anxious people holding their breath in the Sit Room, dealing simultaneously with two potential catastrophes. The U.S. Pacific Fleet and the Chinese fleet were now eyeball to eyeball in the Straits. Here, the clock was ticking relentlessly. Over the next few minutes, Hawke would have to parse out unfolding information carefully. Avoid false hopes or unrealistic expectations.

To be honest, he dreaded telling them what he was thinking at this very moment.

Another tug, the *Diane Moran*, was positioned amidships on the starboard side. The swiftly running tidal current complicated her mission. The tug skipper's job was to keep the ship backing straight out. Once the liner's stern had cleared the berth, the pier itself would be used as a pivot. A tug pushing against the side would shove the stern upriver. That would swing the bow out into open water so that she was headed south toward the Statue of Liberty and the Ambrose Channel.

At that point, according to Hawke's hastily thrown together plan, there would be six of the bright red tugs pushing and pulling *Leviathan* out to sea. Two up front with hawsers, towing. Two angled on either side, steering. And two at the stern, pushing. A book Hawke had read as a child popped into his brain. *Little Toot*. It was about a little tugboat with a big heart. He hoped like hell he had six little *Toots* on his side right now.

Karen Moran had dropped off two pilots. Bob Stuart, the Moran harbor pilot, was assigned to steer *Leviathan* out to the 20-Alpha buoy. At that point, he'd relinquish the helm to a New York state pilot, the "hooker," he was called. The Sandy Hook pilot was responsible for the ship's safe passage through the Ambrose Channel. Once they'd safely left the Ambrose Light astern, *Leviathan* would be in open ocean. There, they might have a chance. A slim one, maybe, but a chance all the same.

They were just now passing the Statue of Liberty to starboard. Hawke checked his watch for the tenth time in as many minutes. He estimated they were doing six knots if they were lucky. Maybe five. He was suddenly aware of Mariucci standing by his side at the rail.

"I don't like this," Mariucci said. "At all."

"It's not going to work," Hawke replied, admitting the truth for the first time. "We've got to go to evacuation. Give me the radio."

"Fuck's sake. You can't evacuate fifteen million people, Alex! You got any idea how many people would die in that kind of panic? Don't even think about it."

Hawke's eyes flashed with anger. "Where the hell is von Draxis?"

"Locked him up in his stateroom. We cut off his phone, took away his cell. Don't worry, he ain't calling anybody about this. And if he gets a call from his Chinese friends, we'll make sure he makes all the right noises."

"Any luck down below?" Alex asked. "The divers?"

"Hell, no. The damn thing is encased in solid lead. No way to get to it. Or even X-ray it! We did insert probes. It's hot all right. And it's got live wires. It's the real deal, Alex. A live nuclear fission bomb."

"What about my idea of cutting out that whole section of keel and just making an offshore run with that? Hell, we could airlift it out of here with a big Sikorsky. Drop it in the trench and be done with it."

"The divers and arc welders tried, Alex. Couldn't cut through. Too thick. Not anywhere near enough time. This is our shot right here, Alex. Tow her out beyond the Continental Shelf where the land drops off and scuttle her. What's the White House say?"

"Hurry."

"Yeah. What are we doing, six knots? That French captain is all right. He was never in on this goddamn thing, Alex. He'd like to get his hands on von Draxis right now—and Bonaparte. He's on the bridge now with the harbor pilots, trying to help. When I left him, Dechevereux was on the radio, coordinating a rendezvous with the sub."

"Sub?"

"A nuclear attack sub the president ordered up to meet us out at the Shelf. The USS *Seawolf*."

"Where's *Seawolf* now?"

"She was conducting an 'emergency blow' training exercise just off Block Island. She's steaming toward the 'Wall' at flank speed. Hey! Where are you—"

"Alaska."

"What? What about Alaska?"

"Let's go see the captain," Hawke said. "I've got an idea."

2:37 A.M., EST

Captain Dechevereux and the two harbor pilots were at the helm when Hawke and Mariucci entered the bridge. Hawke went first to the two pilots. "I want to thank both you guys for all your help. And your bravery. I know you volunteered. As soon as we get to the Ambrose Channel, call one of the tugs alongside and hop off. All right? Go home to your families. And put in for hazard duty. You deserve it."

"Yes, sir," they said, practically in unison. "Thanks a lot."

"Captain Dechevereux," Hawke said. "Just curious. Did your great hero Bonaparte include nuclear terrorism in your job description?"

"He is no longer my hero, monsieur. If that monster knew about this, he should be shot."

"He bloody well knew about it, I assure you. The question is, did you?"

"I am a professional seaman. I have a seafaring tradition in my family that goes back centuries. I am insulted by your question."

"My apologies. Captain Mariucci is convinced of your innocence. I had to find out for myself. Tell me again how much damage the Chinese technicians did in your engine room?"

"As I told you, monsieur. They didn't harm the reactors. No need. They simply short-circuited the computer monitoring systems. The short-circuit presented itself as a 'malfunction' warning, which in turn triggered a shutdown of the reactors. A crew of nuclear engineers would need hours to get them up and running again. Hopeless."

"You can't just give new computer instructions?"

"The technicians destroyed the computers. Backup as well."

"Captain, listen to me carefully. I believe you told me you plan to sail in environmentally controlled areas. Alaska, for instance."

"We do."

"You must use auxiliary engines—"

"Yes. Gas turbine engines, Mr. Hawke. Basically jet engines converted to marine use."

"Her speed with those engines?"

"Thirty knots is not inconceivable. But I've just come from the engine room. The turbines, too, are disabled. Bastards removed the igniters and smashed the fuel pumps."

Hawke smiled at Mariucci for the first time in recent memory.

"That big Coast Guard kid you had watching the gangway. Is he still aboard?"

"Yeah. Tynan. He did a sweep of the ship. Found a bunch of Chinese stowaways. Nuclear techs who worked in the reactor rooms. I got him posted amidships, keeping an eye on them for me."

"I saw a rating on that boy's shirt. Some kind of machinist, right?"

"Yeah. He only pulled guard duty because of his size."

"I want Tynan in the engine room. It's our only shot. Let's go."

"Alex?" Mariucci said, grabbing Hawke's arm. "We were supposed to call the president three minutes ago. You have to—"

"You call him," Hawke said, handing him the radio. "Tell him to cross his bloody fingers."

2:44 A.M., EST

The president turned and looked at his colleagues assembled at the long table in the Sit Room. You could calculate the degree of tension by the permanent smiles frozen on the faces of the Filipino staff clearing the table of dishes and pizza boxes. The wood-paneled wall slid back to display a projection map of New York Harbor. The blue icon inching southward toward Sandy Hook with six red satellites was *Leviathan* and her tugs.

"Six knots? This isn't even going down to the wire," McAtee said, picking up the laser pointer. "I just heard from *Leviathan*. They're still nine miles from Sandy Hook. Seven more to the Ambrose Light. And another twelve to the 'Wall.' Twenty-eight miles at six knots is not going to make my day."

Charlie Moore said, "At six knots, it will take them roughly five hours to reach the 'Wall.'"

"Right," McAtee said, "And we've got less than two."

"Mr. President," a senior staffer said, "I've got the governors of New York, New Jersey, and Connecticut standing by. All state, local, and federal emergency medical services have ramped up. I think it's time to cut and run—"

"No, John. Let's give him ten more minutes. Talk to me about Carter and Taiwan."

"Yes, sir. In the spirit of pushing every possible Chinese button, former president Carter is arriving for a courtesy visit in Taipei. He was on vacation in Bali and we're flying him in. We've invited all the worldwide media. A symbol of American commitment to Taiwan independence. Ratchet up the pressure on the Mandarins."

"That will rattle them. Good idea. What else?"

Kevin O'Dea from NSA spoke first. "Mr. President, NSA has redirected our satellite over the emerging battle zone in the Taiwan Strait. We have real-time battle management, sir."

"But no battle yet, I trust?"

"We're muzzle to muzzle with the Chinese fleet. Three French destroyers and two of their cruisers are steaming alongside the Chinese. We are just waiting for the tipping point, Mr. President."

"Gentlemen, and ladies," McAtee said, "until when and if a Chinese laser decides to interrupt satellite communication, you've all got a front seat at the next world war. Charlie? You're up."

General Moore stood. "Sit report from the admiral of the bridge, USS *Kennedy*, sir. He reports PLA missile batteries on the Chinese mainland coast are lighting up, sir."

"Response?"

"We've got waves of recon flights going in over the top. Low-level haircuts, Mr. President. Right down on the deck."

"Shave 'em close. That'll keep their heads down. Good."

The door was opened and the Marine guards admitted a very anxious-looking young navy officer from the Pentagon, Captain Tony Guernsey.

"Mr. President," Guernsey said, "I am receiving word now that Chinese surface-to-surface missiles are locking on to the fleet. We could lose—Christ—we could lose—"

"We're not going to lose a goddamn thing, Tony," the president said. "Charlie, step up the fighters going in over the mainland coast. One hundred feet. Let those bastards know we mean business."

"Yes, sir!"

"What the hell are they thinking right now, John? The boys in Beijing."

"Five or six in the room, sir. Total panic over Wild Card. But they think they've got us by the short ones with that ocean liner."

"They haven't got us yet. What about the goddamn tankers? Who's on that?"

"I am, Mr. President," an attractive blonde NSC staffer, Pam Howar, said. "The *Happy Dragon* was boarded by a Coast Guard cutter off Fort Jefferson in the Florida Keys en route to Miami. The captain and crew put up fierce resistance. The survivors were off-loaded immediately and she was towed to deep water and scuttled. *Jade Dragon* met a similar fate off Port Arthur, Texas, sir. It took three cutters and two choppers to subdue her. She's already gone to a watery grave in the Gulf of Mexico."

"Well, that's some good news isn't it, Pamela?" the president said. "What about the other one? The *Super Dragon?*"

"That dragon has been slain, Mr. President. Local fishing fleets report a huge explosion in the North Atlantic. One hour ago, one hundred miles due east of Cape Farewell, Greenland. She simply disappeared off the screen."

"Accidental?"

"I doubt we'll ever know, sir."

"This tanker explosion had a nuclear signature?"

"I'm afraid so, sir."

"Okay, so nobody's blowing smoke. General Sun-yat Moon and the Mandarins are sending us a very clear signal. Anything else? Anybody?"

"Captain Mariucci just calling from *Leviathan*, sir. He says they've got her two gas turbines up and running. She's making for the Ambrose Light. Their current speed is almost thirty-one knots."

The president looked up and smiled.

"Well, God bless America," he said.

The room burst into loud, sustained applause.

"Uh, Mr. President?" John Gooch said when the room fell silent.

"Yes, John?"

"It's *Seawolf*, sir. Her skipper reports he is flat-out en route to the Continental Shelf rendezvous."

"And?"

"At this point, sir, there's no way he can make the 4:00 A.M. deadline unless he pushes that monster way, way beyond her approved performance parameters."

"You tell Pokey Fraser I said forget the goddamn parameters. The taxpayers gave him a two-billion-dollar undersea Ferrari. Tell him it's time to damn well use it."

"Yes, sir. I suggest it's also time to tell him about the nuclear device aboard *Leviathan.*"

"Does he have a Wild Card ticket?"

"No, sir."

"He does now. You tell him to move his ass."

Chapter Sixty-three

The North Atlantic

3:34 A.M., EST

A THIN RED SLAB OF LIGHT LIT THE RIM OF THE BLACK world. USN Commanding Officer Persifor Fraser, standing in the bridge position atop the fairwater of SSN-21, the nuclear attack submarine *Seawolf,* was not happy. His command wasn't the usual boat on the New London waterfront. She was the quietest, fastest submarine on the planet. No submarine, and few surface boats, could cover more ground more rapidly than *Seawolf.* En route to Block Island Sound, she'd gone halfway across the Atlantic in roughly forty-eight hours!

Suffice it to say that CDR Pokey Fraser was a man unaccustomed to being late for an appointment. Now the president himself was on his ass and justifiably so. The Red Chinese had embedded a goddamn nuclear device in an ocean liner's keel and were threatening to blow up New York City.

And his beloved *Seawolf* might be just three minutes too late to stop them.

The huge bow wave rode halfway up the sub's fairwater. The sharp salt spray stung his eyes, whenever he lowered the heavy binoculars to look at his watch. Goddamn it! He had the pedal to the frigging metal and he still might not make it!

Fraser had to make it. Aside from the enormity of this mission, he owed it to his men.

His crew of fourteen officers and 124 sailors had been at sea at the time of September 11. Because of the nature of submarine operations, his boys had extremely limited access to real-time events.

Crew emotions had been all over the map. Many had friends and family in New York and at the Pentagon. Their country had been attacked, and they were in a good position to do something about it. The ship had sortied from Scotland, moved halfway back to the East Coast, when she received urgent orders to move directly to the Med to increase the number of Tomahawks and launch platforms in that theater of operations.

She'd acquitted herself admirably.

Now, Fraser's destination was the "Wall," an area of the Atlantic due east of the Ambrose Light, seventy-one degrees longitude, forty degrees latitude, right at the undersea edge of the continent. The seabed dropped off dramatically there and a deep underwater canyon known as the "Wall" gashed the slope, plunging to a depth of two and a quarter miles.

If you had to get rid of a large nuclear bomb in a big hurry, it was as good a place as you were going to find.

Fraser cast a sidelong glance at the two young sailors standing alongside him beneath the small forest of search-and-attack periscopes, the ESM, radar, and communications masts. The fresh-scrubbed and eager faces of his topside watch captured his entire crew's present mood perfectly. Just like their comrades half a world away in the Taiwan Straits, they planned to stick it, in very short order, to those who would terrorize America. The goddamn Red Chinese.

Fraser gripped the rail, his knuckles white. Six miles. That was the outside range of his Mark 48 torpedoes. He just needed to close within six miles. That wasn't too much to ask for, was it? Six lousy miles? He leaned into the stinging spray, willing his submarine onward.

3:39 A.M., EST

The president stood erect, helplessly watching the seconds disappear from the digital mission clock on the wall. Until he took *Leviathan* off the table, his hands were tied. The long knives were out. The Pacific Fleet and the Chinese fleet were at each other's throats, waiting for him to make the next move. How fascinating it was to be held to account by history. To realize that a wrong word, even a wrong gesture, had enormous consequences. It took every ounce of concerted effort he could muster to keep his true feelings out of his voice when he spoke.

"John?"

"Yes, sir."

"Twenty minutes. Somebody has to blink. Talk to me."

"Everything's up for grabs, sir."

"Granted. What do they want?"

"They want us out of Iraq."

"Tell them to get out of Oman. What else?"

"Commander Fraser reports he has closed to within twenty-one miles of the target area."

"And the target?"

"We've got an SH-60 Seahawk helo en route now, sir. That chopper should have visual contact with the liner shortly. If she maintains her current speed, *Leviathan* will arrive at the 'Wall' eight minutes from now at 3:47 A.M."

"Range of *Seawolf*'s torpedoes?"

"Mark 48ADCAPs, sir. Heavyweight torpedoes. Range six miles."

"Tell Commander Fraser to launch two torpedoes the second he closes to within ten miles of the target. Knock her wheels off right over the canyon."

"Sir? Ten miles is pushing the—"

"You heard me."

"With all due respect, sir, we've got three good men on that boat, Mr. President, and I think—"

"You think I don't know that! Damn it, man. Do all you can to warn Hawke. Keep trying to get him. But I can't risk the lives of hundreds of thousands for—just do as I say."

"Yes, sir!"

Gooch watched the man scurry away and then caught the president's eye.

"We're looking at rapidly evolving time and distance calculations here, Mr. President. *Leviathan* will have barely reached the 'Wall' at that point. If we miscalculate even slightly and she goes down on the lip, or in shallow water, the nuclear explosion will trigger a wall of dirty water fifty feet high. People will be swimming down Fifth Avenue. And glowing in the dark."

"We'll just have to take that chance, John. I need that vessel on the bottom."

3:47 A.M., EST

"What's his bloody problem?" Hawke asked Mariucci. Hawke had sounded the recorded "Abandon Ship" alarm repeatedly throughout the ship beginning at 3:30 A.M. Word of the impending nuclear disaster had spread throughout the ship rapidly. Chinese nuclear reactor technicians, reluctant kamikazes all, had been ordered to remain hidden aboard by their superiors in Beijing. Now they came crawling out of the woodwork—and made a mad dash for the promenade deck. Bright orange-topped, motorized lifeboats, thirty on each side of the ship, hung fifty feet above the water.

Two full lifeboats had already been dispatched and disappeared over the horizon. The third and last one was ready to be lowered away. Captain Dechevereux, who had originally stated he was staying with his ship, had understandably changed his mind. He was now seated in the bow of the lifeboat smoking furiously and cursing the name Bonaparte. Von Draxis had gone missing. Hawke thought perhaps the man had done the only sensible thing and jumped overboard.

Hawke had the controller in his hand, ready to push the button that would lower away the lifeboat. The last to board, an overwrought Chinese technician, was bouncing up and down on the deck, screaming.

Mariucci, climbing into the boat, said, "He says he's not getting in the lifeboat without the rest of his colleagues."

Hawke looked at the man. "You've got one second. In or out."

The man turned on his heel and ran off toward the stern. Hawke looked at his watch and said, "Twelve minutes."

"Okay. That's it," Mariucci said. "Climb in and let's get the fuck out of Dodge." Hawke didn't move. He was looking at him funny. Something was wrong.

"Where's Tynan?" Hawke said.

"Hell, I don't know," Mariucci said. "I figured he was coming."

"Where did you last see him?"

"In that bar, directing the Chinese to the lifeboats."

"Which bar? There are about thirty."

"Where we first met von Draxis."

"Normandie? How quickly we forget."

"Alex. We got to go. Now."

Hawke pushed the button and the lifeboat jolted into movement, rapidly dropping away down the side.

"Jump in!" Mariucci cried.

"No man left behind, John. I'll catch the next boat." Hawke ran up the nearest stairway, taking them three at a time. He remembered the Normandie bar as being one deck up, overlooking the bow. He had less than ten minutes now, to find that young Coast Guardsman and get the bloody hell off this ship.

Chapter Sixty-four

The North Atlantic

3:48 A.M., EST

"MR. PRESIDENT," JOHN GOOCH SAID, "SEAWOLF IS AT TEN miles and closing. *Leviathan* is one mile from the 'Wall,' proceeding on autopilot at thirty knots. ETA two minutes."

"Is everyone off that boat?"

"We can't get hold of anybody on board. Coast Guard Search and Rescue helo approaching the target area from the north reports two lifeboats in the water. Riding low. Full."

"Full?"

"That's what the *Yankee Victor* pilot said, sir."

"So they're probably all off. Inform *Seawolf*. Launch torpedoes."

"Yes, sir."

"Is the Chinese premier on the line?"

"They're getting him now, Mr. President."

"Good. Get Hawke on the radio. Make sure he's safely away."

"Trying every twenty seconds. He's not responding, sir."

"Probably a little busy. Keep trying."

3:50 A.M., EST

Hawke burst into the Normandie bar, his eyes scanning the large room for any sign of movement. Deserted. Tynan could be anywhere. He had nine minutes. Less. His mobile rang again. It was incessant. What the hell did they want now? He had nothing to report except his imminent demise. He heard a soft moan coming from a banquette to his left and sprinted through the sea of empty tables. He saw Tynan spread-eagled on the floor. He was on his back, staring upward, his eyes unfocused, his chest heaving rapidly. His shirtfront was a bloody mess.

Hawke bent down and spoke softly to him.

"Tynan. If you can hear me, clench your fist."

His right hand opened slowly and closed tightly.

"Von Draxis," Tynan croaked. "He . . . had a knife and he . . . I didn't see him, he just—"

"Hold on, Tynan. I'm going to get you out of here," Hawke said, getting his arms under the big man.

"Ready? Here we go."

It took every bit of Hawke's strength to stagger to his feet with the dying man in his arms. He ran for the door, knocking over any tables and chairs that got in his way, stumbling, almost going down twice. He stayed on his feet. Ten yards and he'd be back on deck. A shadowy figure appeared in the doorway, lurching toward him with his head down and his heavily muscled shoulders bunched.

Von Draxis. How had he escaped? An enraged bull, his white dinner jacket spattered with Tynan's blood. Hawke kept moving forward, somehow heaving Tynan up on his right shoulder to free his left hand. The German still had the knife. A big one, and it was coming up in his hand as he recognized the man coming at him.

"My Lord Hawke!" von Draxis said, sputtering furiously, his eyes dancing, "I've finally figured out who you are. General Moon told me. You're not George Moran. You're that bastard Hawke, aren't you? You're the one who—"

"Get out of my way," Hawke said and kept moving.

"Ha! You think you're leaving? Deserting the ship like those Chinese rats? I told Luca we could never count on the Chinese! Come here! You're not going any—"

Hawke's left fist flashed out, connected with the man's nose, and there was a soft crack of bone, a dry twig snapping in two. Von Draxis dropped the knife. His hands flew to his face, blood trickling from beneath them, and his legs gave way. He went down hard. He was trying to get up but he couldn't get anything to work. He looked up at Hawke, blood streaming from his nose.

"You think this is the end?" he said, red bubbles forming on his lips.

"Don't you?"

"Bonaparte and I, we are invincible. Unsinkable, just like this beautiful ship I built. We—"

"Bonaparte is going down, just like you and your boat. *Auf wiedersehen, Baron. Schlafen Sie gut.*"

Hawke paused at the top of the steep stair leading down to the lifeboats. There was no way of descending with Tynan over his shoulder. He had five minutes now. No time to lower the boat anyway. No. He would have to—his mobile was ringing in his pocket and he fished it out.

"Hawke," he said, his mind racing ahead, searching for a way out of this.

"Alex, it's Jack McAtee. You're in the lifeboat? You're away?"

"No, sir. Not in the lifeboat at all, I fear, Mr. President. Are we—are we over the—over the 'Wall'?"

"Alex, the torpedoes are launched! Yes, you're well over the 'Wall.' Get off that boat now!"

"Right. Good idea. It's just that unless you sink this bloody ship . . . I don't know—she's got to go *down*! To the bottom, or—"

"That's my problem! Listen to me, damn it! You get your ass off that—"

"Mr. President. I've a badly wounded man here. He's not going to make it unless he—medical attention. Or—"

"Alex, do you see the chopper? There's a Coast Guard—hold on—somebody get that pilot to drop a goddamn rescue sling . . . Hawke is still aboard the damn boat—Alex, listen to me. Get somewhere where you can—"

Hawke staggered beneath the weight, his strength all but gone. Searching the skies, he moved forward toward the rail and open deck. He simultaneously heard and saw the chopper to starboard, coming in low over the water. Orange-suited crew stood in the open bay and paid out line.

"Alex, are you still there? You've only got one shot at this!"

"Yes, sir, I—" a sharp blow from behind. Like a blow from a hammer. A searing pain in the small of his back. The bloody German. The bloody knife. He went down hard on his left shoulder and rolled, trying to hold on to Tynan, trying to break the gravely injured man's fall.

_____

3:52 A.M., EST

"Coast Guard helo *Yankee Victor*, this is the president speaking. Copy?"

"Roger, Mr. President, sir, this is U.S. Coast Guard *Yankee Victor*. I now have your man in sight, sir. He's on the upper deck forward atop the forepeak. Some kind of a struggle going on—he's, uh, he's down, sir."

"Listen to me, son. You've got three minutes before that ship blows sky-high and takes you with it."

"Less than that, I'm happy to say, sir. I've got two torpedoes a couple of miles out and closing fast. I'm going in now. One pass. Okay, this is it. He's, uh, he appears to be on his feet again. He's . . . I, uh— can anybody tell what's going on down there?"

"There is no time, *Yankee Victor*. Get him off that deck. And get your medic ready for that wounded man. Do it now."

"Aye, aye, sir. Two-man rescue net is deployed. We're going in now."

_____

3:54 A.M., EST

Hawke climbed to his feet. He was reaching behind his back to see if the knife was still there as he faced the grinning German. The man's nose had swollen to twice its size and coagulated blood clotted his lips, teeth, and chin.

"I get off," said Von Draxis. "I must get off this—"

"Certainly," Hawke said, lunging forward, lifting the man in one fluid motion from the deck, and heaving him over the rail and into the foaming sea far below, "I insist."

He turned to his right at the whumping sound of the approaching helicopter, swooping in and out of a sharp bank and heading straight toward him. He bent and picked up the unconscious American, surprised at how easily he was able to get Tynan's body up onto his right shoulder again. Directly overhead now, the chopper was slowing and flaring. The bright red rescue net hung from the hoist in the open bay and was swinging in elliptical loops. Trying desperately to keep Tynan balanced on his shoulder, he braced one foot against the rail and stretched out his right hand. The net was tantalizingly close. He was tempted to lunge for it—no, wait! Christ, he'd missed it! Missed his chance!

Still, the chopper hesitated above, whipping left and swinging the basket back once more—

What the hell? Two white torpedo trails just beneath the surface of the black water, racing toward the ship. One veered sharply toward the stem, the other continued straight toward the bow. A hundred and fifty yards . . . ye gods! They were seconds from impact and—there was the rescue net, swinging right toward him!

He reached up and snagged it. Wrestled with it a second, got the net's hard square base down on the deck, managed to heave Tynan inside the opening as gently as possible under the circumstances . . . and climbed in after him.

"Tynan!" Hawke shouted at the man cradled in his arms over the deafening roar of the chopper's engine. "We made it! You're going to be all right! Just hold on!"

Then, at the precise moment the first two heavyweight torpedoes impacted the ship and exploded, Hawke felt the net jerk suddenly upward. The chopper lurched violently skyward, as if lifted by the horrific explosion below.

3:57 A.M., EST

After the first two torpedoes struck, the Mark 48s kept coming. One narrowly missed the bow, swung hard left, circled, and slammed into the port side, successful on its second attempt. The torpedo salvo unleashed by *Seawolf* had already caused horrific but not imminently lethal damage. It wasn't over. One more trail, another explosion. Then two, three, four huge explosions as more blackened holes appeared amidships. The center of the ship buckled. Her entire stern, blown off by the very first torpedo Fraser fired, to take out her propulsion pods hanging below, was still afloat, drifting way from the main body of the ship. What remained of the great liner, roughly two-thirds of her, lay dead in the water.

Hawke watched *Leviathan* founder from his lofty perch. He was still dangling twenty feet below the navy helicopter as the hoist reeled his rescue net upward. She had a slight list to starboard, but she was still pretty much balanced on her keel. Watertight compartments made the water rush from the starboard quarter to the port and then back again. This was probably what kept her remains on an even keel.

God almighty, it was just as he'd feared. Torpedoes, no matter how powerful or how many, were not enough to sink the damn thing! She had watertight bulkheads from stern to stern! It would take a bloody—wait! His peripheral vision had picked up something.

Hold the phone, the president had not let him down after all.

There, screaming across the water about thirty feet above the wavetops, was a squadron of Navy Tomcat F/A18 Super Hornets. He saw two spurts of flame beneath the wings of the lead jet. Two white trails streaked toward the liner. Two Onyx missiles had been fired. Then the fighters flanking the lead fired. Deadly and unstoppable, six Mach 2.9 ramjet antiship cruise missiles skimmed the waves and slammed into the great ship. The sheer force of the missiles, each with the impact energy of fifty-five hundred pounds striking at terminal velocity of 2,460 feet per second, literally vaporized the entire center section of the hull.

The bow section and stern section angled upward and started their long slow slide into the sea.

Leviathan's keel, which, after all, was made of lead, was borne down to the depths below. The unexploded bomb, compressed and buckled by the enormous pressure, plunged two and a half miles down the face of the sheer wall at the edge of the continent, straight to the bottom.

Chapter Sixty-five

Washington, D.C.

THERE WAS A STUNNED SILENCE IN THE WHITE HOUSE SITU-
ation Room. Everyone had his eye on the monitor showing a live feed
from USCG *Yankee Victor,* the bright orange helo now hovering at
one hundred feet above the scene. The ship had finally sunk. No trace
of an explosion. No underwater mushrooms. Everyone held his
breath.

"Mr. President," John Gooch said, "the Chinese premier is still on
the line."

"What's his mood?"

"If Wild Card's intent was to create psychological paralysis at the
top, we've succeeded beyond our wildest expectations. Premier Su
Ning's afraid to breathe at the moment."

"Good. Keep him holding. Get Hawke on the speaker. Get someone to hand him a radio."

"He's on, sir."

"Alex?"

"Yes, sir."

"Any visible or audible sign of an explosion from the keel? As it
descended?"

"None at all, Mr. President. The impact of the ramjet missile
would have sent what was left of the keel straight to the bottom."

"It's on the bottom."

"Affirmative. If it still exists at all, the bomb is two and a half miles
down, sir, and rendered inert by the massive damage to its internal
mechanism."

A spontaneous outburst of applause and loud cheering filled the
room.

"Good. That's very good news. If you could stay with me, Alex, I'm going to inform the Chinese of this latest development."

"Yes, sir. I'm not going anywhere."

"How about *Seawolf*?" the president said, turning to General Moore.

"Mr. President, *Seawolf* reports no acoustic signature of any explosion. No shock waves, no tremors. They have a confirmed sonar location of the keel on the bottom. Based on sonar imaging, deformed pieces of the keel are scattered on the ocean floor. Crumpled and buckled. Nothing remotely large enough to indicate a viable nuclear device. No trace of radioactive leakage, sir."

"Your assessment?"

"The nuclear threat to New York City no longer exists."

The president took a deep breath and took the receiver the Marine guard handed to him.

"This is the president," he said.

"Yes," said the premier, "I've been waiting. My patience is wearing thin."

"Mr. Su, the Chinese device in New York City has been neutralized. I have a demarche. A new list of American demands. Are your aides prepared?"

A moment of stunned silence followed.

"Neutralized? What do you mean?"

"You're no longer in a position to threaten me. You got that?"

"Wait, I want to confirm—"

There was some loud background shouting, muffled and heated conversation, and then Su said, "Go ahead. We will listen to what you have to say."

"Good. I'm now going to give you a list of American demands. Once they are met, and this has been wholly verified by the United States, I will consider taking Operation Wild Card off the table. Do you understand me?"

"What are these demands?"

"You are shouting, Mr. Su."

"I apologize. Your demands, Mr. President?"

"That's better. First. I want you to now order Chinese naval and air forces in the Strait of Taiwan to stand down. I want your shore batteries to stand down. Now, Mr. Su. Are we clear? My patience is wearing thin."

The president could hear a hurried conversation in Chinese. Then the premier was back.

"Yes. They are standing down. Please continue."

"I need to know that it's being done. Now."

"It's being done, Mr. President. Orders are going out to the commanders in the field now."

"Good. Second. This is a long one, so pay very close attention. I want you to guarantee immediate withdrawal of all Chinese military and political personnel from Oman. I want a stop to Chinese migratory forces infiltrating the Sudan. In addition, you will inform President Bonaparte's French government that you no longer support their presence in Oman. Make it crystal clear to him that the United States and China are wholly unified on this issue. We are both firm in our insistence that all French naval and ground troops withdraw immediately from the Gulf. And that the sultan's family, now en route from Masara Island to Muscat by sea, is guaranteed safe passage home."

"Yes. Just one moment. We have that."

"Good. Lastly, I want China to cease the perpetual harassment of Taiwan. It is not China's property. If you have any desire to see China continue our mutually beneficial economic détente, you will see the wisdom in this demand."

"Yes, Mr. President."

"One further demand, Mr. Su, on a personal level. Four people from our side have been deeply involved in this matter. If any harm should come to them as a result of our actions here today, all bets are off. Their names are Brock, Congreve, Jones, and Hawke. Do you have that? Yes, that's right, Hawke, with an e."

The president listened for a few minutes, murmuring assent or dissent, and then said good-bye. He handed the phone back to the young Marine standing at attention nearby. He looked up at all the faces, brave men and women who had stood with him, helped him weather this storm.

"He's giving the order to stand down immediately," the president said.

"Thank God," someone said.

"Verify all that, would you, Charlie? Hard confirmation. That they're standing down?"

"Aye, aye, sir," General Moore said, a smile breaking across his face.

There was no applause now, just a flood a relief sweeping across the tired faces. John Gooch put his hand on the president's shoulder.

"Mr. President, what was the response to the Oman demand?"

"He said he was ordering Bonaparte to withdraw his troops immediately. He said, very diplomatically, that Bonaparte is coming unglued. He's holed up inside the Elysée Palace, surrounded by his Imperial Guard and heavily armed loyalists."

Gooch said, "We've got to do something about that situation. Interpol has a warrant charging the president of France with first-degree homicide. Rock-solid case. There is an eyewitness confession. Tough part will be bringing the bastard in."

"You like the idea of an American infantry division marching up the Champs Elysées, John?"

"Damn right I do," General Moore said, smiling.

"Not even slightly, sir," Gooch said, pushing his clear frame glasses up on the bridge of his nose.

"Is Hawke still on the air? Alex, you there?"

"Still here, sir."

"Is your Oman team still intact?"

"It could be in twelve hours, Mr. President."

"Good. I've got one more urgent matter that needs mopping up."

"Paris, sir?"

"Paris."

The stern was the last remnant of the great vessel remaining on the surface. There was a slight increase in ambient light and in that faint rosy glow of dawn, Alex Hawke saw her name, picked out in glints of gold on the massive stern.

Leviathan. The sea monster.

A large wave came awash of the monster's deck and a small gath-

ering of survivors who'd ignored the "abandon ship" and were clinging to the rails were now carried off and under the tumultuous seas.
Hawke watched for them to reappear but they did not.

The net had now been hoisted to just below the helo. The deep
wound in the small of his back burned like hell but there wasn't
much he could do about it. So he just took it, waiting patiently as
Tynan was lifted out of the net and up into the chopper. The boy was
still breathing, but he'd left a lot of blood in the basket. Hawke could
do no more for him.

For now, he was content to hang there in the sky and watch
the end.

Hawke watched the huge liner's death throes with both horror
and a grim sense of satisfaction. Rows of lights still winked from the
portion of the black hull that remained visible above the water. He
gauged the stern's downward progress by the illuminated portholes
that were snuffed out as she slid under. You could almost imagine
them hissing and popping as they went out, although most probably
remained alight for some time.

The ship's after-quarter rose to a precipitous angle and then rose
higher still, until it was standing upright like a huge black column.
This would not be an agreeable sensation for any man still remaining
aboard. He would be clinging desperately to anything bolted down
to stay alive for an extra minute or two. Hawke could make out a few
more struggling figures on the deck, and some bodies perhaps, entan-
gled in lines or in mangled metal.

The stern quarter, perhaps a good 150 feet of *Leviathan*'s remains, stood outlined against the star-speckled sky, looming black in
the darkness. It hung there for a few brief minutes and then, sinking
back a little, slid forward rapidly through the water and plunged
straight downward.

There was no great noise. Only the slight sound of a gulp marked
the end. She went quickly under and the water swirled and finally
closed over her golden name.

Unlike most such disasters, this one did not leave the sea filled
with panic-stricken survivors crying out for God's mercy and gasping
for air; there were no agonized cries of death from a thousand
throats. No, after *Leviathan* was gone, only a thin whitish-grey vapor
remained. It hung like a pall a few feet above the broad expanse of

sea. For a while, you could see an undulating field of flotsam and jetsam that had bobbed up from somewhere far below.

By tomorrow or the next day, this slate of the ocean would be wiped clean. Above him, *Yankee Victor* angled up and away, bearing Alex Hawke toward the shimmering glow of the distant New York skyline. Hands reached down inside the net for him. As they lifted him up, he took one last look at the great liner's grave.

It was over.

Tomorrow morning, no trace would remain of all that had happened here.

Seabirds would circle and spin above the Atlantic swell.

And the sun would shine down on waves like blue glass.

Epilogue

PARIS HAD DANCED ITS LAST TANGO.

Somebody had flipped the wrong switch, forgotten to turn on the City of Light. The blackout was no mistake, of course. It was Boney's last stand. A week earlier, the Chinese had left him to the wolves and now the wolves were at his door. On that blackest of days, Bonaparte decreed that every light in Paris be extinguished at 9:00 P.M. Suddenly, it was 1944 all over again. There was a nine-o'clock curfew. Anyone caught on the streets after that hour without good reason or a government pass was arrested.

Jet had a good reason. She was running for her life.

After Hong Kong, she had fled to Paris. It had seemed a brilliant place to hide. There was a flat there, a modest love nest she'd shared with Schatzi. A decade earlier, after a row, he'd told her to clear out. He cut off the rent, the lights, the heat. She stayed, and eventually bought it under an assumed name. It was her safe house. A place where no one knew her name.

Only a few other automobiles were on the streets when she fled her dark and shuttered building at 88, avenue Foch. She jumped into the Mercedes, took a deep breath, and forced herself to drive slowly away from the curb. Every car, including hers, was blindfolded, the taped headlights showing only a sliver of light at the very bottom. It made driving very tricky.

Heading south and east toward the Tuileries, she saw the Eiffel Tower in the distance, standing like a thin black finger pointing at the heavens. A tiny aircraft warning light, blinking red at the top, was the sole illumination. Blackout curtains hung in every window. The venerable chestnut trees lining her street were black against the starry night.

She glanced nervously at her rearview mirror. A police car had been following her closely for two blocks, then, inexplicably, it turned off into the avenue George V. Gripping the steering wheel with her left hand, she noticed her right hand shaking badly as she held the car's lighter to her cigarette. Her nerves were understandably frayed. This morning, Te-Wu plainclothes officers had come to her apartment.

She'd escaped down the service staircase with only the clothes on her back. Six hours later, she'd gone back. She watched the entrance from a bench situated in a small park across the street. After four long hours, she'd decided to take a chance. She raced across the boulevard and inside, taking the stairway to her third-floor home. It was destroyed, but she paid no attention to it. It took all of ten minutes to get what she wanted—money and her gun from a safe hidden in the floor beneath a mountain of shoes. Some irreplacable jewelry.

On the way out, she scooped up the new Sharpei puppy that she'd named Stokely. Now, the dog was in the black Hermès bag on the seat next to her. In her lap, she had her Chinese Te-Wu shield and her small handgun. If anybody stopped her, she'd already decided to shoot.

After wandering the streets all morning, afraid to return home, she'd taken a room under another assumed name at the Ritz. She called the number Stokely had told her to use in case of just such an emergency. Surprisingly, Stoke was in Paris. He wouldn't say exactly why, but she could guess. Bonaparte was holed up inside the Elysée Palace. There were snipers on the roof and tanks in the courtyard. No UN resolution was going to get him out any time soon.

Stoke said it was a dirty job but somebody had to do it.

She told him she had to get out of Paris. Tonight. Right this minute. He said he understood. He'd figure something out. He'd call her cell after nine tonight and tell her what to do.

She kept her speed down en route to the location Stoke had given her. Memories stirred, not her own. Newsreels of Paris during the Nazi occupation. Shadowy people hurrying through the darkened streets, anxious to be home, to be safely inside. She passed a CNN crew on a street corner, using available light to shoot a reporter's account of the grim darkness that gripped Paris. In the near distance, a muffled boom and a flash of lightning bloomed on the horizon.

The camera swung crazily around trying to capture the moment. Déjà vu, she thought.

Jet knew what the American reporters were saying on the radio. There were many conflicting rumors and points of view of the current impasse. The Loyalists believed the embattled president was the last, best hope of the nation. But the noose around Bonaparte's neck was tightening. The anti-Bonapartists claimed he'd paid men to roam the town, shooting anyone who didn't have the right answer to their questions. They said the president blamed Anglo-American bombers that no one ever saw. Planes no one could see. He initiated the blackout but the bombs kept exploding.

It was whispered Bonaparte himself was blowing up the buildings, so his military police could clamp down even tighter. So more loyalists would take up arms in his defense. So he could keep the dark city under his thumb while he plotted with his generals, all of them cloistered in the Elysée Palace, desperately clinging to power.

The people who spoke such treason against Bonaparte disappeared nightly.

The bridge was coming up on her right. Jet swung the sleek black Mercedes right onto the Pont Louis Philippe and across the Seine to the tiny island called the Île St-Louis, just south of the Île de la Cité. There was a parking place just after the bridge and she took it. She hit the key remote as she walked away, locking the car. She walked quickly, eyes moving rapidly side to side. No one else was on the streets. No one she could see, at any rate. Since *les flics* had turned off, she didn't think she'd been followed, which was a small comfort.

Stokely had given her very precise instructions. She hurried down the steps leading to the lower quay. Then she walked along the tree-lined pavement toward the western tip of the island.

She reached the designated spot at the end of the island. Stokely had told her to wait here. That was it. No further instructions. She stopped and lit a cigarette. The twin towers of Notre Dame, with the floodlights extinguished, looked black and oddly forbidding against the sky. She could make out the hunched figures of the gargoyles and a slight chill went up her spine. She looked back up at the bridge she'd just crossed. Empty.

Quasimodo's bell in the south tower of Notre Dame suddenly chimed. It was fifteen minutes before the stroke of midnight. She paused and looked out across the river, not knowing what to look for or who might be meeting her. The Seine was dark and glassy in the moonlight, not even a ripple on the surface. No activity on the river at this hour. No *bateaux mouche* steaming her way. Nothing. She felt completely alone.

Then, a faint, droning buzz from upriver. Somewhere to the west of the Île de la Cité. It didn't sound like a motorboat. It sounded more like a small airplane, flying very low. Whatever it was, it was hidden by the trees and buildings lining the Quai aux Fleurs just across the river. She glanced nervously up at the bridge again and then turned back to the Seine.

Yes, a plane, she could see it now. But friend or foe was the question that caused her heart to knock in her ears.

The small seaplane was flying on a slight angle east just above the river. It seemed to be headed directly toward her. It cleared the Pont d'Arcole by maybe six feet and then suddenly dropped. She saw the plane slow, almost to a stall, and then the nose came up a fraction just before the floats touched the water. The pontoons splashed on the glassy water, throwing up a wide spray to either side of the fuselage. Instantly the pilot throttled back and coasted to a stop.

Jet froze. My God, she thought, if someone aboard that plane meant to harm her, there was absolutely nowhere to run, no cover.

The seaplane, sleek and silvery, roared once more and accelerated toward Jet. It made a fast taxi over to the quay, then swung around with the nose pointed west, toward the Pont d'Arcole.

The pilot's window slid open. Jet's hand slid inside her bag, her fingers searching for the gun. A familiar face appeared in the open window. Curly black hair. He was smiling and motioning for her to come aboard.

"Come on!" Alex Hawke shouted above the engine's roar. "Hop on, we've got company!"

"What company?" Jet cried, instinctively looking up at the bridge behind her. A black sedan screeched to a stop and all four doors were flung open. She didn't have to see their faces. She already knew. Te-Wu.

Hawke had climbed down onto the pontoon and had his hand outstretched toward her. The little plane was drifting toward the quay. Only a few feet of water remained.

"Jump!" Hawke said, "Now!"

"Take the dog!" she said reaching the bag across.

She looked over her shoulder just before she jumped for the pontoon. She saw them now, the men on the bridge. There were four of them, all leaning out over the parapet of the Pont Louis Philippe. One of them had his arm extended toward the plane.

Pointing?

No, shooting. Small geysers were erupting near the pontoons.

She scrambled inside. The cockpit was tiny. She threw herself into the righthand seat. Hawke was instantly beside her, shoving the throttles forward with his right hand as he pulled the door shut with his left.

"Nice to see you again!" he said. The roar of the engine was enormous for such a small plane. They were already racing away from the quay. She felt rather than heard small but troubling noises coming from the wing just below. She saw a line of small black holes suddenly appear stiched in the thin aluminum. The seaplane was accelerating rapidly now, zigzagging, as Hawke tried to avoid the weapons fire from the bridge behind them.

"You, too!" she cried, as the plane rapidly gathered speed across the mirrored water. She craned her head to look behind them and saw all four of the men in black with their arms out, firing at the seaplane. She looked back at her pilot and saw a grim smile.

"Buckle up," Hawke said. "Not a lot of room to get airborne here. Sorry."

"Sorry? I'm amazed you're here—"

"This will be tight—hold on."

A bridge was coming up fast. The Pont d'Arcole. A black sedan screeched to a stop in the middle of this bridge, too. Men were jumping out and pointing at the oncoming airplane. Crouched inside, she felt as if the tiny aircraft was about to fly apart. The vibration and noise were tremendous, the strain on every seam and bolt horrific. She clenched her jaw to stop her teeth from rattling.

For a second she thought Hawke was going to zoom right under the arch of the bridge. But, with their wingspan and height, going beneath the bridge didn't seem remotely possible. Or *over* it, for that matter. Suddenly, the nose came up. She felt the water lose its grip just as the bridge filled her view. She held her breath, afraid to look over at Hawke. A surreal beat of time, and she knew they'd made it. The pontoons couldn't have missed the car by more than a foot.

They screamed over the Pont d'Arcole just low enough to make the men dive for the pavement.

She waved an ironic good-bye to the Te-Wu men as the seaplane suddenly lifted and roared away into the nighttime sky. She looked down at the city while slipping on her headset. Paris looked even blacker from above than it did from the ground.

"What are you doing here?" Jet said, looking at him now. "Shouldn't you be storming the Bastille?"

"Something like that."

"You took time out from that to save me?"

"Stokely said you were in trouble. By the look of things, he wasn't exaggerating."

"Thank you, Alex. I hardly know what to say."

"Don't say anything. We'll catch up later. There's something on the radio we have to listen to."

"What is it?"

"I had an idea. If it works, it might save a lot of innocent lives. The president agreed to give it a shot tonight. All the radio and television networks have agreed to the broadcast. We'll see . . ."

Hawke reached over and twisted the radio receiver knob.

She heard a burst of static and then the modulated voice of the BBC announcer saying, "And now, from the White House, the president of the United States."

"Good evening. I speak tonight to America's oldest ally, the brave men and women of France. Frenchmen shed blood in the cause of our own Revolution. Americans died fighting for French freedom in 1917 and 1944.

"In a garden in Normandy stands an American memorial to peace. On it are a few simple words this American president would like you to hear.

> *"From the heart of our land*
> *Flows the blood of our youth*
> *Given to you in the name of Freedom.*

"Tonight, the lights no longer shine in Paris. Fear roams her streets. But I say France has nothing to fear. Not from America or those who stand with us. Your distress at this hour can be laid at the doorstep of one man. A traitor to the noble ideals of France, a tyrant accused of willful murder, a man who now cowers behind darkened palace windows.

"Make no mistake. I ask no one to take up arms against this evil man. I ask only for a show of hope. A visible sign that the citizens of Paris still cherish the rule of law. Our prayers tonight are that a liberated France soon regains her rightful place among the fraternity of free and lawful nations.

"If you cherish freedom and democracy, show it. The eyes of the world are riveted upon you. I urge you now, every man, woman, and child, to go and make a light to shine in every window. Go out into the streets, climb up to your rooftops, not with guns, but with candles. Set your city aglow with candlelight. Light up the sky with your hope.

"You will see, the whole world will see, that tyrants cannot abide your light of freedom. Tyranny cannot survive the will of a free people seen so clearly set against it.

"So, tonight, I urge everyone, men, women, and children, go now, show the world that Paris is still what it has always been—a shining beacon of democracy and hope—still that beautiful City of Light you call home.

"Thank you. *Bon soir et bonne chance.*"

A few moments later, Jet reached over and squeezed Hawke's hand on the throttle.

"Alex, look. Just down there. And over there beyond the river. It's amazing. . . ."

Hawke rolled his plane left. Below, he saw it beginning. It started with a few scattered pinpoints of light here and there, then small patches of brilliance were shining in the blackness. It began in the center of town and rapidly spread out to the farthest perimeter. Whole streets were lit up one at at a time, becoming grids of light. Soon, a rolling wave of light swept across Montparnasse and the Latin Quarter to the Jardin des Plantes and the Champs de Mars, and swept over the river to the Marais.

What had started with a single lit window spread, as whole sections of the city were illuminated, until the city was a dazzling spectacle.

He buzzed the crowded rooftops, saw the people of Paris cheer and hold their burning candles aloft. He saw streams of people in the streets below, their candles and torches held high, snaking through darkened sections of the city, creating living rivers of fire. Within no more than a few minutes, the entire city was blazing with light. He dove and flew low over the treetops, headed for the lone blinking red light atop the great tower that remained unlit, looming dark in the distance, a finger pointed at heaven.

Hawke flew in great, swooping circles around the Eiffel Tower. The lights, when they came on, started at the bottom and rushed upward to the very top. The tower was soon glittering, blinking, putting on a dazzling show for the city, its brilliant lights now dancing across every surface, and racing each other all the way to the top and down again.

"I think it worked," Hawke said, as he raced across the sparkling city and steered a course northwest for the English Channel and home.

Behind him, Paris began a slow and painful return to normalcy. Neither Hawke nor his passenger ever saw the orange licks of flame climbing into the sky above the Elysée Palace. But he knew that somehow the group of brave men led by Stokely Jones, FitzHugh McCoy, and the Frogman would carry the day.

After all, the City of Light was on their side.